05/06 donation 8.95

EMPIRE
BUILDERS

HEART OF INDIA SERIES

Silk
Under Eastern Stars
Kingscote

THE GREAT NORTHWEST SERIES

Empire Builders

LINDA CHAIKIN

EMPIRE BUILDERS

BETHANY HOUSE PUBLISHERS
MINNEAPOLIS, MINNESOTA 55438

With the exception of recognizied historical figures, the characters in
this novel are fictional, and any resemblence to actual persons, living or
dead, is purely coincidental.

Copyright © 1994
Linda Chaikin

Published by Bethany House Publishers
A Ministry of Bethany Fellowship, Inc.
11300 Hampshire Avenue South
Minneapolis, Minnesota 55438

Printed in the United States of America.

Library of Congress Cataloging-in-Publication Data

Chaikin, L. L., 1943–
Empire builders / Linda Chaikin.
     p.   cm. — (The great northwest)

   1. Frontier and pioneer life—Northwest, Pacific—Fiction.
2. Pioneers—Northwest, Pacific—Fiction.
I. Title. II. Series: Chaikin, L.L., 1943–   Great northwest.
PS3553.H2427E47 1994
813'.54—dc20   94–25696
ISBN 1-55661-441-1   CIP

Thanksgiving Day 1994

*Her children rise up
and call her blessed.*

PROVERBS 31:28A

For Henriette Marie Loiselle Chaikin

Mom, with love and appreciation
we dedicate this book to you.

LINDA CHAIKIN is a full-time writer with seven novels published in the Christian market. She is a graduate of Multnomah School of the Bible. She and her husband, Steve, are involved with a church-planting mission among Hindus in Kerala, India. They make their home in San Jose, California.

CONTENTS

PART TWO

Railroad and Timber
1874–1883

CAST OF CHARACTERS

Tavish Wilder • Expelled from West Point through treachery, he ended up a track layer swinging a hammer while his father preached in the train camps. But Tavish had big dreams of becoming a powerful tycoon one day and marrying Ember, heiress of the Ridgeway Timber Enterprise in Washington.

Kain Wilder • The father of Tavish. Kain had sealed his fate the night of the Great Chicago Fire of 1871. Could God forgive a past shattered by dreadful secrets?

Ember Ridgeway • The vivacious niece of railroad tycoon Mack Ridgeway. The road bringing her to spiritual maturity proved a difficult one—and so was the twelve-year romance with Tavish.

Lottie Ridgeway • Ember's cousin married the wealthy son of a San Francisco shipping owner—and trusted her future as an expectant mother to God. Together with Ember, she faced Cheyenne warriors in Yellowstone country.

Wade Ridgeway • He had started out at West Point as a friend of Tavish and ended up his enemy in the Pacific Northwest. What secrets did he hide that threatened to surface?

Julot LeBrett • The fiery French-Canadian cousin of Tavish. Together they swung hammer, fought Cheyenne, and searched for the shrewd enemies who had shanghaied them to sea!

Cleo Ridgeway • Known as the timber queen, she was Ember's aunt and guardian. Someone was blackmailing her, but her secret must not come to light! She had tossed aside her Christian faith, and now the winds of adversity blew cold.

Amity Clark • Growing up as the daughter of a tavern owner on the wharf of Port Townsend had involved her in the dark side of life. Would she ever escape a life of abuse?

Mack Ridgeway • He was determined to climb his way back up to the top of the NP railroad, at any cost!

PROLOGUE

THE BELL OF PORT TOWNSEND

Shrouded by fog and in jeopardy of running aground on the rocks, the steamship *Liza Anderson* sounded the distress signal. The hull creaked in the murky water, but no response to the signal was heard. Silence stole over the ship as the captain ordered the engines to be stopped.

A man who had boarded at Victoria for Seattle felt the dampness seep through his coat as he squinted into the thick white fog and felt the fate of his fellow passengers weigh like an anchor on his soul.

Ira D. Sankey, soloist, hymn writer, and colleague of D.L. Moody in Chicago, stood on deck lost in thought. Slowly he became aware that the wind had shifted as easily as if the Lord had whispered a command.

Then, drifting across the water from the little white church on Port Townsend's bluff, came the clear, sweet ringing of the harbor bell through the fog, guiding them safely into port.

In Seattle, facing his audience, Sankey told of his experience

aboard the *Liza Anderson* and how the hymn "Harbor Bell" had
been born:

"We were nearing a dangerous coast, and night was drawing
nigh. Suddenly a heavy fog settled down upon us: no lights had
been sighted; the pilot seemed anxious and troubled, not knowing how soon we might be dashed to pieces on the hidden rocks
along the shore. The whistle was blown loud and long; but no
response was heard. The captain ordered the engines to be
stopped; and for some time we drifted about on the waves. Suddenly the pilot cried—'Hark!' and far away in the distance we
heard the welcome tones of the harbor bell, which seemed to
say—'This way! This way!' Again the engines were started; and
guided by the welcome sound, we entered the port of safety."

Then his resonant singing voice broke forth:

> Our life is like a stormy sea
> Swept by the gales of sin and grief
> While on the windward and the lee
> Hang heavy clouds of unbelief.
>
> But o'er the sea the call we hear
> Like harbor bell, inviting voice
> And tells the lost that hope is near
> And bids the trembling soul rejoice.
>
> A thousand life wrecks strew the sea;
> They're going down at every swell,
> Come unto Me, come unto Me,
> Rings out th' assuring harbor bell.

PART ONE

BEGINNING OF AN EMPIRE
1871–1874

A Boy's will is the Wind's will,
And the thoughts of youth are
long, long thoughts.

—Henry Wadsworth Longfellow

1

GREAT CHICAGO FIRE

October 1871

A dry easterly wind plaguing the Windy City through the summer and now the fall tugged at his black hat and sent the frayed edge of his knee-length coat flapping.

In his late thirties, tall and lean like a willow bending in the wind, Kain Wilder stood beside a horse-drawn coach across from D.L. Moody's Illinois Street Independent Church. Concealed within a shoulder holster was his pearl-handled derringer, taken years earlier from a dead Yankee officer near Bull Run. The derringer had served Kain in and out of gambling dens from St. Louis to New Orleans. He hoped Vonette wouldn't notice it.

From farther down Chicago's Illinois Street, music from a tinny piano and ragged voices drifted through the open door of a tavern: ". . . you are lost and gone forever, dreadful sorry, Clementine. . . ."

Opposing voices sounded from within Moody's church:

Our life is like a stormy sea
Swept by the gales of sin and grief
While on the windward and the lee
Hang heavy clouds of unbelief. . . .

Like drawn swords the voices dueled:
—"Oh, my darlin'! oh, my darlin'!"—
—"Swept by the gales of sin and grief!"—

A dust devil whipped brittle leaves from the unpaved street and stashed them like kindling against the wooden sidewalk. A scrap of paper flitted along until it snagged on the carriage wheel near his feet.

Kain felt the wind buffet his face. Sun lines lingered in the tanned skin roughened by work on the Kansas Pacific Railroad, and a scar from a hand-to-hand fight with a riled Cheyenne marked the side of his neck. The Indian was dead.

For those in Chicago who didn't know much about the Cheyenne or Kain Wilder, his quiet manner and his handsome and somewhat boyish features could be mistaken for an easygoing personality; the scar as a mark of patriotism won in the War Between the States. Except he had fought on the side of the South, and his temper, once riled, rushed along as strong and deep as any river.

For those who knew him outside Chicago—who had confronted him in the struggle to fight his way up from the dust and sweat of the railroad—no such mistake would ever be made.

His eyes, like Lake Michigan in a freeze, fixed upon the church where Moody was preaching. Seated inside, Vonette would be listening with rapt attention.

It had been three years since he had seen his wife, though he managed to see his son Tavish more often. Kain took satisfaction in the one fine thing he had been able to accomplish as a father—his son's education at West Point. Tavish's education meant everything to Kain, who saw it also as a gift to the boy's mother, with whom he wished to be reconciled. West Point represented a promise that both father and son would make good one day, would make her proud and bring joy to her heart. So far Tavish had excelled; in fact, his high grades had placed him on the honor roll. He had become quite a gentleman. That was due more to his mother's having taught the Bible to him at her knee than anything Kain had been able to do.

What have I taught him? Kain became aware of the derringer under his coat, and a deck of cards in his pocket.

He reached for the makings of a smoke but he was out of tobacco. Kain's thoughts turned back to his wife. What would she say to him after three years?

"You two-bit gambler, you dare come back to me?"

The piece of paper that had caught on the carriage wheel flapped in the wind. Kain snatched it, intending to let it blow. Before he did, he caught sight of a picture of Moody, and he read a few lines of what was written:

"If Christ is what He is represented to be in the Bible, He is worth standing up for; and if heaven is what we are told it is in the Bible, it is worth living for."

Kain subdued the internal struggle voicing objection to the neglect of his own childhood faith and turned the tract loose. It tumbled and flapped its way across the street, where it stuck among some yellow-brown leaves.

Again he glanced down the street to the tavern. There was still time before Moody's preaching would be over. He was thirsty, but if he expected to impress Vonette with the changes he anticipated making in his life, he must refrain.

He leaned against the carriage, waiting for her to come out, but told himself that if he wished to make a strong impression on his wife, going inside and sitting down in front would catch her eye.

He walked across the street to the lighted building, but his booted steps slowed at Moody's voice.

" . . . What men want is the power to overcome temptation, the power to lead a right life. The only way to get into the kingdom of God is to be born into it."

Kain lingered in the shadows outside the door. As prayer was made, he retreated and crossed the street to wait beside Vonette's carriage. Emptiness plagued his insides, but he had long ago discovered that if he ignored it, the feeling would subside.

He mused over whether or not to tell her he had big plans of investing in the Northern Pacific. He had lost money in the railroad before. Even now, he had money socked away in worthless bonds in Thomas Durant's troubled Union Pacific Railroad.

Talk of Durant's financial woes and his trouble with Congress was circulating among Chicago's entrepreneurs and gamblers. Kain was one of those silent gamblers, but he was going to quit. If it killed him, he would get out.

He watched the crowd leave the church, women in bonnets and men carrying Bibles, with children running happily at their heels. Most disappeared into the night, some entered nice carriages, and for a few minutes the street was clogged with traffic. *This is the kind of life I want,* he thought.

A raven-haired woman in a long cloak emerged with a Bible in her arm, talking with an older woman. Kain's heart thudded as he stared at his wife. For a moment she stood on the sidewalk, then as the older woman departed, Vonette crossed the street and walked toward the carriage.

He watched as she neared, the heels of her shoes raising a wisp of dust. He waited, remembering happier days. *She walks with the confidence of a queen, the innocence of a child,* he thought wistfully.

He tensed but didn't move when she stopped abruptly, her eyes discovering him there, leaning on the carriage.

The hot wind touched them and he saw it playing with her hair and the hem of her cloak. He straightened, not trusting himself to speak. Her voice cut through his trance.

"Kain," she whispered.

It was all he needed. The catch in her voice and the look on her face brought moisture to his otherwise granite eyes.

They touched at the same moment, embracing in the dry wind, and he felt her sobs, felt her tears against his rugged cheek, and he was saying over and over, "I'm sorry, honey, I'm sorry . . . sorry . . ."

She clung to him as though a whirlwind would snatch them forever apart.

"I'll make it up to you and Tav. I swear I will. I'm through with gambling, with drifting. I've come home. I've done well for myself."

The moments flew past them until she lifted her face, moist with tears, and he read the joy in her eyes, felt a pang when disbelief struggled with her hope.

"You've said the same before. You mean it?"

The lie caught like a knife in his throat. He had no more than fifty cents in his pocket. *But I do have money. Ten thousand dollars wrapped up in worthless UP bonds.* He had just left Granger at the hotel where the railroad financier had broken the murky news. The UP was facing bankruptcy.

"Nothing's any good without you. I'm going to make good."

The anxiety in her gaze prickled the back of his neck. In fear that she might draw back from his embrace, his lean fingers gripped her forearms snugly.

"It's different this time, honey."

He found his voice calm and it reinforced his confidence. He heard himself speaking words that came like a sudden summer squall, words born of desire but as fleeting as dreams.

"I'm going to make a fortune. I know the big man himself, Jay Cooke. His Philadelphia enterprise is buying the Northern Pacific Railroad. Know what that means? He's going straight to the top and I'm going with him. Sure it's true. I've come for you and Tav."

She hesitated as though mention of their son troubled her. "Tavish is at West Point. I don't want him mixed up with the railroad. But he needs you," she said softly. "He needs you to stand tall with your allegiance to God unshakable."

Kain blinked. "Sure, honey. We'll start over. The three of us. It's what I came back to Chicago to tell you. That, and about a fortune to be made in the railroad. Like I say, Jay Cooke's mighty big, and he's taken to me. There's land belonging to the railroad. Rich timberland. All in Washington Territory. And the railroad's going straight through the Northwest. We've already hammered the first spike at Carlton, Minnesota. We're laying track to Duluth, Fargo, Bismarck—straight to Port Townsend."

She frowned, and he knew she didn't want to leave Chicago and her recent work within D.L. Moody's church.

"You'll like Washington Territory. Townsend's already port of entry for foreign ships. The way I figure it, the NP terminus is bound to go there. We'll build us a fine house, honey, and if I make it big like I think, we'll build a mansion. Tav will marry a daughter of some railroad baron or timber magnate."

She smiled. "You'll have a hard time breaking in your 'cub.' Tavish is as independent as you. He'll marry whomever he wishes."

Her words caused the adrenaline to begin working in him. She hadn't refused.

"I've a letter from Cooke himself." He reached beneath his coat and accidentally brushed his hand against the cold derringer. As though burning his fingers, he jerked his hand away. "I forgot. The letter's at the hotel. Before this is over we'll be wealthy. You'll wear the prettiest frocks in Seattle."

Her eyes softened. "It's not wealth I want, Kain, it's you— to believe in you. No more gambling, no more drifting, no more guns."

"It's over, honey. I swear it."

Her searching gaze ignited a feeling of guilt. He rushed on. "I've been to a meeting. I've heard how a man can change with the help of God. Why—see that tract? It blew from my hand, and I did what it said, honey. Wait here, I'll get it!"

He was back in a moment, brushing the dust off the tract. "Give me one more chance to make good, Vonette. Just one more! You know how I feel about you. There's been no one else. There never has been, never will. Even when I was away drifting, laying track, it was you who kept my strength going when other men fell like flies. But I'm through swinging a hammer. There's millions to be made in the NP."

She looked at him a long moment as though trying to decide. "I want to believe you, Kain."

He was beside her, his lean brown fingers gripping her shoulders, a smile on his face.

"I won't disappoint you this time."

But no sooner had he boasted of big plans than desperation set in, causing his heart to sound in his ears. He had backed himself into a corner. He needed a large sum of money. Could he convince Granger to give it to him? Granger, he knew, was leaving on the train tonight for Philadelphia.

"I'll meet you tonight. It may be late, but wait up for me. Have your bag packed. We'll go to West Point and see Tav, then to San Francisco and Seattle."

She threw her arms around him and he felt like a man again.

"We'll try." He smiled, but his belly ached. "I'll meet you later."

"Aren't you coming in the carriage?"

His throat was dry. "I'll walk back to the hotel. Feel like a long walk. I'm too excited over the turn of things."

She kissed his cheek. "Don't forget where we live."

"Ohio Street."

"I'll be waiting."

He held her shoulders. "We'll make it yet."

She nodded and smiled. "I love you."

He held her as though she would vanish. "I won't fail you, Mrs. Wilder, not this time."

"Yes, Kain," came the whisper tinged with sadness. Their eyes held, then she looked away.

He stepped back and started down the street, feeling the wind in his face. He turned and stopped, staring at her.

"Don't move, just stand like that for a moment. I want to remember the way you look until I'm gray and senile."

She laughed, and her eyes misted. "Go on with you now. I'll be packed and waiting."

He smiled and walked off into the Chicago night, quickening his steps against the head wind.

He thought of railroad financier Cyrus Granger, and the old man's face that his mind conjured up through the darkness turned his hopes into wooden ducks ready for the sportsman's rifle. His steps slowed.

Kain felt sweat on his forehead as he struggled to envision some way to melt the old man's icy grip on his pile of gold.

The Sherman House, one of Chicago's finest hotels, stood five stories high on the northwest corner of Clark and Randolph streets. On the top floor, Cyrus Granger sat hunched behind a walnut desk so shiny that his white walrus mustache reflected in its surface. His hollow-cheeked face looked bored, the bulging brown eyes doleful. He removed his solid-gold-framed spectacles and held them while his right hand, missing two fingers, managed to hold a quill. Before him was a meticulous ledger. The finances of the troubled railroad under Thomas Durant.

"You know I think the world of you, my boy. We didn't work together hoodwinking Congress all those years without you earning my highest regard."

He grinned, as though expecting him to be amused, and Kain noticed that even when measuring friendship, Granger spoke of "earning" it.

"I could wish to help you, Wilder, but things are tight at the moment. Very tight."

"I'm only asking for five thousand back from the ten. I've worked hard for the UP. The railroad ought to take care of their own when the foreign investors fall through."

"I quite understand. Quite so, yes. But it's out of my jurisdiction, you know, and . . ." he droned on in a disconcerting fashion, "nothing that so much as flirts of impropriety can be permitted at this—ah, delicate time."

Kain's smile was chiseled in stone. He had no liking for the man. Until Kain had been fired for his gambling five years ago, he had spent several years under Granger learning the railroading ropes, though it was more like high-stakes gambling than anything else he had been involved in.

Granger was an expert at successfully manipulating an excited cry among the settlers in the West for the coming of the railroad. Once they had the legislature believing the settlers were clamoring for the golden track to be laid, huge land grants from the federal government were given to men like Durant, Crocker, and Gould. The "robber barons," as they were called in the press, had managed to gain 116 million acres for laying track. Free land twice the size of Utah, much of which was given to friends and sold to speculators at a huge profit. No matter that since 1850 there was only one skinny line operating from Mississippi to the Pacific Northwest.

Along with the land grants from the government came the taxpayer's money to build the line. While working with Granger, Kain had witnessed certain railroad lobbyists spend up to $500,000 at every session of Congress for graft, bribery, and corruption, buying votes and public endorsements for the railroad. Kain's own plans had continued to enlarge as he rubbed shoulders with the clever empire builders, but his weakness for gambling had ruined his fortunes several times until he had ended up borrowing. Now he had lost even that as the UP faced financial ruin.

"What's five thousand when millions have been spread around Congress? Especially when the ten thousand was mine."

"I sympathize with your loss, my boy."

Kain found his tone sickeningly sweet. "I didn't come here asking for a grandfather's shoulder to cry on. I came for my money."

The tone of his voice must have alerted Granger, for he truly looked at Kain for the first time. Whether Granger understood the tinder-dry situation he was in could not be guessed by his poker face. The old man, too, was a gambler, and he knew his powerful position gave him the upper hand.

But beneath Kain's outward stillness was a desperate will that refused to be beaten. His future was being held to the burning flame and he felt the heat beginning to singe his hide. And what made it all the worse was that this shriveled old miser was the one holding him on the spit.

Contrary to his personality, Kain breathed with passion, begging for understanding. "Have you ever loved a woman, Granger? I mean *really* loved her? Enough where you can't live without her?"

Granger looked startled, then lifted his deformed hand to bite the end of his quill as though searching through the library of his mind for some cold fact to hold Kain at bay. Something that would steer them back to a businesslike atmosphere, where it was safe.

"I never married, my boy. Never had the time. Too busy making money." He chuckled like a vaudeville comic, a cue that said he expected Kain to smile.

Granger's facade faded under Kain's chill gaze. "Truly, Kain, I always regretted being denied a wife and family, but it wouldn't have been fair to them, now, would it? Leaving the house at four A.M., not returning until midnight. So many out-of-town meetings." He sighed. "But I admit, when a man gets old he thinks about his gathered riches. Where they will go . . ."

"Back into the ground, I suppose. Anyway, most of us don't have two cents to leave even if we had a dozen kids. Look here, Mister Granger—"

"So you heard him too, did you? Ought to be arrested."

"Heard who?"

Granger jabbed his gold quill toward the hotel window. "That revivalist, Moody. He bribes street urchins with rides on his pony to his Sunday school. Clamors up on barrels and throws out his words as if planting seed. The other day he had a singer named Sankey with him to attract crowds."

"No, I didn't see him," Kain said impatiently.

"It was all emotional tomfoolery. 'They shall cast their gold and idols into the street and none will gather them.' Bah! Such foolishness should be outlawed."

Kain sat down quietly on the edge of the man's desk, holding his hat on his knee. He saw Granger's eyes take in the frayed edging on his cuff, and Kain's mouth formed a cool smile.

"The look of a man with a Chicago fortune," said Kain with soft venom, fingering the worn edges of his own coat lapel. "Someday I'll have one as fancy as yours."

"You're a clever young man. I've every assurance you will." Granger drew a solid gold watch from his satin vest.

Kain absently picked up a pencil, watching him. *Fool.*

Granger frowned, "I fear, my boy, I've no more time. I've a train to catch. As I said, my heart goes out to you, but we all took our chances in the UP. I lost a great deal myself."

The pencil snapped in two between Kain's fingers. Granger looked at him.

"I doubt if you'd allow yourself to lose a dime," said Kain too quietly. "You, Durant, Crocker, Oakes—you always manage to walk away from a gutted railroad with pockets stuffed and jangling. The Union Pacific lies stripped and bleeding until some other high financier comes along to buy her up, certain he can revive her to produce a few million more from Congress and gullible investors. But me?" Kain gently laid the broken pencil on the desk in front of Granger. "I'm taking the money you owe me and buying into Jay Cooke's Northern Line. I too will be rich one day."

Granger's brows furrowed like the back of a riled cat. "Look here, boy. You played the railroad game same as the rest of us. Had it paid off, you wouldn't be spouting self-righteous words about greed and unfairness." He calmed himself and let out a breath. "Unfortunately, it worked the other way this time. The UP is going broke and there's not one of us who won't lose money."

"I want mine back. And I aim to get it."

In the windy Chicago night a fire bell clanged.

It was no more than a mindless reflex, yet Kain tensed. The

sound did something inside of him that went beyond logic. He didn't know how he knew, but the bell warned him of a danger far more ruinous than a fire. Like a still small voice the warning to his soul came like a call.

His eyes shifted across the room to the window. Outside, the fire bell clanged again in the warm night. Granger hadn't appeared to notice and continued arguing.

"No one twisted your arm to sink money into UP stock. I'm sorry, Wilder."

Granger snapped his ledger shut and placed it inside his leather briefcase. The finality of that gesture told Kain he had lost the game. He had lost more than money.

Vonette . . .

Granger stood, reaching for his blue derby hat. "I've a train to catch. If you're ever in St. Paul you might look me up for a job—" His voice fell like a bucket of rocks. Kain remained seated on the edge of the desk, but now there was a derringer in his steady hand.

"Don't be a fool, Wilder. This is the Sherman House. You try to rob me here and every policeman on horseback will converge on you in a moment."

"I've already played the fool. There's no mending fences for me now. Men like you and Durant will walk free with millions. Some of that money is mine. Like I said, I aim to have it. Tonight, Granger. In a bank note."

Granger's forehead shone with sweat beneath the gaslight. "Now, now. Nothing is worth hurting a fellow human being for, least of all money."

Kain offered a slow smile. "You sound mighty pious all of a sudden. You thought nothing about lying and cheating to pigfat your own bank account. Now you have the gall to draw the rags of morality around you. Grasping them to hide behind for the sake of your own skin won't save you, Granger."

"I stole nothing in my life. Not one thing! I'm a good, upstanding citizen! I abide by the law, I give to charity, I've created jobs for immigrants going west, I've helped build this nation!"

"You've gotten rich on your so-called patriotism. What has the nation gotten in return? Mislaid track with ties made of white pine lumber that will rot in a few years! But you won't be around when the cry comes for the need to rebuild the line. Like the others, you'll be avoiding the press inside your mansion, drinking wine and smoking cigars."

"Your rantings mean nothing, my boy."

"The rails are poorly laid, just waiting for a train to jump track. If the *Chicago Tribune* smells graft they won't let up on you. If you get into trouble, Durant will drop you and let you bleed. I've also heard the *New York Sun* is poking around."

Granger's eyes hardened, but uncertainty began to deepen the lines in his face.

"Sit down, Mr. Granger," Kain told him.

Granger eased himself slowly into the chair, his hands clutching the armrests. "Very well. We won't quibble. Five thousand."

"Make it ten."

His head jerked. "Ten—! You said you needed five."

"Did I? I was wrong."

"That's outright thievery!"

"Spoken by an expert. I'll remember your fatherly warning, Mr. Granger. Tell you what, for saving your reputation from the *New York Sun* you can add another two thousand dollars."

"That's blackmail!"

Kain picked up the gold quill from the desk and handed it to him.

"No, best make it another four thousand, Mr. Granger. The newspapers are onto this story like a vulture on a dead donkey. It could blow wide open in the next few months. If you want to escape detection, seems to me you'll need time to pay off your friends around Congress."

Granger leaned his gangly frame forward. "I warned Durant you were a dangerous upstart."

Kain picked up Granger's immaculate derby. "Always did like these. They belong on a man with the taste for a railroading fortune." He set it down carefully on Granger's head. "You're right, Granger. If circumstances warrant, they say I can be as heartless as a hungry rattler about to swallow a rabbit."

"Extortion will see you in prison."

Kain took out his plain pocket watch and looked at the time. "Train is soon leaving. You best be scurrying on your way. I too have an appointment. Now write your signature on a bank draft for fourteen thousand."

Kain reached across the desk and lifted the lid on a silver box. He removed a fat Cuban cigar, bit off the end, and struck a match. The derringer glinted.

He heard the bell clanging a third time. It must be a serious fire.

"We're wasting time."

"You won't get by with this. Making money is one thing; pulling a gun is another. In the railroad business we play it smart. The line of legality is rarely crossed."

"Sign it," said Kain, his jaw clenched.

Granger held up his hands. "Of course, my boy, of course . . . take it easy. We're old friends, you and I. To prove it I'll throw in a gift from my personal account, say, another thousand? How does that sound, Wilder?"

"Now that would be right friendly of you, Mr. Granger, right friendly."

Inside, he scorned the man for cringing. He had no intention of pulling the trigger.

The ostentatious gold quill scratched across the paper. With shaking fingers Granger slid the bank note across the shiny desk, leaving a trail of moisture from his sweating palm.

Kain glanced down. *Fifteen thousand dollars.* His throat went dry. Enough money to do him and Vonette well in the Northwest, and to pay the final year for Tavish at West Point.

He swept the note off the desk and placed it inside his coat. "Thank you. Now, give my deepest regards to Durant."

"Anything you say, Mister Wilder."

Granger's rattler-like movement took him off guard. He had drawn a pistol! From where—? A blistering shot cracked with a puff of white, grazing Kain's shoulder and thrusting him backward. Kain fired his derringer.

The pistol slipped from Granger's hand and slid from his thigh to the rug. His glassy eyes locked with Kain's, then he slumped forward, almost gracefully as though taking a nap.

Kain stood without moving, fighting off shock. His left shoulder felt like an explosion. The beat of his heart silenced the growing noise on the street below.

The bells ringing out of control stirred him back to sanity. From his subconscious, a game he had played as a boy reared up in his mind, the little boy's voice petulant: *But I done shot you, Kain! Game's over fer you.*

Below on the street a crowd was gathering, voices and horses and carriage wheels filling the night with babble.

"FIRE, FIRE!"

The bellboy banged on the door. "Mr. Granger, Mr. Granger—fire, fire, get out!"

Kain kept silent. No one had seen him come up to the room. If only he could escape without being recognized. . . .

2

ASHES TO ASHES

If they caught him, he'd hang.

Kain stood at the door listening. Outside in the hall voices had ceased—his chance to escape. The icy fist of fear slammed against his insides. How could he cash the note now? He must if he and Vonette were to have a chance. The word pounded in his mind like an Indian war drum: Run, run . . . RUN!

He snatched the room key from beside Granger's satchel, opened the door, and glanced out. Empty. He shut the door and locked it, then slid the key under the door. He turned to flee and was confronted by several men just coming up the stairs.

"Better get out fast, mister. Fire is moving with the wind."

"Yes."

"Is Mr. Granger in there?"

"What? No. He left for the train."

They rushed past, banging on doors. A door opened and a stout woman poked her head into the hall. "I heard gunshots!"

"No, fire bells. Get out quick, lady!"

Another man stood farther back in the hall shadows, unnoticed. His pale fingers ran along his frilled white shirt to a side pocket, brushing against a marked deck of cards. He pulled out a white handkerchief and dabbed his brow as he watched Kain race down the stairway.

"Well, I declare. That was blood on ol' Kain's coat. Now why would he go an' slide that key under the railroad dandy's door?"

The stranger from Kansas City thought he knew.

Below in the spacious lobby people mingled. A man dashed in from the street. "It's a whale of a big one, gents! Whole of the sky on the West Side is glowing. It's racing straight for us!"

Kain rushed out the front door and was struck by a strong wind that boasted to suck him away. A carriage! A horse! He had to locate Vonette on Ohio Street!

Men and women crowded the walk in a daze; others grabbed carriages and clattered off, nearly running down pedestrians. Kain lunged to snatch the reins of a horse, but a man scrambled into the saddle ahead of him. His boot shoved against Kain's chest. The horse galloped away.

Weakness from loss of blood drank away his energy, and determination alone prodded him forward through Clark Street in the scowl of the wind.

He staggered past Follansbee's bank, his arm numb, the beat of his heart making waves in his vision. What if she was trapped and he couldn't get through to her?

The color of the sky loomed a malevolent orange. Sparks and ash were falling like sooty snow. His leaded footsteps brought him past a Methodist church where the strains of a hymn could still be heard from the people inside. He stopped to draw in a breath. His conscience prodded him. He imagined that angels were swarming through the open windows to seize him—the fiery swords of Eden drawn to halt his progress.

"Maybe it was me, not Granger, who died. Maybe I'm in hell!"

His feet kept rhythm with his heart as he struggled forward.

Curtains drew aside, faces peered through windowpanes, doors opened, and people wandered into the street. "How bad is the fire? How close?"

At the roaring wind, they ran back indoors to gather their belongings.

Jostling crowds converged from buildings onto the streets while red-hot cinders illuminated the night. Men stopped to help women whose flowing skirts ignited. With the clatter of horsehoofs and the whir of wheels, many came from the direction of the fire, carrying whatever they could.

A man stood on the roof shouting down, but his voice was lost in the din. Then his words broke through: ". . . fire on both sides of the river!"

Kain could think only of Vonette. He elbowed his way through, and a policeman on horseback rode up waving a red flag. "Too late! That way is cut off. Go back!"

Panic erupted in the throng. Kain staggered back in the direction he had come. *Vonette!* Store awnings and business signs were burning. Flames shot from rooftops and cinders danced about in small devil-winds.

At State Street Bridge he hoped to cross the Chicago River. One of the planks was smoldering. Tugboats ignored people waving money on the bank. "Take us to the other side!" Kain felt the crowd surging onto the bridge and it swayed beneath his feet.

Faintness caused flashes in his vision as he fought his way across, and won.

Ohio Street! The heat was intense, the neighborhood in pandemonium when he arrived. Trunks, furniture, and piles of clothing cluttered the street. He saw her. "Vonette!"

He ran as though dead, feeling no pain now, stumbling and getting back up in an attempt to reach the house.

Autumn leaves blown by the wind under wooden sidewalks served as kindling. Flames sizzled up through the gaps in the boards. The roof of their house was on fire but had not yet collapsed. Vonette was standing in the street while a boy tried to steady the frightened horse.

"Vonette!" he shouted again, surprised by the strength of his voice.

She turned, and as if by magic, new hope spread through her face. "Kain!" She came running toward him and they met in the midst of her cry as he crouched to smother the flames on her skirt. A whirlwind of smoke and fire converged around

31

them. He grasped her, fearing separation, and heard her voice whispering, "Jesus."

"Hold the horse!" he shouted to the boy just as the terrified animal bolted and galloped away.

A carriage came by, loaded with household goods. The driver saw him waving but was determined not to stop.

Kain lunged at the driver and caught him, dragging him down from the seat. He struck the man, tossing him into the brush.

"Kain, no!"

"Quick! Climb up!"

He applied the whip to the horse and they surged ahead. As they neared Illinois Street, she cried, "Look, Moody's church is burning!"

Kain's jaw set hard with impatience. He turned the carriage back onto Superior Street, but it was also blocked by the huge waterworks building where flames leaped against the sky.

Vonette leaned toward him, raising her voice against the noise. "Take Clark Street to the Kinzie Bridge."

New throngs of carriages and people on foot merged toward the bridge, their faces wearing masks of fear and confusion. "All Chicago is on fire!" someone yelled. "This is hell!"

Kain might have thought so. What if he had eternity to struggle endlessly without hope of escape? To face one dead end after another, his soul empty, his throat parched, and his eyes smarting from ash and smoke.

Whirling embers blinded them. He glanced at Vonette to see if she would panic. The calm determination in her face fed his confidence. Their clothes were full of burn holes on their backs and laps.

Kain knew he would use the whip on anyone who sought to steal the horse. He fought his way through the crowd as though wrestling cattle in Texas. Nothing mattered but getting through.

"Look," she gasped, clutching his arm and pointing.

He saw a ball of fire gathered by a gust of wind and whirled overhead. The horse became skittish and wild-eyed. As Kain maneuvered the carriage down the crowded street, people on both sides were running in and out of their two-story houses carrying out treasures and heaping them on lawns, offering large sums of money to anyone with a wagon. Kain glimpsed furniture, oil paintings, crystal lamps, ornate trunks, and armloads of suits and glittering dresses.

In contrast, a lone barefoot child ran down the street, leading a scruffy brown dog on a short rope. Scurrying behind came an old woman holding a birdcage with a canary flapping from perch to perch.

Women knelt to pray in the street, only to have their hems catch fire.

"We are like Sodom, burning," said Kain.

Vonette's fingers tightly enclosed his arm, and he winced. She hadn't noticed the sticky dark stain yet. . . .

"Then don't look back, Kain. Our treasures are not here."

A man emerged from the faceless throng and neared the side of the wagon, waving his wallet. "Your carriage for any price!"

"Out of the way," Kain commanded, moving the carriage through the crowd.

A once-white satin gown with French lace and ribbons lay blackened beneath wheels and hoofs. Had some debutante waltzed in that very frock the night before? All dreams were now dead. Ashes to ashes, dust to dust. Yet Kain inched the carriage closer toward the bridge. The horse was becoming unmanageable.

He turned to Vonette. "Hang on. If I don't lead him he's likely to buck. Don't get out for anything, understand?"

She nodded, pale in the firelight.

Kain wrapped a cloth around the horse's eyes and tied it into place, but heard Vonette's startled yell: "Watch out, Kain!"

A dray full of burning baggage smashed into their carriage, shoving him aside. With the reins lost, the frightened horse reared and lunged forward, throwing Vonette to the ground.

Kain scrambled to his feet. The crowd had pushed back amid the hysterical shouting. Vonette lay in the street, her hand stretched toward him. She tried to crawl. "Kain . . ."

"God, please—" he choked. He thrust forward to reach her, each step seeming too slow.

Someone shouted, "Watch out!" and he turned his head sharply to look behind them. A runaway horse dragging part of a wagon bore down on them, heading straight for Vonette. In an instant her body was beaten into the ground by heavy hoofs, and the broken wagon crushed her in its path.

Kain stared, stricken. Then he found himself fighting his way through the crowd that surged around.

Vonette was a crumpled figure in a bloody blue cloak when he reached her, the once-lovely dark hair matted into the dust.

Blood and dead dreams stared up at him. He sank to his knees beside her.

"Get up, mister, or you'll soon be trampled. There's no stopping them."

Kain couldn't answer. Dazed, he stared. A black book lay in the street a few feet away—her precious Bible; he grasped it and placed it inside his coat.

A burly man gently lifted her up into his arms and Kain stood, his eyes fixed on Vonette.

"God's pity to you, mister," he said, and there were tears streaking the soot on his cheeks.

Kain had no tears. His insides were a tomb. He took her limp body from the man's arms into his own and stood there. There was no time to even mourn. The crowd and the wave of traffic were pushing him forward and he had to keep moving like a crazed man, knowing she was dead, yet he could only carry her, his precious wife, broken and bloody. Like everything, dead. He trudged on.

He remembered nothing until he found himself stopping to stare up at the Sherman House Hotel. Had fate brought him back?

The flames were leaping high, the structure crumbling, and Vonette was hanging loosely across his arms. His mottled face was streaked with sweat, his eyes like glass.

"All for nothing."

Granger's body was not likely to be found. And if it was, no one would know he'd been shot. He was simply another victim caught in the Chicago fire.

He looked down at Vonette. Where was her spirit? Where had she gone? A moment earlier she'd been beside him, sharing his dream to begin again. Full of life, full of hope.

He sank to the side of the street, cradling the lifeless body to his chest. And he sobbed.

A lifetime passed before he left her body with the others that were laid upon the grass in the courthouse square. He stood watch for some time, reluctant to leave her. He removed her wedding ring and begged a knife to cut a lock of sweet black hair that had once draped his chest as they lay in each other's arms.

Then Kain Wilder found himself beginning the long, torturous walk to the west side of the river.

Exhausted, his arm numb from the wound, he trudged on, pausing to rest on street corners as he maneuvered his way out of the city.

He stumbled on through the late hours, arriving at a little depot in the outskirts of Chicago where others also waited for the departure of the last train.

The conductor noticed Kain's dazed condition and took over, summoning a doctor. Kain remembered little except being tended by a man with his white sleeves rolled up.

"Looks like a bullet wound. Must have been set upon by robbers. World is full of all kinds."

"Wherever he's going, I hope he makes it."

"He will, or he wouldn't have made it this far."

The train gave a long, low whistle. The conductor cupped his mouth and cried from the door: "ALL ABOAARRD!"

The train let off steam. Its big wheels began to turn, slowly at first, groaning but gaining as the rhythmic speed churned faster and faster. They rolled across the track, the whistle blowing. The engineer leaned out the window and gazed at the fiery sky, then tipped his hat as the Windy City fell behind.

When the October sun broke over the hills, scattering light in the coral sky, the train rolled on with a cloud of whitish gray smoke spiraling up from its engine. It rolled past flat Illinois wheat fields, rolled by green trees and little brown hills and patches of pale sky.

Kain awoke to the aroma of hot black coffee.

"Looks like you're going to make it just fine, sir, just fine!"

All for nothing, thought Kain again. Then he thought of his son, Tavish. He had his mother's rich dark hair and her smile.

Tavish Wilder . . . his one remaining treasure.

Fear of even more loss attacked his courage. "God, don't take him away from me. God—I vow to raise him right. I vow to make amends for my wicked ways."

His hand, weak and trembling from exhaustion, found its way under his soiled coat until he touched what his emotions were looking for.

Vonette's Bible. His fingers tightened around the worn leather—leather caressed by her hands, washed with her tears—how many prayers had she sent as incense toward heaven concerning her husband, her son?

He brought the book out and tried to focus his blurred vision. He turned the delicate pages covered with black words—eternal words? Words that were spiritually alive, that breathed of heaven?

She had written in the margins; verses were underlined, but he couldn't read them now. His head throbbed, his eyes smarted.

Kain found his name written on a forward page, with a verse of Scripture beside it. He would look up the verse later. He found the birth of Tavish recorded, also a date that confirmed the time when as a small boy Tavish had confessed Jesus Christ as Savior.

He gripped the Bible. This was the doorway by which he could discover truth—and the way to find Vonette again; a means by which he could hold on to his son. These words were now his bridge, the signposts along the troubled road of life, his light for each uncertain step. But—

A sickening dread squeezed his heart until he thought it would burst from his chest. What of his sin? What about the man he had killed?

What now? Could he be forgiven? Should he return to Chicago and turn himself in?

But I can't go back! What if they hang me? How would my death for murder affect my son? It would ruin his life!

He groaned inwardly. No turning back.

A troubled road stood before him, its end winding too far into the distance for him to guess the outcome of his quest. He would begin the journey with sorrow and dread, holding no confidence of acceptance when he reached the final end. On his way he would seek the Jesus he remembered from his childhood days, whom Vonette had spoken about with such confidence.

Into the shambles of a ruined life, a tiny hope bloomed.

Maybe, in knowing Him, he would not only learn the truth of where Vonette's soul had gone, but discover a way by which he too might follow and find not only his beloved again, but the very One who made a happy ending possible.

Kain wondered: With God, could there be a happy ending? Or were such endings reserved only for fairy tales?

Kain was still clutching the Bible when he lapsed back into a tortured sleep. He dreamed of angels with flaming swords, and sledgehammers ringing out in the desert sand; men groaning and sweating beneath a brazen sky, and peace surrounding him like droplets of sweet water.

When he awoke it was night and stars winked down from the now soft black sky.

But if happiness waited beyond the stars, surely this life was made up of minutes ticking by, full of deadly thorns. A bitter harvest was sure to come from the wicked seeds of his actions. Chicago authorities would still hang him if they caught him. And if Tavish found out about his father, it would damage his future, his life.

Kain could find neither the desire nor the will to go back to Chicago.

He would walk on into tomorrow and hope his past remained buried in the ashes with Granger. *God, my future is yours.* . . .

3

YOUTHFUL BEGINNINGS

Ridgeway Lodge, Upstate New York
December 1871

Icy starlight reflected from the blue-black sky above a meadow of white, encircled with pine and hemlock. The snow was newborn, the winter stillness pure.

In a guest bedroom in the pinewood lodge belonging to railroad financier Mack Ridgeway, his niece stood in stocking feet and petticoats trying on the hat that she would wear on the upcoming sleigh ride and gala New Year's Eve dinner-ball. If she had her way, Tavish Wilder would again be her escort.

She tilted her head from side to side to see the effect. In the lamplight her waist-length hair shone like the warm colors of autumn. Her delicately winged brows, several shades darker than her hair, knitted into a disgruntled V.

The hat was ghastly! How young it made her look! She heaved a perplexed sigh, undoing the hat pin with a disconsolate jerk and tossing the expensive piece of high fashion onto the floral-quilted walnut bed.

"It's no use, Sassy. Being fifteen and a half is a horrid age, and the hat doesn't help. I'll need to impress Tavish Wilder some other way."

She glanced at her confidante, a lanky woman close to fifty, big-boned, and nearly six feet tall, with braids wrapped about her fine head like polished beads. Sassafras—or "Sassy" as Ember called her—wore an immaculate chocolate brown satin high-neck dress without a bustle, and tightly buttoned kid boots. She had worked for Ember's maiden great-aunt since the end of the Civil War, and now had been sent from Tacoma to care for Ember while she was away attending the elite Chadwick Female Academy near West Point.

"What if Mister Wilder don't take you on the sleigh ride and ball?"

Startled, Ember looked at her. The thought had never crossed her mind. A lump she couldn't swallow lodged in her throat. "The New Year's Eve ball is the biggest celebration of the year. Why wouldn't he? He's been my escort all season." And wishing to dismiss the small fear that Sassy's question had stirred, she sat down before the vanity mirror and changed the subject.

"For the ball, I'll wear my hair in the new French fashion called hugs and kisses, and I want lots of gold dust sprinkled on too."

"Hugs and kisses, my big foot! What's with them French? Leave it to Paris to think of all kinds a' ways to torture a girl's hair!"

"Oh, Sassy, please, I've a picture right here—I found it in *Vogue* this morning."

Ember handed her the high-fashion magazine. Sassy took one glance and winced.

"No, ma'am! Won't do it, no way. Looks to me just like them awful wigs the French used to heap white powder on. An' that Mister Wilder, he don't like girls with big white-lookin' wigs—all head and hair and no neck."

Ember became alert. Her eyes lifted from the photograph of the model to fix upon Sassy. She knew better than to fall for Sassy's trap. Ember, however, couldn't resist. If Sassy knew something about him that she didn't . . .

She cast a side-glance, watching Sassy smooth the white ermine fur on the edge of the discarded hat as though it were a kitten.

"He isn't the sort to discuss French wigs," stated Ember. "But even if he did, how would you know? You've never spoken to him."

Sassy smiled mysteriously. She placed the hat inside the box to be shipped back to Fifth Avenue. "Ain't so. I spoke to him comin' out of church on Sunday last." Her dark eyes flickered with a change of thought. Ember knew that look and wanted to squirm.

"Now if you'd gone and paid heed to the Almighty's good words like you is supposed to, 'stead of sleepin' in bed all mornin' long, you'da seen Mister Wilder too. And that fine, pert girl he was with. Now her hair was dark like a raven's wing and just as smooth and shiny. No awful hugs and kisses to ruin her locks."

Ember's honey brown eyes narrowed. She felt a brick fall into the pit of her stomach. "What girl? Who was she, do you know?"

Sassy's expression turned gentler as she focused on Ember. "Was Miss Sara, that's who, a sweet little thing who ain't missed a church service by sleepin' in on Sun—"

"Sara Brackston, the colonel's daughter?" breathed Ember.

"Only Sara I know. Ain't no secret Mister Wilder's been to the colonel's house a dozen times for supper. Afterward he takes Miss Sara out in her carriage."

Not a secret? She sat in mute silence, her schemes and dreams scattering into a whirlwind of doubt and confusion. *He's never asked to take me out in a carriage.* Why hadn't Tavish mentioned the colonel's daughter before?

The truth dawned on her, as freezing as the blustery wind. Why should he discuss the colonel's daughter with her? What did she know of his personal life, his goals? His secret wishes?

For the first time she considered how he had shared little of his private life, or his thoughts. He had played the role required of him, that of a mandatory escort but nothing more. And Ember had been so concerned with trying to win him with her charms that she had never stopped to give his silence a serious thought. Even when his mother had died in the October Chicago fire, Tavish had kept his grief to himself—though Ember had seen the pain in his eyes whenever the tragedy was discussed.

She tried to analyze the memory of his smile, the sometimes subdued flicker of amusement in his eyes, and how it always left her confused and uncertain. Had he been laughing at her, seeing through her attempt to make him fall in love with her? Perhaps he saw it as a childish game on her part. She suspected that he considered the debutantes of rich families spoiled and frivolous.

He does care, I know he does, even if only a little, she thought. *I can win him away from Sara Brackston.*

Her troubled thoughts wandered back six months earlier to the time when she had first seen him at Saratoga at the height of the entertainment season.

It had been at the Grand Union Hotel, where wealthy socialite families went to show off their daughters. The entire affair reminded Ember of the proud owners of show horses who pranced them about to be judged for the coveted prize.

Ember was considered too young for the "coming out" social event, but was permitted to promenade the verandahs and hotel parlors and keep her nervous cousin Lottie Ridgeway company, who was of ripe age for marriage.

The Saratoga excursion had been arranged by Mrs. Ridgeway, Lottie's mother and Ember's guardian, for the sole purpose of capturing a suitable marriage match for Lottie. They had traipsed about arm in arm, showing off gowns and jewels with a dozen other hopefuls. It was all a spectacle fit for Queen Victoria, one well chaperoned by eagle-eyed dowagers who vied to have their own daughter or granddaughter pushed forward. The audience, of course, consisted of young gentlemen from prominent and wealthy families. And because Ember was more outgoing than Lottie, she was permitted to stay with her through three wonderful weeks of waltzes and polkas, the dancing going on for hours each night in the hotel parlors.

It was then that she had noticed a military student from West Point who appeared to find the spectacle amusing. Later, she learned from Lottie that his name was Tavish Wilder and that he had not come with his family but had traveled as an aide to his commanding officer.

Ember had been taken with the young man from the moment she first saw him watching her, but all of her vague flirtations to encourage him to ask her to waltz had availed nothing.

Whatever business brought him to the hotel had not kept him long, and the next day he was gone, returning to West Point.

When Ember and the family returned to the house on the Hudson, she began to look for a discreet opportunity to meet Tavish Wilder again. Since escorts were often needed for less-sought-after debutantes, it was a socially acceptable custom for families to quietly seek them from among West Point cadets. Because Ember was not yet "available," but permitted to attend functions with Cousin Lottie, she too needed an attentive young gentleman, preferably an honor student. So, she secretly arranged with Lottie to have the family request Tavish Wilder.

Throughout the hot summer of '71 and into the winter holidays, he had been her dutiful companion at outdoor barbecues, lawn parties, canoe rides, walks on the green, and the Christmas dance. For months, she had tried to make Tavish fall in love with her, all to no avail. He behaved impeccably, seeing that she danced the appropriate number of times, received her refreshments and moonlight strolls—strolls in which nothing ever took place. It was maddening! At times Ember didn't know if she loved him or hated him. Nor was she able to guess by his behavior if he knew whether or not she had requested him as her seasonal escort.

Now Ember thought she knew why the well-plotted romance had never bloomed. The colonel's daughter, Sara Brackston!

Sassy's unexpected news of seeing them together cut through Ember like a knife. She turned away, knowing her expression often became a mirror reflecting her heart. If Sassy could read her thoughts, what of Tavish? The thought that he might brought rosy tints to her skin.

"What does she look like, Sassy? Is she pretty?"

"Pretty ain't everything. Not to a man with good sense and godly values. I hear his mother—rest her soul—was near' a saint." Her frown deepened but there was understanding in her eyes. "Honey, you need to stay away from that Mister Wilder. You going to get yourself hurt, and him too. I done tole you so from the beginning. It weren't wise for you to be scheming to have him picked as your escort these months."

Ember winced at the suggestion that she had connived. She loved God, she told herself defensively. She said her prayers. And there was rarely a Sunday when she deliberately overslept. When she did, she tried to appease God for her lack of dedication by dusting off her mother's Bible and reading a psalm. However, Sassy usually caught her and would immediately launch into her speech about Jacob trying to bargain with God. *"Didn't trust the Lord like he should and schemed to get his way. Sleepin' in and then tryin' to appease the Lord with a psalm ain't goin' to bring His blessing neither."*

Ember sat down glumly on the blue needlework cushioned stool before her vanity table, chin in hand, half listening to Sassy talk while she wrapped the string around the hatbox.

"Now Miss Sara seems a nice girl, but I has no sympathy for that Mrs. Brackston. Heard say she nags her husband even on the Lord's day about gettin' himself rich. All so she can up her head to the clouds an' traipse her daughter around London."

Ember glanced at her wearily. "To search for a rich husband."

"She aims for a title."

"Titles," repeated Ember, wrinkling her nose and feeling bored. "She can have them all, far as I care. All I want is—" She stopped suddenly, catching herself from saying "Tavish Wilder," and stole a glance at Sassy, but the older woman was scowling to herself and didn't appear to notice.

"That Mrs. Brackston would most likely sell her reputation for a voyage to England if she could promenade Miss Sara. Now, that Mister Wilder, he's a fine young man, but you pay him no mind, chile. He ain't got no money neither."

"I don't care if he doesn't."

"You says that now. But that ain't to say the family will agree, or pay your mind any heed," argued Sassy. "They has big plans for the Ridgeway Timber Enterprise, and a few well-met marriages is what they's concerned about."

Ember stirred uneasily. It was her misfortune to have lost her Christian parents in a train accident when she was five years old. It was of little comfort to be reminded that others, more like strangers than family, held the keys to her future.

44

The robust and quarreling Ridgeways, who had claimed the Northwest as their own, thought nothing of using their blood kin as pawns on a chessboard while they gambled for bigger and bigger stakes in the wheeling-and-dealing world of railroad and timber. Ember and her cousins Lottie and Wade, as well as the other more distant cousins who lived year-round in New York and Philadelphia, were viewed simply as commodities for economic advancement.

There was nothing unusual about her situation. Most of the social families she knew frowned on serious involvement with a young man who had few prospects. Now and then Ember would hear of a secret romance between a girl of wealth and a West Point student without means; such affairs would bloom for a season, only to wither and die. The debutante would return home to her family, and the military graduate was invariably sent west, where wars raged with the Sioux and Cheyenne.

When Sassy had gone, Ember walked to the bed and stood with hands on hips, gazing down upon the sweetest-looking French ball gown she had ever seen.

Ember lived in a period of time when a woman's fashion was considered the barometer of her status as a high-class "lady." She knew of many households where a private seamstress appeared once a week to keep the wardrobe of the ladies of the house in full bloom, with a wide selection of new afternoon dresses and evening gowns.

Even though Port Townsend was her home, Ember fit easily into New York society, which held high interest in fashion. She adored the bold colors that were so popular: apple green, lapis lazuli, deep red, garnet, cardinal's purple. It was a period of time, too, when the cut of the fabric was lavish; some of Ember's carriage dresses required twenty yards, her favorites made with brocades and velvets.

For evening wear, silks were the fashion favorite, but in more subdued colors of cream, white, pale yellows, blues, and greens, all trimmed lavishly with bows, laces, ruffles, ruching, and beadwork.

Crinolines and the billowing skirts of the Civil War era were "out" and the bustle was "in." Ember's French ball gown was the new rage. The dress had a low, rounded off-the-shoulder bodice in the close-fitting polonaise style. Attached to this tight bodice was an overskirt, elaborately looped up at the side, edged with a frill. The underskirt was long and trailing, also heavily flounced. The lace-frilled sleeves were short and puffed. Two colors were always used for important occasions, and she had chosen shades of blue that reflected well with her hair. Because the sleeves were short, something new was introduced to fashion: long evening gloves of silk. Her slippers were made of soft glacé kid with high heels and pointed toes, and she would carry a small fan—an item that women in 1871 were rarely seen without.

"It's perfect," she murmured. "If only I can get the waist taken in an inch."

She snatched up the gown and went out the door in search of Sassy.

The heavily beamed hall, bright with crocheted rag rugs, greeted her with a spicy scent of cedar. It was empty. Apparently the other girls invited from Chadwick, sleeping three and four to a large bed for the weekend, were busy preparing for the gala event.

Ember's bare feet made no sound on the hall floor. *I should have worn slippers,* she thought, feeling the late December cold. Her thoughts were interrupted when she neared the spacious dressing room. The door stood open with bright light spilling out across the hall floor. From inside, she heard a familiar, dreaded sound—whispering and giggling. Ember's eyes narrowed, and she halted, instincts warning her that this time Lottie was not present to defend her against "cat talk."

"I'll wager he isn't!"

"He is!"

"How would you know? You've never been friendly with Sara, and she wouldn't tell you anything."

"A little bird told me," came the silly singsong voice of sixteen-year-old Hedda.

"Meaning her mother," came a sarcastic reply from another girl.

"My mother knows everything there is to know, and she's found out he's already asked the colonel's daughter."

There came a gasp from the girls. In the hall, Ember painfully held her breath.

"To marry him? I don't believe it! He has two years left at West Point."

"Who's talking about marriage, you goose! He asked her to the sleigh ride and ball. I'm glad he did. The way Ember chases him is positively shameful!"

"You're just jealous, Hedda, 'cause he never looks at you."

"I am not! I wouldn't look twice at a man who had no family background—"

"Tut, tut, listen to Miss Green-With-Envy."

"It's Ember who is as jealous as a cat, and all the time pretending to be *sooo* religious. But it's all an act. My mother says Christians are mostly hypocrites—"

"Oh, Hedda, be fair."

"Ember's been sending messages to his commanding officer, mind you. 'Requesting' Mister Wilder's services on matters of serious business."

Laughter erupted.

"Shh, Lottie will hear us. You know how she always defends her. But listen to this—first Ember needs a qualified male escort to bring her to the stables so she can check on the boarding of her horse. Imagine! Then she needs an escort for this, then that—and no one in all West Point will do except Mister Wilder. It's positively hilarious!"

Ember felt sick. She began to back away.

"If you ask me, Tavish Wilder doesn't seem to mind at all. I think he's sweet on Ember but won't show it. He has no money. What chance does he have with her family? He doesn't want to get involved, is all, and he's playing it safe. If Ember had any heart she'd leave him alone."

"You make me die laughing. As if she could capture his heart. He's as cool as a cucumber. He'll arrive with the colonel's daughter—wait and see if I'm not right. I can imagine her expression now when she finds out. Wouldn't it be fun if she couldn't even get an escort in time? Then she'd have to stay upstairs."

"You're as mean as a boat rat, Hedda. If Lottie knew you spoke like this about her cousin—"

Ember's hands were cold as she fled silently back down the hall. So Hedda's gossipy mother knew about the letters sent to West Point. Had she nothing better to do than spy? She tensed with shame. If Lottie's two-faced friends at Chadwick knew about the letters, did Tavish? She made it back safely to her room and quietly shut the door, feeling the stinging slap on her wounded pride. Did he secretly laugh at her while he behaved the gallant officer and gentleman? Her damp palms formed into fists. "I've a mind to let him know exactly what I think of him."

But she couldn't do that either, since she would need his cooperation to save her reputation.

Tavish's image came before her and her anger melted as swiftly as it had risen. She did love him, didn't she? Or was this passion that bordered on agony simply what they called "growing-up love"? An infatuation that would suddenly die? He did care about her, and she must find some way to make him say so. She must find some way to keep him from escorting the colonel's daughter, thereby proving Hedda a false gossip before the Chadwick girls. "If I don't, I'll be the brunt of secret laughter. How can I ever face them again when classes resume in late January?"

As she stood there Ember quenched the reminder of the danger in relying on schemes to solve her problems. "In the future I'll try harder to obey God," she soothed herself. She would spend more time in prayer. Her eyes fell on her Bible, where she'd left it undisturbed for the two weeks since she'd attended Sunday services.

A light film of dust had formed on the leather cover and she felt a prick to her conscience. The minister had spoken of the dangers from worrying incessantly about life's vanities.

She was thinking this, scowling at her image in the mirror, when she heard echoing horsehoofs below. *Who would be coming to call at this hour?* she wondered and went to the window, feeling the cold penetrating the glass pane, aware of the sparkling snow outside the isolated wing of the pinewood lodge.

In the frozen silence of the moonlit night, she saw the driver stop the carriage, its black roof dusted with snow, and climb down to open the door. Ember was surprised to see Cousin Lottie in a fur-lined cape and hood.

What is she doing out so late? Ember wondered, and waited, expecting another member of the family to step from the carriage, or perhaps Major Prescott Hollister, the West Point officer whom Lottie was engaged to marry. Apparently Lottie was alone, for she hurried to the front door and the driver brought the carriage toward the back of the lodge.

Ember's curiosity grew when she heard rising voices in the downstairs hall. Someone had lighted the gas lamps in the front parlor and the snow glistened on the front yard.

Slipping into a straight dark skirt and white blouse that she had worn earlier in the evening, and leaving her long hair unbound, Ember hurried from her room.

The rugged oak stairway was carpetless and descended to a wide entranceway that ran the length of the house, with bulging bay windows dressed with garnet draperies. The drapes were drawn back, but the view of pine trees and winter-white hills lay in darkness.

Lottie had just entered with a cold draft of wind when she glanced up and saw Ember on the stairs. Lottie came toward her, sweeping back the fur-lined hood to disclose blue-black hair brushed into a smooth chignon covered with a white silk net.

Her Christian name was Charlotte Anne but everyone called her Lottie. Her dark eyes reminded Ember of still forest ponds reflecting an uncluttered heart. Frail health during childhood had kept Lottie quiet and introspective, and she was never more at peace than when alone in her world of literature and music. Ember often wondered how Lottie could be so different from the strong personality of her mother, Cleo Ridgeway. Aunt Cleo could not walk without crutches, due to a terrible accident in her youth, but she had risen above her physical disability to become known affectionately to family and friends in Washington Territory as the "timber queen." But if Lottie was retiring and uncertain of herself, she chose to believe in others. Her quiet faith in the Scriptures often cooled the willful Ember like dewdrops on an evening rose.

"Where have you been so late?" whispered Ember. "If the family finds out—"

Lottie hushed her to silence and took hold of her arm, leading her up the stairs.

"I went to meet Prescott," whispered Lottie. "He had some disconcerting news he wished to tell me . . . about Tavish Wilder."

Ember's gaze swiftly met her cousin's. The uneasiness in her chest swelled. She thought of Sara, the colonel's daughter. "Yes? What is it? Is he taking Sara to the ball?"

Lottie looked embarrassed and troubled all at once. "I wish it were as simple as that. This isn't easy to tell you, Ember, but Prescott found out tonight that Tavish was expelled from West Point. He left yesterday. He won't be back."

Ember felt the breath knocked from her. "Expelled!"

Lottie bit her lip. "Evidently he received his high grades by—by cheating. This time they found a copy of the final exam in his desk."

Devastated, Ember stared at her.

"Oh, Ember, I'm sorry. He did it for his father, I suppose. He wanted to make him proud. It's a pity! To be expelled from West Point is such a disgrace."

Ember's insides felt like a tomb. Expelled. Gone. . . .

"Where did he go?" she found herself asking dully.

"To join his father. They say Mr. Kain Wilder is following the train camps." Lottie's face tinted with what must have been a feeling of embarrassment for Ember. "Prescott said that Tavish will work laying track for the railroad."

Late that night in her room, Ember rested her head on the pillow as Sassy sat beside her on the bed.

"Always did say you and him carin' about each other was jinxed. Now I know it's so. There ain't no way your family is goin' to let you involve yourself with a poor track layer. It's best this way, though it hurts now."

"I won't forget him," wept Ember.

"You says that now, but tomorrow has a way of healin' itself when it's given to the Lord. You should have hearkened to ol' Sassy. There's a heap I knows of life you don't. I been around close to fifty years and has me a bunch of scars and bumps to prove it."

Ember had heard the story before of how Sassy grew up a slave in New Orleans before the war. She had worked as a cook in what Sassy called a "slop house"—a brothel—and fed a passel of "no-goods" till she was freed.

"I seen plenty. Shattered women and broken men with no hope, sometimes with no longin' to change even if they could. When the war ended I left New Orl'ns and worked my way into Washington Territory, thinkin' I might start my own Creole restaurant, but things went from bad to worse. I was out of work an' on the street when your great-aunt Macie found me in Tacoma. The two of us was together ever since.

"I says all this because you is only a girl like I was. The man I loved was killed back then . . . used to cry myself into nightmares. Now I don't even remember what he looked like. . . . Two, maybe three years from now you won't even remember Tavish Wilder."

4

THE LONESOME WHISTLE CALL

1873

The Northern Pacific boxcars, filled with tired and silent workers, rumbled toward a little-known site recently named Bismarck on the wide Missouri River just below Fort Abraham Lincoln.

Tavish Wilder was sprawled in the crowded railcar, which stank with a mixture of stale sweat and tobacco. His granite green eyes were almost as dark as his rich hair, held back with a leather cord. He wore dusty black jeans, boots, and a torn denim shirt, and he owned a buckskin jacket that kept him warm in the winters when the snow outside kept the boxcars as cold as the frozen north. A guitar in a canvas satchel was slung over his muscled shoulder.

Tavish leaned his head against the boxcar wall and squinted beneath slashing dark brows in the poor light of the swaying lantern. He held a torn page from a newspaper advertisement he had found trampled underfoot in the train building back in Fargo. The writing had caught his interest because it spoke enthusiastically about the Pacific Northwest, and Tavish had dreams of returning one day.

WHAT IS IT? FOR HEAVEN'S SAKE, WHAT IS IT?
The Banana Line
The TREE is known by its FRUITS!

Tavish squinted at a sketch of a tropical banana tree with its roots growing out of the Missouri River and its leafy palms stretching across the Great Northwest into Oregon and Washington territories.

He restrained a smile, remembering the snow and ice of his boyhood home. Another colorful flyer read

QUIT THE STRENUOUS LIFE!
CORNUCOPIA. NO TORNADOES OR BUZZARDS.
Are you tired of working for others?
GO WEST! Buy five or ten acres of
WASHINGTON FRUIT LAND!
Information mailed free on request.

Tavish nudged his young French-Canadian cousin, who mumbled something but continued snoring, pulling the blanket up around his head. Tavish's father, Kain Wilder, had ridden into Tucson to claim guardianship of Julot after his father had been killed in a gunfight. Julot, then a belligerent young man of nineteen, had been living alone in a small run-down shack in Mexican Town with a Negro friend, Lazou, when Kain had found him.

Grudgingly, Julot had surrendered to his uncle—a recent circuit-riding preacher among the train camps—and had joined him on the journey. Lazou, too, had hitched his two donkeys to a weather-beaten wagon and followed, and was now one of the Northern Pacific cooks. After being expelled from West Point, Tavish had made the group a foursome.

They had followed the grimy Northern Pacific track layers, graders, and surveyors across Minnesota and here to Dakota, working for the railroad baron Jay Cooke, who was building a transcontinental line from the Great Lakes all the way across the Northwest into Oregon and Washington territories. While his father preached the hope of the Resurrection, Tavish earned their meals by swinging a sledgehammer. After two years at West Point he hated the work, but did it without complaining much because he respected the new change in his father. By the time they had arrived at Bismarck they had completed 450 miles of track on the northern route. Another 165 miles were finished in Washington Territory and the railroad had received ten million acres for its progress, more than a fifth of its federal land grant, and word was out that immigrants by the hundreds were arriving to buy the land from the railroad.

At night by the campfire Tavish read his logging books and dreamed, looking up at the stars in the soft Dakota sky. By day he laid track and swung the hammer. The only good the hammer had done was to give him rock-solid muscle in his arms, shoulders, chest, and back. All six feet of him was enough to silence anyone who thought his satchel of prized books was funny or his father's preaching nettlesome.

In the boxcar, directly across from Tavish, a bitter-faced man in his thirties, with small eyes and a hawk nose, rested his shoulder against the wall. Tavish tried to ignore the man. He'd prefer to bust Riley on the chin, but the man was the Northern Pacific's head track layer and Tavish recognized that his own behavior reflected on his father's ministry.

Riley mumbled something to himself and glanced about at the men under his charge, his eyes coming to rest on Tavish. Riley drew the makings for a weed smoke out of his wrinkled gray duster. He spat the distaste for whatever gnawed at him into the sour hay.

"Railroad baron, eh? Jay Cooke's plain stupid when it comes to Injuns."

Tavish lowered his hat, settled his back against the wall, and shut his eyes.

" 'Course the Big Man doesn't need to worry about his scalp—he's sittin' in his mansion up in Philadelphia's Cheltan Hills entertainin' President Grant. Fifty rooms, it has."

Fifty rooms, thought Tavish, too overwhelmed with the idea to begrudge the railroad baron his earthly treasures. *I'd be content with a fox's lair if I didn't need to share with fifty other track layers. What does a man do with fifty rooms?*

"But the NP surveying crew better worry," continued Riley. "Them Injun chieftains are all out there in Yellowstone country—Sitting Bull, Crazy Horse, Black Moon—I'm crazy too, drawing pay for this kind of work!"

In the spring of 1873 at the request of Jay Cooke & Company, the War Department ordered a military force to leave Fort Lincoln and protect an engineering survey party in the valley of Yellowstone. One of the men commanding the expedition was Lieutenant Colonel George Armstrong Custer of the Seventh Cavalry.

Tavish had heard that Mack Ridgeway would be arriving at Fort Lincoln with engineers and 350 civilian mule drivers, guides, and interpreters for the expedition. Surveyors would map a new route into the Northwest where track would eventually join up with the track being laid in Washington Territory. Several preliminary surveys had already been made for the route, but no matter which way the railroad was built, it would continue to cross hundreds of miles of buffalo-grazing grounds in Minnesota, Montana, and Dakota territories—some of it treaty land for the Sioux.

"Heard Sitting Bull's in Canada," said a sleepy-eyed Virginian. "He won't bother us none this time. We got the Seventh Cavalry."

Riley's look was hostile. "Lemme tell you gents somethin'. Back in '71 and '72 I was with the NP surveyors when we met up with Sitting Bull. He ain't in Canada powwowing with them half-breeds. He's in Yellowstone country. An' we're likely to meet him again." He struck a match and lit the end of the paper, his eyes coming to Tavish's hair. "Better watch that fancy hair of yours, boy. Crazy Horse might like it."

Tavish held back his temper, feeling like a powder keg waiting for a match to light the fuse. If he responded, his father would hear of it. The former Kain Wilder would have smiled faintly and leaned back to watch his son teach Riley a lesson, but not the new Kain Wilder! The look of disappointment in his father's eyes would have bothered Tavish's conscience for hours.

Riley was looking for an opportunity to make light of the older Wilder's Christianity. Kain had never said anything, but Tavish guessed the two men had known each other in years past. He could imagine Riley's bitter tongue: *So you're a preacher now, eh, Kain? When you goin' to teach that hot-tempered son of yours some respect for his elders?"*

Tavish concentrated on the advertisements, folding them with care and placing them inside his beat-up satchel. To forget Riley, he took out one of his logging books. Though he couldn't concentrate, he turned to where he had left off reading the night before.

Riley's voice droned on like an irritating mosquito. "Know what Jay Cooke calls this spot, gents? Bismarck. Got one thing on his mind: greed. Hopes to get that German chancellor's money. Got news for him. The NP can call this spot Bismarck, but Sitting Bull won't be impressed. White man's railroad is still 'bad medicine.' He won't like Ridgeway's surveying party heading into Yellowstone country."

"Then why don't you saddle your horse and ride back where you came from?" drawled Julot.

Tavish had thought his young cousin asleep and had nudged him with his boot. Riley turned his head toward Julot with a rooster eye.

"I'm thinkin' 'bout it, Frenchie. Ridgeway better too—if he wants to live and get rich. Heard he has his eye on all Washington Territory. Wants trainloads of immigrants to farm there so he can sell 'em useless railroad land. But money's not in buying, gents. Nope, it's in selling it to half-wit immigrants expectin' to make good."

As if expecting to be challenged, Riley glanced around at the men, too weary and beaten to do much talking and too poor to own land, railroad or otherwise.

Riley sucked on his smoke. "NP's got forty-seven million acres. You kin thank Abe Lincoln and the Congress for that act of benevolence. All the NP needs do is lay a line from Lake Superior to Washington Territory." He gave a dour smile. "While you build it, they'll sell their free land along the way. Them immigrants got a rude awakening. Ain't nuthin' there but rain and snow."

Tavish felt Julot move his long legs restlessly but before he could stop him, Julot spoke. "Tav was born near Hood Canal. There's a lot more in the Pacific Northwest than rain. There's good land out there an' his pa owns some of it."

The boss-man looked at him over his smoke. Julot's black

eyes twinkled. Tavish knew that look. When Julot refused to be stared down, Riley drew on his smoke.

"What do you know about it, Frenchie? Thought you came from Quebec—or was it from them half-breeds so friendly with Sitting Bull on the route north of Yellowstone?"

Tavish saw Julot start to move, but he clamped a strong hand around his cousin's arm. It seemed he was always restraining him. It wasn't too difficult when he was in a quiet mood himself, but at the moment he too had about as much as he could take of Riley's mouth.

Riley turned his head. "If Kain owns land out yonder, what's he doing in Dakota Territory lettin' his two boys sleep in vermin-infested boxcars?"

Tavish hated being called a "boy," especially after West Point, but his cousin would fight about it. Tavish kept a hand on Julot's wrist as a reminder that they must avoid trouble.

"I'm here by choice," said Tavish. "One day we'll go back to Washington and lay claim to our land."

"Yeah," said Julot, leaning forward. "And since you hate the NP so much, why don't you do the same."

"I don't need some kid to advise me. I was a lieutenant in the Confederate Army while you was still bein' weaned. As for that railroad land you're both keyed up about, you ought to know something before you go hightailin' it out there."

Tavish might have told him it wasn't railroad land his father owned, but he kept silent.

"Before Jay Cooke took over the NP from the other busted barons, he bought half of the company sellin' railroad land. That's how they can sell farms and town sites along the track. They advertise 'big' profits for the immigrants who buy, but it's *theirs* to stash away. 'Safe! Profitable! Permanent!'" Riley said derisively of Cooke's advertisements. "Puts everything in them big capital letters. 'Fertile Belt!' he calls it. Tell these trackers here how cold it gets out in the Pacific Northwest. You can't grow nuthin'." He drew on the smoke.

Tavish watched him, hands behind his head as he rested, one boot drawn up. He didn't have a farm in mind, but again, it wasn't any of Riley's business.

"You can grow plenty," argued Julot. "Old Lazou is headin'

to the Northwest to start an apple orchard. He's even got some saplings with him."

"Lazou's a freed slave from Mississippi. What's he know except cotton? Besides, Negroes can't own land in the territory."

Julot leaned forward ignoring Tavish's grip. "Yes he can! Lazou's a friend of mine, an' I don't like you sayin'—"

"Take it easy, young man," came a quiet voice from a darkened corner of the boxcar. An older man smoking a pipe pointed it in Julot's direction. "Everyone's bone tired and hungry to boot. It's been a long, uncomfortable ride. But I feel the train slowin'. I'd say we're nearing Bismarck. Soon we can get some fresh air."

Riley lifted the smoke from between his stained teeth. "Fruit orchards, eh? So you and Lazou know about Jay Cooke's famous banana belt?" he chuckled. "Doesn't surprise me yer pa would swallow that fairy tale stuff."

Tavish thought of the advertisement, and although it had nothing to do with growing apples, he felt uncomfortable, and he resented the slur on his father's credibility.

"That banana belt ain't the only land no good fer farmin'," said a freckle-faced kid, lanky and baked brown from a mixture of dirt and sun. "You been down to the railroad land on Red River? My pa bought some after the war."

"Mighty fine farmland, ain't it?" said Riley with a sour smile.

"Most of all, we was sceered of the Injuns," said the boy. "They don't take kindly to track runnin' where buffalo roam. My ma and pa were both kilt."

Riley grunted in disgust and shook his head. He threw the remains of the smoke onto the floor and stomped it. "And we're gettin' together an engineering expedition into Sitting Bull's backyard."

"It ain't his backyard," said a narrow-eyed man. "Where'd he come from, and who gave him all this land anyway? Before Injuns fought the white man, they fought the other tribes over it. One white man can take ten acres, work the soil and build a ranch, but the Sioux and Cheyenne just roam the plains, needing two thousand acres of hunting ground per man—and claiming it all. Let 'em settle down and farm one spot like we do."

The train was grating to a halt and the men stirred from dozing, or dreaming of kinder days. There were voices outside the boxcar and the door slid open, allowing fresh air in. A brakeman cupped his mouth and sang out, "Hot coffee, corn pones, and red beans at the chuck wagon. Come'n fill yer belly befer it's only a memory of home!"

The grimy men filed out into the dusky rose twilight of the Missouri River outpost. Alternately called "Edwinton" and "The Crossing," the cluster of buildings was now named after German statesman Otto Von Bismarck. The strategic name change by the Northern Pacific was to entice German immigrants to settle here and farm, and to encourage the German government to invest in the enterprise.

While the tired men streamed to the enticing aroma of coffee, and Julot scrambled to roll up his blanket, Tavish sat lazily contemplating the advertisement.

Safe! Profitable! Permanent!

Fertile Belt!

He leaned against the boxcar wall feeling the cold beneath his jacket.

"How big is forty-seven million acres?" he mused to Julot. He did some quick figuring on the back of the advertisement.

Julot, four months his senior, mumbled something in French, gave him a hard look, and jammed his floppy hat over his head.

"Big enough," said Tavish. "It's worth billions, that's what. A kingdom vast enough to take in all the New England states and leave room for Maryland. The money that could be obtained from sales in timber, farmland, and city lots is staggering."

Julot sighed. "A lot of good it does us, *mon ami*. As much as we talk about heading to Oregon and Washington to smell sweet pine, we breathe dust. For the rest of our lives we shall swing a sledgehammer." Julot flexed his right arm until the muscles bulged, growling in a threatening way as he did. "Boxing— maybe I can make gold nuggets by boxing. We both can. We shall hold a circus. One night I am winner, next—maybe you." He smiled down at Tavish with even, white teeth showing against his olive complexion.

Tavish smirked.

Julot's black eyes were merry as he ran his fingers across his clean-shaven face. "Too pretty to be scarred even for gold. I shall stay with the hammer." He dug into his canvas bag and brought out his harmonica. As the boxcar was emptied of its last track layer, Julot cradled the harmonica to his mouth and let out a spine-tingling burst of music that would have silenced a songbird. He weaved and turned as he danced about, adding rhythm with his dusty boots.

Tavish picked up his guitar:

Dey took John Henry to de graveyard
An' dey buried him in de san',
An' every locomotive come roarin' by,
Says, "Dere lays a steel-drivin' man,
Oh yeah! dere lays a steel-drivin' man."

Tavish let his hand rest quietly on the guitar as he thought of the land grant his father had received years ago from the federal government. If the Northern Pacific did choose Port Townsend for its transcontinental line, the grant would be worth a fortune. But it wasn't the railroad he was interested in. It was the bountiful stand of timber he remembered as a boy, before they moved to Chicago. Pine branches heavy with chattering blue jays and clear rivers jumping with salmon. . . .

For a moment he dreamed big, his mind wandering the silver tracks, hearing the call of the train whistle.

Julot's harmonica joined in, sending a melancholy strain floating on the breeze. The sun was setting over the wide Missouri River and Tavish felt the wind like some pied piper tugging at his coat sleeve, and mimicking, "Come, come, come . . . whooo-ahh-woooooo."

"Hey, Tav! Wake up," called Julot with a tinge of amused irritation in his voice.

Tavish looked up to see that the boxcar was now in shadows. "Supper sounds mighty good. Let's go," he said and grabbed for his hat, pushing himself up from the hard floor.

Outside the railcars, the men were lining up for supper. Others in Bismarck were celebrating the track's end. There were decorated boxcars, lit-up tents, some wooden buildings with lanterns. The men wore expensive frock coats, boiled shirts with gold watch chains on the vests, and derby hats. Across the dusty lot were shabby gambling tents where cards shuffled, dice clicked, and liquor poured. Painted prostitutes trying to cover their wrinkles with rouge loitered about, and con men tempted the rail workers to gamble their hard-earned pay. And somewhere in the carnival atmosphere, his father, Kain Wilder, would be offering the parched souls something better than the prodigal's corn husks: living water to quench the fire of an endless thirst.

God bless him, Tavish thought. There wasn't a better man anywhere in sight who was going about the one business that was essential.

Julot was pulling ahead to the chuck wagon like a fearless dog straining at his leash, when suddenly he stopped. Tavish, deep in thought, nearly collided with him.

"There's your pa . . . and he's handing out invitations to the revival meetin'. Nobody will show, Tav. Not on a celebratin' night like this.

"Now take my pa," Julot was saying as they walked on. "He was gunned down in the Quartz Saloon in Tucson by six men. Took all six to do him in! You ain't lived yet, Tav. Not till you seen Tucson. You should aim to ride with me."

Tavish gave him a narrowed look and strode on. "I don't *aim* on riding anywhere. And seeing Tucson's gunfighters isn't one of my passions. I have bigger and better plans than settling for dust, sweat, and a bullet in my back."

"My pa drank brew with Spanish Jack. Could shoot straighter, faster, and never wink an eye."

"And got himself buried for it. Don't forget that part. It takes more courage to ride into sin holes and preach," argued Tavish, settling his hat lower and glaring at him.

"Your pa ain't the only preacher."

"It's hard to stand alone, to walk away and forget an insult. Like putting up with Riley's mouth." He snapped off a leaf from the tree branch he ducked under. "I'd sooner bust him wide open as exchange the time of day. Never heard a man boast so much and say so little as Riley. All the way from Duluth he jawed, and he wore me out listening."

Julot pulled out the huge, deadly Spanish spurs he carted with him in his beat-up pack wherever they traveled. "See these?"

Tavish restrained a smile. "Too many times."

"Pa took these off Spanish Jack. A mean one, him. Now the spurs are mine."

"You can have 'em."

"Now your pa, well, Uncle Kain is mighty good, and don't I know it. But he don't tote a gun, only the Book, and well—"

Tavish looked at him in his cool, quiet way, his eyes glittering. "Anyone who lays claim otherwise to the courage of Kain Wilder might find himself spitting sand."

Julot grinned at him victoriously, his eyes snapping with pleasure. "*Mon ami*, see? And you say you're a preacher's kid. *Oui!* But you take after your French blood, after me and my pa."

"No. I don't," Tavish said flatly. "And don't you take to calling me a kid. I'm only four months younger than you."

Julot turned grave. "Four months is a mighty long time, Tav—especially since I been in Tucson."

Tavish smirked and gave him a shove on the shoulder. "Get moving. Lazou's red beans will be gone by the time we get there. You forget I'm two years ahead of you in education."

"Tav, you should've clobbered that spoiled Ridgeway when he lied about you cheating on that exam. If I was in your spot I'd be plenty bitter. I'd be just waiting for the day when I found him again. You settle your score with Wade Ridgeway, then we'll go to Tucson and take 'em all on. There's six men who shot bullets in my pa."

The suggestion that he settle his score with Ridgeway was closer to how Tavish felt than Julot realized. The ugly head of revenge had reared itself from the wilderness more than once in the last two years of swinging the hammer. And now, the goading words seemed to make the dust and sweat sticking to Tavish more bothersome.

He glanced in the direction of the river as though it offered cool relief from his emotions. He aimed to bathe before the revival meeting. Someday he'd own his own private tub with lots of hot water and white towels.

"Wade Ridgeway is stationed at Fort Lincoln, serving Colonel Custer," said Tavish. "And I've not forgotten. He'll be with Custer when they escort the NP into Yellowstone."

A voice interrupted from behind them: "Who'll be with Colonel Custer?"

Tavish turned his dark head toward the Missouri River, where a man stood in the shadows.

5

NORTHWEST DREAMS

The river was grayish red in the fading light of the setting sun as Tavish faced his father.

Kain wore a dusty frock coat that was thin at the elbows and a derby hat that had seen better days. His eyes, an icy gray-blue, were in contrast to his son's deep green, a color Tavish had inherited from his mother, Vonette. Kain's hair was also lighter, and ruffled the edge of his collar in the river breeze.

Had his father overheard about Wade Ridgeway being at Fort Lincoln? Tavish met his father's eyes and the silence between them grew.

Julot cleared his voice and began to whistle, digging into his pocket for his harmonica. Tavish heard the soothing chorus carry on the air—

"Man of Sorrows!" what a name, for the Son of God, who came. Ruined sinners to reclaim! Hallelujah, what a Savior!

Tavish saw his father's eyes twinkle, as though Kain had guessed Julot was trying to ease the tension by playing his favorite hymn.

"Well, boy, I see you've been practicing for tonight," he told

Julot. His eyes came back to Tavish with a smile. "Who'll be with Colonel Custer?" he repeated smoothly. "Not looking to hunt up Sitting Bull at Yellowstone by any chance?"

The casual humor typical of his father caused Tavish to smile. "I'll leave that to you. You're the preacher."

"Not much of one, I'm afraid."

Tavish pushed back a damp tendril of dark hair from his forehead. He recognized the hint of discouragement in his father's tone, knew that his lack of seminary education bothered him. Quickly he came to his defense with a light remark.

"Oh, I don't know," and he deliberately looked over at Julot. "You brought that ornery one to the Lord and he was about as wild as you can get."

Julot looked up, surprised, and Tavish smiled. Kain chuckled. "I thought *I* was the wild one."

Julot laughed and Tavish looked at his father. The man was so different from what he remembered as a boy that the spiritual change never ceased to amaze him.

Soon after he had arrived from West Point, he discovered there was little of the preacher-type about his father. He relied on the life-giving power of the Scriptures rather than on highstrung preaching. Tavish had examined the books his father had brought with him and was pleased with his choice of C. H. Spurgeon and John Calvin. In the evenings, Tavish would see his father at the campfire reading the first volume of Spurgeon's *Treasury of David,* an exposition of the Psalms. Included at the end of each psalm were "Hints to the Village Preachers." These were outlines and notes that Spurgeon enclosed for young men who could not attend seminary.

"Better get your supper while there's time," said Kain. "We've a large group tonight. Even the soiled doves are coming."

"Soiled doves" were what gentlemen had taken to calling the prostitutes who always followed the railroad camps.

"If they're doves, I'd hate to see a chicken," quipped Julot.

Tavish masked a smile and gave his cousin a whack with his wide-brimmed hat. The dust floated off in the Dakota breeze.

"Let's go," said Kain, throwing a strong arm around his son's shoulders.

Julot strayed a few steps behind, clutching his harmonica in one hand and the beat-up Spanish spurs in the other. Kain paused and waited for him to come up on his left. He threw his other arm around Julot's shoulders, walking on with them both.

"A man's mighty blessed of the Lord having two sons to his name. I've a feeling there's enough sand in both of you to make a man proud when he's too old to preach."

"Listen to him," taunted Tavish. "He's not even forty yet and he's hinting for a rocking chair."

The aroma of supper cooking drifted their way, and Julot surged ahead, impatient as always to eat.

Kain paused to speak to Tavish alone. "I expect to see you with your guitar at the meeting tonight, son. Then be sure to come to the campfire afterwards. I've something to discuss with you," he said, the humor gone from his eyes.

Tavish stood with hands on hips watching his father walk back toward camp. Even if he'd overheard the talk between him and Julot, the mention of Wade Ridgeway's name would mean little. He'd never told his father who lied about him at West Point. If Kain had begun to guess, he didn't let on. But then, his father was a cool one when it came to masking his thoughts.

The silence between them over West Point bothered Tavish at times. When he had first walked into the train camp two years ago, wearing not an immaculate uniform but a frock coat, hat, and jeans, his father had stared at him without moving—stared long and hard.

"I've been expelled," Tavish had said tonelessly, glossing over the pain and anger he felt deep inside.

"For what reason?"

At first the despised word would not come. "Cheating."

The look on his father's face told Tavish to prepare for a blow, but that flicker of disappointed rage melted like ice in a desert sun. In its place came a new expression that he'd never seen before on his father. *Compassion.* It too didn't last long.

"Is the charge true?" Kain had simply asked.

Tavish let out a small breath and shook his head.

"I want to hear it, son."

"No."

The tension had passed. After calmly explaining that he'd been falsely accused, his father had lapsed into silence. The matter was never mentioned again.

Now, as Tavish turned and headed toward the chuck wagon, he thought, *It's almost as if West Point never existed. Chicago too, for that matter.* A tiny flame of frustration flickered deep inside.

The supper line was thinning out when Tavish neared the chuck wagon, still musing over what his father wanted to discuss at the campfire.

Several big pots blackened by years of use were strung out on a chain over a glowing bed of coals, and the aroma of salt pork and beans filled the evening breeze. Tavish hated salt pork. He remembered his mother's cooking during the first eleven years of his life, many of the fine recipes from Quebec. *Buche de Noel,* a jelly-roll cake with chocolate filling was his favorite. He sighed.

As the line of hungry track layers dwindled, Lazou momentarily left his cook station to haul a bucket of water from the Missouri for his scrawny apple trees. Tavish smiled to himself. The sight of the big man nursing his dozen saplings along the difficult journey from Duluth was familiar to Tavish and the other men. Lazou faithfully doctored and pampered his trees, guarding them as a miner his gold.

"I'm mighty hungry for fresh fruit, Laz," Tavish called out. "Think those trees are going to make it to Washington Territory?"

Lazou was busy checking every leaf and testing the soil for proper dampness. "They got ter make it," he replied, smiling up at Tavish. "This here's my El Dorado."

Julot was sitting on a nearby rock, hungrily putting away a generous helping of salt pork and beans, and a stack of corn pones. Tavish smiled at his cousin and grabbed a plate for himself, heaping it high with beans and corn pones. He heard someone walking up from the river and turned his head.

Riley approached, his shirt-sleeves rolled up and his hair wet from washing. He glanced at Julot's plate and stopped.

"Frenchie! Put them pones back! You know better'n to take double!" He looked around sharply for Lazou. Seeing him stooped over his trees, Riley shouted, "Stop your messing round with them blasted trees! Get back to work."

Lazou turned his head, his expression expecting trouble. "There's a whole nuther pan of pones in the stove brownin'."

Riley swore at him. "Git over here! When I say now, I means *now*, you worthless nigger!"

Tavish felt Riley's words slice through his own soul, but before he could respond, Julot jumped up and banged his tin plate down, spilling the beans. He spun to confront Riley.

"Take that back!"

"You talkin' to me?"

"You bet I am! Take it back! He ain't worthless! No man's worthless! There's no more slavery, and you got no call to speak to him like that."

"I'll speak any way I got a hankerin' to speak, Frenchie, an' if you don't like my manners why don't you teach me to shut up?"

"I will!"

"Julot!" barked Tavish.

But his cousin was yelling at Riley: "Come on, come on, then!"

Riley's eyes glittered with cold hatred. He spat, then walked straight toward Julot. "You need a lesson real bad, Frenchie. It's time I taught you one."

Lazou ran up. "Wait, Mr. Riley, he's jes a boy—"

"He's been askin' fer this a long while, and he's goin' to git what's comin'."

"Don't touch him," came Tavish's cool voice.

Riley turned his head. He paused, then smiled. "You're next, Sunday school boy."

Tavish saw Riley reach under his shirt and slip something over his knuckles, still smiling.

"We're all alone now. The others are havin' their supper. Time I'm through with you two, you'll be wishin' you hadn't messed with me."

Lazou was wrestling Julot, trying to stop him from reaching Riley. As they struggled, kicking up dust, Julot kept hollering at Lazou to let him go, but the muscled black man held on tight. "No, no, son, no, I kin handle my own battles. He'll kill you, he's got iron knuckles on—"

Riley had lost momentary interest in Julot and came slowly toward Tavish, his eyes cold and hard, licking his lower lip. "Well, boy? What ya waitin' for?"

"Riley, I'd love to see you spit your teeth out." Tavish smiled as he removed his canvas satchel holding the guitar, set it against the tree, and threw aside his hat.

An uncanny breeze stirred overhead through the cotton-wood trees. Tavish thought he heard his mother's voice calling, and suddenly he was a boy again, wrestling an Irish immigrant along the bank of the Hood Canal. The boy had insulted his French-Canadian mother. He felt his mother's hand pulling him away from the boy, tasted again the blood on his cut lip. *"Tavish, that's no way to handle frustration or pain. Let God handle your anger."*

The Missouri breeze touched Tavish's sweating forehead as he stared hard at Riley.

"Come on, don't disappoint me," breathed Riley. Tavish was aware that Julot and Lazou had ceased their own struggle and were watching him.

A sneer touched Riley's face. "Well? You goin' to let me whip you or not?"

"No."

Riley's pleasure showed in a look of triumph.

"I won't fight you," said Tavish.

"Knew you was a yella coward all along. You and yer pa both. Go on, boy! Get outta here, and take him with you." He gestured with disgust at Julot. Riley turned his back in contempt and walked to the coffee urn, taking his time getting his supper.

Julot sat in the dust with Lazou kneeling behind him.

Tavish stood motionless, his heart thudding. Becoming aware of Julot's stare, he looked over at his cousin to confront an expression he would never forget—disbelief in his dark eyes, and disappointment.

Julot dropped his gaze to the dust and lowered his head. *He's not ashamed for himself but for me,* thought Tavish, and found that Julot's disappointment goaded him far worse than anything Riley had said.

Tavish looked at Lazou. There was sympathy in his sweating face, and something else—understanding.

Riley left with a tin plate heaped with pones and beans, without another glance in their direction.

"Tav, you backed down," choked Julot, clenching a fist of dirt. "You just took all his words like a man lets a rattler just go ahead and bite him!"

Lazou got to his feet, staring down at Julot with a frown. "He ain't got no yella bones in his body."

"Yes, he does! You backed down, Tav. You're just words." He pushed himself up from the dust, grabbing his hat. "Riley has nothing but contempt for the three of us now!"

Frustrated, Tavish grabbed his satchel from the tree. "When I get ready to silence a man's mouth, Julot, you'll be the first." He turned on his heel and walked down to the river. He threw his satchel down by the banks of the Missouri and stared into the water as it rolled along, dark and vibrant beneath the summer sky.

Tavish knelt and splashed water against his face. It was cool and refreshing, taking his breath away. "I did what was right," he gritted. "I could have busted him easily enough."

He smashed a rock into the river. It splashed and was quickly smothered by the deep water.

An hour must have passed as he sat by the water, looking up at the stars all bright and shiny. He could hear the river flowing by and it brought an ache to his heart, echoing the music drifting down from the camp.

Oh, Shenandoah, I long to hear you,
Away, you rolling river,
Oh, Shenandoah, I long to hear you,
Away, I'm bound away,
'Cross the wide Missouri.

He felt a longing, but he didn't know what it was, or perhaps he did. The feeling stirred in the sound of a harmonica, the sigh of the wind, the moving of the river, the silence of the night.

Tavish enjoyed the solitude and dreamed of being a railroad baron like Jay Cooke of the Northern Pacific, or maybe a "timber wolf" like the lumber magnates from Washington Territory where he'd been born. . . .

He had spoken little of his dreams to his father—once a railroad man himself—but he wouldn't have exchanged the new Kain Wilder even for Jay Cooke & Company.

Kain's rugged gentleness and his passion for intimacy with his Creator had convinced Tavish that his father's faith was real. Tavish's one regret was that his mother hadn't lived long enough to see the change in the man she had loved and prayed for to the end. Tavish's fondest memory of Vonette Wilder was of her sitting in a chair by the kitchen table, reading the Bible. Every night she would call him to her side to pray for his father.

Tavish's own dreams could wait a little longer. He would be patient; somehow he knew they'd still be there waiting when the sun came up. And at night? He could dream . . . listening to the lonesome whistle . . . trying to forget the bitterness he felt toward Wade Ridgeway, and the image of Wade's cousin, Ember: a spoiled, rich debutante in satin and lace framing alabaster skin, with autumn hair piled high. It was an image that grew stronger in the dust and sweat of the railroad.

Julot walked up but didn't say anything. He sat down on the riverbank and began tossing pebbles into the water.

"I'm not mad," Tavish murmured, leaning on his elbows.

Julot turned his head and looked at him. A sheepish smile showed in the moonlight. "You're madder than a rattler." He looked up at the stars. "Don't blame you, though. Sorry, Tav, I know you're not a—"

"Forget it."

There had been many other moments like this between them in the past two years. While Tavish watched the light reflecting on the river, Julot brought out his harmonica and began to play, the rhythm of the harmony rolling along with the Missouri.

Tavish knew his cousin was doing some powerful thinking. Tavish too hadn't decided if he was completely squared away with his father's new belief in walking away from trouble. At least not all trouble.

Then there was the matter of not carrying guns. Tavish ran his hand through his dark hair. Why, a man needed a few bullets handy just to kill a rattler if he bumped into one. But Tavish wouldn't admit his thoughts to Julot. It would only give his cousin more reason to go storming off to Tucson.

Tavish had his own plans, and if possible he would avoid trouble in order to let them live. He looked over at Julot.

"I've often thought that if you're as smart as you claim, you'd string along with me to see big dreams come true. One day I'm going to claim that land in Washington Territory. I'm going to be a timber baron."

Julot stopped playing. He was quiet and looked up into the velvety sky.

"I'm going to move among gentlemen," continued Tavish. "Men with money and power."

Tavish didn't know if his cousin believed him or not. He wasn't altogether sure he believed his own words. But they sounded good.

"When we going?" asked Julot, as though willing to play along with him.

Tavish lapsed into silence. Laughter erupted from one of the gambling tents. Julot's question had an uncomfortable way of reminding him that to keep his eye on his dream he must disappoint the man he respected above all others. If he could bring himself to say goodbye, he'd feel as though he were saying it not to his father but to the Lord. To say he wished more from his life seemed to suggest that his father's was unproductive. Tavish sometimes had the notion that Kain would never feel satisfied with his labor for the Lord, as if he had a debt to fulfill with his Savior.

Kain never said anything, but Tavish knew his father blamed himself for his wife's death in the Chicago fire.

"My father has plans to return to the land in Washington one day."

Julot sighed and looped his thumb over his fringed buckskin belt. "That's like saying never, Tav, and you know it. He won't ever leave his preaching."

"He'll go north like he said. He knows the land's there. He knows it's ours. There's something he has to do first. When he's done, we'll ride out of here—for good. No more sledgehammers, no more stinking boxcars, no more Riley."

Tavish looked at him, his eyes flickering with green determination. He could tell Julot was trying hard to believe him. "Remember that timber grant along the Hood Canal?"

"Been telling me for two years. Ain't seen it yet."

"Patience. That grant belongs to my father, and nobody can take it away—not legally anyway. It was given by the federal government."

"I hope it means more'n the government's land treaties with the Indians."

"It's more land than you ever laid eyes on. Big trees! Big rivers!"

"Is that why you keep studying those books about lumbering?"

Tavish nodded. "And we can buy us a stern-wheeler to haul timber down to San Francisco. Maybe start a sawmill like the one in Seabeck. We've a French-Canadian uncle there. He knows about logging."

Julot considered the idea, a glow of hope in his eyes; then the glow faded, and his face, tired and streaked with dust, took on the pallor of the moonlight. "But if he don't want to go back? We're likely to be playing harmonica and guitar for the next ten years!"

Tavish smiled and stood, catching up his bag with his guitar. He slung it lightly over his shoulder. He didn't mind playing but said with wry humor, "Just as long as you do the singing."

"Aw, come on, Tav! You know I hate it worse than when your pa's working on my teeth! Harmonica's one thing—singin' words by myself is another."

"That girl with the yellow rat-nest hair last night seemed to take a shine to you."

Julot stood. "Her! As if I'd ever take to a kid in dirty overalls."

"She didn't look much like a kid to me," teased Tavish. "Kind of nice, I thought."

"Yeah? Well you just go right ahead and keep smiling at her."

"I've other plans. I'm going to marry one of those daughters of the tycoons, the kind who wears buttons and bows and silks and satins," said Tavish.

Julot just smiled at him with innocent black eyes. "I'm going with you, Tav, wherever your big dreams lead."

Tavish flashed his best smile. He'd heard his father remark that it could "win over Queen Victoria."

While Julot stayed to bathe in the river, Tavish walked back, surrounded by the warm night and the sounds of the railroad camp. Tavish knew that he'd finally won the battle with Julot over who was going to be the boss. *I am,* he thought. *And it's just as well. Julot would go straight for trouble. Me, I know when to leave unpleasant things with God.*

Tavish headed toward the chuck wagon to grab a tin mug of Lazou's coffee. The wagon was empty. He reached for the blackened pot and poured. "Looks like Missouri mud," he mumbled.

He paused, hearing what sounded like a moan. He tensed. *If Riley has come back and laid a hand on Lazou, I'll—*

Tavish set his mug down and walked quietly toward the muffled sound. He found Lazou behind the wagon, kneeling before his saplings. Five of the best and strongest had been uprooted from their buckets, the trunks broken in half. Tavish watched him reach into the dust and pick up the leafy branches, gently touching them.

"These was my best ones, Lord, and Riley killed 'em!" Tears streaked down his deeply etched cheeks.

Tavish silently walked back to the front of the wagon, his jaw set with anger, his green eyes glittering. He finished the coffee, set the mug down, and went to find Riley.

6

Shadows From the Past

Out-of-tune piano music drifted from a large tent. Tavish neared the brightly lit opening. Tommy, a Scottish immigrant near his own age, held on to a post, swaying to and fro as though on the deck of a heaving ship. The stench of whiskey was still wet on the front of his torn shirt.

"Where's Riley?" demanded Tavish.

Tommy wobbled toward him, his young life already well on the way to ruin. He reached to straighten his missing hat, yanked at his red hair instead, and pointed behind him to a stack of wooden barrels.

Tavish brushed past him and walked to the rear of the gambling tent. Riley was sprawled on the ground with his back leaning against a barrel, his head tilted back, mouth open, an empty bottle in hand.

Tavish studied him, then turned and walked away.

Late that night around the campfire, it was plain his father didn't believe Tavish's sparsely worded excuse for not having shown up with his guitar at the revival meeting, but he didn't corner him.

Smoke drifted from the campfire and the wood crackled. Coffee was boiling in the familiar dark blue enameled pot that had served them at a hundred other campsites. . . .

"Son, carrying a rifle to hunt game for food is one thing. Toting a revolver is something else. Where did you get it?"

The question took Tavish off guard and he looked at his father, masking his surprise. *How did he know about the gun?* He looked back at the red-hot coals. Curls of gray woodsmoke drifted slowly toward the wide Missouri, which rushed along like time, changing everything.

"I've known all along," said Kain. "I was waiting for you to tell me you had it."

Casually, Tavish removed the gun from his satchel and brought it into the open. His father's dislike for guns puzzled him because as a boy Tavish remembered seeing his father's shoulder holster with a pearl-handled derringer.

"Seemed wise to become good at it," stated Tavish easily. "At West Point I came in first hitting the—"

Kain interrupted. "Did Julot give it to you?"

While Tavish watched his father, he ran his thumb over the shiny barrel. "Julot?" *No, he has a Colt .45* he wanted to say but silenced himself. That too was a secret. "I bought it from one of the soldiers at Fort Lincoln, thinking we might need it out here. Some of the men laying track are troublemakers, and we're in Indian territory." He looked across the fire at him. "I've been catching up on my practice since West Point."

A smile showed on Kain's tanned face, and the scar on his neck showed faintly in the firelight. Tavish recalled how his father had told him years ago where the scar had come from. *"A riled Cheyenne,"* he had said. *"We had us one cruel fight."*

There was no humor in his father's smile.

"Good with a gun, are you, son?"

Tavish ignored the baiting question. "Uh-huh."

Kain's gray-blue eyes froze. "What for?"

The soft-spoken question cut through Tavish like a surgeon's knife. His father's Bible sat on the smooth rock, its edges worn from use, its margins filled with preaching notes from men like D.L. Moody.

Tavish shrugged and slid the revolver into its holster and put it back into his satchel. "You heard about trouble in Yellowstone. Some railroad surveyors were killed by the Sioux. Sitting Bull's warned against the railroad going through. All we have is your Winchester."

"One rifle is plenty. As for trouble, the world's full of it. Soldiers are paid to carry guns. Since you're no longer a West Point student—"

Tavish's gaze rose from the fire to confront him. The tiny flame of frustration grew and flared out. "You're disappointed in me, aren't you?"

"No," came the quick, decisive reply, followed by an even stare. "Not at all."

"I would have graduated this past June," challenged Tavish, wondering if he believed him.

"I told you I understood."

"I would have been stationed at Fort Lincoln—probably with the Seventh Cavalry."

Kain gave a laugh. "You don't know me yet, do you?"

Tavish tossed a pebble in the fire and watched the sparks. "You forget . . . until two years ago I didn't see you very often. You were gone a lot."

He hadn't meant to bring up old frustrations. He sighed. "I'm sorry. I know the death of Mother—"

"She's with the Lord. I know where to find her again. And I have you with me. I wasn't the father I should have been, or the husband."

"I'm sorry I brought it up."

Kain watched him, and Tavish felt the silence between them declare an uneasy peace.

Waiting to fill his mug with the brewing coffee, his father leaned back against a rock and sighed, as though it soothed his soul with some longing for home.

Tavish said quietly, "I've heard talk of a railroad surveyor who was captured. Staked out and gutted on the rocks."

Kain remained silent.

Tavish leaned toward him, his eyes sparkling green. "Carrying a Bible doesn't impress the Sioux! They'd as soon gut you open and fill your belly with rocks as look at you!"

"No doubt. But I won't have my son carrying a gun."

"That makes little sense to me."

"It's too easy to depend on it and start drawing it when you get riled. One moment a man's anger is seething like coals just ready to be stirred into fire, the next—a gun's in his hand and the trigger's squeezed. The result," he added flatly, "lasts for eternity."

Tavish scanned him. Knowing how his father felt on the matter, he didn't pursue the discussion.

Tavish recalled that the soldier who had sold him the revolver had said, "Got to be even-tempered about it, boy. Nice and steady. Takes nerves. Got to get both the draw and aim down mighty fine, mighty fine. Seen a body kilt on the Fraser River gold rush 'cause he drew a mite faster but hit the man's arm. Now the other feller? Sure—he was a shade behind, but he didn't miss. Took that extra second to get it right, you see. He's alive."

The coffee was done and his father poured for them both. Tavish felt the heat warm his hands while the wood sputtered. According to nightly custom, his father picked up the Bible. "Where's Julot?"

Tavish shrugged, feeling troubled by too many things.

His father turned to read what he called "a psalm to sleep on." His resonant voice now took on all the dignity of his education as the speech of the Western man was set aside.

"O Lord, thou hast searched me and known me. Thou knowest my downsitting and mine uprising. . . ."

When the book was closed, Tavish felt his father's eyes upon him, quiet eyes, like a stream, so unlike his own that often flashed with inner storm. He sensed his father watching him thoughtfully, knowing how to measure him and judge where he was at.

"Guns and a restless spirit go together like wood and fire. Unless you want to ignite the kindling, it's best to keep them separated." He added softly, "I don't talk about West Point because I know it's left a wound inside you, not me. You'll need to live with the injustice, to leave it with the kind guidance of God. He knew. He allowed it. I suppose there was a girl too?"

Tavish hesitated. "She was a Ridgeway debutante. There could be nothing between us, even if I had graduated from West Point." Tavish tossed the dregs of his coffee into the brush. He pushed himself up. "About guns. You'd think I was seeking trouble the way you talk."

"Trouble is buried in man's heart, son. You're no better. Just a bit wiser since you know what the Word says. But any man can choose to forget who he is in the Lord, or neglect what he already knows. 'Let not the sun go down upon your wrath,' the Word says. There's a good reason for that. Anger, bitterness, resentment—if you don't take care of them, they'll grow roots in a man's soul. They're twice as hard to pull up as time passes. When he does forget the truth, trouble is more likely to rear up." Kain leaned forward from the boulder and looked at Tavish. "Just like a rattlesnake with two heads."

Tavish let out a quiet breath and looked off toward the river. He waited, willing to listen, anxious to agree with what his father had said, but full of questions that argued inside his soul. If there were double-headed rattlers slithering around, then a man needed to protect himself. He could handle the responsibility of carrying a gun.

"Hanging around with crusty old soldiers who enjoy spinning yarns about how brave they are and how fast they are with a gun is sure to lead you where trouble broods," his father continued with a note of bitterness in his tone. "I knew a few of those talkers myself. Thank God that's one sin not on my conscience. I never boasted to my son of my devious ways. I wanted you to turn out like your mother."

"The man I bought the pistol from is nothing to me. Only warned against Indians is all. He noticed the three of us didn't carry guns."

"We don't need to. Did you tell him that?"

Tavish held back a retort, then said calmly, "A man might wish for peace, and hate war, but it never keeps him out of trouble. Riley turned on Lazou tonight. Julot wanted to take him on, but I stopped him. Riley called me a coward. I took his insult and walked away."

"You were smart. You could have sent him to the dust easily."

His father's statement made Tavish feel better.

"But walking away to cool at the river didn't help Lazou. I came back later and found out Riley destroyed some of his apple trees."

Kain frowned and stood, looking lonely in his long black coat.

"I looked for Riley," admitted Tavish. "When I found him he was passed out drunk."

Kain tossed the dregs of his coffee into the fire. It sizzled. "And I suppose a gun would have helped Lazou keep his apple trees."

Tavish met him at eye level, the wind touching his face, his hair. "If Laz had one, it might have caused Riley to think twice about it."

"And get Lazou strung up probably. Better to lose a few apple trees than get lynched. Slavery's over, but a black man still doesn't have much opportunity. Far better to seek the law's protection. Have you and Lazou gone to the NP authorities?"

"No," he admitted wearily.

Kain appeared satisfied that he had won the point.

"But they wouldn't have listened to a black man over Riley anyway."

"Sadly so. But they might listen to me, or you. I'll talk to them tonight. We have a responsibility to step in where others can't. But don't pull a gun. They go off too easily, too fast. Before you know what's happened, a man's lying dead in the dust."

His father kicked dirt on the fire, and his sudden gravity alerted Tavish. He studied him thoughtfully.

"But you're right about one thing, son. A wish for peace doesn't make it happen. A man can walk into a situation thinking he can handle it, only to have it blow like dynamite in his face. Injustice and evil surround us. Only when evil is silenced once for all in the pit will there be peace in the world." He looked at Tavish. "There's a place for guns, for strength, to stand up against evil, but the man who does so better make certain he isn't masking self-vengeance. Personal injustice is to be left for the Lord to work out."

Tavish grew impatient. He already knew that. He didn't respond.

His father watched him. "There's something I never told you before—a reason why I don't carry one, why I don't want you to."

Tavish was curious, waiting. The silence surrounded them. Then Kain stooped again before the last tendrils of smoke. "I was once close to someone who shot a man."

The wind rattled the trees.

"Did he die?"

His father looked at the flickering coals fading into darkness. Tavish waited.

Kain ran a hand through his hair. "Yes."

His words were so quiet that Tavish wondered if he had heard correctly. When his father stood again to face him, only the starlight illuminated the horizon of the sky along the river.

"You don't need to worry about disappointing your old man about West Point. It's me who worries about shaming you."

Tavish felt his soul wrench. He was about to throw his arm around his father's shoulder, when Julot walked up.

"What? No coffee?"

Kain straightened and turned away toward Julot, his voice a little sharp. "Where have you been, Julot?"

"Thinkin'."

"You didn't come to the Scripture reading." His voice softened. "I want you to turn out better than your uncle."

"You?" Julot laughed. "There ain't none better." He squatted down, picked up the empty coffeepot, and glanced at Tavish with a scowl.

Tavish sat back down on the boulder with his guitar, absently plucking a tune. Julot sat next to his cousin and quietly sang along.

Oh, my darlin',
Oh, my darlin',
Oh, my darlin' Clementine—

"Don't play that!" Kain demanded.

Tavish stopped and looked at his father, surprised.

In the starlight, Kain's voice unexpectedly announced, "We'll be leaving in the morning for Fort Lincoln."

At the mention of the fort, Julot glanced at Tavish. Tavish thought he knew what flashed across his mind. *Wade Ridgeway.*

Tavish felt the quickened beat of his heart.

"What for?" asked Julot.

Tavish thought he already knew. It had nothing to do with Wade but the NP's expedition into Yellowstone Valley.

"We're leaving the area," said Kain.

Surprised, Tavish watched him, wondering.

"You mean we're quittin'?" came Julot's hopeful voice.

Kain smiled. "I'm certain you're disappointed, but yes, I've already informed Riley. I think the man is only too pleased to be rid of us. After his trouble with you two tonight, I know why."

Tavish felt Julot's glance but ignored him.

"We'll be riding with the NP's crew of surveyors," said Kain. "I've been asked to join the expedition as chaplain."

"Chaplain!" Tavish studied his father, pleased.

"I thought you'd be proud of the idea. I'll be paid a regular wage. That means you and Julot won't need to lay track. I was told tonight that Bismarck is as far as the track will go for some time. There's rumblings of the financial downfall of Jay Cooke and the railroad. Another baron to hit the dust."

Tavish caught something in his voice. "You sound as if you know them. Did you ever meet Durant, Cooke, or Granger?"

"This expedition into Yellowstone is Jay Cooke's idea. He's looking for a better and closer route to join up with the NP's line coming down from Kalama, Washington." Kain stretched. "It's time to turn in. We'll be riding out early."

Tavish noticed that his father had avoided his question. "What about Mack Ridgeway? Do you know him?"

His father showed none of the earlier tension. "I know him." He added with a wearied smile, "Who doesn't? The Ridgeway name goes with the timber business in the Pacific Northwest. But I've heard Mack's real interest is in the railroad. I'm told his daughter will soon be joining him at the fort."

Tavish recalled Lottie Ridgeway, Ember's cousin. His next question came casually, but he was certain his father would recognize the eagerness that stirred just beneath the surface. "Did Mack ask about our land grant along the Hood Canal?"

"He wants to buy us out."

Tavish gave a pluck to the guitar. "What did you tell him?"

Kain smiled. "I told him it wasn't for sale, and that if it ever was, he'd need to do business with you."

Tavish relaxed, aware that Julot sat watching them both with excitement. "Then you was tellin' the truth all along, Tav. There is a big stretch of trees, and money to be made."

Tavish looked over at him with a satisfied smile, but it was

Kain who answered. "Lots of money, I'm thinking. Even more than I'd thought years ago."

Tavish suspected his father had a new concern over how well his son could handle success and money if it came.

"I'm thinking of a lumber company at Seabeck," said Tavish. "I've already explained it to Julot. I'd like to build a sawmill and eventually buy our own ships to work on the Hood. We've access to the rivers. Until we can afford the stern-wheelers, we can float our logs straight into the Hood for Seabeck or Union. And I want to protect our stand of trees from the cut-and-run practices of some of the quick lumber companies."

Julot was on his feet, his black eyes snapping. "When we goin'?"

A heavy silence held between the three men; then Kain answered. "As soon as I finish this last work as chaplain on the NP expedition. I'm beginning to think the Lord wants me to concentrate on the future of you and Tav. I've decided to return to Washington, and while you cut timber, I'll have time to do some more serious study. That is," he said with a smile, "after we build a cabin to live in."

Tavish stared at his father; then as Kain studied him, alert to his response, Tavish smiled. Julot let his enthusiasm break loose with a "YAHOO!"

Only after matters quieted down did Tavish pursue the question on his mind. "Why would Mack Ridgeway's daughter be coming out here now? Especially after the skirmish with the Sioux."

"She's married to a West Point officer—Prescott Hollister."

"Is Prescott in the Seventh Cavalry now?"

His father watched him. "Yes, a lieutenant, I think. Graduated with honors. Did you know him at West Point?"

Tavish shrugged indifference. "We were friends once."

"Seems Mack's son Wade has been with Custer in his Indian battles at Cheyenne, Wyoming. He'll be going on the expedition into Yellowstone."

Casually, Tavish picked up his guitar and slung it over his shoulder. "Morning comes fast. I'm turning in."

As he lay beneath the stars, hearing the river and the lazy

chirp of crickets, Tavish told himself that Wade no longer mattered to him. Yes, he had lost his honor at West Point, but he had something else to build his future on now. His father was willing to return home to possess the land. Tavish told himself he'd work hard, fight hard if necessary to keep it, and one day he'd become the timber wolf he dreamed about.

Then he remembered her, as he always did, even if he wouldn't admit it—Ember Ridgeway. If her cousin Lottie had married Prescott, what of her?

But Ember was younger, with a year left at Chadwick when he'd been expelled. Had she graduated in May and returned to Port Townsend?

In the far distance he heard a train whistle calling, wooing its way along through the night.

Would she remember him? Probably. What would she think of a track layer in dusty jeans and hat? Did she know he had been expelled, accused of cheating? The thought stirred the coals of anger again.

He wouldn't think about it. If his plans went as he now intended them, when she saw him again Miss Ember Ridgeway would see a young man on the way up to the top. Maybe he'd take on the Ridgeway timber just to prove himself. *T.D. Wilder Timber Enterprise.* He smiled and settled his hat over his face to fall asleep.

7

YELLOWSTONE COUNTRY

It was July 1873, and they rode with the railroad surveying team guarded by troops from the Seventh Cavalry.

Tavish rode to the right of Kain, Julot to the left. On his father's head sat a black derby hat with a bullet hole through its crown. He joked that he had earned that mark of distinction by his preaching, and wasn't about to get rid of it, but Tavish knew it was because he wouldn't waste their hard-earned money on a new hat, and there were few who cared among the men who rode railcars and slept in the shanty camps along the progressing route of the railroad. Certainly the large numbers of Oglala and Brule Sioux wouldn't have been impressed, nor would the Cheyenne and Arapaho Indian tribes who had come to join Sitting Bull in his determination to remain free of the reservations. Sitting Bull judged a man's skin color as the mark of a killer of buffalo, an invader into Yellowstone country, a maker not of rain but of the "bad medicine wagon" that raced along iron tracks through the great buffalo herds.

Commanding the expedition was General David S. Stanley, and Lieutenant Colonel George Armstrong Custer, who three years earlier had fought the Indians in Minnesota, Dakota, and Wyoming. It didn't take long for Tavish to discover that the two officers despised each other.

Tavish was uncinching his saddle after a long day of riding, when Julot ran up, his excitement showing.

"No time for that. We're heading out."

Tavish was rankled. "Now? We've ridden all morning."

"We're riding with Custer."

"Custer!"

Julot's eyes danced. "Thought you'd be glad. Wade's with him."

Tavish showed no response. He hadn't run into Wade Ridgeway yet and wasn't sure he wished to. "Why's Custer taking out on his own?"

"General Stanley's furious because Custer took command during the general's last drinking binge. He ordered a court-martial but changed his mind. Conflict's been settled by the two of 'em agreeing to split up."

Tavish wasn't certain he wanted to ride with Custer. "I'll stay with the main troop."

"There's no action here, Tav."

Tavish looked bored. "Just the way I like it."

Julot settled his hat with a gesture of righteous indignation. "You can't stay behind."

"Who says I can't?" Tavish's brittle eyes reflected green in the sunlight. He reached for his canteen with a jerk.

"Aw, c'mon, Tav! This is *Custer*. Why, he's already got himself a fancy name as an Indian fighter!"

Tavish smiled coolly. He tipped the canteen and quenched his thirst, looking about at the soldiers in blue with yellow ribbons. He didn't see Wade anywhere.

"And Custer's taking his regiment ahead of the cavalry's main column," pressed Julot. "We're more likely to see Sioux."

"More reason to stay put," said Tavish dryly, and beat the dust from his hat. He squinted up at the steely gray sky. "I've heard a few things about Custer that aren't so heroic. And if Wade's with him—then I know we're in for trouble."

"You can't stay. Your pa's opted to ride with Custer."

Tavish stared at him, surprised. "Now why would he do that?"

Julot shrugged, then looked satisfied. "Better saddle up. Mack Ridgeway's going too." He turned to amble away to his horse.

Tavish hadn't spoken to Wade's father, but there was a hungry spirit about the big man that made him uneasy. It was Mack's money and power that had helped Wade through West Point. *At the expense of my honor,* thought Tavish.

An officer in meticulous uniform trotted by on horseback, raising a small cloud of Montana dust. He shouted in their direction: "You two track layers! If you intend to ride out with the colonel, mount up!"

Tavish turned, his even gaze fixing on the officer.

Wade Ridgeway, holding his saddle horn, had turned to gallop on. A faint look of surprise crossed his face, then his features settled into military aloofness as he looked back and met Tavish's gaze. "I heard you and your father were here."

Tavish folded his arms across his chest, his smile disarming. He scanned him, then said in Julot's direction, "Julot—take your hat off."

Julot scowled. "Huh?"

"You stand in the presence of a military genius," Tavish told him, gesturing toward Wade. "This man had a reputation for scorning study while at West Point—yet look at him now. First thing I hear, he's a captain. Now he's a major. You take my breath away, Major Ridgeway. You're moving fast."

Julot laughed. "Say now, Tav, General Stanley had better watch out. The major will soon take his place before we ever get back to Fort Lincoln."

Wade flushed. "I'll warn you now, Wilder, you and this gunfighting cousin of yours. If you think to make trouble for me on this expedition, think again."

"Trouble?" breathed Tavish. "A preacher's kid? Why, shucks! Now what kind of trouble would I make?" His smile left and his eyes turned granite. "Congratulations on your graduation from West Point, Wade."

"I'm a major in the Seventh Cavalry. That demands respect. I have friends," warned Wade. "Custer himself is one of them."

"Good friends. Your father's money helps too. So far it's done you well. But you've a lesson to learn—one you failed at West Point."

"You think you're the one to teach me? It would be better if you climbed on your horse and rode back to Bismarck. Both you and your father—a two-bit gambler turned hired preacher."

"If you step down from your mount we can talk about it," said Tavish.

Julot caught his arm. "Not now—look, here comes the colonel himself."

George Armstrong Custer rode toward them. Wearing a fringed buckskin jacket over his uniform and a wide-brimmed hat, his blond hair, shoulder length and slightly curling, shone like Sir Galahad's in the Montana sun. Beside him rode his two scouts, Bloody Knife and Charlie Reynolds.

"Major Ridgeway! Get your men mounted. We ride out soon!"

"Yessir, Colonel!" Wade parried a bitter glance at Tavish. "Later, Wilder. There'll be plenty of time on this run to teach you some manners."

"I'll be around, Major."

Wade snapped his reins and galloped ahead.

Julot chuckled. "That, he did not like, mon ami."

Ember Ridgeway felt the discomfort of the July evening, hot and dry as dusk settled like a smothering blanket about the small, dusty railroad caravan. A few flimsy tents and some supply wagons were drawn into a circle. In the wagon she shared with Cousin Lottie, now Mrs. Prescott Hollister, she tried to ease her anxiety by listening to the calm voice of Lottie reading from Psalm Twelve in Spurgeon's *Treasury of David*: " 'The words of the LORD are pure words: as silver tried in a furnace of earth, purified seven times. Thou shalt keep them, O LORD, thou shalt preserve them from this generation for ever.'

"And Mr. Spurgeon says—'What a contrast between the vain words of man, and the pure words of Jehovah. Man's words are yea and nay, but the Lord's promises are yea and amen. For truth, certainty, holiness, faithfulness, the words of the LORD are pure as well-refined silver.' "

They had traveled by hired stage from Seattle to Steilacoom and then to Fort Benton. They had been nearing an outpost called Miles City on the Yellowstone River when the driver had become deathly ill, vomiting and shivering with a high fever. Between Lottie and her they had done what they could for the poor man, but nothing helped. Sassy insisted it was his appendix.

The seasoned scout named Samuel, whom the family had hired to bring them to Fort Lincoln, had come across a rail caravan heading back in the direction of St. Paul, Minnesota, and he had brought the stage to the safety of their small camp. The nearest trading post was farther away on the Missouri River, and the scout had ridden there for help.

Sassy's voice interrupted. "It's time you put the Good Book away, chile," she told Lottie. "Come sit in the evening air. You too, Ember honey. Ain't healthy for us to be cooped up in here all day and night too, even if there is Indians."

Indians. Ember shuddered and glanced at Lottie. As usual, her cousin wore the honorable face of courage.

"You musn't frighten Ember. Not after she's sacrificed to make the journey with me. You've sacrificed too, Sassy. What would I have done without you?"

Ember drew the canvas aside and crawled through the opening, feeling a tug of summer wind. "You speak as if the ordeal is over," Ember told her. "What if Samuel doesn't return with help?"

Lottie smiled gently. "He will."

Ember marveled at her faith. She hoped she was right. Her own faith seemed to shrink as the hours crept by.

"Let's don't talk 'bout it now," said Sassy with a frown. "Both of you, come sit outside while I gets our supper. That cantankerous ol' cook better have more'n beans tonight!"

Inside the covered wagon it was stuffy and cramped, and Ember welcomed the relief of being outdoors. With Lottie, she sat on the step and inhaled a breath of evening air, but found no relief from the prickly sensation that inched its way along her back. She turned her head and glanced behind her. The hot wind ruffled the curls at the back of her neck. She glanced at Lottie and whispered, "We've made a dreadful error coming here, Lottie."

Lottie's brown eyes shone like pools in the starlight. "Oh,

Ember, don't even whisper it. I prayed so earnestly before I decided to join Prescott at the fort."

But did that mean they would escape trouble? wondered Ember.

Lottie laid a hand on her rounding stomach. "Prescott will come with the soldiers from Fort Lincoln, you'll see. Samuel will get through. If there are Indians out there, the army will chase them away."

Does she truly believe her words or is she trying to make me feel better? Ember smiled ruefully at her cousin. Lottie too smiled and sighed, looking up at the stars. "I wonder where Prescott is now."

Ember determined to shrug off the unease that pricked at her. *Lottie is right. We musn't behave like frightened children. We pray and read Scripture every night. Surely the Lord is with us. Everything will be well.*

But her heart continued its odd little jerks. The day had been hot and breathless beneath the Montana sun, but now the last rays of a crimson sunset were slipping over the hills, and soon the expanse of the big sky would come alive with star diamonds. Ember listened for sounds coming from the frontier wilderness surrounding their small camp. Cousin Wade once said that Indians sounded like coyotes.

Nothing moved, nothing stirred inside the circle of wagons. Even the wind stopped abruptly. The crickets began to sing and filled her ears with shrill music.

Her heart pounded so hard that her bodice stays cut into her, and she squirmed, trying to get comfortable.

Even as darkness settled, the searing heat was oven-dry and sucked the moisture from her skin, making her constantly thirsty for something cool with ice. . . . Ice! She closed her eyes, imagining Mount Ranier with its cap of white and the crystal wind that blew in winter.

"I keep thinking of spooning soft snow into a tall, frosty lemonade," murmured Ember.

Lottie groaned.

"Nothing but that horrid black coffee for days," said Ember.

"And so muddy with chicory I had to spit it out," said Lottie.

Stew, hardtack bread, and Texas chili had been their diet

since leaving Fort Benton. Despite her decision to remain calm, Ember again found her mind traveling the same path it had traversed for days. Why did she ever agree to accompany Lottie to the home of the Seventh Cavalry at Fort Lincoln? Self-doubts plucked away pieces of her armor.

Suppose Lottie had a miscarriage? Suppose they were attacked by Indians? What if they were captured!

Ember, of course, knew why she had agreed to journey with her. It was because of these very concerns. Lottie was like a sister and needed her. If anything happened, Ember would never forgive herself for not being by her side.

Ember had graduated from Chadwick Academy in May and returned home to the Pacific Northwest to visit Great-aunt Macie in Tacoma for two weeks, when Lottie arrived from Port Townsend with the news. She would journey to Fort Lincoln to join her husband.

"Ember, I'd feel so much better with you and Sassy along. Please say you'll come with me and stay until the baby is born."

Ember had grown up with Lottie and Wade at the main family house of the Ridgeways near Port Townsend. The frail childhood health of Lottie and the moody disposition of Wade had bonded the three of them together into a family unit of their own. For Lottie and Wade, growing up in a powerful family had been difficult, and they both struggled with feeling rejected by parents who were aloof and distracted with the task of making the Ridgeway name a success. For Ember, it was loneliness, of having no parental love at all, and growing up feeling disjointed, belonging to no one in the family. She was only one more cousin drifting from one wealthy house to another, smothered with sympathy, beautiful clothes, and well-wishes, but emotionally isolated.

When Lottie arrived in Tacoma and appealed to Ember for help, she had rallied to her request, knowing that she would also do the same for Wade if he ever asked, confident that they would come to her side as defenders when she needed them.

And I've ended up with little for my loyalty but being trapped in Indian territory, she thought dourly as she sat on the wagon step fanning herself.

For Lottie, that long-ago vacation at Saratoga had proved successful where a marriage match was concerned. As planned by her mother, Lottie met Prescott Hollister and the relationship had flourished. Lottie married him in a gala wedding at West Point soon after he had graduated. The lieutenant was twenty-seven, which to Ember was very old indeed. Fortunately, nineteen-year-old Lottie was in love with the man the Ridgeway family had intended her to marry.

And no wonder the family was pleased. Prescott was heir to the largest shipping operation in San Francisco—a definite benefit to the Ridgeway Timber Enterprise. Even though he had opted for a military career, the Ridgeways expected to change his mind by working through Lottie. Since Prescott had three years remaining in the cavalry, there seemed time to convince him to go into the timber business in Oregon and Washington.

The night closed in about Ember, rich darkness that smelled of pungent woodsmoke and frontier grasses, dry and dead on the wilderness floor.

Some distance away from camp, harmonica music wafted along on the breeze and she imagined a homesick railroad worker thinking of his sweetheart. The tune drifted through her jumbled thoughts, whispering . . . *Youth is pleasant but short; eternity is forever. What will you do with life, Ember? How will you spend it—if it's not shortened?*

"Lottie? That tune—do you know it? What are the words?"

Lottie looked up at the stars. "Something about a harbor bell, I think."

Ember thought of Wade, who with Prescott was stationed in the Seventh Cavalry at Fort Lincoln in Dakota Territory. He had recently been promoted to a major and she was proud of him.

Was his father proud? She wondered. Mack was also at the fort, leading the team of surveyors into Montana's Yellowstone, searching for the easiest route to the Pacific Northwest. While Mack sought to make it good in the railroad, Cleo Ridgeway was driven to maintain her success as the family "timber queen."

Sassy returned with three plates of beans, but Ember had little appetite and Lottie only sighed. "I can't eat, Sassy," she said.

Ember sat listening to the distant harmonica, glum with her adventure gone awry.

A wiry old man strode by in fringed shotgun-flaps and a faded red shirt, a beat-up hat on his grizzled head. He tipped the hat without removing it when he saw Ember and Lottie.

"Evenin', ladies."

He walked on with a little rise of dust from his boots. Ember lifted her head and looked in the direction of the chuck wagon, where a fire blazed and workers gathered to have their tin plates filled. She picked up her fan and swished it rapidly.

Sassy made a throaty sound over her forkful of beans. "Ain't nothing like good cajun hot. This here is just plain hot."

Ember tensed and sat, her back straight. She stared into the darkness, listening.

Sassy's fork halted between the tin plate and her mouth, and Lottie too turned to look at her.

"Did you hear it? A gunshot," breathed Ember.

"Thunder?" said Lottie.

"The sky is clear." Ember stood and walked a short distance from the wagon, staring out into the dark miles of barren plain. A soft footfall!

She whirled. A railroad worker stepped out of the shadows near a supply wagon.

"Didn't mean to scare you none, Miss Ridgeway, only you best not be out here alone."

His presence had startled her, and she said a little shortly, "I'm only a few feet from my wagon."

"Yes, ma'am, but a few feet can make a big difference out here in Injun territory."

She felt a shiver and glanced out on the plain. "Have you heard from Samuel yet?"

"No, ma'am, but he'll be ridin' in soon."

"The stage driver, is he feeling any better?"

"Afraid not. He's mighty sick. Shall I get you some hot coffee, Miss Ridgeway?"

She rubbed her arms, glancing about. "Yes—yes, please."

"You wait in the wagon, ma'am," he said again politely, but his tone made it clear he wouldn't leave until she did.

Ember walked the short distance back to the covered wagon, where Lottie stood waiting with Sassy.

"It was nothing important," said Ember with a brave smile, but before climbing up the step to take refuge inside with the others, she looked back over her shoulder onto the hot Montana plains.

They rode out with Colonel Custer ahead of General Stanley and the majority of the Seventh Cavalry. Julot's Colt .45 was hidden in his saddle pack wrapped in a worn-out change of underwear.

Wade remained unapproachable, formal, rarely seen apart from Custer himself. They rode in their saddles "boot to boot," as Custer put it. Tavish and Julot were seen as outsiders, mere track layers. Anyone who wasn't an officer in the Seventh Cavalry was treated with casual indifference. Tavish resented Wade's superior attitude as the days drifted past, yet he restrained his feelings. Nothing more had been said between them since their first meeting.

In the weeks that followed they made their way through canyons and cliffs, and at night sat about the campfire with Custer and other army men reminiscing over battles fought in the Civil War and with the Indians.

Tavish listened, lounging against a tree in the shadows, his hat low, and was surprised by Wade's question.

"What of you, Wilder? Have you any ambitions since leaving West Point other than following your pa around?"

Tavish wondered that he had the courage to mention West Point. *He must feel quite confident in the shadow of Custer,* he thought. At the tinge of sarcasm in Wade's voice Tavish tipped back his hat and looked across the campfire at the "elite," who were drinking coffee and enjoying their own private supper. Tavish hadn't been invited to share their meal, cooked by Custer's own private servants, a Negro woman named Mary and her husband, Ham. The two accompanied Custer on many of his expeditions.

The eyes of the other men turned to him. Cool eyes, somewhat mocking, convincing him that Wade had informed them of his expulsion for cheating.

"I have plans. I'm going to Washington Territory as soon as this surveying expedition is over."

"To do what?" asked Wade with a faint curl to his mouth.

He was a handsome man with rusty brown eyes and jet hair like his sister Lottie.

Tavish met his amused gaze evenly. "I've decided to give the Ridgeway family some competition in the timber industry." He smiled. "Maybe I'll see you around Port Townsend, Wade."

Tavish's challenge clearly startled Wade, and he gave Tavish a measured look.

Tavish didn't wait for his reply but stood and walked away. He was certain Wade would relay the Wilders' timber interest to his father Mack.

Which could mean trouble ahead in Washington with the powerful Ridgeway family. He suspected that they had most of the leading citizens in town under their influence.

Before he climbed into his bedroll that night, Tavish looked at his rugged and dusty clothes. One day he would dress as fine as any West Point graduate, he told himself. And he might just see that he and Julot were invited to Ridgeway House for dinners and balls. There was a question he had hoped to ask Wade about his cousin Ember, but Wade would be the last man to ask.

They reached the mouth of the Bighorn River on the third of August. Tavish had noticed a buzzard some time ago and it worried him. The sun grew hotter as it climbed. Tavish wiped his sweating palm along the thigh of his black jeans. There was no need to be tense, he told himself. Colonel Custer would recognize the danger signs. Yet, he would have felt better had the cavalry stayed together. Custer had ridden ahead to scout along the mouth of the Powder River, taking with him his brother Tom, his brother-in-law James Calhoun, and his favorite Indian scouts.

Nothing moved beneath the vast copper sky.

Nothing but that wily buzzard, thought Tavish, and lowered his hat against the sun's glare to watch the fowl. He squinted. Something out there was "mighty" dead, as cousin Julot would say. Tavish's eyes squinted. *Maybe not dead yet, but dying.* That buzzard wasn't sure, either.

Out here, west of the Black Hills and along the Powder, Tongue, and Bighorn rivers, Sitting Bull's Sioux and many of the Cheyenne who had rejected the government reservations had gathered to avoid the white man. The other chieftains had joined Sitting Bull in Yellowstone country, where they journeyed back and forth to trade with Canadian half-breeds. The Sioux and Cheyenne hated the agency trading posts along the Missouri River, and Sitting Bull wished to be left alone.

The river was clear and reflecting topaz beneath the deep sky. In the trees lining its banks birds tittered. Bees hummed, crawling over the golden pollen in the August wild flowers.

Julot edged his horse up beside Tavish. "That buzzard's itching to land. Saw one like that in Tucson once."

The wind tugged at them as they rode slowly along. Tavish didn't say what he thought; Julot already knew.

Julot's black eyes were sober. "My pa always carried himself a Winchester in one hand and his Colt in the other when things were lookin' a bit tight."

Tavish scanned the cottonwood trees along the other side of the river.

Julot murmured, "Pa would sooner be a plucked hen in winter than be caught out here in Injun territory with no gun."

Tavish sighed. "I think I know how he felt about that plucked hen. I'd feel better if we were with General Stanley."

They rode on. Julot turned his head to look over his shoulder. "Look, Tav, I'm serious about this feelin' ridin' up my back—like we're bein' watched."

"Uh-huh. I feel it too."

"Seen your pa?"

"Not since morning. He rode ahead with Mack Ridgeway."

"Seeing how that buzzard's awful worked up, maybe we ought to say something about trouble ahead," suggested Julot.

"Sure, 'Major Wade' is just waiting to hear what the two of us have to suggest."

"You're right. He's so proud he'd never listen. He's ready to burst his polished buttons."

"Anyway, he's seen it," said Tavish, glancing at the buzzard in the distance. "If he hasn't by now, there's no polite way of saying that he should have stuck with timber."

"Me," said Julot, "I'm ridin' back with the wagons and unpackin' the Colt. If your pa finds out and lands into me about it tonight, so be it." Julot turned his horse. "You comin'?"

"Later. I'm riding ahead to find him. He has the Winchester."

Buttermilk clouds churned on the horizon, gold and cream against pale blue. Some distance ahead, a small group of railroad surveyors rode together guarded by a dozen cavalrymen. Kain wasn't among them.

Wade saw him and turned his horse out of the column. "What are you doing up here, Wilder?"

"Where's the colonel?"

Tavish could see he didn't take to explaining things. Wade's face showed impatience, yet he seemed to pay closer attention to him this time, scanning him thoughtfully.

"He and a scouting party have ridden ahead of the main body."

"I'm not one to second-guess any lieutenant-colonel or his major," said Tavish, "but it seems to me the distance between us and General Stanley is uncomfortably long."

Wade's irritation showed, but he smiled thinly. "Then I suggest you ride to the rear—where it's safe."

"It's not my safety I'm worried about. Where are the civilians you're guarding?"

Wade's eyes turned cool. "If you're asking about your father, he's probably up ahead."

A soldier shouted that a wagon lost a wheel and Wade galloped back toward the supplies. Tavish turned his horse to ride ahead when a yellow-haired corporal came galloping toward him from the front of the column.

The young corporal saw him, recognized him as Kain's son, and gesturing, turned aside to the bank of the Yellowstone.

While the others passed on two and three abreast, Tavish joined him, holding the reins steady, his eyes scanning the cottonwood trees on the other side. The corporal was a young man, not much older than Tavish.

"I've only got a minute, but I was hoping maybe you could thank your father for me. I think I kept him up pretty late last night, but he sure did answer my questions. I'm grateful."

Tavish thought back to the night before but didn't recall having seen the man with his father. "I'll tell him. What's your name?"

"Corporal Will Hollis. He'll remember." His eyes misted.

"What he said about Jesus made a whole lot of sense to me."
He turned to ride, smiling. "Say—you got yourself a fine father.
I'd wait to tell him so myself, but I'm being sent back to General
Stanley with a message from Custer. A ways ahead, Scout
Bloody Knife spotted a handful of Sioux—"

The sickening thud of an arrow piercing the corporal's
throat happened too swiftly for Tavish to react. One moment
the young man sat his horse, the next he had dropped over the
front of his saddle. A rifle shot cracked the air, and Tavish felt
its impact as the bullet careened off the cantle of his saddle.

Tavish turned and shouted "Sioux!" barely getting out the
warning before the spine-tingling Indian war cry shattered the
morning, echoing off the banks of the river. Sioux and Cheyenne warriors were spilling out of the trees.

The Seventh Cavalry's bugle blared, its golden mouth lifted,
the proud trumpeter sitting tall.

Like water heated to a rolling boil, the war cry intensified as
the Indians charged, feathers bright, drums pulsating, toma-
hawks raised, bowstrings drawn back, arrows whizzing. The
dozen soldiers fought back, rifle bullets blistering the air,
horsehoofs beating the ground, men falling.

The Sioux kept coming. So did the Cheyenne.

Tavish saw Sitting Bull astride his painted horse on the other
side of the bank, sitting straight, his feathers moving in the
breeze. As though in contempt he sat smoking his pipe while
drums reverberated around him, and Custer's bullets sang by.
The next moment Tavish scrambled to retrieve the repeating
rifle of the dead corporal, hitting the dust beside the horse as
he did and narrowly escaping an arrow. Tavish came up on one
knee, his eyes coolly scanning the tall grass along the bank,
knowing the Indian couldn't be far away. Less than thirty feet
ahead, a Sioux warrior raised up with his bow drawn tight—
Tavish had the rifle directly in front of him and fired just before
the arrow flew past. The bullet struck, jolting the warrior backward into the tall grass.

Taking time to unloose the corporal's gun belt and grabbing
the supply of bullets from his saddle, Tavish scrambled for the
safety of the rocks, leading his horse.

Julot! Was he safe?

And his father! He hadn't been with the railroad surveyors.

He recalled that Kain was last seen riding with Mack Ridgeway toward the Powder River after breakfast—in the very direction from which the Sioux had poured forth on their ponies.

That buzzard! Revulsion swept through him. Something was out there either dying or dead—and Ridgeway and his father were still missing.

His father's words flashed through his mind: *The secret of genuine faith is knowing how to rest easy even when life hurts.*

8

PRELUDE TO LITTLE BIGHORN

Tavish knew of the gruesome torture tactics used by certain Indian tribes. Sometimes a man was staked to the ground and left to die with his belly slit and filled with rocks; other times a captive might be smeared with honey and staked to ant holes until he went insane. The captive they now held up in the rocks was his father, Kain Wilder.

Tavish had argued for a search party, but Wade had appeared unnerved during his first command in an emergency situation and had opted to pull back, choosing to believe the report of Kain's capture and death. Where Wade's father might be, no one knew for certain, but word had circulated that he had made his way back to Stanley's troops. Colonel Custer and his two scouts had last been seen with Sioux warriors on their trail, and Wade made the decision to search for them.

Tavish didn't believe his father dead yet because the buzzard still circled, so when Wade ordered the troop to move out, he managed to slip away.

He followed the pony tracks of the Cheyenne until they entered the river. The next morning he saw the buzzard. Soon afterward, he saw his father, heard his agony, but two Cheyenne had picked up his own trail in the process.

The handful of warriors who had his father knew that Tavish was close-by, and knew that because he had risked coming alone, his emotions were bound to the grotesque sufferings of their captive. They would use Kain's suffering to draw him out.

Tavish was on his own, for he knew there was no chance that Wade would risk lives to come back to search for him, and would report his death along with Kain Wilder's.

How many Cheyenne were there in the rocks waiting for him to make a move? There might be as few as three or four, or as many as a dozen. The sun was now high. It was the second day they had held Kain.

He was close. So close that he could hear him. Tavish didn't shed tears, not because he thought himself too much a man, but because it might cause him to miss his father's voice should he speak, and he knew he'd never hear it again. If he made any noise, the Indians who watched his father would find him, and they were searching, coming closer.

Below him lay a vast plain with pale sky. Overhead the sun glared down. Tavish's heart beat like a war drum. Sweat covered his body, and his fingers dug into the rocky soil. His soul reached out to grasp for his father's voice. The voice that became the family harmony over the evening campfire, the words read from the Book he carried, worn and underlined with faded ink. His mother's Bible. . . .

Tavish strained to hear like a thirsty man dying for water. *One more time,* he thought, *if I could speak to him just once more. . . .*

His fingers clenched, his nails cutting his already blistered palm. There were a few bullets left, not nearly enough. *If I could—God forgive me—I'd be willing to shoot my own father to end his misery.*

Kain cried out, and Tavish knew his father thought he was alone out there, otherwise he'd never voice his agony. The sound cut through him and Tavish felt his emotions snap. He inched forward over a rock. A pebble loosened by his foot dropped. Immediately he stopped, lying flat against the broiling rock.

An Indian spoke in a low voice to a fellow brave, the sound

just audible to Tavish. He waited, holding the gun steady over his left wrist. He must be mad. They'd catch him easily and cut him open as they had his father. It would be considered good medicine to have both father and son.

Stillness surrounded him again, and the heat coming from the rock burned through his clothes. He blinked back the sweat stinging his vision. With emotions spent like a howling storm, a dazed composure descended to wrap around his wounded soul like the embrace of angels' wings.

Another cry stabbed the afternoon. Tavish clamped his jaw to hold back the rage he felt. Every nerve in his body begged him to charge madly in the direction of his father's cry.

Hours passed. The sun was setting, flowering the sky with rose tints. No further sound came from his father. Then—

From behind him the faint tread of moccasins whispered upon rock from two directions. Tavish rolled sharply, repeating rifle lifted. Two Cheyenne appeared to come right up from the rock. Tavish fired consecutively, the bullets ripping through them. They fell, tumbling below into the valley.

More gunfire!—but not from him. It all happened in seconds. A ring of rifle shots split the twilight, and it wasn't clear who was doing the shooting. The Indians? A warrior at his right fell from a bullet. Tavish saw his wild eyes scream rage as he leaped at him.

Tavish felt the muscles of the heavy warrior tense, jerk, then cease to struggle. Tavish rolled him aside and was up from the ground on one knee, but the other Indians were dead or had slipped into the shadows of the rocks. He didn't move.

Then a familiar voice called, "You all right, Tav?"

He turned to Julot, who crouched a short distance away in some rocks, his grave face smudged with sweat and dust. He carried his Colt in one hand and a Winchester in the other. His dark eyes were intense with emotion. "Good shootin', Tav. I got three of 'em up there!"

Tavish felt nothing. He reloaded as Julot climbed toward him.

"And—Kain?" Julot breathed hesitantly.

Tavish tightened the grip on his emotions. "Up there."

Julot touched a hand to his shoulder and moved forward cautiously, his Colt ready.

Tavish slipped to the other side of the crevice and inched forward over the rock, his flinty gaze scanning the rim.

The Cheyenne were gone.

They found him—and he was yet alive, just barely. Shocked by the sight, Tavish could not move. They had staked him to the ground, tied by wrists and ankles. Tavish felt Julot's restraining hand, but he jerked free and moved toward him.

Julot was beside him. "That ain't your pa."

Tavish didn't recognize the unfortunate soldier. Then where was his father? A cold sweat covered his body and he felt the wind blowing against his soaked shirt. His hat blew off and he lifted his gun.

Tavish stood, slowly scanning the rock face until his gaze confronted another prisoner, his father. Kain was spread-eagle over a firebed built to slow-roast its victim, but this one had never been lit. Tavish ran to him, heart pounding. Was he alive?

"Father?"

Kain didn't move. It appeared he had died before they were able to torture him—or had there been some other reason why they had left him alone? There were two arrow wounds, one in his chest, the other in his back. *He must have died before the grueling process began,* Tavish thought. His eyes hardened. What a disappointment that would have been to the Cheyenne.

He reached a hand to touch his father's face and was captivated by the peace radiating from his expression. No hate contorted his strong, handsome features, no grimace of horror and pain.

Something else caught his attention. The Cheyenne had placed his father's Bible on the coals with an arrangement of their arrows—a sign of respect. Had they simply honored him by not torturing him?

"Tav!" whispered Julot. "Let's get out of here. There are more around."

A faint movement, then a raspy breath came from his father—or was it the whisper of the eerie wind?

"Your knife, Julot, quick."

Julot rushed to his side. "He's breathing!"

Tavish wiped sweat mingled with tears from his face and worked quickly with Julot to cut Kain free. God had spared his father a tortuous death, and had touched Tavish's heart with an overflow of gratitude and something more—a passion to know this Christ more deeply who had heard his prayers for his father.

"It's all right, Father. It's me, Tavish."

Kain tried to speak but his throat was too dry.

Julot stood, making a quick search for water. "There ain't any!" he whispered with frustration. "I'll go down to the horses—"

"No! Not alone. We go together—the three of us." Tavish drew his father into his arms. Kain choked something and Tavish bent his ear toward his cracked lips.

"N-no re-grets . . . I h-elped poor soldier die—"

Yes, thought Tavish proudly, touching the matted hair. *You would manage to help him.*

Out of respect for the memory of the soldier and Tavish's own days at West Point, they stayed to bury the young man of the Seventh Cavalry.

Tavish scanned the horizon. "Smoke-talk" danced on the hills, telegraphing Sitting Bull's victory against enemies bringing the Ironhorse. Soon more Sioux, Cheyenne, Arapaho, and other Indians would be on their own march.

The ride would be brutal for his father, but there was no choice; they couldn't remain where they were. The Cheyenne knew they were in the area, and by now Indian war parties would be between them and the Seventh Cavalry.

Kain lapsed back into unconsciousness as they cleaned and bound the wounds.

"There's no hope of catching up with the cavalry now," said Tavish. "They're days ahead. They'll march to winter quarters at Fort Lincoln." He scanned the range dusted with purple and black hues. "Yellowstone will soon be swarming with Sioux. We'll head in the direction of Miles City."

9

RED SKY

Fall rode the wind. Ahead, the land lay sun-blistered by day and frostbitten by night. Renegade Sioux moved silently across the plain, joined by Cheyenne and remnants from other tribes, their shadows merging with the darker splashes of the hills.

Tavish had watched the sunsets flare and fade into twilight against the plain. No sound but the wind and the passage of their horses disturbed the stillness. They had a chance to survive if they could reach the nearest fort.

Somewhere ahead, gunshots cut through the stillness. It was nearing sunset, and water was ahead. He guessed that whoever fired had been heading there. He waited, but there were no other shots, nor dust from horses on the horizon.

The sun settled, leaving streaks of orange scribbled across the shadowed sky. They came to a rise and, pausing, were confronted by an unexpected Northern Pacific railroad camp and several covered wagons.

To his left on the ridge of hills, smoke curled against the horizon. Were warriors hidden in the flat brushland between them and the makeshift camp? The camp was likely to be attacked by morning. That rifle shot could have been meant as a warning, he thought, but from whom? Someone else trying to make it to the safety of the camp?

From where he and Julot sat their horses, the railroad camp did not appear to be aware of their danger. Some wagons were drawn into a circle, and in the vast stillness he could hear faint sounds carried on the dry wind. Tavish knew that when Julot felt either excited or tense, he played his harmonica. With Cheyenne appearing to sprout up out of the ground, he could do neither, so he talked softly.

"My nerves prickle. Just like a rabbit 'bout to be skinned and hung to dry in some teepee."

"You talk too much," breathed Tavish. Unlike Julot, his moods were cool and silent. He glanced at his father strapped to the saddle. He was certain now that he would live, and just as certain that he would never be a strong man again. In the days since his capture, Kain slept most of the time. Tavish worried about infection and fever.

His brittle gaze fixed on the distance between them and the safety of the camp. He made no sound as they rode forward, one hand holding the reins of the horse carrying Kain. Julot, equally tense, continued: "Did you see that pretty blond girl at Bismarck?"

"Nope."

"You blind?"

"Thought you said she was a kid in dirty overalls." Tavish smiled faintly to himself, resting the muzzle of his Winchester across the top of his saddle. Indians had a way of lying flat on the ground so a person couldn't see them until they were eye to eye.

As Julot talked he appeared not to be alert, but Tavish knew his cousin better and wasn't worried. Julot would know that the shooting would be his responsibility since Tavish had to lead the horse carrying his father.

Julot's rifle came up to fire at a pile of bunchgrass. Tavish knew why and was ready. He spurred both horses forward into a dead run, lying low in the saddle, one eye on his father. The shots blasted like quick spurts of dynamite in his ears. Julot rode beside him all the way. Behind them an arrow whizzed. To Tavish's left, an Indian came up from the ground and lunged toward the side of Kain's horse, but Tavish struck him with the butt of his rifle. They raced forward.

Nearing the camp, Julot let off the yell of a French-Canadian mountain fighter to alert the camp of their arrival. As they rode closer, Tavish slowed, bending low in his saddle to get a better view of a man staked and tied to the ground. One glimpse as he rode by convinced him the man could not be alive. He recognized him as a scout and was troubled.

They rode into the camp scattering dirt and drew up near the chuck-wagon fire. Railroad men looked up and began to walk forward. In a sweeping glance, Tavish took in the condition of the men to determine how well they could defend themselves. His gaze collided with a mirage. . . .

A young woman in a blue velvet dress with autumn-colored hair stood in front of a covered wagon. Their glances caught. A flame ignited, followed swiftly by concern, then frustration. *Ember Ridgeway.* What was she doing here!

Tavish lowered his hat, scanning her. She hadn't changed in two years except for the better—if that were possible. His eyes narrowed. Did she recognize him? He looked anything but the suave young gentleman from West Point. But she responded enough to study him before she turned away with an elegant sweep of her skirts and mounted the box step like a princess en route to her throne. She glanced back briefly, saw that he continued to watch her, and entered the wagon with a disdainful jerk on the canvas.

Tavish smirked. *Haughty and spoiled as ever.* He remained in the saddle, and feeling that circumstances were worsening by the hour, he turned toward the old chuck-wagon cook. "Who's in charge here?"

The cook was pouring Tavish and Julot a tin of hot coffee. He chucked a thumb over his shoulder toward another wagon. "Smith is, but he ain't hirin'. North'n Pacific's done busted. Ol' Jay Cooke picked up his money bags and headed home to his mansion in Philly. We're all headed where the wind kin take us. Say—is that feller wounded bad, or plain already dead?"

Tavish followed his glance to Kain. "Alive. He's my father. Do you have a place I can rest him?"

"Sure. That wagon there—hey, Red!" he called. "Man's

hurt. See to him!" He cocked an eye back toward Tavish. "Injuns?"

"Yes. There's a war party of Cheyenne out there with their sights on this camp. You'll have a fight on your hands by morning."

"Why I'll be a dry-gulched lizard. Wuz hopin' them ornery cusses was headin' fer the reservations by now. Thought Mister Custer would teach Sittin' Bull a lesson."

"It's not that easy." Tavish took the cup of coffee. "Thanks. I need to speak to your boss."

"He's comin' now. Musta heard you stormin' in."

The mild-mannered foreman with the face of a poet walked up. "No work, young men. Railroad's been shut down. We're on our own. Have yourself a plate, though, and feed your horses. You look like you've come a hard way. Heard a man's hurt. We'll see to him as best we can."

Tavish didn't want Ember to know who he was yet, so as he offered his hand to the foreman he used his mother's maiden name and said easily, "Thanks. Name's LeBrett. This is my cousin, Julot."

Julot shot him a glance over the use of their French name but went along with it, remaining silent, and Tavish continued: "We were with an NP surveying party when we ran into Sitting Bull's warriors. You've got more trouble than you can handle. There's Cheyenne out there. And if I read the smoke signals right, more will be coming in tomorrow. It'll be a gamble, but if I were you, I'd move out tonight."

The foreman frowned and rubbed his nose. "We've been here for a few days. They haven't bothered us yet."

"They will." He drank the bitter coffee and looked toward Ember's covered wagon.

The foreman looked edgy. "How many out there, do you suppose?"

"More than you want to fight off. I advise you to pack up and get out while you can—especially with that woman."

"Three women."

"Three!"

"We can handle the Cheyenne. I've got fifteen who can use a gun."

Tavish stared at his coffee. "That won't be enough." He took off his hat and beat off the dust, feeling the night wind in his dark hair. "Tell him, Julot."

Julot sat back on his bootheels before the fire, holding out his tin for more coffee. The cook filled it, nervously watching them.

Julot smiled, his handsome French face showing in the firelight. "Ornery as wild broncs, sir. Soon as cut you open as look at you. We buried a man back yonder."

"The Cheyenne waiting out there are seasoned," said Tavish. "Each one is a veteran at war. They've been fighting all their lives, and they'll die fighting before they allow the government to herd them off to some reservation."

"You sound sympathetic," said the foreman with an unpleasant accusation in his voice.

Tavish's eyes turned cold. "They held my father prisoner. When we rescued him he was barely alive. He was a chaplain with the NP's expedition. Another soldier was tortured to death. I've little sympathy left."

The foreman was silent for a time. "That's miserably tough, young man. I'm sorry, I didn't realize." He looked toward the covered wagon where Tavish had seen Ember. "Heard of Mister Mack Ridgeway?"

"Who hasn't?" asked Tavish dryly.

"Mack is the father of one of the young women I mentioned. Her name's Mrs. Hollister. Her husband's stationed at Fort Lincoln. You aim on riding there?" asked the foreman.

"That's right. If we can get through."

"We've a month's pay to pick up," added Julot. He frowned. "Is Riley still in Bismarck?"

"Riley? He took off for Oregon."

"That wily jackrabbit," scoffed Julot. "And after all his jawing about there being nothing up there. He must have taken your advice, Tav."

Tavish's dark brows lowered, but Riley was the last problem on his mind. How would they get Ember and Lottie safely to the fort?

The grizzled chuck-wagon cook scratched his beard. "Hate to say this, fellas, but even if you survive them Injuns, you won't get yer pay. Them railroad gents just folded camp and took off, leavin' us high and dry. I lost me two months' pay!"

"Riley didn't lose his," a lean track layer spoke up. "He was paid plenty by Mack Ridgeway to head to Washington Territory. Something about timberland up there along the Hood that he aims to have for the railroad."

Tavish glanced at him. His own land was located on the Hood Canal.

"Riley jawed that he'd done logging in Idaho Territory before turning to the NP, and Mr. Ridgeway hired him to do a big job."

"Ferget Riley!" someone interrupted. "What about us? What about them Cheyenne? And what about them women? They're in a dandy fix!"

Tavish looked toward the covered wagon. "How did they end up here?" he asked the foreman.

"They were on their way from Fort Benton when the stage driver turned yellow-sick. Don't think he's going to make it either. And if we need to make a run for it, he'll die. He shouldn't be moved."

Tavish finished his coffee. "Any guards with them?"

"One. He must have suspected Indians all along. With the driver sick, and no one to help him protect the women, he feared to go on. He saw our camp and brought the stage in."

Tavish held out his cup and the old cook refilled it. He remembered the man he'd seen on the way in.

"Where's their guard now?"

"Sam's due back from the trading post anytime."

The cook scratched his whiskers knowingly. "He's a mite late."

"I'm riding out tonight, Julot with me. You and the camp better know what to expect," he told the foreman.

"If a fight comes, we'll be ready. But get the women out of here."

And Cheyenne crawling around as thick as fleas! Tavish looked toward the wagon. "Better introduce me. I've a notion she'd fire a pistol if I went near her wagon."

Tavish walked beside the foreman in silence, his mind out there on the plain where the Cheyenne were having their pow-wow. They probably already knew about Ember and Lottie. They knew how many horses and mules there were, and how many men guarded them. If his guess proved right, they'd attack by dawn.

He saw the stage, with its team nearby, that had brought Ember and her cousin here, and he walked over to check out the horses. They were in good condition and strong enough for a run, but what about the women? If they panicked he wouldn't be able to save them. He thought back to the parties and dinners along the Hudson when Ember had been wrapped in silk and satin and smelling like a French garden.

There was only one thing to do besides resting his own horse for a few hours—warn Ember of the nightmare that waited. In New York there wasn't any need to know where she stood when it came to having courage. Strange that they would meet again now, amid dust, sweat, and a terror that was certain to break with the dawn. He needed to see if she possessed more than outward beauty. If she didn't, they were in big trouble.

10

BLACK SKY . . . WHITE STARS

Lottie was asleep behind a drawn curtain at the back of the wagon, and Sassy was with her, but Ember was feeling too restless to sleep. The interior was stuffy and she had opened the canvas flap and stepped outside just as the two strangers raced into camp.

She noticed one of the men at once. She blamed this on the haste with which he and his friend had dramatically made their entrance, but if she were honest with herself she would admit that even if he had passed through as silently as the Montana wind, she could not have avoided him. Although unable to see his face clearly from this distance, this particular man had a cool and laid-back way about him as he sat astride the sweating horse, his dusty hat lowered.

Sassy heard the horses too and, clutching her wrapper tightly about her, came to Ember, frowning worriedly. "You come inside. They wouldn't have stirred up all that dust if there weren't plenty to worry about. Thank goodness Lottie's sleeping like a log. I done tole the both of you that we should've waited at Fort Benton till one of the Ridgeway men come for

117

us. Never did see rhyme nor reason why she was to meet her Lieutenant Hollister at Fort Lincoln. Indians everywhere!"

Ember wasn't listening. The stranger on horseback continued to watch her evenly from beneath his hat. *Why he almost behaves as if he knows me,* she thought. Good breeding told her a woman never gazed back at a man for long, and Ember dragged her gaze away with just the right amount of finishing school dignity, lifted her velvet skirts, climbed back into the wagon, and closed the flap.

Once out of sight, however, her wide eyes met Sassy's. "That gunshot earlier this evening," Ember whispered, afraid she would awaken Lottie. "I was right. I told you the harmonica stopped too abruptly."

Voices and hurried footsteps filled the night. Ember heard horses and wagons being moved closer into the camp to form a tighter circle. Other footsteps stopped outside. Her eyes fixed upon the canvas entrance.

"Ladies? Are you awake?"

She recognized the urgent voice of the foreman. Sassy was about to answer, but Ember took the lead. "Yes?"

"We're movin' your wagon center-camp, ma'am. Don't worry yourself. It's just a caution."

She tensed. Caution for what? She thought she knew, and a sick feeling churned in her stomach.

"I'd like to speak with you if I could, Miss Ridgeway," came the foreman's voice.

Ember hesitated, then drew aside the flap and looked down, seeing the foreman's grave face. "Yes?" she said with a calm voice that contradicted her fears.

He tipped his hat. "Sorry to disturb you, miss, but there's been some trouble."

His voice was apologetic and she guessed that he was trying to shield her. "What kind of trouble?" she asked warily.

"An Indian attack. The sooner you and your cousin meet up with the Seventh Cavalry the better we'll all feel. I'm suggesting you don't wait for a military escort to arrive, but ride ahead to meet them. You best leave tonight."

"Tonight!" Then she was right about the gunshot, she thought. "But how? What of the stage driver and our guard?

Has anyone heard from Samuel yet? There was a rifle shot earlier. . . ."

"Yes, ma'am. I heard it. About your leaving, I'm recommending two trusty men who just rode in from the Bighorn area. They were with your uncle's railroad surveyors when Cheyenne attacked. They're bustin' to get out of here, and so should you."

Her heart stopped beating. "An Indian attack! Is my uncle safe?"

"I don't know, ma'am," came the evasive tone. "You best talk to the men themselves who rode in—"

"But what of Samuel? He should have made it back from the trading post by now. You don't suppose that shot—?"

The foreman hesitated, and the way he silently stood there set her nerves on fire. "That rifle shot," she demanded, her eyes searching his. "Was it Samuel?"

"I'll let him explain, Miss Ridgeway. This is LeBrett."

The introduction was unexpected, for she hadn't realized that another man stood there while she spoke with the foreman. Her head turned in the direction of LeBrett.

The name was French and a vague bell sounded in her mind. Where had she heard it spoken before, or was it her imagination?

She scanned him cautiously, but he stood back in the shadows leaning against a supply wagon, a ruggedly built silhouette without a face. His bootheel was hooked onto a large rock behind him, a hand rested across his gun belt, and the pulled-down brim of his hat was low, the breeze moving his jacket. Although she couldn't see his face, she knew it was the young man she had seen ride into camp earlier. She brushed a strand of hair back uneasily and said nothing.

"Did Mack Ridgeway hire Sam?" he asked smoothly.

She noted that there was no French accent in his voice, but rather a resonant drawl that suggested deliberate Western usage. His earthy presence set her on guard. Vaguely she wondered how he knew about her uncle Mack, and decided the foreman must have told him.

"Yes, he hired Samuel at Fort Steilacoom in Washington Territory. He brought us to Fort Benton, intending to bring us on to Fort Lincoln."

"There wasn't a finer scout than Sam. I met him at Bismarck."

Ember felt a quiver of unease. *Wasn't* a finer scout?

"He did well to leave you here before trying to reach the trading post."

Her skin crawled in the warm wind as she glanced about the distant darkness. "Will he make it back tonight?"

His voice came as calmly as the whisper of wind ruffling her hair. "Sam won't be bringing you anywhere. He's dead. You're in real trouble, Miss Ridgeway, in case you haven't figured it out yet, but I think you have."

The atmosphere of danger, like choking fingers, made it difficult to breathe. Anything as unpleasant and irrevocable as death could not simply barge into her life and scatter her plans to the desert wind, leaving her defenseless.

Feeling cornered and trapped by the raw truth of their danger, her emotions recoiled and she refused to admit it.

"But he can't be dead," she insisted, the accusation in her voice only thinly veiled. "What makes you so certain?"

"You guessed before the foreman did. That rifle shot. It was a warning to the camp from Sam that Cheyenne are out there."

She wanted to draw back horrified, now that he had calmly but bluntly brought her earlier suspicions into the open. But he continued to lean there, looking relaxed, and it was needling to her when her own knees were so weak that she doubted if she could stand. He radiated strength to her in the form of a challenge, and she lifted her head, her voice steady. "But someone else might have fired the shot," she persisted.

She sensed that he was evaluating her response. Well, she hadn't screamed or fainted yet.

"Maybe. But I saw Sam on the way in. He's lying outside camp not far from here."

His easy reply rankled her still further. "You—saw him—?" She stopped, confused, then added accusingly, "And you just left him lying out there unattended?"

"Uh-huh."

Thinking she hadn't understood him, that she was being a little rude to this handsome young cowboy—for she assumed he was either a railroad track layer or a ranch hand passing through—she went on to suggest the proper response for him:

"What you mean, Mr. LeBrett, is that you stopped to make certain Samuel was—was dead."

"No, what I mean is, I didn't stop, no need to," came the lazy voice.

Even though she sensed a baiting quality to his tone, her eyes narrowed with self-righteous indignation. "Then I suggest, cowboy, that you ride back out there *now*—and bring my guard safely to me."

He made no response and just lounged there against the other wagon. She stared at him, feeling warm when she envisioned a smirk on his face.

Her head jerked toward the railroad foreman. "Maybe Samuel's only wounded!"

The foreman cleared his throat. "I'll be needing to take his word for it, Miss Ridgeway. Don't worry, though. LeBrett here, he'll see that you and your cousin get to the fort."

And just who was this LeBrett that she should entrust herself and Lottie, who was five months with child, to him?

"Sir, as fast as you rode in tonight, I'm surprised either you or your partner were able to see anything. Least of all be able to identify the victim. I suggest you're mistaken. Samuel only left us yesterday. Nobody dies so quickly."

"The West is a brutal land when you're not prepared for it. It's my opinion you should've stayed in Saratoga sipping lemonade and strolling under silk parasols. Don't tell me you've come here to marry a rich soldier? There couldn't be another one like Prescott Hollister in all the Seventh Cavalry."

Saratoga. . . . What did he know about her time spent at the resort? For that matter, what did he know about Lottie and Prescott, or her own plans?

"My plans, Mr. LeBrett, are my own. I don't discuss them with strangers." *Especially arrogant ones,* she wanted to say but refrained. If Samuel was dead, then the foreman was right about her and Lottie needing this man to help them escape.

"As for dying 'quickly,'" he went on, ignoring her rebuke, "out in these parts when a man's left to himself with Cheyenne on the warpath, circumstances don't leave him much choice. Not even a good scout like Sam has much chance to survive. We don't either, but I don't expect to surrender easily."

As he continued to talk, Ember tensed, for although she was

unable to see his face, there was something about him that had begun to awaken old memories. That voice . . . if the Western drawl was missing . . . something about his manner—she could almost vow it was—

"Cheyenne are warriors to be respected in a fight. They're the best fighters around. Like Apaches, they're able to sneak up on a man without a sound. They use sagebrush to hide behind. The brush gets closer and closer and a man could swear it wasn't growing there a minute ago, but he's never quite sure, so he doesn't do anything about it. But you're right about a man not dying fast. They like to see how long he can endure torture without screaming and begging. The longer he holds out, the more warrior in his blood. When he does die, he becomes part of the Indian warrior. Sam was lucky . . . they killed him quickly."

Ember couldn't move. She stared at his silhouette, wondering. Somehow she suspected he was saying all this to discover if she had nerve. She might have saved him the trouble of trying to find out. At the moment, she had none.

The foreman wiped his brow. "Why did they move on Sam so quickly? He has a big name, even among the Cheyenne."

"My guess? They have other quarry on their mind. This camp holds interesting prospects."

Ember went cold. She was aware that LeBrett watched her.

"Had I stopped to bring Sam's body in I'd be the same as he is—without my hair."

Her breath released with a blow. *Scalped!*

In an abrupt reaction to the horror she felt, Ember jerked the canvas shut and leaned back. Scalped! Her cold, shaking fingers ran along her waist-length hair. She let out a wail, not caring if they heard her or not.

Sassy threw strong arms around her as they knelt together. From outside, the foreman called, "Miss Ridgeway?"

She managed to regain her poise, drew in a breath, and pulled away from Sassy. Reluctantly she opened the canvas. She had the suspicion that her uninhibited wail had not taken the young man named LeBrett by surprise.

"LeBrett will get you out," said the foreman. "If there's any way to do it, he and his partner can. I'll let you two work it out as to wages. If you'll be excusin' me, I've got to see to these wagons."

Her eyes trailed after him until he was gone, then slowly she turned her head toward LeBrett. He hadn't budged.

"Step forward," she said uneasily. "So I can see you."

"Is this an auction?"

She drew in a breath. "Sir! If I'm to trust myself to a stranger I should at least see what he looks like."

"That will help, you think?"

He walked up to the front of her wagon and stood there.

Her eyes stumbled over him. The lantern light above her wagon fell on a wide-brimmed hat and a poncho worn over black jeans. His hair was rich and dark, longer than that of the young men she had met at West Point—

West Point! Tavish Wilder!

Stunned, she stared down at him, her awakened emotions tumbling in every direction. The warmth rose to her throat, her cheeks. Yes, it was he . . . and yet, Tavish was not only a stranger in appearance but in his manner. His hair was tied back with a leather cord that moved in a gust of wind. As she looked into dark green eyes, they became all too familiar.

The warm softness in their depths took her by surprise. He had sounded hard when he had spoken from the shadows, but the way he looked at her now was anything but ruthless. He did recognize her; he had to. Why was he pretending otherwise?

"You see? I'm human, and my father is a minister. That should make you feel better."

Ember stared at him, struggling against a torrent of contradicting emotions sweeping over her like a heady wind. Dread that he had walked back into her life so unexpectedly, excitement at his presence, anger that he had not contacted her before he disappeared from New York without so much as a simple goodbye! Perhaps it hurt even more to admit that for months after he left West Point she had secretly convinced herself that he would write her at Chadwick and explain everything—and even more; she had expected a confession of love, however vague. And a promise that he intended to see her again, one day.

One day . . . that day hadn't come until now, by chance. She didn't believe in mindless fate, but had God brought them back together again for a time like this? Seeing him now did nothing to suggest her past feelings had been a girlish whim. As she watched him standing there, the glowing embers from the past were reluctantly stirred back into a flame.

What did *he* feel . . . anything? He couldn't, not when his manner appeared as if the Ember Ridgeway he had known in New York was a total stranger.

Her own appearance hadn't changed as much as his had, and she'd been sitting in the lantern light all this time, while he held back in the shadows using a Western accent—and had he not addressed her as Miss Ridgeway? Also, the mention of Saratoga, Lottie, and Prescott Hollister all made sense now, as did his use of the name LeBrett. Had it not been his mother's maiden name?

She remembered something else. He had been expelled from West Point for cheating on the final exams. The word "cheating" provoked a wince, and as she studied him, trying not to be obvious, a bewildering pain wormed its way through her soul. There wasn't a cowardly bone in his body; nor could she believe there was character weakness, except for his arrogance. How could he have done anything so dishonorable as to cheat and lie and blame her cousin Wade?

Wade had been a friend of Tavish and they had roomed together. "He was like a brother who turned against me," Wade had informed her. "I'm sorry, Ember. It turned out badly for you too. It's best it ended now. I found out his father is Kain Wilder, a gunfighter. It's no wonder he would cheat to achieve his purpose. Bad blood runs deep."

Bad blood. She saw little evidence of that now in the strong young man standing below her wagon, and yet her own pain kindled fresh resentment. Her eyes dropped to his gun belt. Wade was right . . . he did look like a gunfighter! *But a darkly handsome one just the same,* she thought with a pang.

So he now claimed to be a minister's son! And his name was LeBrett? Well, she'd play along with his masquerade if that was his wish. She'd never let him know how much she had once cared, or how his abrupt disappearance had hurt.

Her eyes turned cool as they met his. "Do I take it from your clothing, Mr. LeBrett, that you are not a West Point officer? Such a pity."

She saw the flicker of irritation as he took her in.

"And do I take it, Miss Ridgeway, that you are an ardent supporter of our gallant men wearing the yellow ribbon?"

"Indeed. I've nothing but admiration for the brave soldiers in the cavalry." She smiled. "Especially since my distinguished cousin Wade Ridgeway is a major in the Seventh Cavalry."

"Is he? Now I wonder how your gallant cousin managed such a feat?"

Her smiled vanished, and she was about to rush to his defense when Tavish said bluntly, "I deplore the need to disappoint your feminine admiration for West Point graduates, but as you can see, I wear patched jeans and a denim shirt. I'm one of the humble and faceless thousands who laid 450 miles of track to the Missouri River. Speaking of your distinguished cousin, the major was also at Yellowstone when the Cheyenne attacked."

Ember saw his eyes harden.

"I had the fortune of being among the lucky group of civilians under his chivalrous protection!"

"Indeed?" She smarted at his sarcasm.

He smiled. "Yes, and you can be sure he was bulging with all his well-learned knowledge of military tactics and courage."

Ember stiffened. She sensed his resentment as strong as her own toward him. Why would he feel such bitterness toward Wade? If anyone had a cause to feel angry, it was her cousin. Tavish had tried to blame the unfortunate incident at West Point on him.

Knowing Wade had been in the fighting alarmed her. "Wade is all right? He wasn't hurt?"

His smile remained. "Major Ridgeway made certain he rode out safely enough."

What did he mean by that? Somehow she was reluctant to pursue the question and challenged, "And—your father—the man you say is a minister—he is well? I didn't see a third man with you tonight."

His expression changed. "He's wounded but alive. If you expect to join Wade at the fort, you'll need to change your plans."

"What do you mean? Lottie is to meet Prescott there."

"Custer's Seventh Cavalry is wintering at Fort Lincoln. So are Wade and Prescott."

He turned his head to look past her into the wagon. "How many are with you besides Lottie? I can't imagine a girl like you journeying all the way from Port Townsend without a handful of serving maids to attend to her whims."

Her eyes narrowed. If anything, he had grown more arrogant since leaving West Point.

"Whims? And what exactly do you mean to imply when you blithely say a girl like me?"

He smiled as though dismissing the importance of the subject, but she believed he was deliberately goading her. Had she rankled him so much with her questions about West Point and Wade?

"You're a Ridgeway debutante, aren't you?" came the smooth reply. "I'm certain you require your little comforts: chocolates, at least three trunks of silk and satin dresses—"

"Of all the audacity, sir!"

He smiled. "Audacity? I thought it was bare-bone necessity that drove a woman to haul everything with her on a trip. May I look inside and see how many trunks I'm expected to haul through Indian territory?"

"You may not! And I didn't bring three trunks."

"No? I confess to being amazed. After all, a Ridgeway has money, reputation, and the ways and means to get what they want. Seems to me you'd be raised in fancy parlors with a passel of West Point cadets swarming around you."

Her eyes narrowed. "I suppose you have something against debutantes raised in elegance? And West Point gentlemen? I should wear spurs?"

"No, you just keep right on wearing velvet, Ember. I like it. I always did."

Ember. The way he spoke her name pricked her heart. So he did remember, but of course he would. And he knew she recognized him as well, and was admitting it.

Their stormy gaze held. The silence between them intensified until Sassy drew back the canvas.

"Is that you, Mister Tavish? I was suspecting I had me a cause to recognize your voice."

Ember wondered at Sassy's friendliness and her warm smile. After all her earlier warnings against Tavish when Ember was a girl, Sassy appeared relieved to see him.

Tavish smiled at her. "Evening, Sassy. How did Ember bamboozle you into coming west to run into a pack of Cheyenne?"

She groaned. "A long tale, and ain't pleasant neither, seein' hows I have Miss Lottie to think of too. She's expectin' a chile. But I'm breathin' a might easier knowin' you're here with that sixshooter."

Ember recognized the increased concern in the way his dark brow shot up.

"Lottie's expecting?" he asked.

"And not feelin' too healthy at the moment."

Tavish turned to Ember. "That presents a bigger problem. We'll need to make a run for it."

Ember felt defensive. "Lottie won't complain."

"If I remember her correctly, you're right. Her Christian character is impeccable. Lieutenant Hollister is a lucky man."

His comment aroused a jab of jealousy in Ember. She remembered back to New York, trying to recall if there had been any time when Tavish seemed more attracted to Lottie than to her. His attitude had been so casual, she couldn't remember, but the idea bothered her just the same. Would he have sought Lottie if the Ridgeways hadn't already planned a marriage to Prescott?

"Don't bother to pack the trunks," said Tavish. "We'll need to ride out of here with what's on our backs."

Ember had recovered. He wasn't going to get by with his cynical attitude, or his masquerade as a minister's son. "So! You're the son of a minister?" she asked suddenly.

He must have recognized the baiting tone in her question, but remained silent, waiting for whatever barb was sure to come.

Ember offered an innocent smile. "Why, Mister 'LeBrett,' I must say I'm surprised, indeed. I would have mistaken you for the offspring of a gunslinger."

Sassy sucked in her breath at Ember's rudeness, but if her little dig got to him he didn't show it.

The green eyes flickered. "Seeing the fix you're in, you'd better hope that I am." He went on as smoothly as though discussing the weather. "But no need to worry, Miss Ridgeway, I'm as gentle as a shorn lamb. It's my cousin Julot who's trouble."

"Your partner? Is he your cousin? Yes, I can see how he'd be your cousin. Is he good with a gun too?"

Tavish scanned her hair. "He's given me a few pointers. About your hair—"

She couldn't resist and interrupted. "And what did you teach *him*?"

"I've tried Longfellow and Shakespeare but he chokes on it." His challenging gaze, tinged with amusement, met hers. "And what of you, Miss Ridgeway? What have you learned in the two long years I've been breaking my back laying track, while you've been breaking West Point hearts?"

Her mind flashed back to a certain afternoon at the house on the Hudson . . . and how a spoiled girl of only fifteen and a half had done everything within her charms to capture the heart of a certain West Point cadet. Her face felt warm as she knew he remembered.

The emotions that flared up were not all that different from those she had felt for him then, and to cover her embarrassment, she impulsively reached to cuff his handsome face.

He ducked, losing his hat in the dust.

"I see your tendency toward spoiled tantrums hasn't changed after all."

She abruptly turned to withdraw into the wagon.

Undisturbed, he knocked the dust off his hat and gestured to her trunk, his gaze even.

"Change into a riding habit and those boots," he ordered.

"I don't take orders."

"If you expect to ride out with me, you will."

She stiffened. He looked past her to Sassy. "And see her hair is covered. It'll catch the sun's rays and shine like copper. I don't want a pack of Cheyenne on my trail."

He looked at Ember, placing his hat back on and scanning her with a faint smile. "I'll come back for you later."

"Don't bother," she snapped.

"But I will. We'll need to slip away unnoticed—make them think we're not on to them. If they believe we're a pack of fools, they might not attack until sunup, but I can't guarantee it. Try and sleep awhile. It may be the last chance you get for some time." He turned and walked away.

She flung the canvas closed and faced Sassy, heart throbbing, her face flushed. "Who is he to talk to me like that?"

"He's right. An' you was bad to try to cuff him—a nice handsome gentleman like him."

"My how you've changed!"

Sassy cast her a glance. "Times are a-changin'."

"Who does he think he is to order me about! 'Wear this, do that, hide your hair . . .' And a minister's son! He doesn't look like any I've ever seen before! How dare he barge back into my life!"

Sassy's expression turned troubled and her dark eyes flashed with sympathy. "Don't go gettin' yourself upset. We has worse problems than the manners of Mister Tavish."

"Of course I'm upset! Why shouldn't I be? Oh! I loathe him!"

"You ain't got over him yet," Sassy countered.

"Got over him? I never wanted to see him again as long as I lived! And now—"

"Life's full of surprises. Least he's tryin' to help us, can't you see?"

Yes, she could see, but if she thought she was in love with the Tavish Wilder from her past, she found the new one even more exasperating.

"He's too sure of himself," she said crossly. "He always was. Imagine! Daring to suggest I once cared about him, when I never told him I did, and I certainly wouldn't now."

Sassy winced. "How you felt 'bout the man back then wasn't no secret to anyone, least of all, him. He knows how you schemed to get him as your escort all those months—"

"I won't hear it. I was only a child," she said defensively, and when Sassy arched a brow, Ember added firmly, "Infatuation dies quickly with maturity."

"And, of course, you is all grown up now," teased Sassy.

"If we didn't need him to help us now, I'd be only too glad to tell Tavish Wilder exactly what I think of him."

"You behave yourself like a lady and be nice to him. We ain't got another friend in all the world, an' Lottie needs him, and that Julot too. Here, you change into this."

Ember snatched the outfit from Sassy, feeling miserable. Her heart felt two sizes too large for her stays.

She had already decided on the sage green riding habit. And

she had no intention of letting her waist-length hair fly behind her like a flag!

Samuel was dead. Scalped! And Tavish had said there were many Indians out there in the dark. She shuddered, her teeth chattering. What if they killed Tavish and his cousin? What if they killed them all—except the women?

But surely the railroad men could hold them off until soldiers arrived from the fort. Uncle Mack was expecting the stage. When it didn't arrive, he'd come with Wade and Prescott to search for them.

But what if they couldn't hold out against the Cheyenne that long? Would the Indians kill her, or take her as a squaw?

There was nothing to fear, she soothed herself. Just a lot of scary talk. He was trying to frighten her, yet she knew better. Danger was real. And whatever Tavish had done in the past, he was trying to save them now. She ought to show her gratitude by treating him "nice," as Sassy put it, even if he had walked out of her life without explanation.

He was back in her life again. For how long?

She snatched up one of the boots and scowled at it. She hated the things. Chunky, stiff leather, big heels. She wrinkled her nose and smelled the leather. They even stank like cows. Cowboys and track layers. "And that Tavish Wilder is the worst of them all," she murmured and threw the boot down.

The wagon was being moved forward to the center of the camp and she heard voices and horses.

Indians. . . .

Slowly Ember gathered her boots and riding habit and glanced at the wagon opening. How could a woman be safe in a measly wagon covered with canvas? It was outrageous.

She snuffed the lantern and, with Sassy's help, grudgingly changed. "You go help Lottie," she told her. "Try not to frighten her. I don't want her to know about Samuel's death yet. Where's the pistol?"

Sassy scowled. "In the trunk, honey, but you let ol' Sassy do the handlin' of it."

"No, I'll keep it with me. Cousin Wade taught me to shoot."

Ember scooped up her luxurious auburn tresses and began the tedious task of weaving them into braids, then wound them around her head and fastened them with pins, her fingers cold and trembling. She crammed on her hat and tied it firmly under her chin, then curled up on the quilt and tried to rest, listening to male voices and snorting horses. Eventually the sounds quieted her. After a time she tried to sleep, but she was too tense.

The camp grew still. Except for an occasional voice or the sound of boots, night deepened. She imagined sagebrush moving nearer toward camp as the Cheyenne crawled closer. How many were there? Tavish and his cousin . . . were they close by?

When the sound of the crickets ceased, she came alert and leaned forward, listening intently. She heard Lottie's quiet breathing farther back in the wagon, behind the curtain. Sassy was with her. If trouble did come, Lottie would need more help since she was expecting.

Ember's misery grew. Confusion filled her vision, blurring everything. She groaned at her own selfish traits, her fiery tongue that too often spoke things she didn't mean.

"Oh, Lord, help me to change," she murmured into the darkness. "Make me more like Lottie. Whatever it takes to help me learn your ways, here am I, Lord Jesus."

The crickets began to chirp again and her breathing eased. She closed her eyes. . . .

Sleep came silently.

Then a noise—so small that if she let out a breath it would hide the sound. She came instantly awake, her heart pulsating in her throat. Expecting to see the glow of the campfire on the canvas, she froze. Fear seized her. The fire had gone out!

11

BLOOD ON THE MOON

What was that sound? Ember's heart pounded so hard in her ears she could barely hear herself think. Had there been a muffled groan outside the wagon? It had to be her imagination!

Her breath came in a ragged gasp. The Cheyenne were out there! Where was Tavish? The groan must have come from him. He'd been attacked. Palms sweating, she shrank farther back. A yell! Then another—then rifle shots. The darkness exploded with violence, the whistle of arrows, a burst of flame as a wagon caught fire. Voices shouted, bullets sang from all directions, then the nervous whinny of horses, and another eruption of fire and the feel of heat. Flames began dancing up from the back of their wagon. The nightmare swallowed her up, spitting her back out with a taste of horror as she understood she was in the center of it all.

"Oh, God, help me," she breathed, terrified, scrambling back into a corner of the wagon and jerking the quilt up around her throat. If she fled, the Indians would catch her. . . . If she stayed here, she'd soon be burned. She hid, immobilized by fear.

Lottie screamed and the horrified sound stabbed through Ember. In a moment she grasped the pistol and was pushing her way forward in a panic to reach her cousin. "Lottie!"

Ember flung aside the curtain, but recoiled in the flickering firelight from the other burning wagons. Sassy was missing!

"The pistol," Lottie was calling. "Where is it?"

A knife ripped across the other side of the canvas and a form crawled through, looming dark and rigid against the firelight. A feather in long hair and the strange smell of grease brought a scream to her throat. The knife was in his hand and it glinted with a flash of silver. The half-naked figure moved slowly out of the shadows, war paint smeared across his face.

Ember froze. Lottie screamed: "Fire the pistol!"

Ember squeezed the trigger—the bullet smashed through the canvas. She drew back, staring into cold eyes that looked at her without pity.

He sprang toward her, and they fell backward to the wagon floor. She felt his rough hand grab her scalp and a scream died in her throat. She stared into the face of death, brutal and pitiless, expecting to feel the knife plunge into her throat. Suddenly, the warrior was jerked backward, his white teeth baring, a look of startled anger across his face. Ember saw another man's arm around his throat . . . then heard a dagger enter his ribcage.

In a dying rage, the warrior tried to thrust his own knife toward her chest, but the gleaming blade slammed into the pile of petticoats beside her as he fell, his greased arm coming across her face, momentarily smothering her.

Ember fought hysterically, fighting and clawing at something that no longer moved—

The arm was pulled aside and other hands were grabbing her. She tried to squeeze the trigger but the pistol was yanked from her hand. She fought like death itself, until Tavish's fingers closed so tightly about her wrist she couldn't move. His other hand silenced her screaming. *Tavish!*

"Let me go! Lottie—"

"Julot has her. Can you make a run for it without fainting?"

She gave a little cry of rage, and he took hold of her arm, snatched up her pistol and pushed it inside his belt. "Let's go."

He swung her down out of the burning wagon, keeping a

firm grip on her arm as he glanced cautiously about.

Ember almost tripped over a dead man on the ground. The Indian had killed him before entering. That was the muffled groan she'd heard. Her throat parched and aching, she became aware of Tavish's arm drawing her against his side, and she clung to him as he pulled her away from the scorching heat.

One hand held tightly to her arm, his other held a revolver. Another man met them—Julot—and Lottie was with him. No words were spoken, and with only hand signals, they were moving and ducking and darting first this direction, then that. Ember felt herself somehow stumbling along beside Tavish, held up by his strength, her knees so weak they wanted to buckle.

Ember thought fear would cause her heart to burst in her chest. An Indian sprang from the darkness—and she nearly screamed. Tavish's gun blasted. Julot shot in another direction. Then they were moving again, this time running into the deeper darkness away from camp, away from the sounds of battle and death. She heard nothing but her breathing. The pins had fallen out of her hair and her long braids swung behind her. She stumbled on something sticking up out of the ground and went down, silencing a cry. Tavish paused to swing her up in his arms and then they were running again. She managed to twist her head away to glimpse the white stars overhead and felt amazed that anything so stable could still be up there calmly staring down.

God. The word sprang like Samson's strength within her soul, and tasted as sweet as the honey he had found in the lion's carcass. God would never abandon her. Her heart felt like an orphan, but she was not alone. Snatches of a psalm raced across her mind—*God is our refuge and strength, a very present help in trouble!*

Someone else was with them. Sassy! "Oh, thank you, Lord!"

Sassy huffed alongside Julot, who had Lottie in his arms.

Now and then Tavish would drift behind Julot and Lottie, go to one knee to fire, then grab Ember again and race to catch up to the others.

As they ran on, Ember's side was splitting with pain. They neared some rocks and Julot scrambled up with Lottie, aided by Sassy.

Ember steadied herself on the boulder as they began climbing.

"Can you crawl between those two rocks?" whispered Tavish, breathing hard.

She nodded, gasping, struggling on hands and knees through the dark opening, and he came in after her.

"Lottie and Sassy," she whispered, clutching his arm.

"They're on the other side of the opening with Julot and my father."

She tried to catch her breath. Dazed, her mind floundered in horror and confusion, filled with the memory of the Cheyenne attack, of the dagger that had nearly plunged into her throat.

"They'll track us," he whispered, handing her a canteen of water. "Come daylight they'll be all around. We won't see them until they're right on us. Can you take it?"

She drank thirstily, then handed the canteen back. She covered her sweating face with trembling palms. "No."

"You'll have to." He was crouching, reloading his revolver. He removed her pistol from his belt and replaced the bullet she had fired. He handed the gun to her. "Where'd you get it?"

"Wade."

"Use it if you have to." He pushed aside the barrel pointed toward him. "Just make certain you don't aim it at me."

She was too exhausted to glare at his smile.

"I had left a guard at the wagon. I should have stayed. Me and Julot. But we had to get our horses hidden, and my father here to safety. I didn't expect the attack until dawn." He wiped his forehead on his arm. "Maybe we can hold out. The chance is slim. Save your fears. Tomorrow you may not need them."

Her face jerked up, seeing little except the handsome cut of his features and the outline of his hat.

He was suggesting they might all be dead tomorrow.

"We won't talk anymore. Even a whisper carries."

12

YELLOW DAWN

The dawn broke a sullen yellow over the hills. In the distance there was a trail of smoke hanging in the air from the burning wagons. A sick feeling fell like lead in the pit of her stomach. What had happened to the others? Were they dead? A few might be alive. . . .

A bird called out of the darkness with startling clarity, but when a hand pushed her down she knew it wasn't a bird.

Silently they waited. Minutes crept by while Ember shut her eyes tightly and covered her head, praying, the face of the rock pressing into her cheek. She tensed, breathing in the danger.

A bloodcurdling yell stabbed the morning.

She heard the ominous thunder of hoofs and what panic told her were a hundred Cheyenne.

A shot sang out from Julot's position. Tavish lifted his hand from her shoulder and his rifle exploded, deafening her ears. Bullets and arrows crackled and whined and the war cries of the Cheyenne seemed to echo all around them. Her heart beat so that she could hardly breathe. Violence made her feel sick. Blood! Death! Fear!

She glanced at Tavish. His expression was both calm and deadly. First one bullet then another, each shot chosen carefully. Between his gunfire she heard Julot's rifle crackling. It seemed to her they were hitting their targets. Then just as suddenly as the attack had begun, silence swept in, stark and vast.

Tavish reloaded his revolver and the repeating rifle. He placed his gun in his holster within easy grasp. She clamped her jaw to keep her teeth from chattering. Were they gone?

"They'll come again" was all he said, his gaze fixed ahead of them.

She counted the beats of her heart pulsating in her ears. Within seconds arrows clattered, striking the face of the rock. One whizzed over their heads, missing Tavish and falling harmlessly against her boot. She pulled her leg forward as though the object would come to life like Pharaoh's snake.

Out there, the high-pitched yelping began again, like crazed coyotes; then horses rode with breakneck speed toward the rocks where she and Tavish had taken cover.

The horses appeared riderless as they moved in, coming closer. Ember scarcely breathed as Tavish held the revolver in one hand and the rifle in the other.

"*Mon ami!*" came a shout from across the rocks. "Shoot their horses!"

Ember glanced at Tavish. The inevitable bothered him; she could see as much. It bothered her too. Death everywhere. It would swallow them up, and who would make them live again? Would horses live again? The Cheyenne—where would their souls go? Here was a young man who could let go with both barrels at charging Cheyenne, yet flinch at killing a horse. Of course the horse wasn't trying to scalp them—

The bullets spat like striking rattlers, horses squealing in pain. Indians broke through, one leaping onto the rock above as a bullet sent him toppling backward. Another came vaulting over the side.

Ember stared in dazed horror as Tavish leaned against the rock, firing in rapid succession. They were breaking through. Another Cheyenne came, and he fired, and another, and he fired. A tomahawk clattered against the rock in answer to a bullet thudding into the warrior's chest.

As Ember crouched against the rock, a tiny movement

above Tavish drew her eyes upward. A painted warrior stood bronzed and muscled, terrible yet majestic against the yellow sky. The feathers in his dark hair ruffled in the breeze. He stared down at her, his face chiseled like stone. She froze. His bow was drawn back tightly. Facing death she could not move, could not think, for it all merged in what seemed a slow moment in time.

In a whisper the arrow came straight toward her, thudding with a force that left her in shock. Her breath stopped . . . then she gave a small gasp. Pain erupted like fire spreading through her chest. She slumped against the rock, limp. Blood seeped through her sage green habit, turning the cloth dark. Her blurring vision fixed on the warrior. He stared at her, motionless.

Tavish had heard the arrow's impact, and his head turned sharply in her direction. He threw himself to the rock beside her. Looking up he fired two shots. The warrior jolted backward and fell from the boulder, his cry echoing.

Nothing moved in the pervading silence.

A buzzard swooped in the distance.

Ember stirred, hearing her name whispered as if from a great distance away. She was in what appeared to be a wagon, or was it the stage?

"Ember?"

Her eyes opened and Tavish was leaning over her. She felt his hand lifting her head and bringing something hot and salty to her mouth—broth? But she remembered little except sinking back into sleep.

When her eyes opened again she saw Lottie and Sassy, fear and concern in their dust-streaked faces.

"Poor Ember," Lottie was saying, and cooled her with a damp rag. "Dear Ember, you mustn't die."

Ember tried to speak but she was too tired. She felt Sassy's hand smoothing back the hair from her face. . . .

"You sleep now, chile. We're on our way to Fort Lincoln."

October 1873

Mack Ridgeway and his son Wade were safe at the fort. Ember learned about her uncle's arrival from Lottie, who had also been reunited with Prescott. Talk of vengeance was everywhere in the fort.

"The army speaks of tracking Sitting Bull into Canada. They say he withdrew there with his Sioux nation."

As Ember slowly recovered, other news drifted in as well, and Lottie kept her well informed, trying to cheer her depressed spirits.

"The financial ruin of Jay Cooke means the transcontinental line into the Pacific Northwest has come to a halt again. Father has lost a good deal of his investment. Mother will be upset. She's always telling him to invest in timber instead."

At the moment, Ember didn't care about Mack and Cleo's investments, and she knew that Lottie understood and was only trying to keep her mind occupied during her painful recovery. The news of the NP's financial disaster settled like a blinding dust storm over the nation's economic optimism. The crash of Jay Cooke was heard from the Northwest to New York, but it was not Sitting Bull and his warriors who had forced the railroad out of Yellowstone that August of '73.

Lottie told her what Mack had been talking about with Wade and Prescott during the weeks Ember had been in a fevered sleep at the fort. On the day before Jay Cooke lost his railroad, he was offering expensive cigars to President Grant in the grand drawing room of the Cooke mansion in Philadelphia. The next day, the great banking house of Cooke & Company was being forced to shut down its operation, and by noon it declared bankruptcy. Before the sun had set that same day, the Financial Panic of '73, the worst economic disaster to face the nation since its birth, crept across the nation like a plague. Banks locked their doors, railroads came to a grinding halt, and the stocks of powerful businesses collapsed in the East and West. But for Ember, the failure of the railroad in which Mack Ridgeway had involved himself was the least tragedy on her heart. Having confronted death, life had taken on a new and sober face.

The Seventh Cavalry's theme song, "The Girl I Left Behind Me," rang out from across the darkened street in the officers' hall as the orchestra played. The dance was underway and the mouth-watering aroma coming from the big slabs of government beef sizzled on the outdoor barbecue pits.

Ember had spent the month of September recuperating in the small house that belonged to Lottie and Lieutenant Hollister. She gazed out the window at the wagons rolling by the front yard and its dusty rose bushes. Voices and laughter sang out as others arrived at the officers' ball.

Wearily she let the flimsy curtain fall back to the windowpane and walked to sit on the Queen Anne bench before the vanity table. Lottie and Prescott were at the dance and barbecue, and as far as she knew, so was Wade.

She stared at her image in the mirror. After weeks of being confined to bed, she hardly recognized the scrawny girl that stared back—collarbones showing and hollow eyes. Was this the same optimist who had left Tacoma three months earlier?

Ember recalled few incidents from her ordeal and the treacherous journey to Fort Lincoln. After her arrival, Sassy told her that the doctor informed the family she was in "very frail condition, and might not survive."

Ember wondered if Tavish had been told. Sassy explained that during most of the journey Ember had been unconscious with fever. They traveled by night and kept out of sight during the day. In the eyes of Sassy and Lottie there were not two finer heroes in all Fort Lincoln than Tavish Wilder and Julot LeBrett. After being saved from the Cheyenne, Ember agreed, but she wondered why there was no message from him in the month she'd been here. Surely Lottie or Sassy would have mentioned it.

Nightmares followed her arrival. Ember would dream of squeezing the trigger while the warrior lunged at her with his knife. She would awaken crying out in terror with the name of Tavish on her tongue, but it was Sassy there to soothe her.

"It's all over, honey," she kept saying. "The Lord took care of us all."

Outside, the muffled laughter reminded her of how depressed were her spirits, and of how vivid were the memories of the Cheyenne attack. The Bible sat on the vanity table and she reached over to touch it, a new tenderness coming to her eyes. She had always believed in Christ, but He had never been more real, more precious to her than He was now after the skeleton-face of death had breathed its foul breath upon her. That breath had not slain her. But even if it had, death could not bind her with its chains to drag her down to the burning coals! Jesus stood between them—her Protector. Death could not feed on righteousness, and Jesus had robed her with His very own.

She was startled from her thoughts as the door opened and Sassy came in carrying a supper tray, her usual smile absent. Ember noticed the difference at once.

"Is something wrong?"

"Mister Tavish done wrote a report of what happened to his father, Kain, at Yellowstone, and Mister Custer has done seen it."

Ember leaned back into the chair while Sassy poured tea, adding sugar and cream the way Ember liked it. The news did little except to inform her that Tavish remained at the fort. She felt a mixture of emotions—pleasure at his nearness and frustration over knowing he preferred not to get in touch with her.

Ember's brow wrinkled, for she saw nothing disturbing in the colonel reading a report.

"So Tavish wrote a report. What of it?"

"It means trouble. After Mister Custer read it, he done called for Mister Wade to answer questions."

From what Ember could grasp of the confusing details, there was to be an inquiry into Wade's conduct. Later that evening Wade came to visit her, and Ember made her own discreet inquiries about the cause for the report.

Wade looked at her. "What did Wilder tell you? That I deliberately left his father to the Cheyenne?"

The defensive edge in his voice didn't surprise her. Recently his emotions were taut and ready to snap. At times, so were her own, but she tried to keep her frustration over the absence of Tavish out of her voice.

"I've not spoken to him since my arrival a month ago. I wouldn't have known about the report if Sassy hadn't mentioned it tonight. No one is suggesting you would deliberately leave Kain Wilder to die. What could you have done once he was captured?"

She avoided the fact that Tavish had gone alone to try to rescue Kain.

"I think you're being hasty about Tavish," she said. "It's true about his father. The chaplain told me Kain is a circuit-riding minister."

Wade smirked. "And what seminary did he graduate from? He's self-appointed."

"Maybe the Lord appointed him."

He turned, surprised, his eyes searching her wearied face. "Am I to understand you to be defending the Wilders against your own cousin?"

"Don't be silly. As far as I'm concerned you don't need defending."

She didn't tell him that what she had heard about Kain Wilder impressed her. Why was it that a former gunfighter would suddenly turn to preaching Christ among the train camps?

"Tavish is a minister's son," she said evasively. "Both of them must have changed since New York. If I ask about Tavish, is that so strange? I knew him once . . . and I'd be dead now if it hadn't been for him."

Wade let out a breath and ran a hand through his hair as though weary with his own habit of rushing to conclusions. "I'm sorry. The family is grateful to Tavish and his cousin." He looked at her rather sheepishly. "Father offered him a generous reward."

"And no wonder. What did he offer him?"

Wade shrugged and poured himself a cup of coffee from the urn on the dining room table. He waved an airy hand. "You know Father. He enjoys waving big bills around." He gave a short laugh, thoughtful and ironically amused. "Tavish refused it. You should have seen Father's face."

Ember didn't think Tavish had much and would have expected him to accept the money to help care for his own father.

"He's either proud," said Wade, "or doesn't want to feel obligated to the Ridgeways. Especially with this inquiry going on as to my conduct."

Ember moved uncomfortably. She knew Uncle Mack well enough to understand that waving "big bills" before Tavish might just be a hint that plenty more would come if he behaved himself. She couldn't envision Tavish buckling under. "You've done nothing wrong. Why would he bring suspicion upon you?"

"He's jealous of me. I graduated West Point and he didn't,"

Wade snapped. He looked across the room at her. "What else would it be?"

She picked up her teacup and took a sip.

Wade frowned, then continued. "The insinuations he's raised about Kain Wilder's capture has provoked needless questions about my conduct. Naturally I find that troubling."

"That's no reason to dislike you," she persisted.

He looked at her, the manner of his thoughts troubling him, for his eyes were cool. "What are you driving at, Ember?"

"I didn't think I was driving at anything. You're very edgy tonight."

"Don't forget he blames me for his expulsion."

The old feeling of unease came back. "Yes—I noticed when we met. He's quite cynical when it comes to you."

"Of course! I'm a major."

"You never did tell me your part in what happened. Why would he blame you when it was his own fault?"

He set his cup down without tasting the coffee. "I wasn't going to tell you, I saw no need. I didn't think your path would cross with his again. I knew how you felt about him. But it was I who found the stolen exam in his desk."

"You?"

"I confronted him about it alone, just the two of us. He denied knowing how it got there." Wade shrugged. "I was willing to forget it, to give him the benefit of the doubt, until there was an announcement that the major's office had been broken into, the exam stolen, and that there were several cadets on the list of suspects. I was one of them. And I wasn't about to take the blame for Wilder."

"I don't understand. Why would your name be on the list?"

He shrugged impatiently and walked to the window to look out. "Some of the cadets had it in for me. Jealousy because I was rich. I was a Ridgeway. They banned together to make it hard for me."

"Tavish used to comment on it being the other way around. It was the wealthy students who had it in for him."

"Tavish talks too much." He looked at her. "I knew what my father would say if I was expelled. I'd never hear the end of it. I'd go home to Port Townsend and be taken to task for my weakness for the rest of my life." He turned back to the window.

144

Ember stared at his back, seeing his strong shoulders give way to a slight stoop. She too knew what his father would have said. She shuddered.

"So I went to the colonel and informed him it was Tavish. Tavish never forgave me for betraying him."

Ember lost her appetite for the tea and set the cup down. How could she ever forget that Tavish had broken into the instructor's office, stolen the exam, and lied about it? No matter that his father was a minister, or that he seemed the essence of courage and honor. The truth was he had been expelled. The scar remained on his character. And now he disliked Wade enough to write up a questionable report about his conduct at Yellowstone to damage his reputation.

"To make matters worse, I questioned him about his ambitions in life on the Yellowstone expedition." He shook his head as though disgusted with himself. "It was a mistake and I shouldn't have done it. I was only trying to get him to face up to his drifting and do something more with his life than swing a hammer. I can tell you it didn't go over well. It angered him. He's hated me ever since."

It was easy to understand how Wade's background might intimidate a man in less fortunate circumstances. Tavish had told her that he had been a nameless and faceless track layer for the Northern Pacific—that he was helping to support his father's ministry. But had Wade's motives been so selfless?

He was pacing the braided oval rug on the hardwood floor, the retrieved cup of coffee in hand. Ember sat, pale and thin in the chair, watching him, troubled by his unhappiness and her own, hearing the distant music that seemed to mock.

She could understand how much his honor in the Seventh Cavalry meant to him. Was it so strange for a young man born rich, having this world's goods within easy reach, to want to distinguish himself separately from his parents' accomplishments? Mack had been exceptionally rigorous with Wade, often belittling his son's efforts when they didn't match up to his expectations.

Wade continued his pacing, looking distraught. Just what did she know about Tavish? He had escorted her during the social season in New York, but had he ever told her anything about himself, his family? It was from Wade that she had learned about Kain being a gunfighter. Tavish was courageous—there was no question about that—and he had saved her life. She was indebted to him, but was he also capable of reaping bitter vengeance against Wade for informing his commanding officer at West Point about his cheating?

"He won't get anywhere with this inquiry," said Wade. "Not that the army has anything to hide in the matter. I have witnesses. I warned him to stay back with the civilians but he seemed determined to stir up trouble, to prove himself." He paused and smiled thoughtfully to himself. "He even threatened to take on Ridgeway Timber in Washington—imagine that! He has some wild notion of becoming a big lumber magnate."

"He said that?" she asked uneasily, wondering what ties he might have in Washington Territory.

"Sounded like a duel. Whatever's goading him, I want no part of it." He walked over to her, troubled, looking down. "Stay away from him, Ember. Father said so."

The warning sounded like a bell. Whatever Mack said was family law—or was meant to be.

She felt a prick of frustration. "I've no cause to see him, except to thank him for what he did back at the train camp."

"I've already done so, and so has the colonel."

"It was my life he saved," she said. "Why should Mack care?"

She knew why he cared, and it was only an excuse. Wade seemed to know too. He walked over to the window and drew aside the curtain, looking out onto the dusty street. "The family won't ever take to Tavish Wilder. Don't allow yourself to get involved, Ember. It will lead to a dead end."

She straightened her back in the chair. "Maybe if I spoke to him he'd withdraw his accusations," she said, ignoring his warning.

"He's trouble. I feel it whenever I'm around him. Even if you went to him he wouldn't accept it. Let's leave it to my father."

That was the last thing she wanted to leave to Wade's father. Tavish wouldn't stand much chance against the aroused anger of her uncle.

"There must be something you and I can do," she insisted. "Lottie too. Surely Colonel Custer understands your position.

He must know Tavish has a grudge against you from the days at West Point."

"Yes, he knows. Truth is, Tavish can do little to ruin me, except cause the Ridgeway name some embarrassment. If Father thinks there was anything to those days at West Point, he'll call me on it. You know how talk circulates. And an officer," he said wryly, "is not always popular with his men."

Yes, words could hurt deeply. One could slaughter a person's character and never be sent to the gallows for it. She wondered what the men under Wade at Yellowstone thought of his ability, then quickly rejected the notion.

"Father will take care of it," he repeated. "The less involved you are in all this, the better." He walked up to her, laying a hand on her shoulder. "You and Lottie are all I have in the family. You come out here to help her and what happens? You get attacked by Cheyenne!" His young face hardened. "The army is getting the Sioux under control. One day, we'll have Sitting Bull, Crazy Horse, and the rest of the chieftains where we want them, on the reservation. If they can't live peaceably with civilized people, then they must live elsewhere. And when they drive Sitting Bull to his place, I shall be there to see it."

Ember shuddered at the gleam of hatred in his eyes. "It does no good to hate. It will destroy you before it punishes the offenders."

"You should have stayed with Great-aunt Macie in Washington," he said wearily. "This is no place for you. And it's no place for Lottie."

Ember disagreed. "I'm not sorry I came. I've learned a great deal. I've seen things and felt things I would never have known if I had stayed in Washington. God is more real, life is more precious."

He patted her hand. "Always looking at the better side of things. I'll leave you now. You need to rest."

A rap sounded on the door and Sassy poked her head in. "A message for you, sir. From Mister Mack."

Ember's curiosity grew as Wade stood pondering his father's words, then folded the message and put it inside his pocket. He smiled. "I told you it would all work out." She watched him walk to the door and pick up his officer's hat.

"Don't worry about Wilder. I've a feeling he won't want to push this investigation much further."

She followed him to the door, not liking his expression. "Why do you say that?"

Wade wouldn't explain, but there was an unpleasant smile on his face. "I've a feeling Father's private talk with Kain Wilder about his days working on the Kansas Pacific might change their plans."

Ember tensed, desperately wishing to read the message, but she knew there was little chance of Wade letting her see it.

"Sassy?" he called. "Better get Ember to bed, will you? She needs rest. And, Ember, stop worrying. It's going to be well enough now. I'll come by and see you tomorrow. Whatever one might think of the Ridgeways, we know how to handle things."

"Wade! What about Kain Wilder working in Kansas?"

Wade smiled and opened the front door, letting in the music from the dance. "Nothing of interest. He worked laying track there once is all. See you tomorrow," he called lightheartedly. "Good-night."

He went out and closed the door behind him. Ember stared after him. What had Mack discovered about Kain that would make Wade believe the hearing into his conduct was over?

Kain Wilder had once been a gunfighter, or so Wade had informed her two years ago. Was it true? How much did Tavish know about the past reputation of his father? He must know, she thought. Yet now he was a minister. When did a man's past become unfair game for hunters like Uncle Mack?

"Wade's right. You come climb into bed an' eat your supper."

Sassy pulled down the quilt and fluffed the meager pillow, and when Ember stood staring out the window, Sassy warned, "Bein' almost scalped and entering the pearly gates hasn't taught you to be sweet-like and obedient yet. If I knows you like I think I does, you'll be thinking how you can talk to Mister Tavish about things."

Ember turned her head, her eyes determined. "Where is he, Sassy. Do you know?"

Sassy pretended to ignore her. "See, chile, I even stole some of that barbecued beef to tempt your appetite."

"I can't eat. I can't swallow a bite." Ember walked to the

center of the room, her nerves taut. "You know where Tavish is, don't you?"

Sassy was silent, then said quietly, "Yes, I know."

Ember was beside her. "That message from Mack was about his father. I must talk to Tavish."

"I thought you would . . . I'll go for him, but you sit down, lest the wind blows you away. You is as thin as a rail."

"He can't come here. They'll see him and Wade will find out. He's asked me to stay out of the controversy."

"And 'course you ain't goin' to do anything so easy as that," needled Sassy.

"No." Ember looked at her squarely. "I'm not. He saved our lives, and I want to know about Kain Wilder."

"Maybe it's best you don't meddle. I 'spect there's plenty to unearth if folk don't mind diggin' up old graves. Me, I'm for leavin' the dead buried. Whatever it is, you ought to stay clear. Your feelings for Mister Tavish ain't changed since you was a girl. But they won't get him to become your husband, neither. Family won't stand for it."

"What I'm doing now has nothing to do with the past. And I don't want Tavish Wilder as a husband. Is he at the barracks?"

Sassy's brows lowered. "No. He's riding out."

Ember halted. "What about the inquiry?"

"Maybe that Mister Kain got a message from Mack too. Anyhow, they was packin' up, so Mister Julot told me this afternoon."

"This afternoon! You knew all this time and didn't tell me? Sassy, I'll never forgive you."

"Yes you will, you always does. Here, drink this beef soup."

"When are they leaving?" demanded Ember. "Did Julot say?"

"In the mornin' he said—but don't you get any notion of goin' off to that dance in search of him. Dancin' is sinful, so I say. I tole you and tole you even at Saratoga—"

Ember wasn't listening. So he was riding out. And again without a word to her.

"And Mister Tavish probably ain't at the dance anyhow, seein' he ain't in the army and his pa's a preacher—" She stopped.

Ember threw open the small closet and searched through

her meager frocks. Of all the darling outfits she had owned and brought with her, they had been left to the flames in the covered wagon. "I might forgive the Cheyenne for nearly killing me, but not for burning my wardrobe," she groaned as she pulled out a homemade cotton frock that Sassy had borrowed from a corporal's wife.

"Quick, fix my hair. I must see him."

"You is makin' a mistake. If Mister Mack catches you—"

"Maybe. I don't believe I am. I may never see him again. What I want to say to him, I must say now."

"Hmmm—an' just what does you expect to say to him?"

Ember remembered his strong arms around her as he rescued her from the burning wagon, and a little smile touched her lips. "Why—to thank him, of course."

Sassy's eyes narrowed.

She sobered. "And to ask why he questions Wade's decisions at Yellowstone. And I want to ask him about the message Wade received tonight. I wonder if he knows Mack sent it?"

"Seems a good question to avoid, if you ask me. You heard Mister Wade. His father's involved. And when Mister Mack does things, ain't no one else to stand much chance. Least of all, folks who ain't got no money."

The thought was unpleasant. "I've a mind of my own too. I'm entitled to make a few decisions."

"Oh, all right, chile, but I'm trailing behind you, and if you do find him, I'll be within sight. So don't get no foolish notions when nuthin' can come of 'em except you gettin' hurt again."

"Don't be silly," said Ember, sitting down before the vanity table and gazing at herself in the mirror, wishing desperately she had eaten everything Sassy had put on her plate the past week, and wondering how she could sneak out without Sassy following.

"Seems to me if Mister Tavish wanted to come see you, he would. He wants to stay away from you is my guess. He's got good sense. He knows you is a Ridgeway with lots of money, an' likely to get richer in the years to come."

She wouldn't think about that. She hadn't in New York, and she wouldn't now. "Hurry, Sassy. There isn't much time."

"Don't you think he could have written if he wanted to?"

Ember ignored her. "Hand me that yellow ribbon."

13

UNFORGETTABLE . . .

Banjo music filled the autumn night along with curls of woodsmoke, while above, the round harvest moon shone yellow. Ember neared the community square but lingered in the shadowed outskirts.

Two boys working near the barbecue pit noticed her at the same moment and swept off their caps, grinning, although one looked so flabbergasted that she imagined him choking on a sour pickle.

"H-howdy-do, M-miss Mack," the boy stammered.

"She ain't Miss Mack, ya bleatin' goat," corrected the other lad. "That there's her uncle's name. It's Miss Ridgeway." He looked at her with ripe eyes. "A perty evenin', miss."

"Why, yes it is. A trifle chilly though."

"Kin we git you a chair by the fire, Miss Ridgeway?"

"You sure done taken a turn from that Cheyenne arrow!" said the other, looping his thumbs under his suspenders. "When Tav Wilder carried you in, we all done said our prayers thinkin' you was done for."

"That Tav Wilder and his cousin," the other bragged.

"When they've a hankerin' fer it, they kin hit themselves a skinny jackrabbit racin' for its hole."

"A lemonade, maybe?"

"Yes, a lemonade would be pleasant indeed."

"You just sit here and we'll be back in no time. You enjoy the foot stompin'."

She watched them scamper off to the long table where barrels of refreshment were garrisoned, each racing to be first to return with the glass of lemonade. Ember quickly glanced about the men in uniform to see if either Tavish or his cousin might be among them, but they were nowhere in sight. Had they already ridden out? But Sassy had said they wouldn't leave until morning.

The boys were back at the same time, both extending a glass. She smiled, accepting both. "Thank you."

"If it ain't sweet enough I'll add some more honey."

"You both know Tavish Wilder and Julot?"

"They been about ever since they brought you and Kain Wilder in on the stage. Saw Kain up and about today."

"Where is Tavish now? I wish to thank him for saving my life."

"Oh, he ain't here no more. All three rode out an hour ago."

"An hour ago!"

"Yes, ma'am."

The wind turned cold, the banjo music faded, and the lemonade turned her stomach queasy. She set her glass down and stood, feeling weak and tired. "Are they expected back?"

"They took to California. Some shantytown called Sac-re-men-toe."

Ember heard the banjos break out again in the cavalry's theme song.

The boy ran his fingers through his yellow hair and frowned. "He didn't say Sacramento. Julot said they was headin' to Seattle. Talked about a big land grant and timber. Trees is the thing, he said. That, and the railroad. I got me a hankerin' to join 'em."

"You ain't goin' nowheres. Pa will beat the cotton out of you."

Ember wasn't listening now, and walked away, but one of the boys suddenly called after her. "Say—Miss Ridgeway—I may be crazy, but I'd risk my neck to a rope that Tav Wilder ain't left yet after all."

She stopped short and turned to look back. He ran up, pushed his cap back, and squinted ahead into the night. "Ain't that him there? Standin' 'neath yonder tree?"

Ember looked across the dirt street to an empty lot where a large shade tree spread its leafy branches. A familiar silhouette leaned against the trunk, watching her—for how long?

Her heart raced.

He straightened from the tree and Ember walked the dusty street to meet him.

She looked at him, the autumn moon falling on his back, his hat so low she couldn't read his expression. She trembled as a gust of wind blew through her.

"I went to the house but you weren't there. So I waited, thinking you might walk by here." When she didn't speak, he added, "For what it's worth, I came back to say goodbye."

For what it's worth. . . .

"I'm pleased to see you're recovering well."

"I'm indebted to you for saving my life."

"I'll come around to collect on the debt one day."

Her breath paused.

"Now, we're riding out again, this time the trail leading into Oregon and Washington."

Her heart skipped a beat. "So Wade was right. You do intend to visit the Pacific Northwest?"

"Not visit, settle there. What did he tell you about it?"

She remembered Wade's remark about taking on the Ridgeway timber dynasty. "He said you had an inclination to try your hand at timber."

A smile seemed to taunt. "Tell Wade he needs more faith in his old West Point comrade. I don't bother with inclinations. I've already set my mind to it. I've had plenty of time to think and plan while I swung hammer and laid track." He leaned back against the tree.

Caution stirred within and she tested his purposes, knowing his resentment against the family. "Wade also said you intended to challenge the Ridgeway Enterprise."

"Pleasant thought." He shoved his hands into his jacket pockets.

"You won't do that, will you?"

"Who knows? If I earn a fortune in timber I may find one of those hard-to-come-by Ridgeway invitations to a dinner ball. Dear old Mack still has one remaining debutante in the family who needs a rich husband."

She smarted under his smooth remark yet felt pleasure too. She offered a quip of her own. "Is that an invitation, Mr. Wilder?"

"You'll have no trouble collecting invitations from the sons of railroad and timber men. Me, I've a hard road to cover. It's a long way from laying down a hammer to picking up a derby hat. You might need to wait a number of years. I can't see the Ridgeways being so patient. They weren't with your cousin."

"Lottie wanted to marry Prescott."

"She was lucky. Even if she hadn't, the wedding would have taken place."

"I'll not marry unless I wish to."

He smiled. "You'll do exactly what Mack and Cleo Ridgeway tell you to do."

"Is that another challenge to prove otherwise?"

"Maybe. Haven't you had enough challenges recently?"

She smiled and tilted her head, scanning him. "I can't imagine Tavish Wilder without black jeans and a dusty hat."

"You've forgotten the West Point gentleman so soon!"

"It was he who forgot, and left without a word."

"He had his reasons. At least his twin in dusty jeans came back to say goodbye."

"I might favor this 'twin' of his . . . and I may not care for the derby hat."

"I'm disillusioned . . . for two years I've slept in smelly boxcars, strengthened by the vision of owning a derby hat and maybe a diamond stickpin in my lapel."

She smiled ruefully. "And Kain didn't warn his hard-working son against the evils of big diamonds and expensive hats?"

"He did," he said dryly. "He still wears one with a bullet hole through the crown. But my dreams made the hard floor a little softer. So did memories of sharing picnics and balls with a certain girl."

"I didn't think the West Point gentleman thought much about her. She was mighty spoiled."

He smiled. "She still is."

Ember was about to protest, but his next words caught her attention.

"He was a master at pretense. He thought a good deal more about her than she ever imagined."

She fought against the magnet that seemed to constantly be pulling her toward him. "And you? What do you think of her?"

"What a question, Miss Ridgeway! I want that diamond stickpin and hat for only one reason. While I laid track I dreamed of escorting her to dinner in San Francisco. A woman in soft velvet, intoxicating me with her with autumn hair and warm eyes that melt like honey."

"Please—we're without a chaperon—"

"Thanks for reminding me."

She hesitated. He took hold of her arm and propelled her behind the tree where yellow moonlight showered down like gold dust.

"A fortune could be made in the Northwest if a man set his will to it."

"Could it?" she whispered.

"Uh-huh. . . . The timber is all there, and ships to haul it can come later. I told that unlikable cousin of yours that I intend to make a fortune in timber, but I didn't say why it mattered to me. I'm going to have you, Ember. And if I need a fat bank account to bargain with the Ridgeways, I'll get it, somehow."

Her breath paused. She looked into dark green eyes that melted her protest, feeble as it was. In her heart that was wounded and in need of solace, pretense vanished. She cared for him with a stronger love than she had felt years earlier, despite her boast to Sassy that it had been infatuation. If possible, she had loved him from the moment she first saw him at Saratoga, standing aside with that enigmatic smile and watching her waltz and polka. And at this moment she not only wanted him but needed him more than ever.

He tossed aside his hat and reached a hand, taking her arm to pull her toward him. "I think I'm asking for trouble."

She felt his arm slide around her waist, drawing her close, and her senses tumbled into a heady perfume. "We both are," she murmured, but her head went back to receive his kiss.

"You'll be trouble, all right."

Their lips met. The moment narrowed the soft Dakota sky and the harvest moon, the distant future and the forgotten past into the immediacy of his closeness. She began to dimly concern herself that the spell would spin her into a cocoon from which she could not fly.

With a small wrench she was free and moved away, her voice low and breathless. "You've kissed me, yet you haven't said you love me," she accused.

He looked at her, and as if surprised by her statement, he let out a breath and rested his arm against the tree trunk. His warm eyes narrowed. "You know I love you, or you should by now."

Ember folded her arms around herself, shaking with the revelation that she could care so deeply. Her mild accusation had been thrown at him as a means to break the spell that left her so frightened.

"You're certain it's me you came back to see and not Wade?" she persisted, aware of the unreasonableness of her question, yet hiding behind it.

He continued to watch her. "What are you afraid of?"

"Nothing!"

"Well, I told you we were asking for trouble." Tavish gave a soft laugh. "And you wanted this two years ago strolling on the green. . . . What would you have done if I had?"

She turned her back, feeling emotionally exhausted.

He came up to take hold of her arm, but Ember pulled away until she saw the amused challenge in his eyes.

"Better sit on this stump and catch your breath. You're looking a little pale."

"You are the most conceited man I've ever met."

A brow lifted. "As I was about to say, you'd better sit down. It takes months to recover from the kind of arrow wound you received."

"Oh," she murmured, realizing she had misunderstood.

He looked amused as he dusted off the stump. "For you, my lady. Spread your silken skirts and rest a moment."

"They're cotton," she said dully, and sank down.

"When I'm rich I'll buy you French silk."

She glanced at him. "I haven't said I'd marry you."

"I haven't asked yet. It's going to take a box of bouillon just to keep you in dresses."

"I'm more concerned about the manner of man who buys them. But surely you don't think I'm so frivolous as to choose a husband based on how well he can keep me in the latest fashions?"

He smiled.

She was chilled again as the wind picked up, and he noticed. He took off his jacket and placed it around her shoulders. "Ermine," he teased, then walked over and picked up his hat, knocking off the dust and settling it on his dark head.

Ember watched him, glad for the quiet moments slipping by, relishing the closeness of what was his. She ran her fingers along the leather jacket. When at last he looked at her again, his expression had altered with different thoughts and his eyes were remote.

"What did Wade tell you was the reason I left two years ago?"

Tension moved through her limbs, and she sat a little straighter. Did he think she could actually bring herself to discuss anything so foreign to his character as cheating?

Ember was wishing she had never heard of West Point. But she was beginning to learn more about Tavish.

"Strange, but I never realized how much you and Wade are alike."

"If that's supposed to be a compliment, I can do without it."

"But it's true. While Wade sought to distinguish himself from his parents' accomplishments, you felt the same need for personal success at West Point, but for another reason. You made the hard-won honor roll to distinguish the Wilder name."

"Only to have Wade tear down the flag. But he had something I never did—money to fight unfairly with. What did he tell you? That I broke into the instructor's office, copied the final exam, and made off with it like a thief?"

"He told me everything," she said dully, adding more gently, "But it hasn't changed my opinion of you."

"You mean you're willing to give me the benefit of the doubt? That's not enough—I intend for him to tell you the truth . . . maybe to all West Point. Getting his face spattered with mud would be good for him."

Her anger stirred. "Wade is like a brother to me. We were raised together. Along with Lottie, all we had was each other. I won't have you attacking him."

"So he told you the same story he reported to the colonel. And you believed it as readily. But of course you would. As you say, you're a tight-knit little threesome."

The silence froze between them. Ember stood. "There's little to say. I'm weary of even hearing of West Point."

"I can see our marriage is going to be one of peace and tranquility."

She was on the verge of reminding him for the second time that she hadn't agreed to become Mrs. Tavish Wilder, but decided against it. It was also true that the only man she had ever wanted stood within reach, and she didn't want to risk losing him to the Dakota frontier again. Too much uncertainty yet remained in their relationship. The chasm leading to marriage was yet to be bridged.

"Oh, Tavish, if you deny the story I'll believe anything you say."

His eyes held hers. "It's true. Everything happened just as he said, except for one important fact: our roles were reversed."

She sucked in her breath. "Wade? He'd never do that."

His eyes hardened. "But you believe I would?"

"No, I—I did have trouble believing it, only . . ."

"Only it was far easier to believe it about me than a Ridgeway."

"That has nothing to do with it."

"It has everything to do with it. Without the Ridgeway name to hide behind, Wade would have been expelled and I would have rightfully graduated."

"Please stop bringing up family!"

"Social position has stood between us from the beginning. Why do you think I stood aloof? I was fully aware of one thing you wished to pretend wasn't there. The Ridgeways will never let you marry a man they don't first approve. They still won't. They'd stop you one way or the other, and you'd let them."

"I'd let them—?" she said, offended. "I wouldn't."

"You might have courage to persist for a time, but you'd soon give in. You were too young to stand for what you wanted. You still are," he said gently.

"I have as much courage to reach out for what I want in life as anyone. It was you who walked away from West Point, from me, without so much as a goodbye. You might have written a letter to explain."

"You're right. But this time I came back. I told myself I'd never walk away again. Back then, I didn't have the means to try to thwart them, and a powerful family is not a force easily reckoned with."

Was he saying he thought he could thwart them now? She wondered about that land grant in Washington.

"I didn't have much determination myself—not the kind to take on the Ridgeway dynasty. Not then. My pockets were empty, and I'd just been expelled." He added ruefully, "Did you expect me to also come to the lodge door and risk my heart?"

"Then why did you come back now?"

"When you were struck by the arrow I believed you would die," he said softly. "I knew then how much I loved you. That I'd do what I must to have you."

She tried to hold back tears but they glistened in her eyes. "I don't care whether you have material possessions. You must know that. It never mattered in New York; it doesn't matter now. Oh, Tavish, I—"

"Don't say things you may regret later. The other reason I came back was to salvage my reputation. I didn't need to steal the exam. I was on the honor roll. It was Wade who was having problems with his studies. I know, because I tutored him."

"You tutored Wade?" she asked, surprised.

"He worried over what Mack would say about his low grades. He began to grow more edgy and took to staying out late and drinking. Several times I covered for him, making excuses. When the time for finals came he offered me money to take his exam. The Ridgeways think all they need do is wave money under a man's nose and they can buy anything."

She resented that, but said nothing when she remembered how Wade told her Mack had offered Tavish money in pretense to drop the inquiry into Yellowstone.

"I had enough of his excuse-riddled attitude. Wade had everything going for him. Money, name, intelligence—yet he squandered it, waiting for Mack to come in and buy him what he wouldn't earn for himself."

"That isn't true."

"No?"

"Wade is actually afraid of Mack."

"Then he needs to learn to stand up for what he believes. I had little, but what I had I used. I admit I got weary of protecting him. Evidently he panicked. He broke into the major's office and made a copy of the final. I confronted him. He became angry. When word got out about the stolen exam he went to the colonel and blamed me."

Ember was torn between believing him or her cousin. "But Wade said there were witnesses."

"He had friends. They planted the exam in my desk and swore they'd seen me with it the night before. It was five to one in their favor. There was something else. Information arrived on my father's past in Kansas. It was time to leave," he said simply.

The Kansas Pacific. She swallowed, wondering if he knew about Mack's message to Wade. But Sassy had said that it was his father who had decided they would leave the fort. And of course . . . the inquiry into Wade's conduct at Yellowstone would be dropped if Tavish rode out.

"The trouble your father had in Kansas, what was it about?"

He looked at her thoughtfully, and she guessed he was deciding how much to tell her.

"You should know the truth. He was a gambler, he made good and bad investments in the railroad. One year we were wealthy, the next we'd be in a wagon in some train camp. He'd promise to straighten out, and he would for a few months, even a year, then he'd come home and tell my mother we were broke again. Eventually it led to a separation. She went to Chicago and became involved with D.L. Moody's work. My father drifted. He took me with him once. But when he came home after being gone two days and found me playing poker with some boys, he cuffed me around, then took me back to Chicago. That was the last he took me with him. After that, he wanted me to attend West Point.

"He worked on the Kansas Pacific, gambled with the big man himself, and won. There was trouble when he came to collect it—my father busted him up pretty bad, I guess. He had to run for it. Some people don't forget."

And so you're leaving tonight to protect your father, she thought, and wondered why she loved him even more. Did Kain realize that Tavish knew what had happened in Kansas?

"My father's changed," said Tavish. "My mother's death in the Chicago fire turned him around. He's dedicated to the Lord. I know what you're thinking, but it's genuine."

She hadn't any reason to believe otherwise and wondered that he would think so.

"I've lived with him for over two years in the train camps, and it's not an act. Christ is real to him. Only thing is—those years of preaching to track layers seemed to me to be a way of trying to pay back the Lord for His goodness. I think of the apostle Paul, who labored to exhaustion. He said he was a debtor to the less fortunate who hadn't yet tasted God's grace of forgiveness. Father feels that way because of his own past."

"You mean his past trouble at Kansas?"

He hesitated. "I don't know." He smoothly changed the subject. "He knows better than most how an unjust man is declared righteous before God—by the work of Christ on the cross, but there's something bothering him."

"There's something you should know," she began. "It's partly the reason I came looking for you tonight."

But when he looked at her, waiting, she couldn't find the words to betray Wade. And despite her boast that she could stand up to the family, that she wasn't intimidated by Mack and Cleo, she was.

If she told Tavish about the message from Mack, he might confront her uncle. Somehow she didn't think Tavish would be afraid of any man, not even a railroad and timber baron like Mack, who bullied anyone in his way.

Tonight's incident, as well as the fermenting trouble over West Point, could lead to something more dreadful than his leaving with Kain and Julot. At least in Washington he would be safe.

"Your father," she said lamely. "I—ah—wanted to ask if he's well enough to ride out tonight?"

He gave her a searching look and Ember felt her face turn warm.

"He's not the man he once was. But he's recovering. It's time to move on. We're heading northwest."

She was certain now that Tavish was protecting his father by his willingness to ride out. Then maybe he did know about the meeting Mack had with Kain Wilder. Tavish would also wish to protect his father's reputation from further embarrassment, especially now that he was a minister.

"And you're willing to let the inquiry drop?"

He casually retrieved his jacket from her shoulders. "That's up to Custer," he said tonelessly. "You already know my estimation of Wade's military prowess."

She grimaced. "If you marry me you'll need to get along with him."

He smiled. "Sorry, but you're moving out of the Ridgeway mansion to the Wilder mansion."

"Confident, aren't you?" she teased.

His eyes smiled. "About you? or making a fortune?"

Suddenly she felt the descent of loneliness, so smothering that she felt she couldn't let him go without her.

"Must you go?"

"Yes, it's the only way. And my father and Julot are waiting. It's time to say goodbye."

"Don't," she whispered. "Stay. Work out whatever problems you have with Wade, no matter who's to blame. I can speak to him, he'll listen to me. If you'd make peace he'd see to it you had whatever you need to go into business for yourself."

"No. If I ever have you, it will be my way, not the Ridgeways'."

Her disappointment kindled anger. "You're too proud, Tavish Wilder! You could make friends with my family. You could work with them, not against them."

"Maybe. But when I call at Ridgeway House in Port Townsend, I'll come as my own man, not as a beggar."

"You'll never be a beggar to me. Take me with you now."

"Don't tempt me. You're too fine to be a saddle tramp, though. Right now I couldn't buy you a decent meal or a place to sleep."

"I don't care!"

He held her face cupped in his hands and her eyes searched his. "But I care, darling Ember. You're not strong and I want you well taken care of until we meet again. At least Wade is good for that. And you have Lottie. Will you be staying?"

She nodded, thinking only that she didn't want him to go.

"For how long?" he asked.

"I don't know . . . a year, maybe two. Prescott is thinking of returning to shipping in San Francisco when his term is up. I may wait until we journey back together."

"That's three years," he said thoughtfully. "If things go well for me . . ."

"Do you always get your way?" she whispered.

He drew her to him and kissed her. Her disappointment went unmollified. "When will I see you again?" she whispered.

He sighed. "I don't know. No longer than necessary."

Her breath stopped, her heart longing.

He touched her hair, her face, studying her, as though he wished to engrave the image on his mind, then he walked away to where his horse was tied.

He mounted and turned to ride, giving her a long look.

"Don't forget to wait for me," he said softly, adding, "I'll write you how things go."

"And if I don't hear from you?" she asked.

"You will."

"If I don't—I'll marry a rich railroad man," she threatened.

He lowered his hat, and his smile was disarming. "I'll be back."

Her heart desolate, she watched him ride away until his silhouette disappeared onto the darkened Dakota plain.

"Tavish," she breathed to the wind. "I'd wait for you forever."

14

THE PACIFIC NORTHWEST

Tavish stepped from the Miles City general store, his poncho and hat dust bitten. Hungry, thirsty, and edgy, his appetites took sadistic pleasure in reminding him of more fortunate days. He carried jerky and cracker-bread called "hardtack" and a lukewarm jug of water.

He saw his father and Julot waiting for him on the boardwalk. Kain was seated on a tilted frame chair with his boots propped on the rail, staring across the windswept frontier. Purple shadows blemished the skin beneath his eyes and his right arm remained in a sling. Tavish had begun to believe that his father could lose its use. Kain had lost weight and developed a cough, but his faith continued to shine like lamps in his eyes. "I feel like Jonah," he had remarked in his quiet, amused way to Tavish. "Half-digested but spat up to walk free."

Tavish moved toward them. Julot sprawled on the boardwalk, leaning on an elbow and softly playing his harmonica while blue-uniformed soldiers rode by on horseback, watching.

Tavish's boots sounded on the hollow wood planks as he

came up and sat on the hitching rail. He tossed Julot his share of the meal and handed Kain his.

Julot scowled. "I could do better than this, mon ami. Eggs, at least, I could have talked the lady out of. . . . Maybe a piece of cheese."

Tavish scanned him wryly. "It was a man." Tavish bit into the spicy meat. It tasted to him like salty cardboard. "We've a job for Saturday night before moving on," he announced.

Kain looked at him. "Doing what, son?"

Julot picked up the baiting tone to his voice. "Yeah—doing what?"

Tavish gave a pat to the canvas bag holding his guitar. "Playing at that German eating place down the road. The man offered twenty-five cents and our supper."

Julot looked at his harmonica and frowned. "You know German music?"

Tavish shrugged. "A polka maybe."

"On a harmonica?"

Tavish smiled. "For potatoes and sauerkraut we'll think of something."

Kain's mouth showed humor. "You have Wilder blood, all right."

Risking attack from the Sioux and the arrival of the first seasonal snow, the three of them rode into Fort Benton toward the end of October. As Tavish scrubbed his faded denim shirt in an oak pail and beat his poncho, sending dust out with the Montana wind, Julot came hurrying toward him, the big Spanish spurs ringing on his boots.

"Leave fate's emergencies to Julot. I amaze myself with my gift of intelligence—all from my French grand'mere!"

Tavish looked up, holding the dripping shirt in one hand, and aware of the fading warmth of sunshine on his muscled back.

Julot kissed his Winchester. "We have a job all the way to Seattle!"

Tavish squinted. It was his turn to be suspicious as he glanced from the repeating rifle to smiling Julot. "Doing what?"

Julot whistled a French tune and, pretending to be a magician, produced apples, bread, and cheese from a beat-up bag.

Tavish caught an apple, weighing it on his palm. Julot crunched into another. "Ever heard of the 'Stagecoach King'?"

"Ben Holiday? Who hasn't? He sold his line to Wells Fargo and Company."

"Yeah, well, there's still a line from Benton to Seattle, and we've a job riding stage all the way to Washington Territory! We start in the morning."

It was the best of news. His father would be better for it. "What happened to the driver?"

"Killed by the Sioux. Guess who I seen in the fort?"

Tavish took a bite of apple. He thought of Ember until reason told him she could not be here.

"Lazou," said Julot. "Has his wagon and those apple saplings of his with him. I played a joke on him. I put one of these apples on his scrawniest tree. You should've seen his face when he came out with a bag of flour. He's followin' us all the way to Fort Walla Walla in Washington. Says there's fruit trees for sale there from some nurseryman with a big name."

"That's one man who deserves his fruit orchard. When I'm rich—I'll help him get all the trees he wants."

The word "rich" hung in the air like the first snowflake. Tavish smiled and Julot gave a yelping laugh. "But now," said Tavish, "I'll ride shotgun. You drive the team."

Julot frowned. "No, mon ami, I ride shotgun—you drive. And Uncle Kain rides inside."

Tavish shrugged and hung his wet shirt on a nail to dry, glancing at the distant clouds. They looked like snow clouds to him. "You got us the job, cousin. It's yours to choose. Where's Laz?"

"He's coming now."

Hearing the slow plod of the two mules and the squeak of wagon wheels, Tavish looked down the road. Lazou sat smiling beneath his hat. In the back of the wagon were his scraggly trees.

From Fort Benton they traveled the winding Mullon trail toward Fort Walla Walla, heading into rain and snow. It bothered Tavish to leave Lazou behind, and he encouraged him to abandon the wagon, sell the mules, and ride the stage. "We'll haul the trees someway, Laz."

But Lazou wouldn't hear of selling the mules. "I'll need 'em for plowing. Don't worry none about me, Mister Tav, I'll get there."

Kain rode in the wagon beside Lazou when he didn't ride up front on the stage. Unable to handle the team of horses or ride shotgun, he spent hours in the Bible and had taken to memorizing long sections from the Psalms.

Reaching Fort Walla Walla in November, they stayed a week, relishing the hotel and its food, then prepared a fresh stage for driving north.

A slim girl wearing a parka and traveling alone boarded in Fort Walla Walla. She rode up front between Tavish and Julot because she was "unacceptable" company for the passengers. Her mother had been a Cayuse Indian; her father, it was said, was Irish. She was pretty, unusual in appearance with blue eyes, Indian-straight black hair, and warm brown skin. Tavish would have ignored her had she not taken out a portion of a New Testament to read. Her name was Kwanita. She was only sixteen and on her way to a logging community in Seabeck, where she hoped to work in the kitchen or wash clothes for the loggers.

Tavish and Julot exchanged glances. They both knew what could happen to her if she showed up alone in a logging camp. Considered a half-breed, she would have little safety.

Kwanita told him that she had learned Christianity from a great-grandmother who had survived the Methodist missionary massacre of the Lee party in the 1840s. She knew little about the Scriptures from her newly acquired New Testament, except the death of Christ for her sins, so Tavish taught her as they rode along, enjoying the opportunity to use his knowledge of the Scriptures.

Matters changed when he picked up on the warmth in her eyes. Sensing that the spark was ignited by more than sanctified enthusiasm for his homiletics, he casually told her about Ember.

Thereafter, he wisely deposited her on the wagon seat next to his father.

"Kwanita has graduated from my Sunday school class," said Tavish, his eyes glinting with humor. "She's now ready for a professor."

"Thanks, son."

Tavish smiled, settled his hat, and walked back to the stage, swinging himself up to take the reins of the team.

They traveled the Steilacoom–Walla Walla road to the fort, then on to Seattle. There, he and Julot collected their wages.

At the pearl gray waterway of Puget Sound, with white gulls circling in savory fingers of Pacific Ocean mist, they bought passage on a stern-wheeler to embark upsound to the Hood Canal and Union. The land grant was located between Union and Quilcene some thirty miles from Port Townsend.

As they prepared to board the lower deck of the stern-wheeler, Kwanita appeared out of the fog like some Indian spirit in fringed buckskin and blue beads. She trailed after them shyly, carrying her meager bundle, embarrassed, yet hopeful enough to approach. She held out her New Testament between them like a peace offering.

"I come with my Christian brothers. I come as a sister. I wash your clothes. I'll work hard . . . for all of you, for our Lord."

Julot whistled as though he'd already guessed what would happen and strolled away, waiting for Kain and Tavish on the stern-wheeler.

The steam whistle screamed. Tavish threw his jacket over his shoulder and met his father's gaze. He believed they both felt the same—a reluctant and troubled responsibility for a lone girl who was also a Christian sister.

Tavish wished to avoid making the decision and walked away from her, casually saluting a goodbye. She followed. He lowered his hat, still carrying his canvas bag slung over his shoulder, and just stood there thinking, looking at his father. If they didn't care enough to aid a girl who'd soon have every lumberjack on her trail, they might as well pack the Bible away.

The next thing he knew, Kain had already made the decision for them. "This is rough country. She comes with us. Always did want a daughter." He added with a lighter tone, "And she brews a better pot of coffee than Laz."

They ran for the boat, with Kwanita smiling shyly and following as nimbly as a fawn, and all three came on board as the whistle cut through the wisps of gray and began its comely move upsound.

Tavish took the steps onto the upper deck and clamped his

strong hands around the railing, looking out across the Seattle waterway toward the distant forest.

The salty dampness caressed his skin, welcoming him home to the emerald land of his dreams. Spicy timber stood like kings and queens with peaked crowns touching silver clouds. Mount Ranier loomed, silent, white frocked, declaring its royal rule.

Timber! Building blocks for turning dreams into private empires.

PART TWO

RAILROAD AND TIMBER
1874–1883

And the night shall be filled with music,
And the cares that infest the day,
Shall fold their tents, like the Arabs,
And as silently steal away.

—Henry Wadsworth Longfellow

15

CRACKED MIRRORS

Port Townsend
1874

I can't ever change, thought Amity, and hated herself because she couldn't. Her emotions held her a slave. She might deny them, shaking her fist in their face, but they grinned back like satyrs:

If you stood free in a prison cell with open doors, you couldn't even walk out.

What still bound her? . . . Fear of failure? Sometimes in her mind she could look out that door and see sunlight falling upon a wide path. Yet uncertainty kept her from walking through. "I'll fail."

There was a certain safety in that room, and satisfaction in simply knowing the doors were open.

"I can't change," she repeated. "My past is my heritage, my memorial."

It was Sunday morning. She dressed hurriedly in a plain skirt and blouse and left for the little church.

When the service was over she walked home to the wharf district of Port Townsend, where her father ran a tavern. She felt cold plops of rain running down her temples and the back of her neck.

Amity's mind began to repeat the long list of "I hate me" feelings she took to bed with her at night and got up with in the morning. It was worse in the morning when she had to look at herself in the mirror. Her eyes were a nondescript brown. Her jaw was too broad, showing a stubborn streak inside a heart that resented her lot in life. Her mouth was too thin, her bust too flat, her feet too big.

Prince Charming would never love Amity Clark. No, not if she were the last female in Port Townsend. She was doomed to bring mugs of stale beer to smelly fishermen and loggers who treated her like a little sister. She often dreamed of a handsome stranger coming into the tavern and noticing her. But only old men came, or married men, or boys.

"If God has a plan for my life, this is it," she murmured. "I am what I am, and will be till the day I die." And then? She would fly away to the Great Divine Supper, but it would be her portion to sit so far from Jesus she wouldn't be able to see Him.

She smiled at her foolish thoughts. No, heaven would be wonderful, and she would have even more of the Lord than she did now.

Clouds thickened and hung low over the water, causing the afternoon to turn to twilight. If she were late to work at the tavern, her father would rant and rave and threaten to forbid her to attend church again.

She began to run on the wooden quay. The hollow clunking sound of the soles of her scuffed brown high-button shoes only reminded her how much she detested them.

If it were possible for anything to represent everything about herself she disliked, it would be the shoes, she decided. If only she could shed her whole self as though removing the shoes. If only.

But the shoes were strong. Her pa insisted they buy shoes that were well made . . . "worth the hard-earned money I put out to keep you from being barefoot like some Injun squaw, and you gripe at your pa!" he had said.

And that was part of the problem, as Amity saw it. The wretched things would last forever.

Amity quickened her steps toward the harbor, and home. Home was her father's oyster eatery, but in reality it was nothing more than a smelly tavern—one she despised. No, worse than a tavern where fishermen and loggers came only to drink beer—there was smuggling, lots of it. Not only of goods, but men, even a few women, mostly Chinese or Indian, though there had been one white girl. Amity shivered. Her pa had even threatened to sell *her*, but said she was needed in the kitchen a heap more.

The drops continued to fall, wetting her long brown skirt and yellow blouse. Amity imagined she owned a pretty blue cloak.

Outside the tavern-inn, a sign hanging on two rusty chains creaked in the salty head wind blowing in from the Pacific Ocean. "Captain Clark's Inn."

Nearing the double-story log structure, Amity paused on the wharf. A few scrawny chickens meandered about waiting for their corn, and behind the tavern a weather-scarred outbuilding housed several small boats that her father used for late-night business deals. Many times she had peered through her small window to see him with a lantern, rowing out to the bay. Now the door to the outbuilding creaked in the wind that swept in from the harbor. Her eyes fell on her cat hunched on the porch to keep out of the rain.

Then she saw her father come around from the other side of the tavern, the wind flapping his black pea coat, the cap pulled low over iron gray locks. His big hands, salt roughened, held a bundle of clothing and boots. She recognized them and felt a strange sensation up her back.

The clothing belonged to the easterner, Mr. Daws, who had been staying at the tavern-inn for the past four days.

Her father's square jaw was covered with a beard, and his deep-set eyes stared out from under slashing brows. He called abruptly: "Don't stand there gaping as though ye never laid eyes on yer pa before. Get over here, gal. There's work to be done."

She held the books tightly and fought the head wind. "Yes, Pa, I'm coming."

He shoved a sack of feed into her hands and cocked his large head to regard her with roosterlike eyes. "What's in your arms? Books!"

Amity glanced about. "Where's Mr. Daws?"

"Where's Mr. Daws?" he mimicked. "What's goadin' you, eh? Can't busy yer hands in honest work without a smooth-faced easterner followin' behind like a pup?" He shifted a calloused thumb toward the books in her arm. "Them church hypocrites been fillin' yer mind with fairy tales again? Don't know why I let you go. Money mad, that's what. That preacher got more loot stashed 'neath his feather mattress than an old hen with thirteen eggs, an' you tossin' in an honest coin."

"Pa, please!"

"I know their kind, gal, and yer wastin' time tryin' to be as fancy spoken as them, tryin' to mince about like some painted lass from uptown. Best shake the words out of yer ears and let 'em crawl away. Yer Captain Edmund Clark's daughter through and through. When it's time fer you to go mincing about in a new outfit, yer pa will see it through." He glanced toward the tavern, shifting the easterner's clothing under the other arm. "Aye, I got me big plans. Fer both of us."

Her heart weighed like an anchor in her chest. She wondered what he meant. Big plans? Since Mr. Mack Ridgeway had fired him as captain of a steamboat at Kalama, her pa had been morbid, hating all the Ridgeways and vowing to get even one day. His vengeance brought a mood of depression to the house. He was a strong man, and venom often filled his mind.

Now his eyes took on a sly gleam. He leaned toward her in a playful gesture. "Har, whose wife has the old parson been seein' lately, eh?"

"Stop it, Pa!"

"Gimme that corn." He snatched the sack from her, spilling some. The chickens rushed in, rummaging about their feet.

His tone softened, as it did sometimes after a show of temper, and he gave her a glance, chuckled, and tweaked her chin. "So ye like that easterner, eh?"

"Oh, Pa!"

"Go on with ye then," he said gruffly and gave her a little shove. "Into the scullery and fix me supper. Likely to be busy tonight. Ship's coming in from British Columbia."

She feared to ask what business he had with its captain, for she thought she knew. It was either illegal immigrants from China to work on the railroad, or contraband. Opium was legal in Port Townsend, but selling it in San Francisco was not. Her father's smuggling friends were on the low end of things, but bigger and more prominent men sold opium through the Barbary Coast into the eastern states.

She turned to walk toward the back entrance when his strong fingers latched hold of her arm.

"Wait, gal. Them books—you ain't said what they be about."

"There ain't a bad word in 'em, Pa, honest. Charles Spurgeon wrote all about heaven. He says even folks like us can go there if we trust Jesus. Spurgeon preaches to four thousand folks every Sunday in London."

"Another preacher, eh? Well what's he got to say fer himself besides passin' the tin cup for an honest man's coin?"

"I'll read 'em for you if you like," she said softly.

He gave her a sharp look, his eyes shrewd and hard. Then he gave a short laugh. "Be poisoning me mind as well as yer own, will you? Want to fill us with big dreams! So they can turn to dust first time you test 'em. Yer pa's too smart fer 'em. Ain't nothing free. Soon as me eyes fell on them blasted books of yours I knew they'd be nothing but trouble since they'd set you to dreamin'. A waste of me honest money."

His "honest" money was made through smuggling, but she dare not say so. "The books are loaned from the church," she said.

"On loan? What fer? Expect you to lose 'em so he can charge double?"

"Pa!"

He reached for the two books clutched in her arm.

"Fairy tales," he scorned as she held them back protectively. "Bah! There ain't no God."

"There *is*, Pa!"

"Your ma was the same—always totin' a passel of books. Ye'll have no time to waste on 'em. Now go on with you."

Amity's heart was beating rapidly. She was ready to fight for her books if he had a mind to take them, but he turned his back to face the chickens.

"Here chick, chick, chick," he said with unusual kindness. "Nice chikee."

She entered the back tavern that had been made into their living quarters, opening windows to allow the wind to clean the scullery of its stale odor of grease and woodsmoke. She found a fish stew in a blackened kettle and dipped the ladle to fill a bowl.

She heard him coming and pulled out a rickety chair, setting the bowl before him and stepping away with hands behind her back. She said breathlessly, eyes shining, "Pa? Remember how I told you about the church folk bein' nice to me and all?"

He grunted.

"Well, they've invited me to a Saturday afternoon gatherin', Pa."

He glanced up, fish between his teeth. "No."

"Oh, Pa, please!"

"You heard your pa. An' don't stand there so high and mighty. Don't ye think I know them hypocrites been puttin' dreams in your head? Just like a gal! Wantin' to see sights. To eat fancy vittles in fancy rooms. You ain't goin'."

"But, Pa—"

"I won't have my offspring shamed by tryin' to be a lady when she ain't."

She felt the wallop of his words.

"You want 'em to laugh at you?"

"No, Pa. I couldn't stand it."

He grunted approval. "Stay away from that church then. You ain't up to their tricky ways. Next you'll be thirstin' fer their uppity things. Then what? You'll be squallin' around expectin' new things yerself."

"I won't. It's only what they call a lawn outing. All the folks stand around outside an' sip tea and eat sweet cakes with frosting."

"Bah! Lawn outings, tea and sweet cakes. What fer, I ask?"

"They're wishing to raise money for new hymnbooks."

He grunted and slurped a mouthful of stew. "On small folks' money and sweat. Underneath their eastern duds they're all snakes, ready to clench their fangs into the first fool who'll trust 'em. Like this!"

Amity jumped as his hand darted to her arm, pretending to

bite her. He chuckled at her response, then his eyes took on a faraway gleam. "Aye . . . I knows me another gent who's back in this neck of the woods and who's been masqueradin' as a preacher . . . be named Kain Wilder. I knew ol' Kain when his boots were run-down at the heel and he had rips in his jeans. We talked and drank together in many a hole."

She sought his eyes. She had never heard of Kain Wilder.

"I got me big plans, gal. Kain and me fought Injuns together once. We was both workin' fer the railroad then, laying track in Kansas. He could throw a mean hammer 'bout as good as yer own pa, but I was bigger. I could outdo him . . . and I will again. That land he's got on the Hood be worth plenty one day and I aim to do some collectin' on the sly."

She wondered what he meant. Did it have anything to do with Mr. Daws?

"Where's Mr. Daws from? Kansas?"

He gave her a sharp look. "Why? You know he's from the East."

"Don't know what part."

"Don't matter. . . . Me and Kain . . . but he went to Chicago. . . ." He slurped his soup thoughtfully. "Me, I come here to work at Kalama haulin' goods for ol' Mack Ridgeway's train. Until that blasted accident. . . ." He studied his stew. "But Kain, he went to Chicago," he repeated to himself thoughtfully. He looked at her, his eyes bright and glittering, as though he knew something. "Only he says he weren't never in Chicago. He don't want it known, but Daws saw him, and I'm movin' in. Just as soon as his land on the Hood fills his pockets with jingling gold coins. Aye, me and Kain Wilder, we're goin' to have us a little chat."

She knew he was up to no good. She could tell by the sly look he wore, the suggestion behind his musing words, the way he stirred his stew when he thought. She guessed that Mr. Kain Wilder didn't want it known that he had once been in Chicago.

"Pa, can I go to the church outing? I like the folks there a lot," she said wistfully. "A nice lady came and sat beside me, said my hair looked pert." She touched it self-consciously. "Said I ought to weave it in braids, even said she'd show me how to do it with a ribbon. Look, Pa!" She rushed to the cupboard where she'd placed the books and, opening one up, carefully brought out a shiny green satin ribbon. "She took it right out of her own hair and gave it me!"

Amity could see he wasn't listening but was enmeshed in deep, secretive thoughts. He slurped his stew, staring at the window with a view of the boathouse. Amity watched him. What was on his mind?

"Aye, Daws was right, and you just might be gettin' new shoes. Maybe a whole lot more 'for this is over."

She moved uneasily, holding the ribbon behind her back. "Pa, I ain't understandin'."

"Don't matter. You'll see when I'm ready fer you to see. Now, go look in on Daws. He's been a hair under the weather since last night. Likely to get sick, so I'm thinkin'."

His tone of voice caused her to glance at him.

"Just like easterners to fold up once they be gettin' a taste of the frontier. Got no sand in 'em."

She quickly left the scullery, going up the steep flight of wooden stairs. Why had Mr. Daws come to rent the room here in the tavern when he might have stayed at the fine new hotel uptown? There was a bit of mystery about it. He seemed to know her father, and they had talked well into the night. At first she had thought it had something to do with smuggling, but Mr. Daws seemed too nice for such things. He had a way about him, though, like her cat when he didn't cotton to strangers. She had also noted that Mr. Daws carried a shoulder holster with a gun in it, and his vest had been expensive at one time. There was a deck of cards in his pocket too, and some old clippings from a Chicago newspaper.

She tapped at the narrow door. Was he sleeping?

Amity opened the door a crack. The room was cloaked in shadows. In one corner the familiar old iron bed that she had changed the linens on hundreds of times faced the door. A figure lay there hidden under an Indian blanket. The clean but limp curtain was drawn closed at the small window facing the harbor. The room was cold and damp with the sea. She looked toward the small hearth built into the corner, its chimney connecting with the one downstairs, but there was no fire.

The least her pa could have done for the ill man was keep him warm. And where was the china teapot and plate of cracker-bread she had left out that morning?

"Mr. Daws?" she whispered.

Hesitantly, Amity went to the side of the bed, the floorboards squeaking beneath her high-button shoes. She peered down. His eyes were open, but they were fixed with an empty stare upon the ceiling.

Amity felt her muscles cramp. She forced herself to come closer. As she suspected, there was no breath. He was dead. Amity backed away.

For a moment she stood without moving, her thoughts in disarray. Then she turned and nearly stumbled down the steep stairs. "Pa! Pa!"

She stopped halfway down, breathless and clutching the old banister as her pa came from the kitchen with a tin mug of ale in his fist.

"Now what be ye squallin' about?"

For a moment she couldn't find her voice, and only pointed up to the room. "He's dead."

She could see his mind was working swiftly, wondering what he might gain from the unfortunate happening. He looked up the darkened steps, raising the mug, took a long swallow, then wiped his mouth on the back of his sleeve.

"Up and croaked on me, did he? Just like an easterner."

Amity stood motionless, hearing the rain tinkling against the windowpanes.

"The man has himself no manners. Worst kind of luck havin' him dyin' on me like this. Don't need no port authorities to come nosing around. You sure?"

Amity's mouth was dry and the words came with difficulty. "Aye, he's dead all right."

He grunted and started up the steps, mug in hand.

Amity leaned against the banister as he trudged up. She listened to him moving about the creaking floor in the room above her head, and her gaze fixed upon the shadowed ceiling. How had Mr. Daws died so quickly?

She listened to her pa's boots move about on the wood floor, pausing now and then. She knew the layout of the room well, and her mind followed his steps to the small bureau, to the closet, and to the bed again.

Several minutes passed before he reappeared at the top of the stairs and looked at her. He came down slowly, and her eyes

181

dropped to the two large pockets on either side of his coat. They were stuffed with several letters, newspaper clippings, and a small leather pouch. She had seen Mr. Daws pay for his room from that pouch. What was in the letters? Why did he want them? What was important about the clippings?

"Pa," she whispered. "Don't take nothing. Mr. Daws was bound to own himself family folks and friends. They'll be knowing he came here. They'll be asking a whole bunch of questions. Maybe hire one of them detectives."

"Do you take yer pa fer a fool? Daws was a loner. A gambler. A fast gun. He knows no folk in Port Townsend 'cept me, and no one knew he came. He made plans to come here. We was both with Wilder in Kansas. Daws knew him better'n me. Daws followed him to Chicago 'cause he owed him, but Daws stumbled on somethin' even more important than Kansas—now I'm the only one who is knowin'."

She was trembling. "Know what, Pa? Trouble? Please don't get caught in it."

"Go on with you. Get the rope in the boathouse. An' the tarp. We be needin' to do some buryin'."

She clutched the banister. "We can't! They'll know! Someone's bound to ask where he went."

"No one be askin'. Do as yer pa tells you."

"But . . . ain't we going to send for Dr. Murphy?"

"What fer, mind you? He's dead, ain't he? Why add to Doc's pocketbook. The ol' horse already be chargin' folks too much. Gets fat rich on folks' pains."

She watched him go down the steps and stand in the small parlor with the rain beating on the window. "We can't just bury him, Pa. We'll get us into a heap of trouble with the law."

"You got much to learn, gal. Do you think I be goin' uptown to find meself held for a passel of foolish questions?"

"But they wouldn't—"

"Be sure they would. And fer what? The man be sick all right. You saw it. Had yellow eyes and runnin' himself a fever. No more gabbin'. Off with you. He's got need of burial and we ain't goin' to get ourselves involved in more trouble than he's worth." He looked up, the oil lantern casting a stark light across his face. "Think I need the port authorities snooping about? Now mind yourself, gal. Your constant wantin' to do good will see us both swingin' from the gallows."

Her emotions withdrew in a panic. *Gallows!* "I ain't done no wrong!"

"Don't be sure, gal. They hang females like they hang murderin' thieves."

Amity stared at him, her hands shaking. "I ain't going to help get rid of his body!"

He walked to the bottom step, one big hand resting on the rickety banister. His eyes narrowed. He took a swallow of his ale. The silence lengthened. "You ain't arguin' with your pa now, are you?"

She shook her head no.

He jerked his thumb toward the scullery. "Wait fer me in the boathouse. When I finish me supper, we'll bring the man's remains to a respectful restin' place in the sea. Best place any good man could be laid to."

The outbuilding was dark against the twilight. Clouds had settled low, like fog, and the rain drizzled in a gray sheet. She sought the boathouse like a shelter offering escape. Escape. . . . How? If she told on him, would they believe her? And she would be left to his anger.

She leaned against the boat. She must pull herself together before he came. Even the damp odor of the boat was more welcome than the tavern. *So that's why he already had Mr. Daws's clothing. Pa already knew he was dead.*

She heard him come out the back of the tavern, heard the door bang shut with the wind, and she snatched the rope. When she ran outside, the wind soaked her wet with rain. He was crossing the yard, his boots squishing in the mud.

He stopped in the middle of the yard. The rain slicked his long hair close against the sides of his head. "Amity!"

"Comin', Pa."

"Best we wait till tonight, when I be meetin' the ship. Get in the house 'fer you catch the sickness."

She hurried past him and up the steps into the scullery. He followed her inside, shutting the door. "There's bread and milk fer you. I know how you hate fish stew. See? Yer pa ain't so mean. Then be off to yer room. Stay put till I come fer you."

She turned and saw by his face that he intended her to take part in bringing Daws out to sea.

"Aye, I mean fer you to be comin' with me tonight. Ye won't like it, but that's the way it is. Sure way to seal a wagging tongue. Now off with you. I'll drink me ale in peace, if ye don't mind."

Amity climbed the steps and closed the door of her small room, hearing the wind and rain from the sea beating against the tavern.

Oh, God . . . let me die too! I don't want to live no more. Ain't nothing to live for. Jesus, if you be there like Mr. Spurgeon says— do somethin' with my life!

In the boat that night Edmund Clark fought the black swells with his powerful arms, rowing out toward the ghostly ship. Amity clung to the side while the icy rain beat against her face and hammered the oilskins she wore. Her stomach came to her mouth as the boat dipped and rose and sank again into watery valleys. Edmund Clark stopped rowing and pushed the remains of Mr. Daws over the side—*SPLASH!* Amity gagged.

The ship was ahead and a signal glowed in the dark. Her father answered with his lantern. She had seen this ship before, but not its captain. She knew only that he did business with her father. How had he known to expect them? Perhaps he had not.

The roar of the wind filled her ears as they struggled back to the quay, then up the creaking and moaning steps. The wind lashed against them.

Amity stood beside her father, both of them dark silhouettes in oilskins.

He chuckled. "Aye, gal, yer Cap'n Edmund Clark's daughter all right, an' tonight you've flown yer colors. Now! Look pert. Soon all you seen and heard will be forgotten."

He threw a heavy arm around her shoulders. "Aye, flighty you may be at times like yer ma was, like a little brown sparrow, but I be bettin' there's more of the blood of yer pa in you than hers. And yer books with all them words didn't help you tonight, nor will they. Ye'll be doing what I tell ye, an' ye always will!"

And you always will. . . . The words echoed in her mind.

"You can't be different, gal. It ain't in you, no more than in me. We're two of a kind, Amity. Yer mold be cast in iron, like mine. Ye ain't no one's child but Edmund Clark's."

16

AN EMPIRE CRASHES

Mack Ridgeway stared at the Port Townsend newspaper headline:

JAY COOKE'S EMPIRE TOPPLES!
NORTHERN PACIFIC RAILROAD ENTERS
RECEIVERSHIP

His throat tasted sour and his belly felt like a pit full of bricks. How much had he lost in the railroad? *Everything*, the mocking voice laughed. *Everything, Mack, you lost it all.*

"But I couldn't have," he told himself.

It was simply a nightmare. He would awake, look upon a new day, and go forth to conquer again.

Weakness assailed him. Gone, all that he had so carefully invested. Every dollar, every dream, every hope—gone. Mack's house of cards—with each card so meticulously placed—spiraling upward, looking so clever and so smart, had toppled to its foundation.

No, there was not even the foundation remaining. He had

built on the promises and skills of the cool-minded financier Jay Cooke. He had trusted his wisdom, his ability to make money, to outsmart the dice. But just as the Greeks said: "The dice of the gods are loaded."

It was Cooke's voice he heard now, not speaking in sympathy but derision: *"Sorry, Mack. Better luck next time. After all, life is made up of luck, isn't it?"*

Next time? thought Mack, sickened. Would there be a next time? He had admired Jay Cooke, an entrepreneur. His empire sprang great and wide like a city of gold, but in the unveiling light of the sun, it became fool's gold.

His eyes flew open. Cleo was leaning over him, her face contorted with sympathy. "Mack, it's all right," she soothed in a whisper, wiping a cloth against his sweating forehead. "It was a nightmare."

The splendid bedroom sprang to light as she turned on the lamp beside their mammoth bed. His hands felt the luxurious velvet cover, and the expensive paintings in silver frames looked back from the walls. His eyes searched hers and found in them a solace. He reached a bronzed hand to touch her hair, and while it was not the hair of a young princess, he would not have exchanged it for any price. "I love you, Cleo," he said with a dry throat.

He saw her tears spring to life, saw her funny smile, and he smiled too. "It's not so bad," he said, "to reach middle age, lose it all, and start over again when a man has a woman like you."

"You flatter me."

He sobered. "I mean it, Cleo. I actually think you're woman enough to start over with me in a covered wagon on a hard road to some new frontier."

She smiled. "You're dreaming again. We *are* the new frontier, darling. Washington, Oregon, the Northwest territories—we'll need to make our happiness here. There isn't anyplace else to go."

He knew that, yet he almost wished . . .

"There's the Yukon. I once heard a man say gold could be found there."

"In Alaska?" she laughed. "Nothing there but snow. We may not have a big piece of the Northern Pacific anymore, but there is timber. You didn't build this house outside Port Townsend for nothing."

Mack looked at her. He had built Ridgeway House between Port Townsend and Quilcene because he intended to buy Wilder's land grant. He had yet to see a better location for logging except perhaps Seabeck. The stand of trees between the two rivers was worth a fortune.

"I need time to rethink things . . . about you and me, about Lottie and Prescott—don't forget we have a grandson now. I can't wait to see Jamie! Two more years and Wade too will leave the army and come home to Washington. That boy better make good. And so had I."

Mack tossed aside the cover and stood, reaching for a cigar from the silver box on the mahogany table. He struck a match, lit the cigar, and glanced at her over its glow. "You've been looking into that grant?"

"I know how much you want to buy it."

"With what!" he said bitterly.

"You forget I own half the Ridgeway Timber Enterprise. You'll find your dream again. The NP might have gone bust, but the Ridgeways haven't."

Mack poured himself a drink. "I want them off that stretch of land. Railroad's going through there one day."

"Ben says Wilder won't budge," said Cleo.

"Your brother's old and sentimental. What we need is a foreman with smart business sense. I've been in touch with Val Cooper. He's due in from Oregon with a crew of new jacks in a few weeks."

"There's none finer than Val," she said. "He was loyal to my father for years."

"He's tough and knows how to handle squatters. That's all that matters to me."

"I don't want any trouble," hastened Cleo.

"And I don't have any particular desire to make trouble for them, unless I'm forced into it. But they'll need to go soon. If not, I'll need to talk to Kain Wilder about Kansas again."

She wrinkled her nose. "Kansas!"

"The man wasn't always a minister. He has a reputation for pulling a gun, and he'd like to forget those days. He doesn't want his son to know."

"I can't say I blame him. I haven't met the man yet, and I don't care to, but I'm willing to offer them a good price if they'll quietly leave."

"They're not the quiet type when it comes to backing off. If you want to try, go ahead, but let Cooper be the go-between. Stay away from there just in case there's trouble. My reputation with the NP is important. I can't allow my name to be dirtied with anything that even smells of scandal." Mack emptied his glass, setting it on the bureau.

Several weeks later Cleo took her crutches and came slowly into the library. At Mack's desk she sat down in the silence of the large mansion to write a letter. When she had finished, she sealed the envelope and addressed it to a family friend in the nation's capital. Hopkins was a friend of President Grant and officials in the Department of the Interior. She reminded Hopkins of a loan her brother Ben had once given him.

Surely there was a way for the railroad to claim that land along the Hood. And when they did, friends in the railroad would sell her the old Wilder claim.

Cleo told herself she would make it up to the young Wilder. There was land all across Washington. Good land for farming. She would double his grant and so make amends. There was Mack to think of.

Mack may have taken a beating with his loss in the railroad, but he would soon be stirred by his old vision. She couldn't imagine a man as restless as her husband giving up his passion for the NP.

She rang the bell for the butler.

Dudlee came in. "Yes, Mrs. Ridgeway?"

"Send for Cooper. I've some work for him."

As far as Tavish could see there was timberland, green to the eye and spicy to the smell. His gaze studied the wooded aristocracy of Douglas firs, hemlock, and spruce, the untouched giants that lifted branches toward the Creator's sky. No wonder

Kain had filed on this section of land, he thought.

He had heard his father speak of the forest stillness as a cathedral. In the deep silence of the dense pine surrounded by mountain ranges and gorges, Tavish understood how a man who knew the God of order and design could sense his own smallness. How dependent he was upon Him! How awesome was the power and creative wisdom of God, but how finite and temporary were his own plans, and those of the empire builders.

A pinecone fell, making a snapping sound as it landed on a bed of dry needles. He looked east where old Indian trails climbed to flowering meadows and alpine lakes. The glacier peaks of the Olympic Mountains stood arched against a blue sky.

The wind from the snowy peaks shook the tassels on his jacket—the chill warning of a short summer, also reminding him of the brevity of a man's youth. Yet the summer that Christ had brought to his soul would never fade with passing years.

Yes, the forest could be a cathedral, and he offered up his thanksgiving. They were in possession of the land that he had thought and planned about for so many years. His father was growing stronger day by day, at peace in the Scriptures. And Lazou, too, had made it to Washington, even though he had lost his saplings in a snowstorm that nearly buried his wagon. At Tavish's invitation, Lazou remained with them. The apple orchard in Wenatchee remained a golden dream, even if it did need to wait for another tomorrow.

Tavish walked his horse along the bank of the Hood, where the saltwater channel ran forty miles through deep forest to the river's great bend at Union.

His land claim stretched between the Dosewallips and Duckabush—the two rivers located thirty miles from Port Townsend. Both flowed into the Hood, giving him access to the waterway. Until he owned his own logging vessels, he and Julot would be their own "boom men," floating their logs out to waiting ships anxious to buy. He was working on plans for their first big cut, but whether or not they could proceed as he hoped depended on friendly contact with his mother's uncle, Mathieu LeBrett, who owned shares in a sawmill at Seabeck.

17

FRENCH LEGACY

Tavish heard the splashing of the stern-wheeler pushing its way up Hood Canal even before the big steamboat rounded the bend of firs. The whistle sliced through the clean scent of pine, announcing its proud arrival at Seabeck. With Julot beside him, Tavish rode his horse along the bank toward the logging town, his mind on his great-uncle.

The meeting would not be an easy one.

Julot was frowning and seemed to have a different matter on his mind. "A load of lumberjacks arrived in Union."

The tent-town of Union was located at the great bend of the Hood Canal where steamers serving the Puget Sound connected with a logging railroad. Tavish wanted to avoid any thought of trouble.

"Loggers? From where?"

Julot rubbed the bruise on his chin. "I didn't have time to ask. But I heard the name of Riley, and Oregon."

So Riley was working as a jack. Tavish remembered back at the train camp months earlier when someone had said Riley had left for Oregon to work as a logger. That Riley was in the Washington area could mean trouble. It was now even more imperative to get a loan to hire his own loggers and get his first cut into the waterway.

"Tav, I ain't a mean one," said Julot with a scowl. "But I just ain't got any more give in me. I'm tired of bein' pushed around."

Tavish smirked and lowered his hat over his eyes, unaware of a gust of wind from off Mount Rainier that sent the Indian feather in his hat fluttering. The leather reins he held in one hand, the buckskin jacket, and the soft boots that reached to his muscled calves had all been made by Kwanita.

"You've never been known for patience, cousin. So don't start making excuses to me about the fight in Union."

"The big jack had it coming," grumbled Julot. "Said the French stole Quebec."

Tavish smiled and scanned the ridge of tall spruce. "And of course that insult to our fine French blood justified the man's missing tooth."

"Next time he'll think twice."

"Next time," said Tavish dryly, "you do some thinking, will you? Especially with Riley in that logging crew."

"I didn't see Riley," grumbled Julot, "nor do I want to."

"He'll hear of the logger's missing tooth," said Tavish. "Your temper will soon give us both a reputation for trouble. I need friends. Good ones, with connections. I've got to get a loan. If I don't, we'll soon be back driving the stage."

The lumber town of Seabeck faced Hood Canal, and he and Julot rode along the bank, slowing their pace to watch the loggers.

Tavish would be content now with an ox team to haul his logs along skid roads. His property was less than a mile from the Hood. Dumped in the salt water, he could use the tides, or chain the logs into rafts and sail them to the mill at Union, Seabeck, or out to the bay, where independent shippers from many world ports waited to buy.

They rode into Seabeck hearing the productive sound of saws and hammers. The clean air held the fragrance of cut pine.

"I used to come here as a small boy, before my father worked on the railroad," Tavish told Julot, who was looking about with interest. "My father knew the four men from San Francisco who came here in '56 to form the lumber marketing firm called Washington Mill Company."

"Looks like they've been right successful," said Julot. He looked at Tavish with expectancy. "Your ma's uncle owns part of this operation?"

"He did back when I was a boy."

Tavish was surprised at how much the town had grown since the early days. San Francisco remained the sawmill's primary market for lumber, but the logging ships also delivered to Australia, Tahiti, Shanghai, and Hong Kong. He dreamed of having his own ships one day. He remembered back to the days of the Fraser River gold strike in British Columbia and how Seabeck's timber had been sent to Victoria to satisfy the boom.

Seabeck far surpassed Seattle in size. He counted eight sailing vessels and a tug belonging to the lumber marketing company. Additional lumber ships were in the process of being built at its own Seabeck shipyard. The town's future seemed assured in the 1870s.

"John?" he called to the foreman.

The muscled lumberman turned and, seeing Tavish astride the horse, squinted.

Tavish smiled. "Haven't changed that much, have I? You used to throw me in the millpond over there."

"You couldn't be Tav Wilder! I heard you were back, you and Kain both. I've been meaning to get over there. What you doing in Seabeck?"

Tavish reached to the strong brown hand John extended. "I've come home. We're going into lumber."

"So far the demand has been good. Say, how's Kain?"

Tavish briefly told him of Yellowstone. "He's got the use of his arm back. I think he'll be his old self soon."

"That stretch of trees Kain filed on is some of the best. You're close to the rivers too. Good setup."

"If I can get gear and loggers," he said wryly. "They don't work without wages."

"Not unless they know the man and what he's made of. They'd need something to make the wait worth their while. You asking?"

"Yes. If you spread the word, I'll be in your debt. I'd make it worth your effort if you'd come. I need seasoned men. I'm learning, but I've a long way to go."

"A man who talks like that will make it, Tav. It's them young know-it-alls that fall flat. I'll keep your words in mind and do what I can. But you ought to know something. Talk is, Mack Ridgeway is claiming that stretch as his own."

Tavish said nothing and noticed that businesses and Victorian houses were going up. "My great-uncle around?"

"Mathieu left Seabeck a few months after you and your parents pulled out. From what I understand he was quite sore about his niece's husband giving up his big opportunity with the land and taking to drifting, as he put it. He hated to see you and Miss Vonette go."

His father and great-uncle had never gotten on well. Mathieu LeBrett, already in his sixties, had turned against Kain when he gave up on the financial opportunity at Seabeck.

"Where is he? Did he return to Quebec?"

"Naw, he sold his interest here and struck out on his own." John gave a chuckle and shook his head. "Got to hand it to the man when it comes to nerve. He went to Portland and, last I heard, was involved with the Oregon Steam and Navigation company and some railroad tycoon named Villard. Thinking of looking him up?"

"If he'll see me."

When Tavish rode out of Seabeck, Julot gave a satisfied whistle. "You thinkin' what I am? Maybe he'll be interested in buying into a new logging company started by his two handsome young nephews."

"Two?" taunted Tavish with a smile.

"Aw, Tav, come on! I'm sort of related. If my mother was your mother's cousin . . . and my pa was your pa's brother . . . then that makes your great-uncle and me—"

"Never mind. You can explain all that to Kwanita and Lazou while I'm away."

"You're right. Say—I saw Kain with a cameo picture of your mother. Better take it with you to help break through to his generosity. One look and he'll soften like a sun-kissed plum."

Tavish smiled. His father wouldn't part with the photograph and locket of hair for even a short time.

Tavish stood on Portland's G Street looking at the sign above his great-uncle's office. He frowned to himself and continued to weigh the cost of visiting him. According to Mathieu, Kain had wasted his ability to make money. He had squandered opportunity. And opportunity squandered was never to be regained.

Tavish's eyes narrowed as he stared at the sign. He stood there, debating his course of action. Horse-drawn buggies trotted up and down the street, the gray sky threatening rain.

Perhaps he best do a little more thinking before he walked into Mathieu's bright, clean office.

He was hungry and tired. There was a small eatery across the street, and he dodged the horse traffic to do some contemplating over a cup of coffee and a bacon sandwich, if it didn't cost more than five cents. What little money he did have, he had left at the house.

The little restaurant was busy and smelling of beef, potatoes, and onions. Tavish sat down and dug into his pocket for coins.

"How much for a bacon sandwich?" he asked the boy.

"How thick ya want it?"

"Give me a nickel's worth," said Tavish dryly. "And a mug of coffee."

The boy started to laugh, met Tavish's level gaze, and changed his mind. He caught up his damp cloth, gave a swipe across the soiled table, and left.

Tavish looked out the window and saw that it was raining, turning the already wet road still wetter. He could see the sign on his great-uncle's office. A man came out in coat and derby, carrying a dark umbrella. A moment later a carriage came for him and he was gone.

So much for meeting Mathieu today, he thought wearily.

"When does Mr. LeBrett come to his office in the morning?" he asked the boy.

"Who's asking?"

"I am."

The boy studied him.

"He's my great-uncle," said Tavish. "My name is Wilder."

The boy smiled and Tavish knew he didn't believe him.

"Mr. LeBrett arrives before eight."

A short time later Tavish picked up the cup of coffee the boy put in front of him. "Thanks," he said, and was surprised when a platter of roast beef with broiled onions and potatoes was placed before him. Next came bread, creamery butter, and a pot of coffee.

Tavish looked at the boy, who gestured his head to the next table. "Compliments of Mr. LeBrett."

His cup stopped midair.

His great-uncle's cheerful voice addressed him: "Hello, Tavish! So you've come home! It's about time."

Great-uncle Mathieu decided that past disagreements within the family were better left buried with the peaceful dead. He had made only one comment when Tavish informed him of Vonette's death: "A pity. If she had stayed here as I suggested, my niece could be alive and rich."

"She is both," said Tavish with a smile. If his great-uncle understood the deeper meaning to his words, he allowed the comment to slip by. Almost at once the bright old bachelor in his seventies began to discuss the fall of the Northern Pacific and the outlook for its future.

"It's not dead, my boy, only dormant. It waits for the right man to breathe new life into it. Mark my words—within a year it will be reorganized and permitted to sell its lands again. Provided with additional cash, the railroad will reactivate a number of new promotional activities. New investors will pour in money, and before long, you'll hear of the NP laying track again."

Tavish listened, paying the old businessman respect as he went on to tell him of a new genius coming on the scene.

"A German . . . Henry Villard. And he's made a good name for himself among financiers for his clever deal with the Kansas Pacific. Villard recovered investments for a group of German financiers. Well, he's here in Oregon to investigate the Oregon and Pacific railroads. They've defaulted on their bonds. Villard plans to work out harmonious business relations among the differing parties." His black eyes gleamed. "One of them is the Oregon Steam and Navigation Company—of which, my boy, I am a heavy investor. Your father should have listened to me and the two of us gone into business in steam transportation on the Hood."

Tavish recalled the long nights of discussion between his father and great-uncle over buying stern-wheelers. Tavish wondered now how many shares his uncle had in the OS&N. It was difficult to judge by his outward appearance, for Mathieu was not one to "waste" money on diamond rings, stickpins, or New York fashions.

"Let me tell you about Villard," he was saying. "The man is smart enough to know what I knew years ago. There is a fortune to be made in controlling transportation in the rich Willamette and Columbia river valleys. Settlers are arriving daily. Villard may have come to work as an agent for unhappy investors, but mark my words, he'll end up staying as president of the railroad and the steamship company. Do you know what that means?"

Tavish had said little during the meal, only listened while he devoured the beef and potatoes. Now he pushed the plate aside and refilled his cup with coffee. "It means you'll be a rich man."

Mathieu LeBrett smiled thinly. "When Villard buys the steamship line, he buys my shares. I shall then take my money and invest in the Northern Pacific."

"Because Henry Villard will want to take the place of Jay Cooke," said Tavish, not sure how he felt about that. The only thing on his mind was a loan to hire some lumberjacks. If he could just get his first logs cut and sold . . . he might be a rich man himself one day.

"Exactly. If you were wise, my boy, you'd sell that land of yours and invest in the steamship company."

"After all you said about the money to be made in timber? I can still remember going to bed at night and listening to you and Father debating the future of Washington logging."

"Logging will always be here. But the railroad's time has come. I tell you, my boy, if Villard gets hold of the steam company and the Oregon railroad—it will be the beginning of an empire that will monopolize transportation in the Pacific Northwest for years to come."

"Uncle Mathieu, I'll be honest. I haven't more than ten dollars to invest in anything. I've come for a loan. I need to hire jacks. The Ridgeways have their eye on the land and I'm not powerful enough to stop them. But if I can get my logs to market, I can at least begin."

Mathieu smiled like a hungry wolf. "Intend to take on the Ridgeways? You'll never beat them out."

"Why should one family monopolize the business?"

"Because they have powerful friends in Washington, D.C. Mack and Cleo are friendly with Charles Hopkins at the government land office. While the land office should be the agent of the people, it bows to the railroads. You'll have a fight on your hands if you try to buck them." He leaned toward Tavish, his eyes shrewd. "If you were smart, my boy, you'd go ahead and sell that land to Cleo and invest in the Northern Pacific. One day it will rise again. And now's the time to buy in."

Tavish was bored. "I've seen enough railroads, thanks."

Mathieu chuckled. "Yes, but you saw it on the wrong end of a sledgehammer. What you need to do is see it from inside one of George Pullman's luxury cars."

"I'll settle for timber, Uncle. And one day a fine house along the Hood."

"Then I'll loan you just enough to hire a crew and your equipment. If you make good—and pay me back—I'll loan you double. We'll take it from there."

"Thanks. I won't disappoint you. You'll get your money back with interest."

Mathieu's dark eyes flashed. "Now *that*, my boy, I shall take you up on."

18

TROUBLE AT UNION

When Tavish returned to the cabin he heard a holler from the direction of the river. Lazou hurried toward him. He'd been in the water fishing and was shirtless. His faded breeches were cut off at the knee and dripped as he carried a wet, sandy bag.

"Done found oysters like I ain't never seen, Tav. Bigger'n those I done gathered recently for that big man from Olympia. Why, they just lie on the flats smilin' at low tide."

Tavish couldn't stomach the thought of the slimy, gooey things. "I feel generous today, Laz," he said, swinging down from his horse. "You can eat my portion."

They walked toward the log house. Kwanita's salmon was basking over an alder fire with the fish held in split cedar sticks.

"You goin' into Union?" asked Lazou, hitching the bag onto his shoulder as they walked.

Tavish detected the change in his voice and looked at him. The care line in Lazou's forehead brought Julot to mind. "Where's Julot?" asked Tavish.

"Union. Rode there this mornin'. There's trouble sure to be had."

Tavish's irritation was kindled. "Did he go looking for Riley?"

"It was Riley who let it be known he was lookin' for Julot. I aimed to go with him, but Julot got away while it was yet dark. And Mister Kain ain't here."

Tavish looked at him. "Where is he?"

"Been gone since you left for Seabeck. Said he was going to the government land office to check into the grant, just to make sure the Ridgeways ain't done messed with it."

The last thing Tavish wanted was to ride to Union. He unsaddled his horse, calling to Kwanita. She quickly appeared with the coffeepot.

Tavish threw off his hat and shirt for a swim in the cold river. "What happened to get Julot riled?" he asked Lazou.

Lazou explained about the men he and Julot had noticed by the Hood Canal while Tavish was away.

"They was lumberjacks from Oregon. A foreman named Mr. Cooper said the railroad owns this land and done sold it to Miss Cleo—that Ridgeway woman. Cooper said he was working for her an' was under orders to clear us out an' start cuttin' trees. Well, Julot, he got all mad and told him to get off the land or he'd bust him one. Some jack said, 'Hey, Julot! Riley wants to see you in Union. And he's goin' to teach you a lesson you failed to learn in Bismarck.'"

Tavish showed no emotion, but his insides tensed. Riley! So the Ridgeways thought they could steal his land by using the railroad?

He drank the hot coffee while watching the river flow past toward the waters of the Hood, aware that Lazou was wondering how he would take the news. Well, it looked as though his cousin might need some help.

"The only way they can take this grant is by 'stealing' it. And they would need the approval of honest politicians in Washington, D.C. at the land office," Tavish said, his voice tinged with sarcasm. "Politicians wouldn't do that to humble folks like us, would they, Laz?"

"Seems to me they do anything they wants to, 'cept killin' a man, and mebbe they can do even that." He hitched the bag of oysters to his other shoulder. "You be careful in Union. Trouble comes huntin' both you and Julot. That cousin o' yours seems to attract buzzards. I done think his mammie had a jinx on her the night he was born. You best be armed if'n you go into Union."

A crow cawed and flew over a tall pine, perching on a weaving branch.

Tavish caught the drift of woodsmoke where the wind walked through the trees. Ahead, the small but rowdy logging town, consisting of canvas stores and shanties, was sprawled on the bend of the Hood Canal.

The haunts of rough and oftentimes violent men were crowded. Men of all ages milled the street where hoofs and boots ground the newly laid wood chips into the damp earth. There were oxen and wagons, a stray dog or two wandering about, some hungry-looking children playing near a covered wagon, and a scrawny chicken sitting on the wagon's canvas roof, soaking up the fast-fading sunshine. It cocked a beady eye toward the billowy clouds hovering above the Olympic Mountains as though it knew a long, hard winter rode the wind.

Tavish sat astride his horse, regarding the scene with a growing satisfaction that surprised him. Union wasn't much; neither were Lilliwaup, Brinnon, Quilcene, nor Skokomish. They were just names that sounded smooth on his tongue, small tent-towns dotting Hood Canal toward Port Townsend. Yet, he felt that he belonged, that he was a part of something growing.

The out-of-tune piano grew louder, and he looked across the sawdust street to the big tent where he expected to find Julot. He recognized the unmistakable click of poker chips, the whirl of a roulette wheel. A handwritten log sign swung from two pieces of rope: "J.P.'s Friendly Gambling House."

A broad-shouldered lumberjack wearing a plaid shirt and denim trousers stepped onto the street. Was this Cooper, the new Ridgeway foreman? He appeared to be in a hurry, and loggers in a hurry worried Tavish. The "cut and run" tactics used by some logging companies could ruin a land for generations, taking the best and easiest lumber and leaving miles of tall dead trunks to stick up and turn black.

Tavish swung down easily from the saddle. The man was so

preoccupied with his thoughts that he didn't see Tavish and purposefully strode on across the street.

As he suspected, Julot was waiting inside the gambling tent and Tavish joined him at a log table. Tavish's eyes narrowed. "There's trouble enough without looking for it. Let's go."

"I'm not running away again. Bismarck was enough."

"Riley's a bigmouth. Why bother with him? He'll trip himself up one day without either of us needing to do it. What do you know about the crew of jacks he's with?"

"The new Ridgeway foreman named Cooper hired them out of Oregon. They've a bad name, Tav. What he wants 'em for is plain to see. He expects to turn 'em on you. Riley would love the job."

"Let them play rough. We have the law on our side."

"Say—here comes trouble now. That's him, the foreman named Cooper. He was here earlier and we didn't get on too good." Julot sat up easily and moved in his chair to keep his gun hand free.

"None of that," gritted Tavish.

Julot cast him an impatient glance, his black eyes brooding.

"I mean it," ordered Tavish.

Julot scowled. "Your pa ain't here to be telling me what to do. You aiming to take his place?"

"If I have to. There'll be no gunplay, Julot, understood?"

Julot looked at him, his young face hard. Then suddenly he smiled and spread both hands. "It's your land, mon ami. If you wish to surrender it without a fight—"

Tavish glared. "Who said I'm surrendering anything?"

"They want that land. They won't take a nice polite no for an answer. He sent his jacks out there to warn your pa while you was in Seabeck."

Tavish waved a hand. "Kain isn't intimidated and neither am I. We can handle them." He snatched up Julot's coffee mug and gestured for the bartender to refill it.

Julot smiled unpleasantly. "You may die early if you wish, but me? I aim to live long and tall and see grandchildren. Besides, these men have guns."

Tavish had his Winchester, and he carried his revolver in his saddlebag, but he would not tell Julot. He glanced across to the board counter where beers were being poured. Five lumberjacks stood there with their backs to the counter, all staring at him and Julot. They were five of a kind—big, rugged, mean, and ugly. One had unkempt hair that dangled in oiled ringlets over his bearlike shoulders.

"Right perty, ain't they?" said Julot with exaggerated Texas drawl. "Looks like a trained circus."

"Look, Julot, just keep quiet, will you?"

"They're not taking your land."

"I can take care of myself. I don't need you to fight for me."

"I don't intend to. We'll fight together." He smiled.

"See here—"

"That one is the foreman," said Julot of a sixth man who had strode in bristling with impatience. "That's Cooper. We had a little trouble earlier about Riley."

"No fighting. I mean it."

"Thinks he owns the world. Just look at him."

"I don't want to," gritted Tavish, not wanting to become angry.

Tavish had sat down facing the door. No one had ever told him, but he knew instinctively that it was always best to sit with a clear eye for trouble. Maybe more of Julot had rubbed off on him than even he knew. His father was right when he had said to watch for the lion crouching by the door. That lion might be his own nature.

Cooper glanced hard at Julot, but then centered his gaze on Tavish. There was a hard, brusque confidence in the way the man handled himself as he walked up to the table. As though on signal, the other five brutes from his crew came up, ranging themselves in front of them.

Tavish sighed.

"Looks to me like he picked the biggest and ugliest bunch of all to put a fright in you," said Julot and smiled at them. "Howdy, boys."

Cooper the foreman strode up to the table. "Are you the Wilder boy?"

The man's tone was challenging. Tavish waited, his expression telling nothing, his eyes measuring the man he'd seen in the street earlier. He appeared to be in his forties, and solid muscle. Tavish looked down into his cup. *I won't get angry . . . I won't get—*

"I spoke to you, boy. Did you hear me?"

Boy. The term rankled Tavish. "I heard you, Cooper."

"You know me?"

"Heard about you. You work for Mack Ridgeway, or the timber queen?"

Cooper didn't like that. "I work for Miss Cleo. She's a fine lady. Now you didn't answer me, boy. I asked if you're the one who lays claim to land between the rivers up the Hood?"

Tavish took his time, staring into his black coffee, then finishing it. He set the cup down too quietly and looked up into the man's eyes.

"I own it." He leaned back, his boot resting on the empty chair in front of him. "And I aim to keep it."

"Is your father that circuit-riding preacher?"

"Only one I know of. There couldn't be two as good as he." Tavish studied Cooper's face, noting the grim impatience in the white around his mouth.

"This is Ridgeway country."

"Actually, this is Washington Territory. It's free country, and I don't settle for surrendering it all to any one family to rule."

"That old claim of your father's has been revoked by the United States government. It now belongs to the railroad."

Tavish smiled. "The railroad doesn't own it. I do. But I know all about the schemes of the robber barons. I worked for the NP for years. I can see how Mack Ridgeway might think he can pay a crooked politician to arrange for the theft. This time it won't work."

Cooper flushed with anger. "Miss Cleo bought it from the railroad honest enough. She's giving you two weeks. After that we're moving in to log it."

"Not on my land you're not. I've a house there. It's mine, legally. We like it; we're staying."

Tavish spoke quietly but with a cool confidence that disturbed Cooper.

"Maybe you don't understand, boy—"

"Name's Wilder."

The foreman measured him. "Look, Miss Cleo doesn't want you roughed up. But I can always tell her you pulled a gun. There's not an authority in Union or Port Townsend who'd say otherwise. The Ridgeways are a powerful family. I don't want trouble either. And these gentlemen from Oregon don't. Do you?" he asked the brutes loitering behind him.

"Naw, boss. We like things peaceful."

"Cooperate and you'll get yourself paid good enough to settle elsewhere. Miss Cleo mentioned western Washington. Good farmland, you can grow wheat."

"Fine land, but I don't want to grow wheat. I'm going to start my own lumber company."

The foreman's lips tightened and the muscles in his jaw began to pulse.

"There's an Injun squaw out there too," said one of the grizzly men behind Cooper.

"You have something against Indian blood?" asked Tavish, a deadly ring to his quiet voice.

Cooper held out a restraining arm toward the men behind him. "None of that. Look, Wilder—"

"We're staying."

The man's anger had been mounting. "One of these days, kid, I'll need to pull you up off that chair and slap some sense into you."

"Want to try it now?"

The man looked down at him, his eyes icy. "Stand up!"

Tavish was rising from his chair when the unmistakable click of Julot's gun startled the tense silence. In a whisper, Julot's .45 was in hand, aimed straight at the lumberjacks.

"Don't waste your time, Tav. That's what Cooper wants. He won't fight. He'll step aside and let his five idiots do it for him, and they have steel chains and bars. They can kill you legal-like and get by with it." Julot lifted the gun a little. "Well, it ain't going to be that easy, Cooper. One thing Wilder didn't tell you gents. His pa is a mighty fine man, but mine—he could shoot a rattler 'tween the eyes and never blink a lash." He smiled. "Always did say I took more after my pa than my uncle." His smile vanished. His black eyes turned hard. "Get out of here. All of you."

The foreman stared down at him, then looked at Tavish. "We'll remember this, Wilder." He turned and walked out of the tent, his crew following like trained goats.

Tavish watched them go, studying the situation in his mind.

"You shouldn't have drawn the gun, Julot."

"And see you get busted?"

"I could have handled him."

"He would have stomped you. Didn't you see their chains?"

"I saw them. I still could have handled him." He frowned impatiently and threw back his chair.

"And I would need to fight too. I wish no scars on my nice face."

"Is that why you came looking for Riley?"

"Riley's another matter. We have something personal to settle from Bismarck."

"He works for Cooper. You start anything, and Riley will be sure to go to him and say you're to blame." He placed his hands on the table and leaned toward Julot. "I think I should go to Port Townsend and talk to Ridgeway myself."

"Miss Cleo?"

"No, the big man himself. I have the notion that while Cooper swears he works for Mrs. Ridgeway, he's really serving Mack."

"The railroad gets what it wants. The only justice is a man's gun. You'd do well to start toting one, mon ami. Julot may not always be here to help."

Tavish ignored his cousin. While spoken lightly, he saw truth to what Julot said. If the law wouldn't protect him, he had an obligation to protect himself.

"I'll make it. I can't say the same for you if you keep waving that iron around at folk. You make them mighty nervous."

"Sure. And if I hadn't been smart enough to have it with me, we'd both be bloodied up by now."

"I won't mind getting bloodied if it will settle matters. It's better than leaving a man dead in the street."

"Best thing I can do is go with you to Port Townsend. Never know what might happen between here and there."

"Get that list of groceries over at the store first, will you?"

"Aw, Tav! That's woman's work!"

"Who said? You want to eat, don't you?" taunted Tavish with a smile.

Julot glowered and stood. "Oh, all right. But if I bump into Riley along the way I'll be a little late."

Outside, darkness was beginning to settle.

Tavish came to where his horse was grazing near the river-bank and loosed the reins, hearing music playing in the distance. He placed his Winchester in his saddle boot.

"Say now, preacher kid, fancy meetin' you in the Northwest. Been a while since Bismarck."

Tavish turned. Riley stood beside a huge lumberjack.

"Me and bossman Cooper, we've had a little talk about you, Wilder."

The big jack stood in a broad stance. Tavish recognized the giant with the ringlets touching his shoulders.

"The boss is thinkin' you might need some persuadin' to git you movin'," Riley told him. "You be squattin' on railroad land."

"Aren't you man enough to do it alone, Riley? You need a bodyguard to protect you?"

Riley's smile washed away. "I don't need him. He just come to watch and see how it's done. I ain't one to hurt a good boy none, but—"

Tavish smiled coolly. "You have my permission."

Riley came toward him. "If I was you, I'd take that Injun squaw you brought back from Yellowstone and that old—"

Tavish struck two hard blows into the man's belly. He buckled with a groan and went down slowly to one knee, clutching his stomach.

"Riley, you're too easy. All talk."

He turned to walk away, but Riley came up and swung viciously. Tavish came back with a sweeping right, followed by a left to the forehead that landed Riley on the riverbank.

For a moment Riley didn't move. Then he crawled up—covered in mud, spitting water and blood—and tried to stand; swayed, then caught himself on a low-hanging tree branch.

"Looks like you done lost the bet, Riley," said the big jack. "You owe me a beer." He snickered and turned to walk off. Riley gritted: "Break him in two."

The jack turned and looked at Tavish.

"Don't try it," breathed Tavish. "I'm in no mood to be nice tonight."

The jack walked on.

"You'll pay for this, Wilder," breathed Riley.

Tavish mounted his horse and rode out of Union.

19

ON THE TIDE

Above the wind-driven rain lashing the waterfront of Port Townsend, Amity heard her cat yowling to get inside. She lit the stub of an old candle and found her way into the narrow hall where the steps led down. Her father's voice startled her:

"Easy with him, lout! Think we be paid fer cracked bones?"

"He's no easterner. The man's a soldier. He won't squall easy. I don't pick weaklings."

She recognized the other man's voice, though she didn't know his name. He often called on her father. His kind were known as crimps—unscrupulous men who prowled the waterfront district like alley cats. They either worked for a bigger man, or were hired by a ship's captain. When there weren't enough sailors available to legally fill out a ship's crew, the crimps would come up with the quota, finding their prey among the many taverns and brothels built along the waterfront. For their night's work they received a fee of thirty dollars a head, and in some cases up to three months' advance on each man's wage. Their victims, rendered unconscious through a dose of chloral hydrate—"knock-out drops"—would awaken some-

209

where off the stormy coast of Cape Flattery, bound on a voyage to the Orient.

As the crimp told her father, the victims were carefully chosen. First choice were seasoned men of the sea. Next came soldiers, loggers, then farmers' sons. Local citizens and Indians were usually avoided. The method of securing the crew for a ship might be as simple as the tavern keeper befriending a new face with a backslap and a few free drinks, or as vicious as jumping a man in a back alley.

"Bring him over here," said Edmund Clark.

"Wait—I don't sidle up none to strangers. Who's that at the table?"

"He ain't talkin'."

"Says who? You hear something? That noise—from the stairs. . . . Where's your daughter?"

"Asleep."

"I'm saying I heard something."

There was no time to make it back to her room. Her trembling fingers snuffed the small flame on her candle and she sank to the step, crouching low.

Footsteps creaked across the wooden floor, and while she could not see the figure of her father, she sensed his presence just below the steps. She felt his eyes straining to peer into the darkness. Did he smell the smoke from the extinguished candle? The wind pulled at the door with a creak and a groan, and beneath the tavern floor, water caused the pilings to tremble. The noise covered her breathing while her silent prayer reached to the throne of grace. *Please, God, if Pa sees me don't let him say anything.*

"Be the storm you're hearin'. On with ye now. We got no time to waste yappin'."

His steps retreated back to the tavern room and Amity feared to move, expecting the sudden thrust of a bright lantern into her hiding place.

No one came. She heard the men moving about in the tavern. She guessed what was happening to the poor soldier sprawled unconscious on the boards with the pilings groaning beneath his ear.

On the sleazy and foul waterfront district most taverns and brothels, called "cribs," had been built with easy access to the water. Back doors opened onto the wharf. Captain Edmund Clark's tavern, like many others, had a seamier advantage: trapdoors were built into wooden flooring for the disposal of garbage into the dark water below. Business could be done secretly behind closed doors and windows in darkest midnight.

There came a heavy scraping noise. Tables, she thought. She heard the trapdoor lift open and imagined her father bending down and thrusting a yellow lantern below. A skiff with silent rowers would be waiting in the water beneath the dock.

She tensed, hearing the soldier being pulled across the floor to the door's edge. Straining sounds came from her father and the crimp as they lowered their human cargo down to men in the skiff who were anxious to row the coveted merchandise to a ship waiting in the night.

Amity was beyond feeling sick. This ugly business had filled her life for the two years they had lived here. She felt numb, disconsolate. Somewhere she heard the patter of wharf rats that lived in the wooden dock. Evidently they expected food to be dumped; tonight it was a soldier. When he didn't return to his post his name would go down as one more deserter, and if he had a family they would never know. Did he have a wife, a child? What would they think? That he no longer loved them, that he had run away deliberately?

Amity found herself praying that somehow they would believe in him till the end. Perhaps if he survived the savage voyage to fight his way back, they would hear from him in several years.

She clutched the dead candle stub, listening to the skiff below the tavern leaving for the ship. All grew quiet and she believed her father to be alone once again. She had no wish to confront him; such an action would prove foolish. Another voice from the next room where her pa was startled her. The twang was thick with a down-south accent. The stranger spoke from somewhere in the shadowed back room, where he was seated at one of the tables. She heard a name spoken—"Kain Wilder." She remembered now. A man had entered by the back door just before closing time. He had worn an old Confederate duster and cap, and chewed on the ragged end of a cigar between his teeth. Her father had appeared cautious when he arrived, yet curious as well. The southerner had called himself "Riley."

His mention of the Wilder name had brought her alert.

"I got me a handsome notion," Riley was saying. "An' I got me a score to settle. I was hired to clear that land an' I aim to get the job done. Now you just come an' sit a fine spell while we dicker up."

Her father's voice was a match for Riley: "I got no call to dip hands in the witch's pot any more than they be wet now. Aye, I've a fancy thing growin' in my mind, and you best not move in to muddy up me waters for fishin'."

"Say now! Supposin' I know what that notion is you have, Clark. A stern-wheeler? You've dreamed enough about it. No one but ol' Riley can get it for you."

"I got me burdensome woes enough without hikin' up with your personal quarrel with Kain's son. If he busted you one in the belly, that be between you and him."

"You're talking mighty fine, seeing how you aim to become a thievin' blackmailer. As I see it, if you want a stern-wheeler and a silk dress for your girl, you'll get 'em when you learn it pays to work with me. If not, my jacks can rough you up a bit and the Ridgeways won't even know it. Now sit down. We need do us a little more conversin'."

Amity heard chairs scrape across the floor . . . a sloshing sound from a pitcher of ale refilling two mugs.

Blackmail? Didn't her pa have enough on his conscience to drive him to the wailer's bench? Must he also cross hands with Riley? And just what did Riley have in mind?

They were talking in low tones at the table. Softly Amity crept down the steps, her heart thundering. She moved through the darkness, her bare feet making no sound, more cautious than she had been earlier. She edged nearer to the wall that divided the tavern from the stairs, and leaned there, feeling the draft of wind from the cracks in the floor. Beneath, the water lapped and the pilings groaned. Insects crawled as stealthily as had she, seeking garbage to feast upon.

"I've no quarrel with Kain's son," grumbled her father over his ale. "It's him an' his big makings on that land I'm waitin' on."

"You've got it all wrong, Clark. There ain't going to be no

big makings, because Mack Ridgeway wants that land and he ain't a man to lose. You want that stern-wheeler and here's your big opportunity. As for Tavish and Frenchie, they're both going to pay a heavy due."

"Aye, I hear you, but how does that thievin' Ridgeway fit into this?"

"Lemme tell you somethin'. By the time my jacks rough the Wilders up a mite, they'll be hightailin' it off that land fast. That'll give me a promotion. I'll have those logs cut and floatin' to the bay before fall. Well, I ain't a man to quit with a job half done. Done too much of that in the past. Lemme tell you somethin', Clark. Ain't nuthin' turned out in life like I thought or planned it when young. I fought in the war on the losing side 'cause Jackson had no guts to keep fightin'. We could've taken to the hills and fought on for years, giving them filthy Yankees as little peace as a hound with ticks and fleas aplenty, but no. I ended up on the losing side. Then I came west to fight them Injuns, saw men die under the stupidity of Wade Ridgeway. I been servin' fools too long. Mack Ridgeway is a different man. I got me a strong attachment to him. He's a man who ain't broken easily. A man who don't lose. Winning is what's important, Clark. Brute strength makes things happen when wishin' and quittin' leave a man in a bear trap."

"Save yer yowlin' fer the bottle. I ain't got no kindness for Mack. I ain't likely to ferget how he sent me down the trail at Kalama. A man don't ferget when he's been shamed."

"Then you know how I feel about the Wilder kid. He stood up to me, him and that gun-toting cousin of his. Wilder made me spit blood at Union in front of my jacks. A man don't forget when his pride's been stepped on. I'm aimin' to see him stomped into the ground for it. I've given orders to the jacks to scare 'em good. Maybe set their cabin on fire."

Her father's voice was wary: "I don't like it. After tonight, I be swearin' off the illegal. I'm makin' a new life fer Amity."

"You'll help me get Wilder. Then we'll both call it quits. You'll be free to do as you wish an' we'll never lay eyes on each other again. I can get that stern-wheeler for you. Like I say, Ridgeway wants that stretch of land. Wait, and you'll be out of dreams."

"All right," her father growled. "But ye best be tellin' me the truth, Riley."

Amity felt the sweat break out on her skin. If her pa cooperated with Riley there was no telling where it would end. Someone could get hurt badly.

She crept back up the steps to her room and stood listening to the wind and creaking timbers.

She might go to Mr. Ridgeway to warn of what his foreman planned, but Riley had said he left Port Townsend and wouldn't be back for weeks. She might go to the port authorities, but that would involve her father—and her. What if they questioned him and discovered about the easterner, Mr. Daws?

The gallows. She touched her throat.

"Oh, God," she prayed, dropping to her knees before her bed, "what should I do?"

She must warn Tavish Wilder, but how? Could she saddle her pa's horse in the boathouse without him hearing? The storm was noisy, and perhaps if she waited until Riley left and her pa went to his bed she could sneak out the scullery door.

It was a thirty-mile ride to the Hood Canal, and even then she wasn't sure where the Wilder cabin was located.

A thirty-mile ride in the dark night in pouring rain! Could she do it?

Her heart throbbed. She knew the area well enough once. Her pa had worked the Hood for years before losing his job as pilot of a steamer. She had grown up near Brinnon, gathering oysters, clams, and blackberries to sell in Union.

Late that night as the storm howled and the pilings groaned beneath the tavern floor, Amity quietly dressed, pulling a scarf over her head and taking a woolen shawl to cover her shoulders as best she could. She soon slipped out of the dark tavern into the driving rain and sloshed her way across the yard to the boathouse.

Words from the pastor's Sunday service tumbled across her mind—words from the Book of Esther: "And if I perish, I perish."

For the first time, Amity felt that her life mattered.

20

TEMPEST DRIVEN

The night wind struck against her face, taking her breath away as the horse raced like a dark phantom through the forest. Leaning forward in her saddle, Amity's eyes stung from the cold wind that numbed her wet hands. The rain that was drenching Port Townsend had not yet sent clouds to Quilcene, and above the tall tops of Douglas fir trees the stars were visible, white and luminous.

The hoofs echoed in the chilling night until they seemed to come from every direction. The horse flitted through dim moonbeams of light screened by partial white clouds. Dark silhouettes of fir trees stared down from overhead where they grew on the banks of the Hood Canal.

The horse raced forward. Amity's heart kept pace with the cadence of its hoofs.

In the forest calm that followed her passing, an owl hooted.

How far was the Dosewallips River? Somewhere out there in the night the old Wilder land claim and its cabin awaited her arrival, but how would she find it in the darkness? Would lights be on in the windows?

She need not have wondered—she saw the glow of fire long before she turned her horse onto the trail that led farther up into the forest. The cabin was on fire!

Tavish read the brief message he'd received earlier from Mack Ridgeway and placed it inside his jacket. "Mack wants to talk."

"When?" asked Julot, seated in their hotel room in Port Townsend.

"Tonight, over dinner."

They had left the Hood two days ago after his fight with Riley, and Tavish had sent word to Ridgeway House that he wanted to discuss matters with either Mack or Cleo Ridgeway.

On the wharf, a gas lantern was newly washed above a recently painted sign, "Edmund Clark's Inn."

Tavish exchanged glances with Julot. They entered and found the large wooden room empty except for a Chinese coolie in black satin skullcap and knee-length tunic. He brought a load of logs to the wall-length fireplace. His cool, furtive eyes cast in their direction, then he went about his business as though alone in the world. Perhaps he was.

A man came from the back wearing a new white apron.

"You be wanting a bit of wine, sirs? A plate of oysters and cornbread maybe?"

"We're expecting company," said Tavish. "Mack Ridgeway."

His head cocked to one side like a rooster eying them. "Aye, the table by the window be a fine view, sirs."

He ambled ahead of them and pulled back a scarred wooden chair for Tavish. "Be seated, sir."

Tavish's attention was drawn to the man's large hands. The long fingers were perpetually moving up and down his shirt.

The man tilted his head as though his neck was stiff with sore muscles. "You be Mr. Wilder? Thought so. Do sit a spell. I'll get some brandy—sent special by Port Townsend's leading citizen, Mr. Ridgeway. He be on his way now."

"Coffee," said Tavish. "Two cups. Make it fresh."

"Coffee it is, sir, fresh-ground beans from South America."

He smiled and ambled off, glancing back over his shoulder before he disappeared into the kitchen.

"There's something I don't like about him," commented Tavish. "Like a beady-eyed rat pattering about waiting for night to fall."

Julot looked at him crossly. "Come on, Tav. Talk like that's enough to ruin our supper."

Tavish sat opposite Julot and glanced about. "Why would a wealthy man like Ridgeway choose this junk heap? I'd just as soon have dinner at Lazou's old chuck wagon along the Missouri."

Julot was staring out at the ships. "Say, Tav, look at that—she flies the flag of France," he said, and there was a slight tone of pride in his voice over his ancestry. "I would like to see Paris someday."

"Better than Tucson," said Tavish dryly. "Your tastes are beginning to improve at last."

Edmund Clark brought the cups of coffee. "I'll wait kindly like, sirs, to see if the coffee's to yer favor."

Julot took a swallow. He shrugged. "No better than railroad coffee."

Tavish met the eyes of the tavern keeper. Edmund Clark walked to the hearth and picked up the steel poker to move the coals about. "A cold night it's turnin' out. Rain yesternight, looks like fog's callin' tonight. Thick as pea soup."

Tavish watched him. Why did he keep turning his head and giving them furtive glances? He finished his coffee and set his cup down. "You're right, Julot. I've tasted better coffee by mixing soot and alkaline water—"

He looked across at Julot and tried to clear his vision as his brain began to weave and sway like a small boat bobbing in the darkened swells.

"Julot . . . quick! Outside."

Julot tried to push his way onto his feet, slurring angry words. "D-D-drugged—"

Tavish squinted at Edmund Clark. "Y-you filthy shark—"

"They be clean out in a minute. Riley! Get the trapdoor ready."

Riley? thought Tavish, dazed. "RILEY!"

Julot lunged at Edmund Clark, who stepped back easily.

Julot landed facedown on the wood floor, unconscious.

Tavish struggled to keep back the clutch of darkness trying to suck up his mind. He swayed, saw the evil eyes of Edmund Clark and then Riley grinning from the doorway.

"Say now," said Riley. "Look who's come to call. The preacher's kid and Frenchie. Ain't this nice and cozy?"

Tavish tried to reach him and fell across a table, bringing glasses and bottles to the floor with a clatter.

Edmund Clark waited to come near either of them, as though they might unexpectedly spring to their feet. He circled them, touching Julot's leg with his toe. When there was no response, he nodded to Riley.

"Take 'em away. An' I be knowin' his father, Kain. The man would gut me like a lizard if he knew. That stern-wheeler best be delivered to me!"

"Don't squawk. A man needs himself patience."

Clark suddenly wheeled and fixed Riley with a riveting stare. "Where's me fruit from the bargain?"

"I said you'll get your boat!"

"Better be," Edmund growled. "If I don't I'll break you in two."

Riley eyed him over his smoke, then knelt and swiftly searched the unconscious men, removing their weapons. "There's more to be collected than a boat."

Clark looked at him with dark musings. He wondered if Riley knew about Chicago, about Granger.

"What be crawlin' round in yer mind?"

"That Miss Cleo sets a fine store by Mack," he said over his cigar stub. "Kinda woman who'd do most anything to protect her man if he got into trouble."

Edmund Clark watched him with wary eyes. He didn't like working with Riley. He drank too much and might open his mouth.

"I want no part of blackmail," he lied. "They'll be on to us. Best keep yer tongue still. You got your revenge, let it be."

There was a door built into the side of the wall that opened onto the wharf. A dark-faced sea captain stood there with his first mate. His deep-set black eyes scanned the floor and fixed upon Tavish and Julot.

"Out deader than a rum-buster." Edmund held out his hand. "Me money, sir."

"Aye, ye'll get it," said the captain. " 'Og-tie 'em both, they be strong men. 'Aul 'em below to the boat."

Edmund Clark stood back, watching. He was uneasy. The men were young and strong. "Make sure they don't jump ship."

"My ship's 'eaded for the West Indies. They'd better be 'ealthy."

Outside in the fog, Edmund Clark said nothing, but his eyes darted to the bodies of his shanghaied bounty. He pocketed his money and watched as the two men were lowered into the waiting skiff beneath the creaking quay.

In the darkness ahead he saw a larger boat with a group of bodies piled on top of one another ready for the belly of the merchant ship the *Dragon Queen,* sailing to the Caribbean.

Riley chuckled. "Say now, that's the end of the preacher kid and Frenchie."

Edmund Clark didn't like the way matters had turned out and he was irritable. "Remember, Riley, this weren't my idea. I had nothin' against either of 'em. Didn't even know 'em. It was the stern-wheeler I wanted, and that matter had naught to do with 'em."

"What's the matter, Clark, losin' nerve after all the wretches you sent to sea? How many have come back to reap vengeance, eh? None, from the looks of you. Be content."

"What'd ya mean, 'content'? Where's me stern-wheeler as we made the deal?"

Riley shifted. "It'll take me more time."

Clark's eyes became evil slits. "There ain't no sternwheeler?"

"You got the captain's money."

"You double-crossin' jackal—"

Edmund's big hand latched hold of Riley's throat and began to squeeze. Riley sputtered and clawed. Edmund's eyes narrowed. He smiled.

A minute later he shoved Riley backward into the barrels. Riley landed with a clatter—gasping, choking, trying to breathe again.

"Now scamper away like the flea-bitted rat ye are. Be hangin' about and I'll wrap yer neck with seaweed and send ye to the slimy bottom of the waves."

He walked toward Riley. "An' if I hear of any blackmailin' goin' on, I'll do ye even worse."

Riley struggled to his feet, stumbling over the rolling barrels. He looked at Edmund as though he thought he were mad, then slunk away into the mist.

21

THE DARK REAPER

Kain lay in the pine needles on his stomach, a bullet in his back. He managed to lift his face from the earth to see bright orange flames leaping throughout the cabin. Acrid smoke burned his throat. His memory found its way along the ugly path leading back to October 1871, to Chicago, to the Sherman House Hotel, to Cyrus Granger. Fire, everywhere.

Vonette! Desperately he began to crawl toward the fiery cabin, certain that he saw her trapped, reaching out to him.

"Lord! Help me—" he breathed, "—must find her—"

His prayer brought relief and his troubled mind cleared, even as his eyes dimmed. A peace came to wrap about his heart. His beloved was safe . . . no need to fear for her.

But Tavish! A stab of dismay pierced his soul. "Don't let my son learn about my past sin. . . . Please—for his sake . . . if you've forgiven me—spare him. . . ."

The fire crackled and spurted, and he heard pieces of wood falling. He looked up at the black sky. If only he could glimpse the stars, but the smoke dimmed his vision.

Death came to mock: *Be sure your sin will find you out.*

"Lord? Am I truly forgiven?" asked Kain.

He no longer saw fire and smoke, but the stars seemed to come from behind the haze to look down on him where he was dying.

Kain's fingers closed tightly about his Bible, Vonette's Bible.

Amity's hands gripped the reins as she nudged the horse forward, its flying hoofs ripping up the earth.

So this is what Riley calls a mere "scare"?

She pulled the horse's reins to an uncertain stop beside the river, and in the protective screen of trees and wild shrubs she held her breath. Too late.

The warm wind of devastation struck against her body. Wood smoldered, and smoke hung above the pine trees. Nothing moved in the barrier of silence surrounding her.

She recoiled from the sight of what must surely be hidden farther ahead in the charred rubble. Kindled coals let off a flurry of red, then settled into darkness.

She held her breath, listening, hearing no human moan nor cry for help, only an ugly sizzling sound as the first scattered raindrops drizzled onto the hot coals.

"Oh, Lord," she whispered, the sight sickening her.

She climbed down and tied the reins to a shrub, cautiously making her way forward. She skirted the charred ruin of what had been the front of the cabin and circled toward the back, certain that if anyone had tried to escape the attack they would have run toward the thick trees behind the cabin.

The song of the river was a lament, tumbling over rocks and flowing down to join the Hood Canal. She nearly stumbled over something in the pine needles. She gasped, stepped back, then gingerly knelt.

Amity's hand shook as she saw that it was a man, his face soiled, his dark frock coat wet with rain. She winced as a spurt of firelight illuminated the bloodstain on the back of his jacket. Dead. . . . *Shot in the back.*

In the man's hand was a Bible.

Amity took the Bible and placed it inside her wrap. She stood to her feet, her knees weak, and began searching. Were there more wounded or dead? Amity suspected this was Kain Wilder, the minister. Had the lumberjacks shot him in the back? Her stomach fluttered and she became nauseated. Had Tavish Wilder and his cousin been able to escape?

Amity stood there, perplexed. She searched the ground around the body, unaware of the falling rain. There were no empty cartridges. He hadn't fired at them, yet they had—

She looked up, startled. Horses were coming! Was it Tavish Wilder?

She ran for the shelter of the trees, taking cover, looking back toward the road. A minute later lumberjacks arrived, followed by another man driving a wagon. Amity swallowed back the bitter taste of defeat. She recognized the driver. It was Cooper, the foreman who worked for the Ridgeway Timber Enterprise. She also saw a woman—Cleo Ridgeway!

Cleo came on crutches to where Kain's body was lying in the mud and knelt beside him. Cooper swung down from his horse and came swiftly to stand beside her.

"I had nothing to do with this, Miss Cleo. I swear it."

"You fools," gritted Cleo. "What have you done?"

A lumberjack stepped forward. "We didn't plan it to end this way, Mrs. Ridgeway—it was Riley. He went after the old black man named Lazou, but Kain Wilder stepped in to stop him. Lazou had a rifle and opened fire. Next thing, Riley fired back, then we all did—Wilder was hit. One thing led to another . . . it got outta hand—we only meant to scare 'em like Mr. Mack said—"

"Silence!" snapped Cleo. "Now we have a killing on our hands. If the authorities discover what happened—"

"They won't," said Cooper with a deadly quiet voice. "We'll cover it up."

"How do you expect to cover up a murder?"

"The black man got away—we'll find him. We'll make sure he doesn't talk. And the woman was only an Injun, a Cayuse. She won't talk."

"There's Wilder and his cousin," she said hoarsely. "Do you think they'll stand by and do nothing? This man was his *father*."

"Riley took care of 'em, Mrs. Ridgeway," said a lumberjack.

"What do you mean he took care of them?" demanded Cleo.

"Him and that Edmund Clark shanghaied them away on an

outbound ship. And Julot's bad blood anyhow—even Cooper heard him say when we was in Union how his pa was a gunslinger. Nobody will miss either him or Wilder. Who's to tell what happened tonight?"

"Blood tells, you blundering idiots. It always does."

In the moment of silence the wood sizzled in the rain.

"W-what do you want us to do?"

"What can be done now? If this burning and killing comes to light, Mack will be held accountable. He's the one who bought the land from the railroad."

"Don't worry," said Cooper. "I'll quiet it down. I'll get the jacks out of town, including Riley." He turned to the men. "Take Wilder away and bury him where no one will ever find him, understood?"

"Yessir, Mr. Cooper."

"And look for that black man who got away. And the girl."

"We'll find them both."

When they had gone, Amity crept out from behind the trees, soaking wet and cold, her teeth chattering. She stood there, dazed. Would they find the old man named Lazou and the Indian girl? Would they be able to escape? She found herself praying urgently for their safety. And what if they knew she had overheard everything? Would they come looking for her too? If they found out . . .

She stumbled along the bank to where her horse was hidden, dreading the long ride home. What if her pa was up and waiting for her? What would he do if he discovered there had been a killing, and Wilder's house set on fire? And Kain shot in the back!

She led her horse down the wet slope covered with slippery pine needles. She reached the embankment, breathing hard. She stood there, her eyes riveted on the water. Above, some clouds scuttled past. A silvery section of the moon shone above the treetops and onto the river that tumbled over small rocks toward the Hood.

She thought of Riley bringing her father into yet another act of brutality, one more sin that mounted up toward heaven. Her pa would be unhappy about Kain Wilder's death because he had wanted to blackmail him. What would he do when he learned Riley's men had killed him?

There would come a day of reckoning for them all. What had Miss Cleo said?

Blood tells . . . it always does.

22

BLACKMAIL!

Cleo Ridgeway stood in the damp drizzle feeling the cold penetrate her black mourning dress. The moisture accumulated on her matching umbrella and rolled off the edge in a monotonous drip. The green grass beneath her feet was sodden, the voice of the speaker with a backward collar seemed as hopeless.

"Ashes to ashes, dust to dust."

The funeral of Great-aunt Macie was coming to its dreary end. What had Ember written from Fort Lincoln? That death for the Christian was only the beginning?

There was little doubt in Cleo's mind that Macie had been a believer in Christ, and so were Lottie and Ember. She wasn't certain of Wade. He was so weak willed that she doubted if he believed in anything. But Ember's confidence in the God who promised that death was only the beginning for those who trusted His Son was not for Cleo.

She supposed that she was a Christian, and in fact, the entire Ridgeway family. They certainly weren't atheists or heathens. What was there left to be but Christian?

Since Great-aunt Macie had died suddenly while visiting

them from Tacoma, the funeral was held in the Port Townsend area. Cleo's brother Ben had managed to find a minister to take care of the burial, but it had been difficult, since the Ridgeways were not known to be churchgoing people. At last they had found one. Cleo wished he would finish with his ritual; the damp weather had started her joints aching.

She looked away from the blanket of flowers that draped the expensive casket, her eyes centering on a fir tree where a black raven sat, and she imagined it cocking its head at her as it cawed. It gave her skin a shiver. Every raven she ever laid eyes on reminded her of Edgar Allen Poe, the murky poet.

Her thoughts switched tracks away from the death of Macie to her beloved husband, Mack.

She had started receiving anonymous messages telling her to ask Mack where he was the night the cabin burned down and Kain Wilder was shot in the back.

A tight feeling welled up in her chest as fear tormented her. She had never truly been afraid before. She was not one to withdraw from a challenge in order to safeguard her emotions, and yet the letters were a different sort of challenge than she had faced as a young teenager falling from her horse. Then, it had taken all her courage to go on living when the handsome Bill Chaudry had broken their engagement and decided that a wife who would be crippled for the rest of her life would be too much of a sacrifice for him.

Cleo, then eighteen, had secretly wept bitter tears. She had turned a stone face toward the church, believing that if there were a God who was love, He surely would not allow so bitter a burden to be placed on her soul. Her conclusion was simple: if He were sovereign, He could have sent angels to keep her from falling from the horse. She could have ridden another horse that morning. It might have rained—the way it usually did in Washington! But none of these circumstances had kept her from the tragic accident. She had lost not only the use of her legs but her youth, her future, and Bill.

She had snapped out of her pity quickly enough, and in its place had come a hard resolve. She could take whatever life threw at her without flinching. She would laugh back in its frowning face, ignoring the cold wind that blew against her. She would overcome all obstacles, she would remain single—so what? She would live with her crutches. She would help manage the Ridgeway Timber Enterprise as efficiently as the men in the family.

And she had done well. Port Townsend had looked up to the young Cleo Ridgeway. She had reached out beyond her own dilemma to cheer others. She had given much to charitable works. She could compliment those more beautiful and lucky in life—and in return, she was respected, praised for her endurance, and if not truly loved, she was liked.

And then cousin Mack Houston Ridgeway had returned from the gold rush in British Columbia and walked into her life. At first she had disliked him. He was too strong, unyielding, even brutal. They had argued in the stock meetings about the Northern Pacific Railroad, and about timberland in Idaho, Oregon, and Washington. Eventually they had become friends; finally they had become lovers.

They married, and for the first time in her life Cleo felt loved. Yes, truly loved. Mack thought nothing of her deformity, telling her she was worth a million belles. The years since their marriage had been satisfying, even if Mack was gone much of the time in his work with the railroad. Life was pleasant.

And now the letters.

They threatened to take Mack away from her, to leave her soul alone again. And suddenly Cleo understood how lonely had been her journey through life until she had become a partner with Mack. She could not—nor would she—live without him at her side.

Anger welled up, then fear blew in like a storm, drowning her rage and resistance with stark apprehension. *It is true Mack ordered the lumberjacks to teach the Wilders a lesson.*

With all the strength she had once used to laugh at life, she would now use to keep him from being hurt. She would see what this fiend wanted. For surely, if he were interested only in so-called justice, he would have gone to the authorities with what was known.

She calmed a little. Yes. Of course. The writer wanted something in return for silence. Money. What else? She would do what she needed to keep him quiet. The voice of the serpent who had entered her garden would be silenced. But who could help her? What one person could she trust enough to keep the secret?

Through the drizzling rain, her eyes scanned the dreary faces of those present at Macie's funeral, and they fell upon the one man she knew she could count on.

He stood well behind the important people who came to pay their last respects to a Ridgeway matron. He was only a worker for the family but a staunch man. Val Cooper had served her father until the elder Ridgeway patriarch had died, then Val had left Port Townsend for Oregon, working in the timber until Mack had found him and rehired him to work as foreman in the Ridgeway logging camps.

Cooper had already come to her support over the ugly incident on the Wilder land. Secretly he had hustled both Riley and the logging crew out of the area and into Idaho until the matter of the fire was quietly forgotten. Since Kain had long been away from these parts and was considered a drifter, there were few to ask about him. Cooper had spread the report that the Wilders had pulled out after the railroad evicted them as squatters, and that a fire erupted when the old black man had stayed behind thinking to live on in the cabin for the winter.

Yes, she would turn to Val Cooper. She would have him make arrangements to find out who the blackmailer was and what he wanted.

And, she thought, her eyes turning cold, *he had best play fair and square with me.*

The dark shape of the coach fled along the trail as if it sought escape from some terrible disaster. In the calm that followed the coach's passing, the rainwater trickled slowly back to mirrored pools on Port Townsend's streets.

Cleo Ridgeway pushed back into the leather seats of the coach to brace herself. The coach slowed, and Cooper's voice rang out as they rumbled to a stop near the fog-shrouded wharf. A moment later she heard his approaching footsteps. He opened the door and leaned in, his face hard in the yellow glow of the lantern.

"He's here, all right, waiting. You sure you want to talk to him, Miss Cleo? I can do it for you easy enough."

She had thought long and hard about meeting him. Surprisingly she felt no fear, only cold determination.

"No, Cooper, I want to see him myself."

Weeks had passed since receiving the last anonymous letter. For a time she had thought the hoax was over, and she had begun to feel free of the prison of fear that was keeping her tense with uncertainty. What worried her the most was that Mack might find out.

He must never learn that I know about Kain, she thought.

Then the letters began to arrive again, more frequently. She had noticed that the language was roughly written and obvious in its intent. The last letter had finally demanded a "gift" to keep silent and gave an address of where to write—a brothel on the harbor. Finally, through Cooper, she had made contact.

She heard Cooper's footsteps; then he looked in. "He's ready."

Cleo felt her emotions harden into ice. Her eyes looked past Cooper into the fog.

Edmund Clark stepped up to the carriage door, hat in hand, and as he emerged from the gray dampness a sheepish grin played across his broad, bearded face. His deep-set eyes could not be seen in the shadows, but she felt them staring at her from beneath heavy brows.

"Get inside," she demanded. She looked at Cooper, who stood close to Clark. "Wait outside the door. I don't suspect this coward will try anything, but if he does, be certain he hangs."

Edmund Clark shifted his feet. "Now, Mrs. Ridgeway, I'm not a violent man. I'm an honest man, I am. I wouldn't be meetin' you like this if there was another way."

"Save your apology for fools. I know who you are, and what you are. Now get inside before someone sees you."

A big gangling man, Edmund Clark climbed awkwardly into the fine carriage, sitting opposite her and drawing up his big booted feet to keep from touching her crutches.

Cleo was not intimidated. She picked up the end of a crutch and held it toward his chest, poking it against him with little angry shoves.

"You are an evil man, Edmund Clark."

She heard him swallow. His long fingers, the nails showing

dirty in the lantern light, crawled round and round the brim of his hat.

"I 'spect so, m'lady."

"Well. A rat admits its bloodline."

"I aim to change, m'lady." His teeth showed in a silly grin.

She felt repulsion. "Cooper tells me you will be satisfied with a boat. Is that correct?"

"A stern-wheeler," he corrected humbly. "Yes, m'lady." He held up a big palm toward her. "I swear I'll never see you again."

She pushed the end of her crutch against his palm with loathing. "What do you know of vows before God or man? Your promises mean nothing. The devil always lies to get his way. Are you any better?"

"I rightly hope so, m'lady."

"You'll get your stern-wheeler—and Cooper will see you have a job on the Columbia River working for the Oregon Steam and Navigation Company."

"I'm much obliged, Mrs. Ridgeway."

"I suppose you wonder why I would choose to look you in the face when I might have simply arranged the boat through Cooper?"

"Why, yes, m'lady. I surely did."

"I'll tell you why." She opened her handbag and pulled out a shiny derringer. The metal glinted in the lantern light. She felt no remorse when he shrunk back into the leather seat, his eyes narrowing into dark lines of uncertainty.

"I want you to know something," she said in a chilly voice. "I've no intention of being bled by a blackmailer. Nor will I stand by helplessly and allow you to torment my husband, should such an unwise thought come to mind in the future. I warn you now, Edmund Clark. If you should awaken one morning and think to yourself that your greedy appetite demands a little more—or if I ever hear from you again"—she lifted the derringer slightly—"you will end up a dead man in the river.

"Now, get out."

23

SHANGHAIED

"Well, lads?" Captain Hannibal roared. "Look into my sweet face and tell your captain what ye see!" He swaggered across the quarterdeck.

Tavish did not flinch but retained his caution.

Since their abduction from Port Townsend two weeks earlier, the first officer, Eli, had commanded the ship. The captain had not shown himself in port, and now, seeing him for the first time, Tavish understood why. He had waited for the storm before making his dramatic entrance on deck. He had walked out dressed in black, with billowing smoke pouring forth from his head, a mask hiding his face. He then tore the mask away, letting it fall to the deck, where seawater washed about his boots.

Tavish stared into the countenance of a leper.

Captain Hannibal smiled, his rotted teeth showing in a bizarre grin under a partially missing lip. His red shoulder-length hair was a mass of bristling braids in the tradition of the infamous Blackbeard, into which he had poked slow-burning hemp cords dipped in saltpeter and limewater. They sizzled and smoked, and the wind caught up the foul odor and brought it to Tavish.

A groan shuddered through some of the new crew, but those who had sailed with him previously were ominously quiet.

"Well?" he roared into the biting wind. "Now you see what you're in for!"

The inky swells rose and fell and were blown on deck as Tavish felt the icy water surge against him trying to suck his feet from under him.

Captain Hannibal stood boots apart, his body swaying to and fro with the ship's movements as if he had been born on the back of a hurricane.

Just our luck to end up with an insane captain, he thought grimly.

"What, me bright lads! Are you not afraid of Captain Hannibal?" he mocked and walked toward the handful of new sailors. They cringed backward as he held out his left hand, showing missing fingers, laughing hoarsely as each man showed terror that he might be touched.

Tavish could see he enjoyed his mastery. His outward appearance mirrored an evil temperament.

The captain's lashless eyes flared as a boy began to weep.

"Now, now, laddie, your master be a kind man, after all. Nay, he'll not hurt ye, laddie," and he walked past him to Julot, pausing.

Tavish held his breath. He released it again as the captain walked on, flipping his whip in a black-gloved hand. The captain halted and fixed Tavish with a stare. He raked him from head to toe, taking in his ripped shirt.

"Aye, a handsome piece of flesh," Captain Hannibal sneered. "But what will the lassies say when they learn you've sailed a leper ship? Do you not fear your life will be ruined by contact with your captain, lad? Best fall to your knees and beg me for mercy!"

His eyes flared. "Did you hear your captain?!"

"I heard. I was shanghaied, as you know. I'm not aboard your ship by choice. And serve, I will—without complaint—but I bow to none but Christ alone."

The captain squinted in a rage. "Curse you! Drag him aft!"

he shouted to Eli. "Lay hold of him! I'll flog his flesh to the bone!"

The first mate held back, his jaw flexing. "Captain, I beg of you. We'll need every man with wit and strength. This storm is sure to get much worse."

Captain Hannibal turned to his mate with a string of diabolic oaths. "Will you contend with your captain? I am weary of your jawing, Eli!"

"Have I refused my duty?" said Tavish. "For what do you flog me?"

The wind whipped at Tavish's dark hair and blew sea spray into his face. Only then did he realize his mistake. Captain Hannibal did not want men; he wanted slaves, and sniveling, cringing beggars!

"So you think yourself brave, do you? We'll see! Nay, I flog you for not bending your knee!"

He shouted to his officers to drag him to the gangway.

"You don't need three men," said Tavish. "I shall walk."

The first mate slipped the irons on, avoiding the even gaze of Tavish. "If you have any sense," he whispered, "save yourself and bow the knee to the captain. Can you not see his mental condition?"

"Are you not next in command?"

Eli's gaze came up sharply, but he looked away again.

"Take me instead, Captain," came Julot's sudden voice. "I'm not afraid of what you'll do to me!"

Tavish shot him a glance of despair. "No, Julot," he gritted as the captain took the bait and turned on Julot.

"Aye, fearless are ye? We shall see! I shall flog you both for insolence! And the rest of you shall watch and know what manner of captain you have for the long voyage to Zanzibar!"

Zanzibar! Their voyage would bring them to the other side of the world!

Tavish was brought between two shrouds and his hands were bound to them, and yet it was not the leering face of the captain that rose to taunt him, but the memory of Riley and the shrewd eyes of Edmund Clark that flashed across his mind.

But he remembered his father sitting quietly before a campfire: *"Whoever said life was fair? It is full of injustice! But we trust the wisdom and grace of God to do something meaningful with our injustices. In all our circumstances we must learn to keep our focus on His eternal plan.*"

Tavish felt his shirt being ripped open and his back exposed. Despite his internal struggle, anger ravished its pathway through his soul.

Captain Hannibal stood on the break of the deck, a few feet from Tavish, elevated in order to better manipulate his whip. His three officers stood with somber faces. A young cabin boy had crawled up a rope ladder and hung there, gaping like a frightened monkey.

"Will you bow the knee to your captain and beg his mercies?" shouted Hannibal.

Tavish responded in silence.

Captain Hannibal swung the whip over his head and brought it against Tavish's back, swinging halfway around between each blow.

"One—" counted the dead-level voice of the first officer Eli. "Two—!"

Tavish remained silent.

"You've got a master over you now! You'll learn to fear me, or I'll flog you fore and aft!"

"Five," called Eli. "Six!"

"Jesus," cried Julot. "Stop him! Please!"

Enraged, the captain turned to Julot with a vicious snap of the whip across his face. "No, not Jesus! Judson Hannibal, that's who! Judson Hannibal! I'm your master now!"

Tavish's fury broke. "You'll call on God in this life or in hell!"

The sound of the whip cracked through the wind. The rain broke in gray sheets. Dreadful silence hung over the ship until the first mate cried: "Captain, you'll kill 'em! Both are unconscious. Save 'em for your sake! We'll need men for the voyage!"

The captain came to himself and with shaking hand signaled the mate to loosen them and carry them down below the forecastle.

The crew was silent while the captain, pompous with his importance, marched the quarterdeck sopping wet in the lashing rain, and at each turn in his cadence, shouted a challenge: "You've a slave driver as your captain. Not even Blackbeard was more of a devil than I. So take heed and be quick to my orders!"

After ranting for some time, he went back to his cabin.

That night below deck, as the ship tossed about in the swells, the crew ate their supper of salt pork and ale in silence. They glanced occasionally toward Tavish and Julot, who lapsed in and out of an unconscious sleep.

It was midnight when the lanky old steward named Tobias crept below, bringing wine and a medicinal salve of balsam.

"It'll soothe the demon-fire a mite. I risk my own skin in showing this kindness, but you seem fair lads. The cap'n swore you'd have nothing until you come and kneel before him."

Tavish gritted as he felt the salve sting. "The captain's insane, or possessed by the devil himself."

"Aye, maybe both. So treat him as he is. He cannot be reasoned with. We've all tasted his wrath. Grovel before him and he'll be appeased."

"I'll grovel before no man. I'll bust the rest of his teeth down his croaking throat," Julot whispered, the raw slice across his face bleeding open again.

"Now, lad, be the nice fellow I can see ye are, and whine just a little, will ye? For your sake! It'll be over a year, an' closer to two, before we dock again in these waters. A word o' wisdom from a soul who's sailed with the captain for many a voyage. He's a lonely, bitter man since the evil touched his flesh in Madagascar."

"Leprosy's too good for him."

"I'll kill him," croaked Julot, moaning softly in pain.

"There's only one way, me lads. Serve him well with fear. Do your miserable tasks till an opportunity comes to jump ship."

"A fine dream," whispered another sailor from the foul darkness. "I've been on board four wretched years."

Julot groaned again. "Four years!"

"Aye, four is enough."

Tavish couldn't imagine being imprisoned so long with the hellish Captain Hannibal. "I'll survive," he said. "For I've an enemy I wish to find, a man by the name of Edmund Clark."

In Dakota Territory on a pleasant fall day in 1874, Ember

sat on the front porch of the wood-frame house at Fort Lincoln. The letters expected from Tavish had not arrived—yet. She fanned herself disconsolately and watched Lottie smiling contentedly into her baby's pretty face. Her musical voice sang a lullaby as he cooed and smiled, reaching little fingers to grab her hair.

> Bye, baby bunting,
> Daddy's gone a-hunting,
> Gone to get a rabbit skin
> To wrap the baby bunting in.

Where was Tavish now? wondered Ember. What was he doing? Did he think of her, or had he already forgotten the night of their goodbye under the soft Dakota sky?

Adjustment to military life at the fort had not come as smoothly for Ember as she had expected, and she admired Lottie's happy outlook—but of course she had Prescott. For Ember, girlish dreams died quickly within the walls of a dusty fort. While Lottie made friends with other wives of career officers, Ember sensed that she didn't belong. She was certain they resented her. She had spoken out at a social gathering in the parlor of Major Sorenson's wife, Dolly, in defense of the Indians' concern over the "Ironhorse chasing away the buffalo." It had been a small discussion that did not even mean that much to her, but still had shut her out. If she hadn't had a headache that day, she was sure she wouldn't have felt prompted to be controversial.

Wade too was disappointed with her. She had embarrassed him, he had said.

"Don't scold her," said Lottie. "She has a right to her opinion."

"Lottie's right. I only spoke out for the poor buffalo—"

"Ember," he said wearily, "your loyalty must be undaunted. There is no sympathy for the Sioux and Cheyenne after raids against settlers. I would think nearly losing your own life when you first came here would have convinced you what these renegade Indians are like."

During her first year at the fort she longed for home. Only the presence of Sassy, her undaunted ally, and Lottie's continued pleading that she stay kept her from leaving. She took solace in Lottie's baby, Jamie, as both Prescott and Wade were gone much of the time.

Then one night little Jamie nearly died after contracting the measles. Ember knelt with Lottie before his crib and vowed him to the Lord's purposes. The baby's decline was the most dreadful day of her life—far worse than when facing the Cheyenne. Now it was the awful prospect of seeing Lottie part with her dearest possession.

"Don't take him, Lord," Ember pleaded. "I know this is an unusual prayer . . . but if in your mercy you let Lottie keep Jamie, I vow to give you the first child from my own future marriage—just the way Hannah did with Samuel. I'll not stand in the way, and I'll teach the child your ways."

Jamie didn't die, and thereafter Ember took more seriously her time alone with God and the Scriptures. Each morning she rose before the others and took her Bible out onto the porch to read and pray. Her favorite book was the Psalms, and she read at least one every morning. She prayed daily for Tavish, and waited . . . but no letter arrived.

"Perhaps," she murmured soberly, "the Lord has someone else He wants me to marry. Maybe He's telling me to be open to someone new who may come into my life."

Ember soon discovered that her restless spirit began to change. She was no longer at the fort out of duty to Lottie but because she believed it was the purpose of God. Like the words of Paul in Philippians, with God's help she could learn to be content in whatever situation the Lord had placed her.

True, she hadn't won the friendship of the other wives, but she had made new friends at the little chapel. They soon ceased looking upon her as a spoiled young girl, bored with the social life at the fort because of her family's status.

24

SWEET SONGBIRDS OF YOUTH

Zanzibar, Isle of Cloves
1875

Tavish could make out the white line of surf on a curving bay, with ragged coral rocks forming a breakwater. The breeze blew gently off the shore and cooled his shirtless torso, deeply tanned by the year that he had sailed the Indian Ocean. The *Dragon* had dropped anchor off the trade islands. The air carried a heady mixture of cloves and sweet tropical flowers to the deck. As the ship gently rolled in pale waters, Tavish looked across the bay at the green-fringed heads of straight palms. The sky still held the faint color of coral and was speckled with blazing stars.

The night, the breeze, the scents that wafted with the rustle of dry palms, was enough to send his mind spinning off into tantalizing dreams of freedom—of standing on the warm white sand with Ember in his arms. . . .

Tavish also dreamed of mutiny, but few of the sailors would join in the dangerous talk. There were weapons in the captain's cabin, but no one was allowed to wait on him except the cabin boy and the old steward, Tobias.

"Mutiny will see us all hanged," Tobias had whispered. "And if we take the ship, it's piracy, no less. Our best bet is to wait till the cap'n dies of his disease. First mate Eli will be a mite kinder."

"He won't die," grumbled Julot. "He gets stronger every day. He's too evil to do us the favor. He knows the entire crew counts the days till we can dump his carcass into the sea."

Tavish and Julot looked for any opportunity to escape, but port call did not come often, and when it did, Hannibal ordered them into shackles.

"Is your captain a fool? You'd jump ship first chance. Nay, you'll sit and dream instead, like I do, remembering better days. There's no hope for me, and there's to be none for you."

Captain Hannibal remained in his cabin and left Eli and the other two mates in command.

The main body of the crew were also not permitted to go ashore, only Eli, and a man named Frost, who was as cold and silent as his name, and the old steward Tobias.

"Why does he hate us so much?" asked Julot.

"He serves the devil," said Tavish.

Tavish didn't understand Eli. The man was civil, yet he refused to oppose the captain. Though the captain cursed him, Eli seemed bound to loyalty. Eventually Tavish learned that Eli was his younger brother.

"We're doomed, mon ami," sighed Julot. "We shall grow old on a leper ship."

Tavish thought of all the weapons stashed away in the captain's cabin. If he could just get his hands on a revolver, even a dagger. Once, near Ceylon, he and Julot had tried to escape. Due to the more civil nature of Eli, Captain Hannibal hadn't been alerted.

Tavish thought much about his father and the land grant along the Hood. Did Kain know what had happened to them? Was he searching? Was Uncle Mathieu? Had his father stayed to work the timber with the financial help of Mathieu?

A thousand thoughts like gnawing rats disturbed his soul, not the least of them being the memory of Ember.

His deep green eyes, as warm as the tropics, narrowed beneath black lashes as he thought of her, remembering the moment he'd held her in his arms, remembering the sweetness of her lips.

He had promised to write her at Fort Lincoln. What did she think of him now that no message had arrived in over a year? Did she believe he had forgotten her? It was the vision of Ember with starlight in her hair that kept him sane after months of toil under the hideous Captain Hannibal. And he had a faith in God that held rock solid, grounded on the Scriptures that his mother Vonette had him memorize as a boy. He remembered, too, his father's torn frock coat, the bullet hole in his dusty derby hat, the Bible he carried as they rode the train camps. As the waves of treachery and evil washed and pounded over his soul, he told himself that God had a purpose in all this, and the angry waves subsided.

But the temptations to doubt, to be bitter, were constant, and the struggle was sometimes hourly, the war never won, for it began the moment he opened his eyes until he shut them at night.

If God had a purpose, it eluded Tavish. How could good come from the year he had already spent on Captain Hannibal's ship? What if he were here for ten more years?

His prayers to escape went unanswered, and the heavens seemed bronze rather than tropic blue. His circumstances made no sense to him, for he could think of a hundred more important things he could be doing with his life than enduring the captain's evil passions for making others miserable.

Perhaps the one good he could see in his situation was the need for endurance in well doing, and the faith to believe that one day he would walk free.

But now, as he felt the heavy shackles on his wrists—for the captain had ordered him and Julot bound during the ship's anchor off Zanzibar Island—the hope of walking the warm white sand as a free man seemed as foreign as the smells of spice that drifted to him, taunting of better things that lay just outside his reach.

He squinted into the deepening twilight of lavender, looking toward Tumbatu Island. Men, dark silhouettes in white garb, were barely visible in the rising of the full moon that seemed to come straight up from the calm sea. They appeared to be loading several small boats, and after a few minutes, one of the boats shoved off from shore and rowed toward them. It was too soon for Eli and the others to be returning. Supplies and cargo for the Barbary Coast would not be loaded until daybreak.

After a time he heard the boat below the ship, the sound of the rope ladder, of scuffling feet and low voices. He came alert. The first man over the ship's rail was Frost, followed by one of the sailors, then the old steward Tobias.

Tavish didn't know why, but his expectations soared like a songbird flying toward the eastern sunrise. He stood to his bare feet, wearing a pair of baggy white cotton trousers.

The steward came toward him, while Frost and the sailor stood guard, hiding in the shadows of the rigging.

Julot, too, stood, catching the silent enthusiasm that gripped Tavish.

Tobias had the key and Tavish felt it turn in the lock that held his wrists bound in chains behind his back. In a moment his hands were free and Tobias pushed a gleaming dagger into his hand. Their eyes met wordlessly. Tobias gestured his head toward the side of the ship and Tavish knew he was to make his escape. He hesitated long enough to see that Julot was unshackled. They went as nimbly as sleek, muscled cats to the rail. Tavish held the dagger, ready to make the plunge into the blue waters of Zanzibar and freedom—then he stopped.

From the shadows of the ship a figure had emerged, a massive ugly form that held a pistol in his one good hand—the hand that wheeled a whip so efficiently. Captain Hannibal stepped into the moonlight, his face contorted with anger, and he pointed the gun at his steward.

"Tobias, you mutinous scum—"

A shot cracked and spat a tiny flash in the darkness, and Tobias buckled. Another shot followed, but from a revolver belonging to Frost. Captain Hannibal staggered forward, shot in the back. He came toward Tavish, his leprous hand outstretched with hate in an attempt to infect him before his own death. Tavish gripped his dagger, but Frost fired again and Hannibal fell facedown, his fingers, like claws, still grasping for Tavish's leg.

Old Tobias had managed to push himself forward onto his knees, and Tavish knelt beside him, ripping his shirt away to look at the bullet wound. He saw little reason for hope but was determined to take him with them.

"Away," rasped Tobias, "before the others come. They'll have heard the shots—"

"We'll take you," said Tavish. "If you die, old friend, you'll do so a free man on the fragrant beach of Zanzibar! Julot! Quick! Away!"

Frost and the other sailor had already gone over the side and were waiting when Tavish and Julot entered the boat, carrying Tobias. They shoved off, the oars slicing through the water.

The old man died in his arms on the way to the shadowed shore where palm trees beckoned. Tavish continued to hold him until they reached a deserted stretch of white sand on the other side of the bay. There, they buried Tobias. Beneath a white moon, a tropic breeze, and the dry rattle of palm branches they had their first wind of freedom.

It was late, and the moon was setting when at last the four of them raced along the white sand that felt warm to their feet. Tavish felt the trade wind blowing against him, felt the waves splashing against his legs. Frost and the sailor ran behind them laughing, throwing back their heads, and Frost extended his big brown hands up toward the smiling stars. It was the first time that Tavish had ever heard him laugh.

They began the trek across the island that set them on a new journey, one that was slow and burdened with risk. Tavish and Julot worked their way below the horn of Africa, across the waters of the South Atlantic, and up the coasts of the Americas to San Francisco. When at last they arrived in early spring, it was 1876, the year of the nation's centennial.

June 1876

While both Lottie and Ember looked forward with anticipation to Prescott's and Wade's release from the cavalry and their return as a family to Washington Territory, neither of them had expected the ominous news of the Battle of the Little Bighorn.

Lieutenant Colonel George Armstrong Custer and the Seventh Cavalry had confronted Sitting Bull and his chieftains at Yellowstone for the last time.

"No survivors," came the mournful announcement at the fort.

Prescott and Wade were dead.

At first Ember felt only numbness and disbelief, then guilt. She blamed herself for not praying enough for the two men. In fact, she should have had a concern for the souls of all of the soldiers who had ridden out that morning. Despondency set in. Lottie was a widow. How would she raise Jamie without a father?

Ember looked around at weeping children, little boys sitting outside with heads hung low, knowing their father would not ride back through the fort's big gates. Black was hung everywhere—black, and yellow ribbons.

Ember watched Lottie smooth the yellow ribbon that Prescott had given her.

"One day Jamie will want the mementos belonging to his father. He'll read about the Battle of the Little Bighorn, of Custer, Sitting Bull, Crazy Horse, and the Seventh Cavalry. And he'll feel proud of his father, who died with saber in hand. Yes, Jamie will cherish the yellow ribbon."

After Lottie carefully packed the ribbon in the trunk with Prescott's other things she burst into tears.

Ember too wept and cradled Jamie, who also began to sob. "Daddy," he kept saying.

Ember sent a telegraph to Uncle Mack and Aunt Cleo in Port Townsend telling them of their son's death, and that she would be making arrangements to journey home with Lottie.

Ember's one desire now was to escape the fort, but their plans were foiled by endless obstacles. Several other women and their families were also making plans to travel home, and this caused her and Lottie weeks of delay—and of enduring vivid memories at the fort and the memorial ceremonies for the Seventh Cavalry. Already more troops were arriving from forts Rice, Benton, and Keogh. Newspaper reporters arrived; so did sympathetic town folk from Bismarck, St. Paul, and even farther east. Until the military could arrange to escort wives and families to Duluth, Ember settled down, resolved to wait.

News of Colonel Custer and the massacre shared the newspaper headlines with the nation's centennial celebrations. When she could no longer read about the massacre, then she read about the thousands of Americans who were said to have ignored the depressed state of the economy and had journeyed to Philadelphia to enjoy the Centennial Exhibition. There, among all the wonders of the new industrial age, they could explore George Pullman's latest train car. The hotel on wheels, which he had fittingly named the *President*, was richly superb and made for ease and comfort.

> "This railroad car foreshadows a new elegance in transcontinental travel. . . . Pullman has spared no expense in outfitting the *President* with exquisite furnishings, filigreed woods, chandeliers, washrooms, and a kitchen equipped with restaurant-size oven and broiler . . ."

At the moment, Ember told herself she would have settled for a boxcar if she could leave Fort Lincoln. At last the day arrived. With Lottie, Jamie, and Sassy, and a number of trunks, they left Fort Lincoln early one morning, traveling in a group of women with a cavalry escort. They arrived in Bismarck only to find they would have to wait all day and late into the night at the train depot because summer thunderstorms had brought torrential rains and flash floods.

"Section of the rail's been washed out," said the agent, "but the delay won't be much longer now."

The storm brought others seeking shelter into the already crowded depot, and Ember paid scant attention to the strangers all wet and hungry until a man entered, alone.

Perhaps it was the way he entered the lobby—sort of cool and unapproachable—that first brought her attention to him. All the others had come rushing in, talking of the terrible weather. He entered silently, as though accustomed to torrential rains and floods, and a good deal more. He stood without moving, scanning the room and its passengers as though searching for someone.

His clothing was rugged. His knee-length dark coat matched his trousers and his stiff-brimmed hat was low. A scar across his chin added to the startling, rugged good looks. Everything about him seemed dark—the hair, the narrow black mustache, the eyes. She wasn't certain about the eyes; they could not be seen.

Ember looked away and drew the blanket up around sleeping Jamie. Thank goodness he remained asleep through the lightning and loud peals of thunder. If he awoke now he would be hungry, and Lottie had nothing to give him but a tin of milk and some hard sugar cookies that Sassy had brought from the fort. She glanced at Lottie and Sassy—they were both sleeping, curled up on the blanket on the floor beside the bench where she sat.

Holding the sleeping boy a little closer, she stole a glance back at the stranger, surprised that she remained the bold object of his attention. She saw him look at Jamie. Feeling a tinge of embarrassment, she turned her head away again, and leaned back against the wall, lifting her hood up over her flame hair as though she were chilled and wished to go to sleep.

Through half-closed eyes she watched him make his way through the crowded lobby full of resting travelers lying on the floor. As he stepped around several others talking in low tones, his coat moved aside and Ember saw a gun belt with a revolver. The holster was tied down—a sign that when he drew his gun, he expected it to come out smooth and fast.

He helped himself to a mug of black coffee and looked back at her, taking a swallow. He said something to the ticket agent, who drew out a ledger and began poring over numbers and names. The agent peered over his spectacles at Ember, said something, and shook his head no.

Ember's skin crawled. What was he asking the agent about her?

A flash of lightning ripped across the dark sky. Seated by the window, the brightness startled her. Above the depot roof a loud crack of thunder shook the building. She looked quickly to Jamie, who stirred in his sleep but thankfully did not awaken.

She tensed, not moving as she felt the stranger's presence. She saw his booted feet in front of her, and glanced up past his gun belt to his open jacket, then his face. The eyes were green. As hard as glass. Almost startling against the bronzed face.

Ember took refuge from the onslaught by slipping into a blank stare.

For a moment he simply looked at her and she hoped desperately that her skin remained pale. His mouth moved into a smile beneath the mustache.

"Hello, Ember."

"Tavish. . . ?"

His present manner had not been all that gentlemanly, but when she smiled, she noted that the gentleness of it affected him, if only momentarily.

"You've—you've—changed," she stammered.

"Must be the scar." He scanned her.

Her heart thudded and she could hardly breathe. For lack of anything else to say, she murmured, "Not from combat with another Cheyenne, I hope?"

He smiled faintly. "Not this time" was all he said. He looked pointedly at Jamie, but his expression could not be read. "Nice-looking boy. At first I thought he was yours. The agent told me he belongs to Lottie."

Did she recognize a hint of relief in his voice? It was difficult to tell for certain, and she was reminded how he had once again simply walked out of her life, this time for three years. If she were married with a child it would serve him right—what did he expect? Not a single letter had come from him in all this time. What was he doing in Bismarck? She had an uneasy notion that he had not come looking for her but someone else—Wade?

She was glad to change the subject. "His name is Jamie. He's almost three."

"I understand Wade is dead, along with Lottie's husband."

She felt a tiny wince at the bluntness. There was a hardness to his voice that surpassed even the tone he had used in the past when speaking of her cousin. After three years was he still angry about West Point? As she looked into the granite eyes she held back a shudder. There was something more now . . . what?

"Wade died with Custer. You heard about the Little Bighorn?"

"It's been in the newspapers for almost two months. Custer and all his fancy soldiers wiped out by Sitting Bull."

This time she had not imagined the cynicism in his tone. There wasn't a bit of sympathy oozing from his manner. The Tavish Wilder standing before her wearing a gun belt and watching her with those riveting green eyes was not the man she remembered—or was he?

She felt herself turning warm. There was something different about him. . . . He was older, of course, and the hard lessons of life would have left some change. But the changes went far deeper.

"I see you're holding up well in the early stages of grief for the fallen hero."

Was that a compliment? She didn't think so. "I would think, Mr. Wilder, that you above all others would know the source of my strength."

Ember drew her cloak about her as if cold and asked the question that had plagued her for three silent years. "Have you done well on your land in Washington? You're married now, Mr. Wilder?"

Mr. Wilder. How false her address sounded, and she wondered if he saw through it.

He lifted the cup to drink his coffee, watching her evenly. "I've been out of the country for two years."

Curious, she briefly let her eyes fall over him. "Oh?" she said casually. "How interesting."

"I wouldn't recommend it to others."

She glanced at the deep scar on the side of his chin. A knife wound? Something else? How had it happened? Her curiosity grew, but she knew she couldn't bring herself to press for details, for he seemed a stranger. Had she really been in this man's arms that night under the stars?

"You went away on business for the railroad?"

"Not exactly . . . shipping business."

"Oh? To Europe?" Was it her imagination, or was there something unpleasant in his smile.

"No. Madagascar, Tunis, Zanzibar—places like that."

Something was very wrong. How had he become involved in shipping, when it was timber that had filled his earlier dreams? Or did that idealistic young man no longer exist? Somehow she felt a pang, hoping desperately that he did, that whatever had hardened him had not left permanent scars on his soul. He was wearing a gun belt. Who did he work for and what did he do? And what was he doing here now at this train depot? Yet it made no sense unless he had come searching for Wade.

"Did your father go to Africa with you?"

"No. Kain is dead."

"Oh! I am sorry—how did it happen?"

"I expect to find that out. He died while I was away."

She searched his face and he seemed to know she did, for a bland expression appeared.

"You no longer work for the railroad?" she asked.

"No."

"Are you here to board the train?"

"I'm thinking about it. I may stay awhile longer. I've recently heard some disquieting news from Fort Lincoln."

Another Indian attack, she concluded, for she couldn't think of another reason why he would be interested in visiting the fort now that Wade was dead and she and Lottie were on their way back to Port Townsend. She didn't want to think about any more Indian attacks, and pushed his reason for staying out of her mind.

"Then you're no longer planning to go into timber? I don't mean to sound probing, only . . ."

"Not at all," came the too-silky voice. "You see, I'm curious about you too. Why you would stay at the fort for three years when you could have made the social rounds at Saratoga and Europe. What caused you to stay so long while Wade pretended to chase Indians?"

He was beginning to nettle her. Obviously not even her cousin's death in the massacre had tempered his dislike, and she didn't like the insinuation that she still required girlish frivolities.

"Lottie needed me to stay with her—and perhaps I preferred the company of a certain soldier."

"He must have been some gallant soldier to keep you there so long."

Her eyes narrowed. There was no particular soldier, of course, only casual escorts to outings, but he didn't know that, and she wasn't so certain she wished him to understand after he had failed to write her as he had promised.

"I suppose he also died with Custer?"

"And what of you, Mr. Wilder? What interesting adventures might you have had on your voyage to such exotic places as Zanzibar?" she asked with acid sweetness.

He smiled. "Adventures I'll remember for the rest of my life."

She had read about the beauty of the tropics and felt irked.

"So you're grieving Wade's death, of course?"

Now why would he ask that? It would be unnatural for her not to grieve her cousin's death. She looked at him curiously and his gaze sobered.

"Both Lottie and I have tried to measure it all in the light of what our faith tells us. You would know perhaps better than I, since you're a minister's son, that trials and hardships come from the hand of God for our good—"

She stopped when his smooth demeanor cracked for the first time. His faint smile was gone. He was frustrated and it took her by surprise.

"You are right," he said. "I would know doctrine better than most. So we needn't discuss it. How much did Mack and Cleo Ridgeway write you about what's been going on in Port Townsend for the past three years?"

She recognized his unmistakable anger just below the surface. "They wrote me occasionally, why?"

"The rich world of Jay Cooke's Northern Pacific came crashing down. Mack was heavily invested in the NP. Did he take a hard wallop in his finances? Port Townsend is in a recession since Tacoma won the railroad terminus. Did either Mack or Cleo write of this?"

Ember frowned. "Not that it's any of your concern, but yes, he did lose a great deal of money."

"And the Ridgeway timber investments?"

She held Jamie closer. "Yes . . . although, we haven't lost as much as Uncle Mack did in the railroad. Why?"

Did she see a faint glimmer of satisfaction?

"Did they write you or Lottie about anything else?" he asked. "News from home? Maybe trouble along the Hood with certain lumberjacks?"

"No. Is there something I should know about?" she asked. "Something to concern me?"

He studied her for a long moment. For the first time his eyes softened.

"No. Nothing," he said.

The rain beat against the windows.

"You seem to know a good deal about the economy of Port

Townsend, having been gone for two years. Have you been back there?"

"I've just come from there, and I went to see an uncle in Portland."

He offered no more and she asked, "You're going back to the Northwest?" After three years absence without a word, she wasn't certain she wished to rekindle old feelings.

"I didn't think I would. Not yet anyway."

She moved uncomfortably on the bench. "You sound as though you've changed your mind."

He scanned her. "I have."

She said nothing and, under his gaze, busied herself with Jamie.

He looked at his empty cup, then out the window. "Rain," he said easily. "I've always liked it."

"You seem to be able to change life's plans very quickly."

"I had no choice. When that happens, they're easy to change."

"You're staying in Bismarck?"

"I've accomplished all I wanted to here. I'll be going to Fort Lincoln for a time."

She tensed, and her eyes came back to his. Searching for what?

"Looks like the workers fixed the washed-out track," he said. "I hear the train coming."

Ember now believed that Tavish had come here expecting her to know something, but what it might be she had not the foggiest notion. Was it her lack of knowledge that now altered his plans about returning to Port Townsend?

"What is it about Port Townsend I'm supposed to know?" she asked bluntly. "What did you expect Mack and Cleo to write me?"

As she stood looking into his eyes the train came grinding to a halt, letting off a puff of white steam. Jamie awoke and began to cry and Ember was distracted. Lottie and Sassy also awoke. She brought Jamie to her and when Ember turned around, Tavish Wilder had gone.

She glanced about the depot but didn't see him. She went to the window to look out, wondering if he would change his mind and board the train going northwest, but he did not. The last she saw of him, he was walking in the opposite direction.

Odd, she thought. *How very strange.*

As the train pulled out of Bismarck, she looked out the window and rebuked herself for feeling a tug of disappointment that he had not come. It was the same feeling that she had felt the night he disappeared from her life three years before.

As the train gained speed down the track, Ember wondered what surprises would await her in Port Townsend. What was it that Mack and Cleo had not written her about?

25

BRADLEY MORRISON

January 1877

Wade was alive!

He arrived in Port Townsend one icy night after the New Year with a heroic tale. Colonel Custer had entrusted a letter to him to bring to the general. Wade was captured by a party of Arapaho, known to be kinder to their captives than the Cheyenne or Sioux, held for two months, and through the mercy of a young Indian girl, eventually escaped and made his treacherous journey back to the fort, nearly dying of thirst.

The tale was riveting to little Jamie. His uncle was a hero, an Indian fighter like Colonel Custer and his martyred father, Prescott. If there were doubts in the rest of the family, or questions about why a major would be sent with a message instead of a corporal, no one cared to ask.

The one thing that mattered to the Ridgeways was that Wade was home safe, his years in the Seventh Cavalry expired, and he was a welcome addition to the family in Washington. Mack set out immediately to involve his son in the business decisions of the timber enterprise that was facing hard economic times.

As the seasons turned to spring, summer, and fall, Ember's frustration with the elusive and enigmatic Tavish Wilder had reached its moment of decision. Once again she had not heard from him since their brief meeting that night in the train depot at Bismarck, nor could she discover any news about him in the Port Townsend area.

Going back several years to search into his past, she discovered little to explain Tavish's behavior at Bismarck. The Wilders had settled somewhere out on the Hood for a few months, then simply packed up one day and left like a passing shadow in the night. No one had heard from them since. They had left a cabin that some old drifter had lived in for a time before it burned down one night.

"I knew he'd never make a success of it," said Wade. "The Wilders are drifters, gunfighters. They blow away with the wind."

As 1877 drew to a dismal close, Aunt Cleo approached Ember on the subject she knew was inevitable.

"The family will want you to marry soon. Wade, too, will need to take a wife, and hopefully Lottie will snap out of her bereavement to marry again in the future. Jamie will need a father. But it's you we're concerned with now."

Ember resented her businesslike approach, and her insensitivity toward Lottie, who sat doing cross-stitching in a chair by the fireplace.

"Whom I marry will be my own concern. I won't be bartered off to the wealthiest bidder," said Ember, standing abruptly and walking to the fire to warm her hands.

Cleo ignored her and tapped the end of her crutch. "There are several men the family has in mind."

"Is that all that matters, who the family has in mind?" snapped Ember.

Lottie bit her lip and tilted her dark head over her work, her needle flying.

"There's a DeWaine cousin in Sacramento in the newspaper business—destined to become rich," said Cleo. "We could use a good newspaper on our side," she mused. "There's also Bradley Morrison in Portland. You met him last week at the dinner Mack gave Mr. Morrison."

Ember knew quite well who Bradley was without being told. The truth was, she had rather liked him. He appeared to be a Christian gentleman and had treated her with care.

"His father's in the NP," Cleo continued.

"Other than money and a family background, does anything else matter in my choice of a husband?" asked Ember wryly. "My Christian faith? Love?"

"Come, Ember dear, be reasonable."

"I am reasonable. It's right that the family should have something to say about my marriage, but the ultimate decision is mine. Good heavens! I'm the one who must live with him when everyone else goes home!"

"Didn't you say Bradley attends church regularly? I'd think he'd be the perfect choice for you," said Cleo. "And he's a gentleman."

Ember scowled a little, for she had no argument against her aunt's comments on Bradley's qualities.

"You're all of twenty-one now; you can't hold off indefinitely."

"Mama, you're heartless," said Lottie with exasperation, laying aside her cross-stitching. "Let her be. You were twenty-eight before you married Father."

"That was different. Most men wouldn't look at a woman with two permanent crutches. Can you see me in a French gown at one of the town balls? Mack was different."

"But if I wait," said Ember dryly, "I may do better than Bradley. Think how pleased Uncle Mack would be if I married the governor of Washington?"

Cleo looked at her, tiny lines furrowing above her dark eyes. "Governor?"

Ember smiled pleasantly. "Of course. One day the territory is bound to become a state."

"You're very amusing, Ember," said Cleo, sighing as she used her crutches to stand up from the divan. "But not very clever. And regardless of your stubborn streak, you'll marry soon. Bradley is coming to dinner tomorrow night."

❖

In the summer of 1879, the talk circulating around dinner tables and ladies' luncheons in Port Townsend was the looming engagement between Bradley Morrison and Miss Ember Ridgeway. Photographs of the two of them together appeared on the society page of the *Leader*, with details of their attendance at prestigious balls and dinners, and on family outings aboard a private yacht off Port Townsend Bay.

Laughing as the sea spray wet their faces, five-year-old Jamie tugged at Lottie's hand, edging her toward the side of Grandpa Mack's boat. They were off Whidbey Island, viewing Port Townsend.

"Look, Mama, boats! Lots of 'em! An' bigger 'an Gran'pa's!"

"What did you say?" cried Mack, pretending to be insulted.

Lottie laughed as Jamie looked ashamed. "But yours is nicer, Gran'pa," he said graciously.

Mack laughed. "I'm glad somebody thinks so," and with a gleam in his eyes he looked meaningfully in Cleo's direction. She sat in a low seat on the windswept deck of the boat, with a blanket around her legs. She grimaced at him, for her dislike of the water was well known to the family.

The sea spray and wind from off the coast of Whidbey Island invigorated Ember. She smiled at Bradley, whose shock of chestnut hair whipped on his broad forehead beneath the tight-fitting surge hat. His brown eyes smiled at her, and she told herself she felt at peace with her decision to marry him the following year.

In silence, they held to the boat railing, gazing across the water to Port Townsend spanning along the shore where the Strait of Juan de Fuca turned into Admiralty Inlet.

"From here we can see every sailing vessel coming in and out of Puget Sound," she told him.

Ember had come to love the town, and her eyes took in the rows of buildings filling the narrow flat between the waterfront and the windswept bluff. In the uplands, fine Victorian homes and churches looked back with an air of sedate majesty.

"Mama, look!" Jamie told Lottie. "A big house on the cliff!"

Ember too followed in the direction Jamie pointed. The mansion was a pretentious Queen Anne style in the last stages of construction, with flaunting gabled windows, intricate wrought-iron work, and a steep roof.

"Hush, don't ruin my surprise for your aunt Ember," said Bradley, and smiled at Ember's gasp.

"Oh, Bradley, you didn't!"

He slipped an arm around her shoulders and drew her to his side as they looked across the water to the cliff. "I knew how much the place had captured your fancy. It's not certain yet, and the builder has turned down other prospective buyers. But I've arranged an appointment to give you a tour. I'm looking to purchase a wedding present," he said softly, and Ember could only look at him, speechless.

The mansion had been a topic of speculative conversation on everyone's list for months, and Ember had fallen in love with it from the moment she saw it.

"Who's the builder? Another newcomer to Port Town-send?" asked Wade lazily, stretching his booted legs out and resting them on a cushion. The sunlight caught his hair, and his tanned face was more smooth and relaxed than Ember remembered seeing it in many years. He lifted his glass and emptied it.

"Henry Villard says she's from Quebec," said Bradley. "A friend of his who's come to the Portland area and become rich in railroad and steam navigation."

Several weeks later, the coach bringing Ember and Bradley to see the mansion came to a stop along the windy bluff. Ember peered out the misted window, feeling the strong gusts from the Pacific buffeting the side of the coach.

"Are you certain you'll like it here with the winds?" he asked.

"It's wonderful," she whispered. "I've always loved the sea."

The wind whinnied around the corners of the coach and seeped through cracks to chill her ankles and hands, but at the moment she hardly noticed.

"Wait here, darling," said Bradley, opening the door and stepping out.

She watched him, in black top hat, gloves, and overcoat,

walk up the cobbled carriageway to the front steps. A servant opened the door.

Ember didn't wait and, lifting her skirt, stepped from the coach. The wind struck her, and she lifted a hand to her hair. It was done in the new style, with long cascading curls drawn to the crown of her head and trailing below her shoulder. She had bought a new sailor-style dress for the occasion. The neck was high, and it had a jacket-type bodice that was hip level at the front and sides. Both her jacket and basque were decorated with wide trimming and gold buttons, with two rows of the gold trim to form the sailor collar. The sleeves were long and flared slightly at the wrists, and the skirt had an attractive tieback that fanned out into a short train.

Ember went up the cobbled walk toward the porch as Bradley returned, a smile on his face.

"The serving man says the owner is here. He wants to show it to you himself."

"The owner is a 'he'? I thought you said 'she' was from Quebec, a friend of Henry Villard?"

Bradley gave a laugh. "A little joke of Villard's. I only just found out myself. The builder prefers to work out of the limelight away from the society page, and Villard covered for him."

Ember stopped.

Bradley looked down at her, smiling, and took her elbow to lead her across the porch through the wide-open doorway where light from the chandelier fell brightly.

"No! I've changed my mind—I don't want to see it, I don't want to go inside." She turned, heart thudding, intent on an escape to the safety of the coach.

Bradley caught her arm, his expression startled. "Ember, what's come over you?"

"I don't want the mansion. I've changed my mind."

"But you've wanted it for months!"

She glanced back. The looming mansion stared down at her, faceless, mysterious, and grand. As clouds rolled in from the sea, fingers of gray mist wrapped about its walls with a secrecy that matched its elusive owner.

"Darling, be reasonable," he said. "We've made the appointment for the tour, and he's come all the way from Portland to meet with us. He knows it's a wedding gift."

He propelled her back up the steps and in through the doors. A flood of light showered down upon her as she stopped beside Bradley in the entryway. A polished mahogany stairway spanned before her. Above, the Viennese chandelier glittered.

Ember looked at Tavish. He waited on the stairs leaning against the banister, arms folded, meticulously dressed in an expensive square-cut black dress coat. His good looks were startling. The sleeves were close-fitting with turned-back cuffs accentuating his masculine build. The waistcoat was single-breasted with a deep V-shaped front, and the trousers were narrow with a braid running down either side from the waist. The spotless white evening shirt had a high, closed collar. A diamond stickpin was prominent on the black jacket and winked boldly at her.

Ember's throat went dry and her heart thudded so loudly in her ears that she didn't hear Bradley introducing her.

There was a mocking hint to his smile as Tavish scanned her, and the warm green of his eyes glittered. He came to meet her.

"Darling, this is Mr. Villard's friend, T.D. Wilder. Mr. Wilder, my fiancee, Miss Ember Ridgeway."

How dare he do this to me? The rogue! Well!—she wouldn't give him the satisfaction of seeing her crumble.

Ember offered him what she hoped to be an affectation of surprise, even as her eyes faintly challenged with irritation. "Why—it's Mister LeBrett—isn't it?" She hesitated then offered a gloved hand. "Let's see now . . . I met you—?" and she allowed her voice to falter as though she couldn't remember. Her soft winged brows formed a pucker.

"Wilder," he corrected silkily. "T.D. Wilder. We met on the night a Cheyenne had high hopes of stealing your hair," he finished, bending over her hand. Her stylish gloves had open fingers and she felt them pressed to his lips.

She pulled back suddenly. His gaze held hers and she flushed angrily when he smiled.

"Then you do remember me, Miss Ridgeway."

Rage flooded in like the waves of the sea as she understood that Tavish had deliberately deceived her, yes even tricked her into coming here with Bradley to look at the mansion! *His* mansion! She would never forgive him for this embarrassment and shock!

As he looked down at her with mocking green eyes, she had the unexpected realization, however, that he didn't care if she did forgive him. As she searched his face she could see that he, too, was angry. She read the cool resentment in his smile.

"Yes, I remember you, Mr. Wilder, though it has been many years. I'd almost forgotten."

"You two know each other?" asked Bradley. "That's pleasant. So this is the man who rescued you and Lottie from the Cheyenne." Bradley turned to him with a smile. "Well, Mr. Wilder, I'm deeply grateful to you."

"Yes, I could see how you would be. I've delivered you a mansion and a bride to go with it."

Tavish looked at Ember. "I understand you're interested in purchasing my house for your honeymoon, Miss Ridgeway."

Ember felt the blood drain from her face.

"I'm charmed that you find my taste to your liking. Permit me to show you the view of the sea from the master bedroom."

Her throat went dry. *How dare he?*

His eyes held hers. And a sardonic smile appeared. "But before I show you about, perhaps we'd better discuss prices. I wouldn't want to disappoint your upcoming groom. You see, I've put a great amount of money into this mansion and I expect to get it back with a substantial profit. My tastes have become rather extravagant recently." He studied her. "Can you and Bradley afford it?"

Ember felt the words strike deeply, bringing emotional hurt. As their gazes held, her feelings rose to the verge of tears, and she turned furiously and sped out the open door, feeling the icy wind buffet her. The tears stung her eyes as she walked briskly to the coach.

On the way back to Ridgeway House, Bradley was silent and Ember stared out the window.

"Why didn't you tell me about Wilder before?" he asked at last, his voice chill and stiff.

Had Tavish said more to him after she left?

"I haven't heard from him in years," she said dully. "We met briefly at Bismarck soon after Custer's battle. Before that he had been gone for three years without a word. And before that—"

"He's here to stay," he said quietly.

Ember rejected the nervous thrill. *No! Not this time! Not again!* She listened to the horses' hoofs echoing over the wet cobbles.

"I don't want to discuss Mr. Wilder," she said. "Not now, not in the future."

He turned his head and looked at her, his jaw line tense. "What about us?"

She bit her lip, then turned her head away to look out the window, feeling miserable. A smothering emotion of anger and frustration descended upon her like the blinding fog that swirled about the coach.

"I've not changed my mind about the engagement," she said.

He took her gloved hand between his, squeezing it so tightly that Ember winced. "We'll announce it in the paper this Sunday. Would that be suitable to you?"

Ember's eyes filled with hot tears. She stared out the window stiffly. "Yes. Quite suitable."

26

STRANGER IN TOWN

Ember wondered how Tavish Wilder had been able to emerge from the dusty black jeans and boots of a track layer to become an empire builder with a classic derby hat. Did anyone in the family know yet who was the mysterious new stranger in town?

It was the generation of sudden giants emerging from what appeared to be nowhere. These men had worked, schemed, and maneuvered their way to the top through a long, arduous struggle. Yet no one noticed them until they were "there," and then people spoke of "sudden successes."

Mack had been one of them, even though he was a distant Ridgeway cousin. The Houston side of the family had never been wealthy, but roamed the gold camps in British Columbia and Alaska in search of a big find. Like Tavish, Mack had come from a rugged background. He had become rich and powerful suddenly—only to lose it all in the collapse of the nation's economy in 1873. Now Mack was again in debt, and the Ridgeway holdings in Port Townsend, Seattle, and Tacoma tottered on a cracked foundation just awaiting the final quake. There was hope, however. Mack had packed his bags and gone to St. Paul to meet with the financiers of the Northern Pacific Railroad. He had written Cleo and the family that the NP was rising from the dust and ashes like the fabled Phoenix. The "Sweet Railroad" was again making a strong showing under its most recent president, a man by the name of Billings, who'd taken the place of Jay Cooke. Reorganization had allowed the resale of its lands, providing cash. Along with newer investors, friends within the government land office had also issued new pamphlets advertising Dakota and Minnesota acreage in order to attract more settlers. "The best lands in the Northwest for general farming purposes are on the line of the NP," they read.

How had Tavish gotten his money? Ember wondered. More importantly, why had he come to Port Townsend?

Since the dramatic encounter at the Wilder mansion on the windy bluff she had not seen nor heard from him. It was just as well that he hadn't tried to contact her, she told herself, uncertain whether or not she would ever speak to him again.

It didn't take long, however, for Ember to discover that she needn't have worried about what her response should be. The stranger named T.D. Wilder appeared to go out of his way to avoid contact. *He's arrogant,* she thought. *His new wealth has gone to his head.*

On a later occasion the following spring, Ember did catch sight of him in town. It was a cool, rainy day with the wind beginning to blow as she rode in the carriage with Lottie and Sassy on the way back from shopping. Ember saw a fine coach parked in front of the Jefferson Courthouse and Tavish was coming down the steps wearing a fashionable overcoat.

Looking more and more like big success, she thought grudgingly. Could this be the same man she remembered fighting the Cheyenne, and the dark stranger in the train depot at Bismarck?

As her carriage passed, she found she couldn't squelch her curiosity and peered out the window. He glanced her way. At the instant their eyes met she knew he recognized her, but he made no indication that he did, and slipping inside the carriage, he shut the door. She caught a last glimpse of his coach disappearing into the rain.

Ember settled back against the seat, fighting a growing sense of unease. Her eyes strayed back toward the Jefferson Courthouse. What would he be doing in the courthouse?

During the next month his elusive presence remained a topic of interest in town. It was said that he came and went, saying little to anyone in town except his banker—and the minister at St. Paul's Church—the little church on the windswept bluff not far from his mansion. The proximity to the historic church with the famous bell that had saved many from shipwreck—including Ira D. Sankey who worked with Moody—had been the cause for Ember wanting the mansion. It was only a short walk from the mansion's front yard up the path to the church.

Whatever her inclinations about Tavish might have been, they came to an abrupt halt two months later. As she left Sunday morning worship at the little church and walked to her waiting coach parked on the bluff, she was hailed by Wilbur Franks from the leading town bank.

"My dear! My dear! Can you spare a moment?"

She hesitated, for the old financial wizard huffing his way toward her seemed always to bring her bad news about her private holdings. And everything either began with, or ended with, words of endearment.

"Yes?" she asked warily. "I haven't much time, Mr. Franks. Lottie isn't well today and she's waiting in the coach with Jamie."

"It won't take long, my dear. It's about the holdings of your dearly departed great-aunt."

"More debt?" she asked uneasily, never dreaming that Great-aunt Macie had left loans due on the property and house she had left her at Tacoma. It was all she could do recently to make the payments to the bank.

"Tut, tut, expenditures is the better way to speak of these delicate matters. I regret to tell you, my dear, that since the shipping interest has been doing poorly it has gone into foreclosure. The other investors have managed to get out with Mr. Wilder's assistance. But he doesn't feel he can continue to prop up your faltering investment unless you come up with a good deal of money between now and the end of April."

Ember stared at him. Then, as though compelled to do so, she turned her head and looked toward the mansion built not far from the church. Usually she managed not to look in that direction, pretending it didn't exist. As her eyes squinted, they fell on the distant but familiar figure of a man leaning against a porch pillar, watching them.

He was deliberately buying the mortgages on everything she owned!

"I've taken the liberty to speak a word on your behalf in the ear of Mr. Morrison, the father of your fiance, but he informs me his own holdings have come upon hard times. He's struggling to stay in the black," continued the banker. "Mr. Villard and his associates are buying them."

Ember wondered if the railroad baron's "associates" might also include Tavish. Was he also out to ruin Bradley?

She looked toward the mansion, but he had gone inside and shut his door.

"How much will I get for the shipping shares, and my store?" she asked coldly.

He sighed. "He's been very generous, my dear, absorbing all the debt."

"That's all!"

He looked apologetic. "We were not able to find any other buyers. He insists it will take months before he will even begin to break even."

"Break even, my foot! He's deliberately taking everything I own. There must be something I can do!"

He sighed. "Times are quite difficult. Perhaps if you went to Mr. Wilder and explained your position—"

"No," said Ember flatly.

On the way home, Ember was silent, not wishing to pour out her woes to Lottie or Sassy, who held Jamie on her lap. *Why is he doing this to me, to the family?* she wondered. *Vengeance?*

Her mind trailed back to that night at Fort Lincoln when a message had arrived for Wade concerning Kain Wilder. After these years, did Tavish continue to blame Wade for his father's capture by the Cheyenne? And then there was the matter of West Point.

But now that he was an important and wealthy man, that

matter would have been forgotten. Anyway, why would Tavish take vengeance out on her?

A fine way for a minister's son to behave, she thought, and was reminded that he hadn't been coming to the church. His behavior disturbed her.

"What could change him so much?" she said to Lottie and Sassy.

"Maybe you ought to ask him," said Lottie.

"Go to him now? After buying me out of the shipping business? The scamp has left me nothing. No. I won't go crawling to Tavish Wilder."

Her ego smarted. Could it be that pride cloaked its face within the secret places of her heart? Maybe she wasn't as saintly as she had thought.

In the days following, her suspicions about Tavish were confirmed when she learned from a tense and angry Wade that many of the family holdings in town and in Seattle and Tacoma were safely tucked away into the company of "financier" T.D. Wilder. With the passing weeks, his comings and goings remained a topic of conversation. Ember heard he was quietly buying up other businesses in town beside the Ridgeways'. The more he owned, the more others submitted, the more they held him in awe. Money meant power. Power meant authority.

Ember was not the only one in the family who was tense. In Mack's absence, Cleo and Wade were taking care of business and it was not going well for Wade. Cleo's bachelor brother, Uncle Ben, was worried. Family arguments broke out over where the Ridgeway money was going.

"The family didn't build the timber dynasty to see Mack squander the hard-won profits on the NP," Ben exploded one afternoon in Cleo's office. "That's my money you're so generously sending to him in St. Paul. Don't we have economic troubles enough in this recession? And Wade's no businessman! He's losing money daily!"

"Don't be a boastful old fool, Ben," said Cleo. "I've as much right to say where the investments go as you do. And my son is heir. Don't forget that."

"Between him and Mack there won't be a Ridgeway Timber to inherit. You married a railroad gambler who dreams of becoming something he'll never be—president of the Northern

Pacific. Don't expect me to use timber money to pay his bills."

There was a loud crash as something toppled to the floor and shattered. A moment later the door into Cleo's office swung open and Ben came out, his leathery face ruddy with temper as he left, banging the front door behind him.

Ember had come downstairs to speak to Cleo about her own difficulties, but after coming upon the disagreement between her aunt and uncle, she knew she wouldn't receive the help she needed.

Prayer, she thought. How long had it been since she had truly poured out her heart to the Lord, allowing all her fears and frustrations to be known? She felt suddenly rebuked by her indifference. Where had all the blessed times gone when at the fort she had met with God every morning?

If God is my heavenly Father, what anxious thoughts about the future should tie my heart and soul into knots like this?

And Tavish? Did he not belong to the same heavenly Father?

Prayer. The Scriptures said that God desires to hear the concerns of His people. Would He work in their lives if she went to Him, not just once, but daily? From experience she knew that God did not pull strings on puppets. He worked and chiseled, sanded and honed. He allowed circumstances to accomplish results in the lives of those who were His own. He was the Great Potter of the Book of Jeremiah. But the clay was also responsible to yield to the Master's touch. And if it didn't? Ember felt a chill sweep through her soul. As unpleasant as it was to think about, she knew that if the clay persisted in rebelling, the potter would cast it aside.

Not me, Father, she prayed. *Don't ever give up on me.*

Nor my family. . . .

And Tavish belongs to you. He knew you when he was a boy. Lord—don't let him slip through your fingers.

That night it rained again, tinkling like pebbles against the gabled windows. Dressed elegantly for dinner, she joined the family members gathered in ritualistic splendor around the large dining room table adorned with silver, crystal, and large quantities of food.

Uncle Ben and Cleo had come to a silent truce over Mack and the railroad. Wade appeared tense and inadvertently turned the conversation to the new Mr. Wilder. Ember pretended disinterest as she watched Lottie cut the ham on Jamie's plate into bite-size pieces.

"I've discovered that the old French tycoon in Portland was his great-uncle," said Wade. "Mathieu LeBrett became a rich man in the OS&N when Villard bought it up."

Ember glanced at him, noting the lines of worry around his eyes. His mouth thinned as he pushed his untouched dinner aside.

"LeBrett made a mint. When he died in '76, he left everything to Wilder." Wade banged his glass down as though the knowledge infuriated him. "He might have told us years ago that he was related to LeBrett. But no! He deliberately kept it a secret, speaking of the land grant instead." He looked at his mother. "That grant, we should never—"

"You worry too much," Cleo interrupted. "I've taken care of that already."

"Taken care of what?" asked Ember, alert.

They looked across the table at her. Wade's eyes faltered, but Cleo smiled. "I've a surprise for you, dear. We'll talk about it after dinner alone in my office."

Surprise? Ember wondered why she suddenly felt nervous.

Wade stood. "No wonder he can make us look like fools! He's got money enough to rub our noses in the dirt! And he's having a merry time doing it!"

"You talk like a fool," said Uncle Ben. "No upstart young tycoon is going to hurt the Ridgeways."

Cleo leaned into her high-backed chair, staring thoughtfully at the table as Wade paced, hands shoved in his trouser pockets. "Just how much money does he have?"

"You figure it out," said Ben, taking out his pipe and lighting it, ignoring Cleo's scowl.

"Ben, must you smoke at dinner?"

Ben lit his pipe. "Villard bought the steamship line and the Oregon and Pacific railroads a few months ago. Wilder seems to have inherited the keen business blood of his uncle. He has a smart way when it comes to multiplying his money. It was you who mentioned his doubled investments."

Cleo's mouth tightened. "Me? Since when would I know of Mr. Wilder's business? You know I've been sick since Mack left for St. Paul. I've never met the man. I've been staying in the house."

Ember looked at her, wondering at her defensive mood. It wasn't like Aunt Cleo.

Ben waved an indifferent hand. "Well then Mack mentioned it before he left."

"Mack doesn't know Mr. Wilder either. He's been in St. Paul for six months now," argued Cleo.

"All right, Cleo! It doesn't matter who told me. Wilder was smart enough to invest in Villard's new enterprise."

"And he's rich," said Wade. "And he hates the Ridgeway name. We must do something soon or he may end up owning Ridgeway Timber Enterprise."

Ember caught her breath. She had never guessed matters had progressed so far or so badly. "That's not possible," she whispered, and felt a shiver when Wade looked at her, his face taut.

"He'll never buy me out," said Ben. "We've been in timber for a generation, and we'll stay in it for a century. There'll be no more loans to Mack and the railroad," he told Cleo. "We'll need it to protect the timber."

"I think you're all jumping to conclusions," said Lottie quietly. "I'm sure Mr. Wilder has no desire to ruin us. Why should he?"

Ember noted that the three faces turned to look at Lottie, but no one responded.

Wade broke the silence hanging like doom over the dining table. "I've learned that Villard's going to issue several million dollars in new stocks and bonds. With his wizard reputation, he'll have buyers fighting to get in line. I doubt if the man will even need to draft a mortgage."

"What does that have to do with Mr. Wilder?" asked Ember stiffly. Her mind staggered at the realization of just how rich and important Tavish had become.

Wade looked at her. "Wilder owns a hefty piece of the operation. I've heard he's going to help Villard build the railroad from Oregon into Washington. But that isn't the half of it. Villard has bigger plans. His eye's on the Northern Pacific. He'll end up its president one day, and Wilder will go along with him to the top." He turned to Cleo. "Tell *that* to Father in St. Paul."

Wade gave a sudden, almost hysterical, laugh. "He might end up working for Tavish Wilder—we all will."

Ember lifted her cup and tasted the bitter black coffee, trying to swallow the lump in her throat. Her feelings were mixed. Awe, shock, and a strange, bizarre pleasure that she couldn't understand.

Wade must have seen her expression and it angered him. "And that includes your husband-to-be. Wilder's buying him out is what I've heard. You may marry a man with empty pockets. So much for the mansion on the bluff, and a whole lot of other things."

The rain tapped at the window and silence filled the dining room.

Ben turned and frowned at Cleo. "I hope the money you're giving Mack to pour into the NP has a bottom to it. He'll lose again if he gambles on Billings. You heard Wade—Villard will oust him. Then what?"

"Mack knows what he's doing. I'm not going to allow you and Wade to fill my mind with panic. Lottie is right. We're all jumping to conclusions."

Ember wondered. She felt the shroud of gloom that hovered over Ridgeway Enterprises. She saw the tension in Uncle Ben and Wade, and Cleo's attempt to wave it aside was a pretense. Cleo was perhaps more worried about Tavish Wilder than they were.

It was later than usual when Cleo and Lottie put Jamie to bed, and saw to his nightly Bible story and prayer. As Ember left them alone and came out of the boy's room to walk to her own, she overheard voices downstairs.

More arguments? She frowned, troubled. The voice below did not sound like Ben's or Wade's. There was a quiet confidence in the tone that made her stiffen. *Tavish.*

She walked to the banister and peered down into the hallway, careful to keep out of sight until she knew the reason for his call. She suspected it was not a friendly visit. But why had he chosen to come himself?

Ben had not asked him inside and Tavish stood in the open doorway with the rain pouring in.

She heard Ben say abruptly: "My niece is unable to see anyone this hour of the evening. If you have a message, Mr. Wilder,

I shall be glad to give it to her in the morning."

Ember debated her emotions. Should she step forward and declare she would see him?

"Tell Miss Ridgeway it concerns the house and property of Macie Houston of Tacoma."

His words stunned her into silence. Her hand gripped the banister.

"What about the house?" came Ben's uneasy voice. "It belongs to Ember now. Miss Houston passed on some years ago."

"I'm aware of that. Are you familiar with another section of property here in the Quilcene area? I speak of a certain land grant between the two rivers. There was a fire there some years back."

Ben stood in a deathlike silence. His shoulders stooped forward a little, then his voice came wearily. "There's a lot of land out there, Mr. Wilder. It all looks the same to me, trees and rivers."

"It's not all the same, Mr. Ridgeway, and I'm sure you know why."

"No, I don't, Mr. Wilder. Should I?"

Cleo had stepped from the shadowed library. "Ben? Who is it?" she called.

Ben didn't answer and Tavish's smooth voice said, "I always liked that section of land. Tell your niece that I also like the property and house in Tacoma. It's going into foreclosure. Tell her I'm going to buy it. If she has any objections, I'll be in town until the end of the week."

Ember stared down into the hall, unable to stir herself.

Ben made no comment and stood looking at Tavish.

Tavish lowered his hat against the rain, slipped his black gloves on, and turned to walk down the porch steps. Just then he seemed to sense her presence and looked up at the stairway. He scanned her briefly and walked out into the rain.

The door stood wide open. The rain beat against the porch. The coach rumbled away with the clatter of horsehoofs.

Cleo came, her crutches sounding lightly across the polished floor.

"That was Wilder," said Ben in a low voice. "You heard?"

"Yes."

"He mentioned the land, Cleo. What now? What are you

going to do about it? You got us into this mess when you insisted on buying it from the railroad."

"Quiet, Ben! Don't speak about that here."

"A lot of good it did us all. Look at Mack—he has no interest in timber. The land sits there untouched, remembering nothing but that evil night—"

"Shut up, Ben!"

"And he's here because of it. What are you going to do? He's ruining me! I had nothing to do with it! I didn't even know un-til—"

"What is it?" cried Ember from the stairs. "What land? Great-aunt Macie's? That was willed to me. And I won't let Tavish have it!"

They turned, their faces stricken under the gaslight.

"It's all right, Ember. Ben seems to enjoy blaming every financial loss in the family on Mack and me. If Mr. Wilder wants the house in Tacoma, let him have it. It's old anyway. Macie never kept it up."

"I won't," she insisted. "I was practically raised there. So were Lottie and Wade. I don't care if it does need paint and fixing, it speaks to me of Great-aunt Macie, and I won't let him take it!"

Ben turned and strode into the library.

In her bedroom Ember paced the floor in the shadows, her heart thudding. Into her feverish thoughts his words returned: *"If she has any objections I'll be in town until the end of the week."*

Of course she had objections! He knew she did! What did he expect her to do? What did he want from the family?

She ceased her pacing and stood there as his words only now dawned on her with their true meaning. What had he said? If *she* had any objections. He had placed the emphasis not on the Ridgeways but on *her*. Of course he knew what the house in Tacoma meant to her.

She couldn't sleep well that night. She lay awake thinking, planning. Nothing seemed to bring peace.

"All right, Tavish Wilder. I'll give you my objections."

27

CHECKMATE!

The next morning's blue sky peered between wool-like white clouds.

Ember took more care dressing than usual. She chose a stunning claret red and black outfit with close-fitting bodice and double skirt. The square neckline was filled with a lace-frilled jabot.

She donned a matching black hat with a high, rounded crown adorned with claret feathers, snatched her suede gloves with eight pearl buttons from a drawer, and tiptoed down the darkened hallway.

She peered over the banister. No one was up yet and the servants were working in the kitchen. She came swiftly down the stairs and sped out the front door, hoping no one would ask where she was taking the coach.

Minutes later, Ember stepped from the coach, her eyes fixed on the mansion. Constructed on a high foundation, the house was vertical in structure with a wide bracketed cornice. Projecting bay windows on all three floors gazed serenely out to face the sea. The wind was chillier on the bluff, and during a storm the mansion would face the head wind, but she assumed he had chosen the location deliberately with that majestic stormy sea in view. The lawn was already in, so were shrubs and bushes. Pine trees had been recently planted. *Their slender cone shape would do well here,* she thought.

Most houses in Port Townsend were wood—the lumber, of course, was easy to obtain. This house was rather unusual, for it was veneered with stone, the style contemporary.

Her eyes followed the stone walk toward the high foundation and up the steps to the porch. She thought she felt someone watching her from inside the house. Her eyes lifted to the second-story window, but there was no one there.

"Just in time for breakfast. I haven't hired a cook yet so I can't offer you anything but coffee."

She whirled, not having expected him to come up behind her. She saw that he had walked from the bluff. In the distance the little white church of St. Paul's stood serene and sedate on the brow of the hill.

She stared at him, careful to conceal her thoughts. He was dressed casually this morning, but immaculately, in what could only be described by the fashion-minded as "rich and name-oriented." Yet he retained that rugged appearance she suspected would always be a part of Tavish Wilder. She glanced toward his coat, almost expecting to see a gun belt beneath a dark blue jacket.

"I've been expecting you." The green in his eyes appeared to soften a little. "Hello, Ember."

She couldn't resist and said, "I once knew a Tavish Wilder, but that was so many years ago he no longer exists. He was the son of a minister. And he could be trusted to do what was good and decent." She might have added, *And his eyes were warm and pleasant to look into, not hard and challenging.*

"Oh, him," came the easy quip. "You must be talking about my unfortunate twin. Used to sleep in a railcar and say 'Howdy, ma'am.' He carried a beat-up guitar and had a tear in his denim shirt. He was last seen fighting off the Cheyenne to save a spoiled girl. His investment was risky—she decided to get engaged to someone else."

"Leave Bradley out of this. And Wade too, in case you—"

"Ah yes, your gallant cousin, the major, who abandoned his

post with Custer and went hightailing it over the hills the night before the battle. What did he tell Mack? That he was sent on a 'do or die' mission to the fort?"

"Yes," she said stiffly. "But he didn't make it. He was captured by Indians and held for almost two months before he could get away."

Tavish smiled. "And 'Pocahontas' fell in love with him and helped him escape one deep, dark night." He laughed softly with malicious amusement. "How romantic and clever of him, but you're too smart to believe a tale like that. So is Mack. How did his relentless father take his son's homecoming with a dishonorable discharge?"

Dishonorable discharge?

She stared at him. She didn't believe all of Wade's story, but she wouldn't give Tavish the satisfaction of knowing, nor did she wish to confront the possibility of the discharge. His behavior left her defensive and without weapons, and she turned and began to walk away. "I won't stand here and be insulted."

He called smoothly, "If you want to keep Great-aunt Macie's house in Tacoma, you'd best reconsider."

She turned to meet his gaze.

"How did you know about Wade? What gives you the right to speak of his discharge? Is that why you were at Bismarck that night? You did say you were on your way to Fort Lincoln," she accused. "Is your grudge against him so vicious that you must pry and snoop into matters that are none of your affair?"

"Wade's courage was the last thing on my mind when I went to find him. I had reasons of my own for wanting to talk to him."

"Will you never forget what happened at West Point? Did you ever consider that had you been the one to graduate instead of Wade, it might have been you with Custer's regiment?"

He scanned her face. "No. I didn't go looking for Wade because of West Point. But you're right. . . . I could have been there."

"And you'd be dead now," she said stiffly, trying to deny the overwhelming emotion that the thought brought to her.

"Because I wouldn't have abandoned my position?"

She looked out to the turbulent gray sea beneath a foggy sky. "Does it make you feel better to call my cousin a coward?"

"It doesn't especially make me happy, and I'm not out to muddy Wade."

She looked at him. "I'm only glad you're both alive. And if an injustice was done to you at West Point, you might consider it one of those hard-to-understand purposes of God that works out for good."

"I've thought of that," he said gently. "I'm pleased you've considered it."

"Why can't you forget past injustices? You've come back to Port Townsend to hold us all accountable for the past."

"Only those involved. When it comes to forgetting, some memories don't deserve to be buried—not yet."

"You're right when you said your 'twin' no longer lives," she said quietly, wondering about the hard glitter in his eyes. "I don't understand you, Tavish. You're successful now, with all the money you could wish for. You have most folks in town awed by your sudden prestige, yet you seem to have tossed aside everything you once believed in when you had little but character and courage. You're bitter, and I can't see why you should be. I don't see that you deserve sympathy."

"Sympathy!" He walked toward her, his jaw set with frustration. "That's the last thing I want from you. You don't know me yet, do you? After all these years we've known each other—"

"Years spent apart from each other, waiting for you to come back. Waiting for letters that you never wrote—"

"Believe me, Ember, I had no choice. I can't explain everything now. I ask you to trust me—"

"No. You never cared enough to inform me of your plans, of how you felt."

"You knew how I felt. I made it clear that night at the fort. I asked you to wait for me until I could make something of myself, until I could stand on level ground with the Ridgeways. I couldn't come as a beggar, a track layer, with nothing but a hammer and a guitar!"

"The wait that has proved endless and destined to go nowhere! You say you're not after sympathy, that you're no longer concerned with Wade and West Point, but you're bitter. What do you want?" she demanded. "Vengeance? Because of what happened at Yellowstone when Kain was captured?"

His eyes flickered, the green turning to dark granite. "The

first thing I want is to know where I can find Cooper."

"The name means nothing." She turned away.

"Your aunt would know where he is. Maybe you do too."

Why would Cleo know anything about the trouble that resulted in his father's capture at Yellowstone?

"Cleo! She's the last person to know what happened. I've never told her. Why should I upset her with your suspicions?"

He squinted at her as though trying to make sense of her words. "Then you do know where Cooper is?"

"He must be dead with the rest of them," she said, thinking of the Indian massacre. She turned away. "Must we discuss this?" The thought brought back the attack of the Cheyenne. She rubbed her arms, remembering that night in the covered wagon, the warrior who had entered with the knife, and how his body had fallen so close to her that his greased arm had smothered her. . . .

He too appeared troubled and turned to look out to sea. "Never mind. I'll find him myself."

"Do you believe Cooper worked with Wade or my family, that they're to blame for what happened? It's not true, Tavish. You must try to forget the past, however painful the memories of death. Don't you see? If you thirst for vengeance it will only destroy you."

"I know the right answers. It's your great-aunt's house and property I wanted to talk to you about."

"One mansion isn't enough for you?" she said, looking about. "You must have my house too? Well, it's not for sale. I'll get the money some way."

His smile was faintly malicious. "Do you know how deeply the Ridgeways are in debt?"

Ember kept silent. She did, of course. "I'll pay off the debts."

"Not a chance. If you want to save the house you'll need to borrow from me." He folded his arms and smiled. "On my terms."

Borrow from him? That was the last thing that she'd expected to hear. She had thought he would say he was buying the Tacoma house and that she had no alternative in the matter.

She regarded him cautiously. "You'd loan me money? Why?"

"I have my reasons and my price."

Her eyes searched his. "I think I know your reasons. You want to use me to get back at the Ridgeways. The price, I am not certain about. What is it? Indentured service, Mr. Wilder?" she asked with sarcasm.

He smiled, and briefly scanned her. "Not a bad idea. But I doubt if you can boil coffee, and I'm even more sure you can't scrub my shirts. Your hands"—he snatched one up and turned it over—"are too small to be wasted on such things."

At his touch she jerked her hand free and stepped back.

"It's time Mack Ridgeway returned to Port Townsend," he said. "We have the past to discuss."

"So you can torment him by threatening to buy up the timber enterprise? No, I won't write him, and I won't let Cleo either. I'll make it on my own first before I take a loan from you. Or I'll get the money I need from Bradley."

"I wouldn't try it," he said silkily. "He's already in hot water. If I were you, I'd hold off on your marriage plans. He's not only the wrong man for you, but if his bank account keeps its downward spiral, you might end up with a track layer for a husband, after all." He smiled, his eyes taunting her with good humor. "Just think, you might need to take a job cooking red beans and corn pones at a train camp."

"That's it, isn't it? You want to see me penniless, and my entire family. You want to get even with them by lending me money. By having me in your debt. Will you never forget what happened out there?"

"I'm determined not to forget. Those responsible will see justice."

"Your justice? Are you also judge and jury?"

"I suppose you think they should go free? Do you think murder is a light thing?"

"Murder! How can you even hint that murder was on Wade's mind?"

"Wade? He wasn't there that night. But Cleo was—" He stopped, as though he had said more than he intended.

She was at a loss and stared at him. "What do mean? What are you talking about?"

"I'll loan you the money to pay the bank," he said, watching her.

"I don't want your money."

His mouth turned. "Afraid I'll reap vengeance on Mack and Cleo's niece?"

"Oh no, never that. You're too cool and calculating to do anything so open. You would prefer a game of chess."

"To place you in my personal debt? Perhaps you have me figured out after all."

"To use me as bait to make others uncomfortable."

He smiled a little. "As you say, the queen is trapped by the bishop. But for what cause? Is the bishop out to destroy, or does he wish the quarry for himself?"

She turned away and looked at the house, cooling her emotions by studying the gables. "Your cousin Julot would take vengeance on us all if he could, but not you. You plan your moves. I saw the way you fought the Cheyenne."

"Maybe I was just trying to concentrate in order to stay alive—and save that flame hair."

She whirled. "I know why you came back to town. But when Wade first told me everything, I didn't believe him. It didn't fit you. Now I'm beginning to wonder."

He looked at her, his eyes narrowing. "Wade told you?"

"Yes, why wouldn't he? He knew what you thought, that he deliberately left you and Kain to die."

"Wait a minute. You're talking about Yellowstone."

"Of course. You blame Wade. You want to get even because of the message that arrived that night at the fort about your father in Kansas. Well, it won't work. I'm sorry about your father—truly I am! But I won't let you use me to get back at them. Mack and Cleo had nothing to do with what happened! You must believe me."

"The truth is, I don't know if Mack was the one, but I think he knew. They all did. And they let it happen. It must be dealt with."

"By harassing us? Making us feel guilty and ashamed?"

"Maybe I don't see them at all. Maybe it's you who fills my memory. I remember a girl with beautiful hair down to her waist. I thought about her when she was the only thing left to fill the darkness of my mind."

"Stop it. I won't listen. Not this time."

She picked up her skirt and ran to the carriage, her heart

pounding. She reached the door when he overtook her, his hand resting against it.

"Wait. I've had justifiable reasons for going away as I did. It wasn't because I backed out of the commitment I made to you that night. I can't explain everything to you now. . . . Trust me, will you? Believe I meant what I said."

She hesitated, aware of the wind touching his dark hair, his coat, the way his eyes were so intensely green.

As though resisting inward frustration, he looked ahead on the windy bluff to St. Paul's church. "Walk with me there."

She hesitated, struggling against the tide of feelings that struck against her will, seeking to demolish her resistance. She stood, her eyes misting, unconsciously twisting the engagement ring.

Tavish held out a hand toward her, his eyes warm, pleading for her willing response.

She refused his hand, and instead made a small compromise by walking past him up the path as he requested.

They walked in silence with the wind blowing against them. As they neared the small white church, he stopped and they stood facing each other.

"You've gotten engaged to Bradley, but it wasn't much of a contest when I was away for three years. Delay the wedding, give us more time."

"Us? I don't know. . . ."

"You don't love him."

"You wouldn't know."

"If you ever did love me, you still do. Break the engagement."

"No."

"Then I'll do it for you. . . . Come with me now. We'll marry today, tomorrow."

She stepped back, confused, overwhelmed, even embarrassed. "You can't be serious. I—I can't do that. What would people in town say if I simply broke off with Bradley and married you overnight? Why, my reputation would be in question. They'd think I did it for money."

"All right, then we'll wait until you think it's safe to become Mrs. Wilder. All I'm asking is that you delay Bradley, then marry me at the appropriate time."

"You're impossible, Tavish. First you're as elusive and hard to catch as a man can be, then you overwhelm me with your zeal to marry at once. Will I ever truly know what kind of man you are?"

"Yes, when you marry me."

"What if you disappear again as soon as I tell Bradley I've changed my mind? It's a dreadful thing to do to him, you know."

"Marriage is forever. You wouldn't want to make the mistake of a lifetime would you? You'll be sorry if you turn me down."

She looked at him swiftly and found a teasing smile, but there was a serious glint in his eyes.

"I'm here to stay, Ember. I aim to win you this time," he said. "I won't give up."

She refused to look at him, knowing that if she did, she might succumb.

"I won't listen to this, Tavish." She turned to walk back, in fear of her own emotions. They were whirling out of control. *Do I love him?*

Yes, she knew she did. She had always loved him. But did she dare?

He had caught up with her. "It won't do you any good to run away."

She looked at him standing in the wind, and wondered with misery why the sight broke her heart. She did love him. Her hands formed fists. "I'll get the money some other way."

"Not a chance." He smiled. "I won't let you. I'll use my influence at the bank."

She drew in a breath. "There's a chance Mack will be successful again. Then he'll take you on. He's the man to do it."

"I want him to. In the meantime, if you don't cooperate with me you'll lose the Tacoma house. And maybe Villard and I will buy a controlling interest in NP stock. You'll be back where you started, Ember, only I'll still be around. Like I said, I'm going to win this time."

Her skin warmed; she tried to drag her eyes from his.

He gestured to the new mansion. "I built it with you in mind. It's yours, but I'll blow it up with dynamite first before I let Bradley Morrison carry you over the threshold as his wife! Want to see the inside?"

"No . . ." Her weak voice was lost in the wind. She turned and started walking swiftly for the carriage.

"Then I'll wait until you take that engagement ring off and put mine on," he said walking beside her. "What would you like? Diamonds, emeralds, or rubies?"

He caught her by the shoulders and turned her around to face him. She looked into his eyes and felt her resistance sinking as he drew her slowly toward him.

"Please . . ." she whispered, "not yet, not now. . . ."

He studied her face a moment, then lifted a brow. "Anything you say. I've already waited too long. What's another delay as long as it's not permanent."

Her eyes lowered. He released her and, taking her arm, walked her to the coach and opened the door.

He helped her inside and she sat down. "And—if I did accept your offer for a loan on the house at Tacoma, what do you ask as collateral?"

He leaned against the coach and watched her with a lazy smile. "Really, Ember, I'm surprised at you. You, of course. Become Mrs. Ember Wilder. Everything I've done so far is toward that goal."

Her stomach sank to her slippers beneath his warm gaze. "You are serious."

"I thought you knew that at the fort."

"I'll need time to think."

He smiled as though he knew he had won. For a moment he stood there, then simply closed the door.

She closed her eyes with relief as the cool shadows inside eased around her. The coach moved forward with the sound of the trotting horse. She looked down at the engagement ring, and in the shadows the diamonds no longer shone.

28

SERPENT'S SMILE

Ember didn't mention the marriage proposal to the family, but it became the last thing she thought of at night, the first thing to greet her in the morning.

There's something troubling him, something I don't understand, she thought, *but what can it be?*

If she did accept his proposal, what would the family think? She had the uncomfortable notion that because of his money and the pressure he was exerting on their peace of mind, they might breathe a sigh of relief. Yet what of Tavish's suspicions about the family? Would he ever accept them?

Would he change if I married him? she wondered. *Can I make him forget his past, his suspicions? He knows the importance of an intimate relationship with God.*

Yet regardless of her love for him, uncertainty loomed.

A few days later, Ember sat with Cleo in the family coach parked beneath the trees by the Dosewallips River near the canal. This piece of land was the surprise that Aunt Cleo had told her about. Ember sat across the leather seat from her aunt and gazed out the open door into the afternoon, deep with forest stillness. She inhaled the pungent smell of pine and heard the murmur of the river.

"I've never seen a more peaceful spot."

Cleo tapped the end of the crutch on the floorboard. "Great-aunt Macie was always smart about investments."

"But I shouldn't take the land, Aunt Cleo, not with you and Uncle Mack struggling with the timber business. You could use this section for logging."

"Mack insists you have it, just as dear Macie wanted. And I wholeheartedly agree. What matters now is that it belongs to you. An inheritance from Macie." Cleo smiled, relief in her eyes. "Mack will be so pleased that it's in your name."

Tavish's quiet search for Edmund Clark, Cooper, and Riley had turned up few prospects. Every path led to a dead end. But he knew it was only a matter of time and persistence. He had plenty of both.

He was certain Riley would be with Cooper. Riley had a tendency to panic, to make mistakes. Cooper and Riley would be in hiding somewhere, and would have changed their names. Tavish had already made inquiries at the local logging camps without success. He now believed he should try to track them down through the Ridgeway family. Whoever had hired them to attack his cabin was now keeping them out of sight.

Tavish had done everything in an unobtrusive manner. They would wonder how much he knew. The Ridgeways were nervous. That's the way he wanted it.

Ember was right; he had changed, and was not pleased with himself. A smooth veneer covered his soul. He was even more determined to find those who had wronged him and killed his father. Kain was dead, shot in the back. But he didn't know who fired the rifle.

Riley? Cooper? Mack? No, Mack would never risk the evil deed himself. Mack Ridgeway would have given the order—or Cleo, maybe even Ben—but one of the jacks would have done the work.

His green eyes flickered. He would move slowly. He didn't want to scare away his quarry now that he had them in his sights. Eventually, he would gain a stranglehold on the Ridgeway investments. Before he was finished, the Ridgeway Timber Enterprise would belong to T.D. Wilder & Company. Already he was making Wade sweat. As for Mack Ridgeway, it was only a matter of time before he would discover what was happening and come scrambling home. Tavish would be waiting for him.

Before it was over, they would all be in his debt. Until then, they would wonder why he never moved to accuse them openly of Kain's death.

He would wait. He was certain that the guilty party would eventually panic. There was only one problem that pricked his conscience—Ember. Whatever he did could come between them in the end. He couldn't yet tell her what drove him to vengeance—*No, justice!*

He might tell her one day . . . after the marriage. If his plans disturbed his conscience, he would not admit it. He avoided dwelling on the goodness of God—which would lead him to trust God in perplexing trials. Words from Scripture tapped at his heart, but he denied their entry. The words asked him to rest, to believe, to leave all the anger and injustice at the feet of a heavenly Father.

Tavish wanted revenge, however wrong it was, but there was no peace in demanding his way. There wouldn't be any fellowship with God until he surrendered his hurts and the desire for revenge, but he couldn't seem to let go. In his mind, the Lord was too merciful and he didn't want the Ridgeways to get off.

Seattle
Christmas Day 1880

The handsome young Frenchman with a scar across his face wore expensive clothing and leaned against the pier railing while the rain sprinkled his derby hat. "There is no sign of an Edmund Clark. The pig I wish to carve for the Christmas platter has put on sheep's clothing."

Julot's black eyes flashed as they came to Tavish. "But find him, I will, mon ami. I am hot on his slimy trail."

Tavish leaned beside him. He didn't feel the rain even

though he was hatless. The ships and boats in Seattle's harbor were from many ports, and the quay was noisy with the babble of voices. The aroma of cooked seafood drifted to them from the little eateries that dotted the harbor. Small boats and larger stern-wheelers maneuvered in and out of the port, with flags ruffling in the wind, and steam whistles blowing.

"Like a rat, he hides in dark places," said Tavish. "You're certain you covered the taverns?"

"Mon ami! I have slinked in and out of every tavern here and in Port Townsend. I've offered money to the crimps. They all say the same. That he and his daughter Amity disappeared from Port Townsend soon after we were shanghaied. They left no word, and no one has seen either of them since."

Tavish's gaze scanned the stern-wheelers. "He's changed his name. If he's come to Seattle, he'll have his daughter with him, and maybe he isn't running a tavern."

"I thought of that. Like I said, Tav, I'll find him. And when I do—"

"Do nothing until you inform me." Tavish met the hard black eyes. Julot smiled innocently.

"I mean it, Julot—nothing. Not a hair on his head, understand?"

Julot's smile was thin and cold as he touched the scar across his face. "Mon ami, would I go and kill a man now that we're rich? I've too much to live for."

Tavish smirked. Julot gave a laugh and they walked down the pier in the direction of their carriage.

Not more than a hundred and fifty feet away a young woman stood, tense, clutching her shopping bags. Amity Clark recognized Tavish Wilder and his cousin Julot. *Dear God, they've found us at last. I knew Pa wouldn't get by with this evil. I knew it!*

The salt-laden wind blew into her face. Panicked, she turned and started swiftly down the pier in the direction of the stern-wheeler *The Olympia*.

Her pretty slippers clicked on the wood as she ran, climbing the quay steps and boarding the steamer.

"Pa? Pa!"

She dropped her bags on the fine wooden table and hurried up the steps to the pilothouse, where her father would be studying his charts for a run to Vancouver. "Pa!"

Captain Edmund Clark looked up from his desk. His beard had been shaved and he wore a walrus mustache; his black hair was cut short and parted in the middle. Alert to the sound of alarm in Amity's voice, he stood, a big man in a tailored pea coat.

Amity stopped in the narrow doorway, holding to the side, her eyes frightened.

There was not much left of the old Edmund Clark that had been her pa in Port Townsend. The outer man had undergone a reformation, but she knew the inner man remained untouched.

"Aye, gal, what is it?"

"It's the two of 'em. I saw 'em on the pier. They've traced us here and they'll find us. Pa! I'm afraid."

His eyes narrowed as her words took root in his mind and alerted him to danger.

"Wilder and his French cousin?"

She nodded, breathing hard. "Pa, what'll we do?"

He stood for a moment without moving, then walked over to the cupboard and opened it, taking out a bottle of ale. He uncorked it and filled a mug.

Amity listened to the gurgle of the ale being poured. Outside the window, seagulls wheeled and screamed.

"They won't find me," he said. "My name is Captain Peter Finch. I've a stern-wheeler from Seattle and been doing business here for ten years. What can anyone tell 'em?"

"Five years, Pa—"

He whirled, eyes blazing. "Ten, gal! Remember!"

With the sudden anger, his old personality came to the forefront. Amity nodded.

"I must think. If they've showed their faces here, it may be the last time they come poking around." He gave her a sharp look. "Where'd they go, did you see?"

"Into a carriage. But they rode down the harbor toward Redeye Inn. Suppose they ask questions about me, Pa? I can't go to work tonight."

He paced, drinking his ale. "They wouldn't know ye. They

ain't never laid eyes on ye." His head turned toward her, his eyes crafty and bright. "Aye," he grunted to himself thoughtfully.

Amity felt uneasy.

"No," he mumbled again. "Ain't never seen you . . . har! 'Tis an idea of mine to find out what they know. You keep your job tonight at the inn, gal. You find out what you can about 'em. What they're doin' here. What questions they be askin'."

"Pa! I can't! I can't! I'll give myself away. I'll be nervous—"

"Nay, ye got a cool head about you, gal. Always did. And they ain't never seen you before. If ye keep a grip on yerself, it'll be fine enough. Aye," he repeated, nodding his big head. "You get ready to wait on tables, gal. There'll be no runnin'. Not yet."

At the Redeye Inn, Tavish and Julot had gone upstairs to their room. The inn had double rooms and a sitting room decorated with Queen Anne furniture and rugs. As Tavish removed his jacket, a serving man in black satin livery entered from their private kitchen with a tray of coffee. The man scowled as he ran his palm along his trousers.

"Merry Christmas, Laz," said Julot with a smile. "Say now, you're lookin' a bit fancy."

"Merry Christmas. Best one in years." Lazou's eyes twinkled as he looked across at Tavish. "I know someone else just itching fer you to hurry up and come see her."

Tavish thought of Kwanita. The night Riley and the lumberjacks attacked the cabin on the Hood, Lazou had fought to protect her. Lazou told him he had wounded Riley, but was outnumbered and couldn't hold off the mob. One thing led to another and Kain was hit, shot in the back. Soon all-out fighting broke loose, ending in the fire. "They saw us run away, but we hid, and I saw where they buried Mr. Kain. I done took her where I knew she'd be safe. To your Mister LeBrett in Portland. He took her and notified the authorities, but the Ridgeways were able to say they had no notion of what happened. Then the men all disappeared. An' your uncle LeBrett, he died."

Tavish and Julot had relocated Lazou and Kwanita upon their return from the sea after they learned of the inheritance from Great-uncle Mathieu. Kwanita was now going to school under a private tutor whom Tavish had hired for her in Seattle.

Tavish took out his watch and glanced at the time. It was Christmas Eve, and he and Julot were soon due to spend the evening with Kwanita and Lazou—the only family they had.

"We've an hour, Laz. Right now we'll have our own holiday toast. Julot and I have a surprise for you."

"Hope it ain't more satin, boss," said Lazou. "I don't go for this fancy duds none."

Tavish and Julot exchanged smiles. "Now I don't know, Laz, you look right handsome," said Tavish with a smooth voice. "You keep it up and Julot and I will lose you to some pretty Seattle girl."

"Not me, boss. Unless she's got apple land, I ain't interested." He set the tray down and poured hot coffee.

Julot grinned at Tavish. "You've got it?"

"Right here."

Tavish reached in his pocket and drew out an envelope. He handed it to Lazou in exchange for the cup of coffee. Outside, the rain tinkled against the windowpanes.

"Merry Christmas, Laz."

Lazou took the envelope. He and Julot watched him open it and take out a land deed for a large apple orchard in Wenatchee. An unjust law barring a Negro from land ownership in Washington Territory had been repealed. Tavish had bought the land and deeded it to Lazou.

Lazou stared at it, dumbfounded. His hand began to tremble and the expression on his face deepened into tense emotion. Tears formed to trickle down his cheeks. He said nothing and glanced from Tavish to Julot.

Tavish set his cup down and went to Lazou, embracing him.

Julot squeezed Lazou's shaking shoulder. "And all the seedlings you'll ever want are just sittin' in Tacoma ready to be shipped!"

29

BLOSSOMS AMONG THORNS

The lumberjack foreman watched the man on horseback ride into the logging yard. If he hadn't known who he was, he might have mistaken Tavish Wilder for a drifter, a jack looking for work. His presence here meant trouble. Wilder stepped down from his horse and his gaze riveted upon the newly hung sign outside the office: RIDGEWAY SAWMILL.

The foreman walked toward him and smiled stiffly.

"Afternoon, Mr. Wilder. Name's Patrick Finney. I'm foreman here."

Tavish turned his head and beneath his hat looked at the ruddy-faced Irishman. The flicker of caution in the foreman's eyes alerted Tavish. He didn't trust him.

"Where's your boss?"

The foreman gestured his head toward the office. "Inside, going over the books."

Tavish walked past him across the yard and up the steps. A squirrel darted away, taking refuge beneath the porch. Blue jays quarreled above in the fir trees.

My trees, thought Tavish, unable to restrain his mood. *My land. Stolen by the Ridgeways. Kain died here. The cabin was burned down not far from this spot. He's buried on this land—and Wade's jacks dare to cut and log it!*

He grabbed the knob and threw open the door. It impacted with a thud against the outside wall. His brittle eyes collided with Ember's startled gaze. He stopped.

She stood quickly, caution in her glance as she scanned him.

She wore a simple high-necked Victorian blouse and a dark skirt that fell in soft folds. Her flame hair was piled high, and unkempt strands fell across her shoulder. He watched as she tried to push them back beneath her combs.

"Tavish," came the surprised voice, somewhat nervous. "What are you doing here?"

He took her in briefly. "What are the Ridgeway men doing now? Hiding their operation behind a woman?"

Her eyes went cool as her fingers tightened around a pencil.

"Thanks for the compliment," she said dryly. "However, I can manage my own sawmill without their help."

Her words set him back. For a moment he looked at her. *Her* sawmill?

She sat down hastily, grabbed the ledger on the pine desk, and pulled it toward her.

He pushed his hat back, leaning in the doorway as he watched her through his narrowed gaze. She kept her eyes on the ledger.

"You nearly busted my door off the hinges. If it's damaged— you'll pay to have it fixed," she said, not looking up.

He smiled wryly. "I expected someone else behind the desk."

Ember laid aside her pencil and stood, facing him.

"May I come in?" he asked with exaggerated politeness. When she made no reply, he walked in and glanced about. "Where are Wade and Ben?"

"Ben's in town. And Wade's gone to see his father in Missoula. Uncle Mack, of course, is a friend of the president of the Northern Pacific, Mr. Billings."

A faint smile touched his mouth. "Is he? A pity Mack always picks the losing side. Billings is out of a job now."

"I suppose you're going to take Billings' place?" she quipped.

He smiled easily. "No thanks. Villard is." He turned his head and looked toward the lumberjacks working on the Dosewallips River. "Nice piece of land."

She said warily, "It's not for sale."

"I wasn't thinking of buying it. I don't need to." Tavish glanced at the bare spot where his cabin once stood. "How did the Ridgeways come by it?"

"They didn't," she said too quickly.

He looked at her thoughtfully. "Did Ben buy it from the railroad?"

"No, he didn't buy this grant." She hesitated, then smiled too sweetly. "If you've come here on business, you'll need to deal with me."

"Why, I couldn't think of another woman I'd rather do business with—evidently Mack thinks so too."

"Mack?" she repeated, looking confused. "What's he got to do with this?"

"But you don't need to work for him. I told you I'd lend you all the money you need."

"Mack doesn't own this sawmill," she stated, and smiled again. "I do."

His smile faded; a subdued glitter was in his eyes. As quickly it came, he restrained himself. He said in a too-quiet voice, "How did you get this land?"

She came out from behind the desk and leaned against it, her arms folded. "The sign says Ridgeway, but I'm having it changed. I'm having one put up with my own name on it. 'Ember's Sawmill,' " she said. "How does it sound?"

He winced. "You're not serious."

"I am! So if you've come to buy my land the way you say you're going to buy my house in Tacoma, you'll need to face your first business defeat." She smiled again. "I'm going to keep my property if I die doing it."

He simply watched her, his body tense with this new knowledge.

"Stop looking at me like that. I almost expect you to draw a pistol!"

She turned her back, but Tavish gently placed his hand on her arm, pulling her back. "Where did you get this land?" he asked again quietly.

"What does it matter to you? Come, Tavish, you have acres! You have houses, and railroad stock, and shipping stock and—"

"It matters more than you think. I want to know."

She sighed. "The land belonged to Great-aunt Macie."

"Macie Houston?" came the surprised voice.

"Yes, she left it to me in her will. I only found out a few weeks ago."

Tavish didn't believe her, yet he said nothing. Slowly his anger began to subside into something he at first could not understand. *I've been checkmated.* "A clever move on his part," Tavish whispered.

"I told you—it was Great-aunt who bought it."

Under her searching gaze he nearly told her the truth. "It's a good section of timberland," was all he said.

She eyed him cautiously. "Yes, it is. I'm proud to own it. Why were you so angry to learn it was mine?"

He arched a brow. "I told you, I was expecting someone else. And that someone expected me to come here, and find you. A smart move."

"You speak in riddles. You always do. What about this land? You expected to buy it? You're disappointed? Poor Mr. Wilder!" Her eyes narrowed. "By the way, just how much money do you have?"

He caught up her left hand, now absent the engagement ring from Bradley. "Ah . . . you told him. It took you long enough."

"Breaking the engagement with Bradley was difficult, but I now believe that I made the right decision."

Tavish ran a thumb over her finger. "Willing to marry me for my money are you?"

She pulled her hand away and ignored his jest. "I wanted to do something on my own—though a sawmill is not exactly pretty like a perfume or dress shop. But I may fail—I'm losing money and I can't seem to hire logging vessels to haul my lumber to San Francisco. They keep telling me there's no demand right now." Her eyes met his. "You do understand, don't you?"

"Yes. I understand. Someone else understood too. They understood how I'd respond to your being here. Who was it that suggested you come here and build a sawmill?"

"It was my own idea."

"Granted. But someone informed you the land was left to you by your great-aunt."

"Yes," she said reluctantly. "Cleo did. She brought me here."

"Ah . . . a woman's plan. Of course."

"More riddles? Will you explain what you're doing here? You asked if Wade were here. Why?"

"Did you say Macie bought this land?"

She flipped her pencil. "Yes."

"And left it to you in her will?" he asked smoothly, watching her response.

"That's right," she said uneasily.

"She died in 1874?"

Her eyes narrowed. "Yes. Why?"

"I have another question," he said.

"You have too many."

"I'm a curious man when it comes to a certain woman."

"I wonder." She looked at him. "Is it about a certain woman? Or is it that you think I know something about the death of your father?"

"What a question! You'd be Mrs. Tavish Wilder at this moment if you'd stop putting me off. Tell me, how did she buy this land before the land office decided to snatch it up and sell it?"

She looked confused. "I'm sure I don't know what you mean."

"This land wasn't railroad land before 1874."

"How would you know that?"

"I know the man who owned it."

Their eyes held. "Are you suggesting Macie stole it?" she asked wryly.

"Perish the thought! Would the family take timberland that didn't belong to them? There's too much honor in the enterprise for anything so dubious."

She folded her arms. "Great-aunt Macie wasn't a thief. Neither are the Ridgeways."

"They're the worst thieves in Washington Territory. Don't look so offended—" He smiled. "I'll soon change your name to Wilder."

"You would know best about the railroad taking land since you own a good piece of it yourself," she goaded. "Do you also call your powerful friends land thieves? Is that what you say to Mr. Villard?"

"So it was Cleo who informed you about the land?"

She flipped her pencil. "It was Macie's lawyer who told Cleo. The land was left to me in Macie's new will."

He reached and plucked the pencil from her fingers and leaned toward her. "New will? You mean there were two?"

"Well, yes—and no, I mean I don't know, but the lawyer found the most recent one."

"You saw this second will?"

"I don't need to see it."

"What's the lawyer's name?"

"I don't remember."

"No matter. I can find out easily enough."

"Tavish! Stop it! Why are you interrogating me like this? What is it about this land that—"

He smiled. "Never get angry with the man you're going to marry."

"I never said I would marry you."

"You wouldn't disappoint a lonely, heartbroken young man, would you? Not when he's been thinking about you for so many years?"

"I'm very busy now, Mr. Wilder. I think you'd better go."

She turned and walked behind the desk, sitting down. She pulled the ledger in front of her.

He laughed. "All right. Let's talk timber instead."

"I don't care to talk anymore. You can go now, please."

He sat down on the desk and leaned toward her. "You wouldn't want to turn down a good business deal now would you, Miss Ridgeway? If you want this sawmill to succeed, you'll need some customers. They're hard to come by now. The San Francisco market is over-logged. You could become successful and leave our future children a prosperous sawmill."

She looked up at him warily. "What kind of business do you offer?"

"Buying lumber, what else?"

"I'm not so certain."

"I've come to the right sawmill, haven't I? Owned by a lovely young woman who haunts my dreams."

"Just how suddenly did you decide you needed lumber?"

Tavish gave her his most disarming smile. "What a question!"

She smiled ruefully, scanning him. Tavish knew she couldn't resist an opportunity to sign a contract.

"Very well, how much do you wish to buy?"

"Did anyone ever tell you your eyes are like warm honey when you're excited about something?"

"No. I'd rather talk timber."

He stood up from the desk and walked to the doorway, studying the trees along the river. "Your foreman, Patrick Finney, what do you know about him?"

"Not much. He's an experienced lumberjack, so I hired him. Why do you ask?"

"Curious. Thought I might have seen him before. Maybe in Oregon."

"He mentioned Idaho. Shall I ask him?"

"No. I'd rather you say nothing to him."

"Why?" she asked bluntly. "What is it you wish to hide, Mr. Wilder?"

He turned, and under her searching look he smiled faintly. "If you want to know all my secrets, you'll need to marry me first."

"That might be dangerous . . . are you interested in buying my timber or not?"

His eyes glinted with malicious amusement. "Yes. Enough to make you independently rich. You see? I've decided not to back you into a corner to get you to agree to marriage."

"How considerate of you."

He folded his arms. "Anyway, I admire a woman with courage. If you can face a Cheyenne and keep that hair of yours intact—you can run a successful business—once you learn how to add and subtract," he said, glancing at her ledger.

She tossed her pencil down. "I'll learn a good deal more than that!"

"I've no doubt. I want lumber—lots of it."

Her eyes gleamed with excitement. "How much?"

"Several shiploads to start with. I'll need more later."

She stared at him, stunned. "But the economy is slow and—"

"Do you want to sell or not? I've never heard of a merchant talking a client out of a sale."

"What do you want the wood for?"

"To sell, of course. What else? Julot owns logging vessels. He has contacts in Quebec. And there are markets in Australia and Singapore. Are you interested?"

She smiled. "You can buy as much lumber as you want."

"I'll need to contact Julot in Seattle and make arrangements. It'll take a few weeks. I'll be in touch with you at Port Townsend."

"Port Townsend? But shouldn't we make the deal now?"

He smiled. "You really are a shrewd businesswoman, aren't you? Don't worry. I've every intention of following through." He smiled. "On everything we've talked about. Goodbye, Ember. I'll see you in Port Townsend."

Ember stood at the door and watched him leave. She noticed Patrick Finney was hanging around outside, and when he saw Tavish, he walked away swiftly as though afraid he might be questioned.

She saw Tavish mount his horse and take the narrow road toward Quilcene.

Well, she thought jubilantly, *the sawmill might just make it!*

As she smiled to herself, a thought stole across her mind, leaving shadows in its wake. When Tavish had first arrived he hadn't come to discuss buying. He had been confrontational. His mood had changed only after he realized that she owned this land grant instead of the Ridgeways. There was more to all this than his interest in lumber.

One day soon after Tavish's visit a foreman by the name of John arrived from Seabeck. He told her he was a friend of Mr. Wilder. Since she hadn't gotten on with Finney, Ember decided that she was only too glad to have the older man to advise her on the business.

Her relationship with Tavish grew more intense as the months passed, and he pursued her relentlessly. He sent her flowers and other gifts and called on her frequently at the sawmill, but as her own happiness grew, Uncle Ben declared his displeasure.

"It was a mistake allowing him to back you financially in the mill. And now the house and property in Tacoma! He's only put you in his debt. I know what the man has on his mind. He intends to marry you."

Ember looked at him and drew in a breath. It was time to announce the truth. "I am going to marry him, Ben. I was hoping you'd give us your approval."

"I'll never do that! You should have married Bradley. Wilder is a clever man, one who will pretend anything to get what he wants. You'll learn to your hurt that he's only used you."

Ember felt the pain of his insult. "I know Tavish better than you do. I've known him since West Point. There isn't a man in Port Townsend who's more honorable, or one I'd rather marry."

"Then you'll go through with this?"

"Yes. I've made up my mind. In fact, I made it up when he was laying track for the railroad. I would have run off and married him years ago, but it was Tavish that wanted to wait until he made something of himself."

His face was hard. "Then you can move out."

Cleo appeared above the stairway, looking older and more weary than Ember had ever seen her.

"I'm surprised at you, Ben. Talking to Ember like this. I, for one, heartily approve of her decision. Do you want Wilder as a family relation or as an enemy?"

"The marriage will do nothing to improve the situation."

Ember didn't stay to hear them argue. She respected Ben, and wouldn't remain in the house if he wanted her to leave, not even if Cleo asked her to stay.

She went upstairs to her room, leaving them to discuss their differences. She wanted nothing more now than to belong to Tavish. She would write him tonight about Ben telling her to leave. Tavish had asked her to marry him again that afternoon. She would say yes.

Downstairs, Ben confronted Cleo.

"Have you forgotten who Wilder is? She's playing with a tiger, and so are we."

"A tame tiger if he falls for her. I'm surprised you don't see it to our advantage. How best to keep matters under control than to have the man in love with her? For her sake, he'll do nothing."

"More conniving on your part? Don't count on your conclusions where Wilder's concerned. He's not going to forget so easily. I say he's using her to lay his trap. How better to do it than bring himself into our very midst?"

"Yes. So rich, and growing more friendly with Villard every day."

"He's not welcome here. He's trying to ruin me."

"Not after he marries her. I detect a difference in his movements already. He's stopped looking for Cooper."

"He'll never stop. Not until he finds out who's responsible."

"She'll keep him pleased and satisfied. He'll forget all about what happened. You've been alone too long, Ben. You've forgotten just how much a man will do for the woman he loves. With Ember as Mrs. Tavish Wilder, she secures our future as well as her own. And Mack will be safe."

"Mack! He's one cousin I wish I'd never met. He's been a curse ever since he showed up here. He's got you wrapped around his finger. Can't you see you're nothing to him? Where is he, I ask you? St. Paul! Is he here with you when you need him? No, you're ill, Cleo!"

She struck him. "It's you who will leave this house, not Ember! You! This is my home, not yours. Mother left it to me! Go, get out!"

"Cleo—"

"Get out!"

30

SWORD OF VENGEANCE

"I think, mon ami, your sword of vengeance is double-edged."

Tavish glanced at him with a warning look that told Julot he could take no more of his words, but Julot kept pressing.

"You marry Mack Ridgeway's niece, and what will you tell her on your wedding night? You married her so you could find your father's murderer?"

Tavish turned on his cousin with glittering rage, his fist smashing hard against the table, sending a Victorian lamp of Viennese crystal crashing to the floor.

Julot looked at Tavish in surprise.

"I'm marrying Ember because I won't have any other woman, is that clear?"

Julot said nothing. Tavish turned abruptly and walked out of the room.

Outside, the raindrops met his face. He walked toward the pier, deliberately getting wet, seeking coolness for his spirit.

What's happening to me, he thought. *There was a day when I wouldn't even hit Riley—who deserved it—now I lash out in anger at Julot.*

He stood at the rail, staring at the dark water, the lights from the ships and boats reflecting on its surface. The cold rain soaked through his shirt. He heard footsteps. A moment later Julot walked up, and without a word threw his arm around his shoulder.

Ember smiled to herself as she looked at her wedding ring. By turning her hand under the gaslight she could make the diamond sparkle like a rainbow. She and Tavish had been married a month and they had moved into the mansion on the bluff.

"I'm too happy. It can't last," she whispered. "Something must happen to burst the bubble. I must come crashing down to hit bottom and nurse some bruises. . . ."

"What are you whispering about to yourself?" asked Tavish, putting on his shirt.

She glanced in his direction. He was going out alone—again. "Where are you going this time?"

"I won't be long. I've some business that won't wait."

"It's late. What kind of business?"

He smiled. "Cloak and dagger business, darling. What else would lure me from your arms to the cold and foggy water-front?"

His eyes glinted with ironic humor, but she believed his remark to be deliberate, to take her off guard. Was it truly a clandestine meeting?

"Who are you going to meet?"

"A spy."

"Do be serious. Must you go now?"

She came up behind him at the door, and he drew her to him, kissing her languidly. "Yes, but I'll be back soon."

He was gone. She stood there staring at the closed door. Why did he never explain what he was about? She heard the carriage leave beneath her bedroom window, the echo of horsehoofs fading away.

Two men. Two legacies, mused Tavish, standing in the wet grass on the Hood Canal. "My great-uncle knew how to multiply gold. My father knew how to look up at the stars and see the Lord's footsteps walking silently through eternity. I am the restless heir of both."

He felt the wind tugging at his jacket. He stood beside Kain's neglected burial site in the forest behind the sawmill. He stooped, brushing away the damp earth and pine needles to read the weather-faded words on the flat wood marker that Lazou had placed there years ago. One day soon he would place a stone memorial here to his father. He would never have known where Kain was buried if Lazou and Kwanita had not informed him. He could still envision his father sitting before the train campfires, reading a psalm to sleep on, as he had done every night.

How long is summer? Only a vapor. Ah, to do the Master's will, his father used to say.

In his memory, Tavish saw Kain upon his horse in his worn frock coat, the Bible in front of his saddle. They were on their way to another revival meeting in some train camp. His father was singing. Julot was playing his harmonica as he trailed after. Tavish rode alongside, his hat low, his black jeans dusty, his beat-up guitar slung over his saddle. . . .

Oh, Jesus is a Rock in a weary land,
A weary land, a weary land;
Oh, Jesus is a Rock in a weary land,
A shelter in the time of storm.

Now Tavish felt the rain on his head, felt the damp soil at the grave. Although he fought to hold back the emotion, tears came to his eyes.

"God, for a touch from that memory when you felt so near!"

But peace remained a stranger. He now seemed to own nothing of the past. His father's blessing had tumbled away with the desert winds; the satisfaction of owning his great-uncle's gold felt more like a bag of rocks shackled to a dying man crawling toward water.

His father had understood. Nothing the world might offer could satisfy the appetite of a sheep but sweet green grass and still waters. However full the cup of success, a sheep in the wilderness found nothing to quench its thirst.

At the end of broken dreams, what? The rainbow is clutched within the fist, the pot of gold sits at the feet, and disillusionment is king.

"Lord! Where are you! Where?" he whispered passionately, his hand clenched.

The answer did not come like messengers from heaven's portal hurrying to his call. It was not angels' wings that brushed past him, only the cold wind. A trumpet call did not echo, only the quiet stirring of leaves.

Emerging from his inner conflict came questions, not answers, but the questions removed from his soul's eyes the scales that had blinded him with bitterness.

"Am I the only one to have suffered injustice by man's selfish greed, or the devil's hatred for a man who bows to God?

"Is it not Satan who charges God? And if I charge Him foolishly, do I not join hands with Satan? As for injustice—was not God's own Son treated so?"

Tavish wiped his eyes, then looked up at the cloudy afternoon sky. "Lord, help me look with the eye of faith beyond this momentary affliction, and trust that you are in control of my circumstances—past and present."

Eternity will tell all. The mystery of adversity, of affliction, of pain, remains a secret, thought Tavish. *Wise men have given their answers, the Word speaks into the problem of darkness, but the why remains unanswered until we see Him on His throne.*

"At the end of life's drama," whispered Tavish, "that's when I will know that trusting Him mattered above all else.

"Lord, I yield the injustice done to you. I'm willing to be cleansed by your Word and Spirit, to be free of my anger and desire for revenge."

Ember had been at the sawmill when Tavish arrived. When he hadn't come to the office as she expected, she followed him. Now, standing unseen behind the trees she watched him stooping before the ground and her heart caught with love. *He's praying.* At that moment she never loved him more. *How strong, how masculine, how wonderful he looks yielded to Jesus Christ!*

"Lord, thank you for my husband," Ember whispered. "Maybe this is the end of his suspicions. Oh, God, may it be so. May we start a new life."

She didn't want to interrupt his time alone with God, nor even let him know she had silently intruded upon his forest altar. As she stepped back into the trees to leave, he stood and walked toward his horse. She watched, somewhat surprised when he mounted and rode away. She had expected him to come to the office to see her.

When he was gone she walked out of the shadows and started back for the mill, wondering, then paused to look back to the spot where he had been praying. Something inside compelled her to go there. Her heart stopped when her gaze fell upon a grave marker. She knelt and touched the wood, reading the inscription.

Kain Wilder!

Her breath caught. She stared, as if caught up in a whirlwind of facts, doubts, questions, fears. Why was his father buried *here,* on this section of land?

Like a crack of thunder overhead, the truth broke upon her soul. This is the Wilder land grant! Kain died here! How? When? Then they had not sold out and left as she had been told! They had lived here at one time!

She understood now what he had meant when he told her he didn't need to buy this land. It already belonged to his father in years past! Why then had Cleo said that Great-aunt Macie bought it from the railroad? No wonder Tavish had been caustic when she spoke about her inheritance!

The blood rushed to her temples. She knelt there in the damp earth, the rain seeping through her clothing.

There was more to the riddle surrounding Tavish than his suspicions about his father's death. And all of them had kept the truth from her! How could they do it? How dare they do it! And how dare Tavish marry her with such secrets still hidden away?

She went cold. Why had he married her? For love, or some hidden agenda cloaked in vengeance? Maybe he hadn't been praying at all, but was simply overcome by seeing his father's forgotten grave on *her* property!

A hundred questions darted madly through her brain. Answers! She would have them this time. She would not rest until she did. The secrets surrounding Tavish would be unmasked, even if she must confront every individual in the family to do it.

She stood, weak with emotion. "Cleo brought me here . . . it was Cleo who spoke of the railroad buying this land. This time she will tell me the truth!"

31

A MATTER OF FAITH

The sky was gray, the air damp but warm for August. Amity left the cabin of the stern-wheeler and came on deck. Quiet happiness wrapped about her heart.

She smiled wistfully and touched her hair, remembering how she had first met him in Seattle at the Redeye Inn. He had never guessed who she was, and for a time she had kept it from him. But as she found herself falling in love with him, she had avoided seeing him again. Little did she know that he would follow her to the *The Olympia* and learn who she was—the daughter of Edmund Clark, the man who had shanghaied him and Tavish to sea.

Julot had been furious, threatening to "wring your pa's neck like a rooster!" Yet as she had stood looking at him in fear, hoping he didn't know she loved him, his mood suddenly broke into something very different.

"Amity, it isn't your fault. I still think you're the prettiest girl I ever laid eyes on."

The next thing, she was in is arms and he was kissing her with a growing passion that had left her dazed. After that . . .

the secret of who Captain Peter Finch was remained just that, a secret.

"What about Tavish?"

"I won't tell him. We'll get married, Amity. I'm taking you away from here. We'll forget the past. We can be free. I've a friend in Wenatchee. He's got his apple trees all planted now. I think he'd welcome us there for a while until I can explain things to Tav."

She was still in her reverie when she heard a sound that made her tense. Stealthy footsteps! The pleasant day suddenly turned overcast with gloom. She turned slowly and started with surprise. A man in a soiled duster stood there, a cigar stump between his teeth.

"Say now, where's your pa?"

Amity gathered her scattered courage and said calmly but firmly, "What are you doing aboard this boat?"

He leered. "You jes tell your pa that ol' Riley's here to see him. He'll know better'n to ask questions. Scat, run find him. I'll be waitin'. Say now! This be a right fine boat, Miss Amity. Right fine indeed. Was smart of yer pa to wheedle it out of the Ridgeways, weren't it?"

She swallowed, fear and dread welling up inside. *Riley!* In her memory she again saw the fire, felt the heat, and remembered the horror when she had touched the dead body of Kain Wilder.

And now he was here to threaten her happiness by unmasking her father.

"Go find yer pa," said Riley again. "And where's his cabin? I 'spect he's got ale below, eh?"

"Go away, Mr. Riley," she whispered. "Please. If Julot and Tavish find you back in the area they'll kill you."

His eyes flickered and he wiped his hand across his mouth. "I'm goin', but not before Clark pays me my due. Without me he wouldn't have this stern-wheeler. Without me he'd still be shanghaiing men from the wharf in Port Townsend. Say now, yer pa's goin' to be a mite kind to me in my sudden need, an' if he don't, it may be Mr. Wilder will get an anonymous letter all unexpected like. A letter tellin' him just who Captain Peter Finch is."

"You're a vile man!"

"And your pa's better'n me now, is he? All spruced up and wearin' fancy duds? He's a murderer. He's no better 'n me, and he better know it. Get him."

He turned and went up the steps to the cabin.

At last she moved, one step at a time, then she was running to find her father.

For once in his life Edmund Clark was speechless when she drew him aside on the wharf. His eyes hardened as he glanced in the direction of his boat, then flickered with genuine fear.

"Har, that wily blackmailer. So he thinks he can scare Edmund Clark, does he?"

"Pa, he means it. I'm afraid. You must go to the authorities this time. Tell them everything. The past must be reckoned with before we're all trapped by it!"

"Shut up, gal. I'll take care of Riley."

Amity hung back, frightened, watching the looming figure of her father in cap and pea coat trudge slowly up the steps to where Riley waited in his cabin.

32

UNRAVELING

The Ridgeway mansion was silent as Ember came through the front door and crossed the entry hall to the stairway. Lantern light fell across the stairs. She climbed rapidly, not bothering to remove her hooded cloak. Finding the glow of light beneath Cleo's door, she called, "Cleo?"

"Is that you, Ember? Come in."

Ember stood in the open doorway facing her aunt reading in bed, the crutches within easy reach. Ember's expression must have given her away, for Cleo laid the book aside and swung her legs to the edge of the bed. Taking up her crutches, she stood.

"I found the grave, Cleo," breathed Ember. "It was in the forest. Did you think the past would remain buried, forgotten? I want the truth. All of it. I deserve to know. I'm his wife!"

Cleo paled, but remained still, her eyes searching Ember's face.

Ember walked slowly toward her. "Did you know the grave of Kain Wilder was there?"

Cleo sighed, closed her eyes, and shook her head. "No, Cooper didn't tell me where he was buried. He took care of it. He

315

and a blundering fool named Riley. It was all Riley's doing. Mack never gave orders to burn the cabin, least of all to harm any of them." Cleo sank into a chair, looking old and beaten.

Ember stared down at her, stricken. "Mack gave the order?"

"He wanted them off the land grant. He wanted to frighten them, but he never wanted Kain to be shot. A tragic affair. Believe me, I've seen his face in a thousand nightmares."

They had shot Kain. Ember's hand went to her chest. "Tavish . . . knew . . . this?"

Cleo looked at her, alert for the first time. "Yes, you found the grave?"

For a moment Ember couldn't speak as emotion tightened her throat. "Yes—I saw him kneeling there."

Cleo let out a wounded groan.

Ember felt sick. *Tavish didn't tell me!* The Ridgeways were responsible for his father's death. No wonder he had hated them . . . and their marriage. . . .

"The land grant first belonged to his father," said Cleo. "Mack always wanted that land, but Kain wouldn't sell it. They came here in the fall of '73 to start a logging company. There was trouble, lots of it."

Dazed, Ember watched her aunt. Cleo was holding her head in her hands now, her voice droning on in a dull, monotonous tone as she told Ember what had happened.

"When Mack lost everything in the railroad, I—I took matters into my own hands. I had friends in Washington assign the grant to the railroad. I bought it from the railroad and gave it to Mack." Cleo looked up at her, ashen, broken. "But I didn't think it would end in a killing. Mack never used the land. . . . He went right back into the NP. He's been there for years. All he does is write and tell me he loves me. But he's never home."

"You stole it from Tavish?" whispered Ember.

Cleo flinched. "I shouldn't have done it. But Mack, he was so disappointed over his losses. I felt I must do something to help him."

Ember hurt inside too badly to shed tears. Tavish had deceived her. He didn't love her. He'd married her to position himself to get back at the others, to avenge himself at her expense.

Cooper and Riley. The names sprang up in her memory.

Tavish had asked her about them at the house on the bluff. Now it all made sense, their strange conversation. Like a fool, she had been thinking his anger was only over Wade and the incident at Yellowstone. But when he had spoken of justice, of murder, he had been thinking of the land, and the evils that had taken place at his cabin. But why hadn't he explained all this to her?

"Who are Cooper and Riley?" she asked flatly.

With shaking hands Cleo was pouring water from the pitcher into a glass. She drank. "Cooper had nothing to do with the fire and killing. He got there after Riley and the jacks had committed their deed. Cooper tried to cover it up to protect me. And I've been trying to cover it up to protect Mack."

Ember lifted her head. "Protect Uncle Mack? Why?"

Cleo looked away from her, then spoke softly, evenly. "A man named Edmund Clark was blackmailing me about the death of Kain. He knew Mack ordered the jacks to go there. I had to protect him. I couldn't let it out. I couldn't lose Mack."

Devastated, Ember stood there, her world blown to bits and scattering in the wind. There were too many pieces to ever pick up again and put back together. Too many.

"You told Mack about the blackmail?"

Cleo shook her head no.

"Who's this Edmund Clark?"

"They have a stern-wheeler in Seattle. He goes by the name of Captain Peter Finch. There's more. Cooper found out that Riley used Clark to have Tavish and his cousin shanghaied. For a while we thought they'd never return . . . but then Tavish showed up in early '76."

Ember gasped. "Shanghaied!"

She remembered his comment about being at sea for two years, about visiting Zanzibar. What misery he must have gone through aboard the ship! She remembered the marks on his back, the scar on his chin—she had asked him about them the night they were married, but he had only made light of it, never giving her an answer. Had he gotten those scars aboard the ship? Had he been flogged?

How his suffering must have been intensified as he wondered about his father. . . . Then he returned to discover his father dead and his land grant taken away unjustly. No wonder he was angry. Who could endure such injustice without the grace of God?

And yet, even devastated by pain, he should have told me. Instead I was the one he used to get even. Tears stung her eyes and she struggled to keep them back.

"And Riley?" she asked Cleo, her voice trembling.

"Cooper paid him off. He's been in San Francisco working the docks. He's a drunk and a bungler. If anything goes wrong it will be because of him. Cooper should have—"

Ember's eyes swerved to Cleo's. "Should have what? Killed him?"

"He was an evil man!"

"How can you! Had Cooper killed Riley, there'd be another death to answer for. It's not that easy. Yes, God can forgive, but He doesn't erase the past. The scars remain for generations!"

"I tell you, Kain Wilder's death was an accident! First one thing, then another happened. I didn't order the cabin set on fire! I didn't tell anyone to hurt Kain. It just happened."

"Nothing will ever be right again," choked Ember. "It's too late for Tavish and me. All of you have lied to me."

Cleo sat motionless, her hands covering her face, the crutches lying on her lap.

Ember turned and walked from the room.

33

REAPING

Night shrouded the wharf. The fog advanced, covering everything with wet gray. Riley sat on the wooden quay, holding a bottle and trying to sing. The words got stuck on his tongue and his brain failed to work. He heard footsteps coming from the taverns where dim lights wavered eerily in the mist.

Edmund Clark walked up and looked down at him with a smirk. "It's all settled, Riley. You be goin' on a bit of a cruise, you are. Our friends be comin' now."

Riley tried to focus on the weaving face. "Eh?"

A wheel creaked and rumbled over the wharf. Two crimps emerged from the fog—big men, hard of face and carrying ropes. One pushed a creaking wheelbarrow.

"Eh?" said Riley again.

The crimps gazed down at him, at each other, then at Edmund Clark. "Him? Ain't a captain about who'd pay us for him!"

"Aye, we made us a bargain," growled Edmund Clark. "I didn't bring him all the way from Seattle to have ye change your mind now. He goes."

Beneath the two men's stare he shifted uneasily. "Aye . . . an' what vile little bugs be crawlin' round in yer minds now?"

Edmund Clark stepped backward, his hand slipping under his pea coat for his dagger, but too late. They jumped him. He struggled fiercely to free himself until a thud connected with the back of his head, knocking off his cap. He fell to his knees.

"Hog-tie him. Quick. Get 'im in the barrow."

"Aye, we'll get us plenty for this big fish. What about him?" he gestured toward Riley who sat in a slumped stupor.

"Let him be. He'll die in his own ale. Clark done sent a message to Mr. T.D. Wilder askin' him to come here. He was going to tell him something about his father and the Chicago fire."

"Do you know what it was?"

"Clark wouldn't talk. Whatever it was, he won't be talkin' now, and Mr. Wilder will have come here for nothing. Let's get out of here. That Wilder ain't a man I wanna fool with. Let him find Riley instead."

"Quick, ship's leaving for Shanghai. This is the last we'll see of Edmund Clark."

The wheelbarrow creaked under its heavy load as the crimps pushed it down the wharf. Fog swallowed them up as their heavy steps died away.

Riley sat there trying to clear his brain. He picked up the bottle and held it to his mouth, taking a long guzzle. He tried to sing, his words thick and slurred. "W-ish—were in lan' o' cotton—times there—ain't fergotten—look 'way, look 'way, look 'way—ol' Dixie lan' . . ."

Riley was still sitting there with his bottle when the ship slipped away into the night, Edmund Clark stashed in the hold.

Riley heard footsteps walk toward him, then pause. He looked up, squinting at a young man in a dark pea coat and hat. Green eyes stared down at him.

"Eh? I know you?"

The man didn't reply, just stood watching him.

Riley spat and attempted another drink from the empty bottle. He tried to focus on the handsome young man. He showed him his precious bottle and grinned, then held it toward him. "S-smile?" he slurred, using the greeting among westerners when offering a drink to a stranger.

"Where's Edmund Clark?"

Riley gestured to the sea. "Shanghaied. Smile?" offered Riley again.

The man stared down at him.

The silence grew. A bell tolled.

The man turned and slowly walked away.

Riley shrugged.

A minute later a coach door shut. The echo of horses faded away into the night.

Riley drew his duster about him with cold fingers and shuddered as the fog became his blanket. He laid down on the wharf to sleep, trying to feel warm.

Lights were still burning their golden welcome when Tavish let himself in the front door and crossed the entry hall to the stairs. He went up to find the one person he needed above all others: Ember.

His heart turned his thoughts toward the Lord. . . . Obedience to Him now made sense to Tavish. He liked life to be reasonable.

But what of trusting God when events in life did not seem reasonable? Injustice without remedy, tragedy without knowing why, suffering that seemed to accomplish nothing but frustration. He thought again of his father's death. Had he lived, would he not have served God longer and aided others to know Him? Yet knowing God was in control of events did not satisfy the questions in his soul. "Perhaps God doesn't intend to tell me the answer. Maybe I wouldn't understand if He did. . . ."

At the bedroom door he paused. He had so much to tell her. Would she understand his reasons for keeping silent about the past? He entered, expecting to see her, but the room was empty. The bed was made. He glanced toward the dressing room, thinking she might be preparing for bed.

"Ember?" he called.

He walked over to the velvet settee, removing his coat. His eyes fell on the bureau. He stopped. A piece of paper lay there. He snatched up the paper and read, his heart sinking.

Tavish,

I saw you at Kain's grave. I've confronted Cleo and she's told me everything. There's no more reason to pretend. You married me hoping to trap those in my family you believe responsible for your father's death.

I won't see you again. I'm leaving. Please don't look for me. Nothing you can say will change what has happened between us.

Ember

Tavish stared at the letter. The bell on St. Paul's church was still ringing, warning ships trapped in the fog off Port Townsend Bay. In disillusionment, he wadded the paper.

Her final words rang in his mind, not like the bell of hope but a funeral dirge.

He felt tired. He walked to the bed and sat down, thinking. He lay back against the satin coverlet, his arms behind his head as he stared up at the ceiling.

He had gained everything a man might want. Wealth, power, success. He had even come to terms with what had happened out on the Hood. He could have killed Riley tonight, but he had walked away. The cords that bound Riley were judgment enough in this life. His spirit of revenge was gone. He no longer cared about Edmund Clark or what he may have wanted to talk with him about at the wharf. *Perhaps another tale about Kain Wilder's past,* he thought. *Let it stay buried.*

Neither did he care where the foreman Cooper might be. Cleo, too, was bound by her own chains. As for Mack Ridgeway . . . greed and lack of self-control had flourished, making a fertile soil for the tragedy that had taken Kain's life.

But now that his emotions were free at last, Ember had slipped through his fingers. Little else mattered now without her.

"Nothing you can say will change what has happened between us."

He could see her as she had looked the day of their wedding. Like Solomon's bride, she had desired only him, her eyes like a dove, full of trust.

He had gained it all, but lost the one woman he truly wanted.

Inside the stern-wheeler, Amity faced her reflection in the mirror. Her father had not returned, nor was there any message. He must have feared exposure and run away, she decided, and wondered that she felt no loss, no sadness. She felt free.

The young woman who stared back at her was not her girlish memory of Amity Clark. Amity smiled at her reflection. "With God's strength you can change," she told herself. "You already have. The prison doors are open. All you need do is take the first small step."

Her hair was arranged high on her head, and she held a new hat.

"Amity?"

Julot's voice called from the deck. "You ready yet? The minister's waiting."

"Coming, Julot! I'll be out in a minute."

She was getting married. She had found love.

Amity smiled at herself. At first she felt silly. Then, as her smile deepened, she felt an emotional release.

"Hello, Amity Clark," she whispered.

"Amity? We best . . ." Julot's voice trailed off as she turned from the mirror to see him standing there, handsome and smiling in his dark suit.

His expression confirmed the hope beating in her heart. "*Ma chérie,*" he breathed.

She walked toward him, her eyes shining. "I'm ready now."

They walked across the deck and onto the wharf. A carriage waited, and Julot helped her inside. She didn't look back at the stern-wheeler. Julot climbed in beside her, and the horses trotted away. The carriage disappeared into the Seattle morning.

Amity took the Bible from her bag and handed it to Julot. "It was your uncle Kain's," was all she said.

Julot recognized it. "Wait till I bring this to Tav! It belonged to his mother first, then Kain. It will mean everything to him."

"Tell me again, Julot," she asked softly, "what does it mean to you?"

Julot's dark eyes flickered. "It speaks of the most cherished years of my life, ma chérie. It speaks of campfires, of Kain, of Tav, of good times and bad, of a time when on the bank of the Missouri I asked my uncle's Savior to be mine."

Amity slipped her hand into his.

On the stern-wheeler nothing was heard but the creak and groan of pilings, and water lapping against the hull. Gulls cried and landed on the handrails. Through a small open window, a letter to Edmund Clark sat on the table.

Today I'm getting married and beginning a new life. Goodbye, Pa.

Amity

A breath of wind came in through the window and stirred the paper. With another strong gust, it was gone.

34

THE DAY THE RAILS MET

St. Paul, Minnesota

Journalists were everywhere. Ember discovered too late her mistake in coming with Lottie and Jamie to St. Paul to meet Mack and Wade. Locked in her grief, Ember had been indifferent about the completion of the Northern Pacific's line from Lake Superior to the Pacific Northwest. Nor was Lottie's father in St. Paul, after all. He and Wade had left a week earlier to prepare for the last spike finale in Gold Creek, Montana.

Henry Villard had arranged for his investors and elite guests, including former President Grant, to travel by special train along the route from St. Paul to Washington Territory. Parades, speeches, and bands waited to greet the whistle-stop extravaganza.

NP officials and journalists assumed she had arrived with Lottie for the historical occasion. After all, she was married to T.D. Wilder, the young tycoon who had made it big with Villard, now the president of the NP. And Lottie was the daughter of Mack Ridgeway, who had survived the new takeover of the railroad by Villard. Mack had been involved in financing the Marent Gulch Trestle, west of Missoula, completed in May.

"The trestle is a marvel," he had written to the family in Port Townsend. "Two hundred and twenty-two feet high and over seven hundred fifty feet in length."

In that year of 1883, the trestle was reputed to be the largest wooden structure in the world.

Ember kept silent about what she knew. Only Tavish could threaten Mack's new success.

She paced the carpeted floor of her suite of rooms in the luxurious Hotel Lafayette as Sassy unpacked their belongings. She had said nothing to Sassy about leaving Tavish or about the information Cleo had confessed, but Sassy suspected trouble and it was difficult for Ember to keep it from her.

"I shouldn't have come to St. Paul," she murmured. "I should have gone to the house in Tacoma."

"Most folks knows you're in the hotel. And Mister Mack and Wade be waitin' for us at the last spike ceremony in Gold Creek."

Maybe Tavish will come.

With Lottie and Jamie, Ember attended the St. Paul parade, estimated to have been twenty miles in length with about twenty thousand people. But the twin city of Minneapolis boasted a crowd of a hundred thousand. Schools and county offices were closed. Streets were decorated with arches of forest pine and bunting.

Tavish did not show up in St. Paul, and the next day Villard's excursion train pulled out amid steam whistles and cheers.

In the Pacific Northwest another train left a waving, cheering crowd, bringing Cleo and the other NP tycoons. Coming from opposite directions, the trains were to meet at Gold Creek, Montana, on Saturday, September 8, for the Golden Spike celebration.

Fargo, Dakota Territory

On Tuesday the train arrived for a brief ceremony in front of the Headquarters Hotel, also Fargo's railroad depot. Then they were on their way again with steam whistles saluting and drums beating.

The excursion rolled westward through land once bloodied by battles with the Sioux, Cheyenne, and Crow. If she allowed her imagination to run free with the train, she might envision ghost warriors chasing after them on the wind as dust devils swirled.

Bismarck

The train rolled to face a dusty Main Street, churned by wagon wheels. The triumphal arch read *1869 JAY COOKE— H. VILLARD 1883.*

More flags. More crowds. More bands. But as they cheered Villard, Ember remembered a young track layer with a guitar here at the track's end in 1873.

That night she slept little.

The festivities began the next morning. A crowd gathered to catch a glimpse of President Grant. The celebration included two important events for Bismarck: laying the new Dakota capitol building cornerstone, and crossing the Missouri River Bridge, the largest steel structure on the NP road.

Again, more bands, speeches, and decorations. If anything differed it was the appearance of Sitting Bull from the Indian reservation. Ember tensed as the chieftain stood before the crowd to address the railroad dignitaries. Here was the victor of the Little Bighorn, but he was no longer the mighty chieftain leading his Sioux warriors to defeat the Ironhorse. Men in suits were his audience.

Lottie and Ember remembered together Prescott, Colonel Custer, the Seventh Cavalry—and yellow ribbons now faded.

Sitting Bull sold his autograph for $1.50, then delivered his speech in Lakota. The affluent listeners in top hats, derbies, and boiled shirts gave the Sioux chieftain a standing ovation, then boarded their Pullman palaces on wheels to journey on. Later, she found out Sitting Bull had given a bitter indictment against land thieves and liars, but the army officer who had "translated" the speech into English had pronounced gracious greetings and bountiful hospitality.

The train steamed ahead over the newly laid tracks across the Great Northwest, over the Little Missouri River, across the Badlands, and into Montana.

Gold Creek, Montana

Cannon boomed their salute. Black trains left white steam clouds drifting away along the blue Montana sky. Ember sat in the wooden pavilion, pine boughs and red, white, and blue bunting moving about her in the breeze. She heard the frenzy of hammers hitting spikes, men shouting, cannon booming, the band blaring tribute. Flags snapped to attention in the breeze as railroad barons began making their speeches.

The Northern Pacific Railroad's victory sign faced the crowd: *Lake Superior 1,198 miles. Puget Sound 847 miles.*

The long, troubled adventure of laying track across the Northwest into Washington Territory was completed. Today the Golden Spike would be hammered. What had begun in 1869, with railroad baron Jay Cooke, ended with Henry Villard seizing the moment of triumph to the salute of the Fifth Infantry Band from Fort Keogh. Strains of the "Triumphal March" paraded across the wind.

If any of Ember's personal dreams remained untarnished along the hazardous route, they no longer mattered. Track's end, like her life, had come to its moment of climax, but for her there was no celebration.

Designer George Pullman's plush cars mocked her from across the track. Chandeliers, Venetian mirrors, velvet upholstered furniture, looped draperies with gold fringe. . . . The Victorian luxury reflected the railroad barons and financiers themselves. Successful, rich, powerful.

Deadly . . . When had it all begun with her family? The deceit, blackmail, even murder. . . . Who was to blame?

Her own adventurous journey through life had begun with the Northern Pacific's, but unlike silver track racing proudly across the Northwest through buffalo herds and Sioux warriors, flaming sunsets and golden dawns, she was left with a fistful of wind.

On this September twilight, the sunset heralded its own

message of glory in scribbled crimson across the golden sky. If she allowed herself to reminisce she might hear the distant war drums of the Sioux at the Little Bighorn. Or if she listened with her heart, perhaps she could hear again the voice of Tavish Wilder, saying quietly: *"I've always loved you. Marry me."*

She heard nothing now but the restless Montana crowd shouting for President Grant to speak. Ember turned away and looked across the plain. The wind whipped a dust devil into its own war dance that settled quietly again, its energy spent. Gone. Everything.

She stirred. English and German financiers, in black derby hats and smart Prince Albert coats with fat gold chains on their vests, were leaving the wooden pavilion. The Montana cowboys whooped: "Beer! Where is it? Ain't a worker deservin' of nuthin' round these tycoons? Who do they think did all the track layin'?"

The shoving crowd lined both sides of the trackbed to watch the last twelve hundred feet of rail get hammered into place. Another whoop and holler sounded, reminding her of Sitting Bull's angry warriors attacking the invading Ironhorse. But this was only a friendly contest. The muscled track layers from east and west would compete against one another to reach the spot where Villard waited to pound in the golden spike. It wasn't made of gold at all. This spike had been removed from a section of track that was laid in Carlton, Minnesota, some thirteen years earlier.

"Them eastern track layers don't stand a chance," hollered the crew from Washington and Oregon. "Stand aside, gents! Let a Pacific Northwestern man show how it's done!"

WHACK! RING! WHACK! RING!

She smiled faintly. She could remember years back when Tavish Wilder in his dusty black jeans and torn denim shirt had watched her, a sledgehammer propped at his boot, a beat-up guitar often slung over his shoulder. *"I always loved you,"* his voice echoed.

She swallowed. The pain was too real to accept now. Like a new cut with stinging sweat running into it.

Ember listened to the frenzy of hammers and spikes, the shouting men. Her gaze caught the shimmer coming from a wedding band on a woman's hand. Ember touched her own, remembering.

Where had the mystery first begun? she wondered again. With the schemes of the Ridgeways? Certainly not with Tavish Wilder. He had been almost innocent then, the young son of a circuit-riding revivalist, drifting through train camps from Duluth to Bismarck. No, the mystery surrounding him and the fragmented pieces of the last twelve years lay scattered. She had been fifteen when it all began—the first time she had met Tavish. She was now twenty-seven. How could a woman gain so much and lose it all?

She stirred, dragging her eyes from the woman's wedding ring and looking toward the train as it stood empty on the track.

A movement on the platform at the rear of the train caught her attention. A man stood there unnoticed by the throng. He wore handsome black broadcloth, a spotless white shirt, a wide-brimmed hat. Well built, his green eyes contrasted with his dark hair. She saw his dark coat move in the wind, saw the gun belt, the holster with his Colt .45 tied down. He didn't look like a railroad tycoon as he stood watching her leaning in the doorway.

Tavish. She stared back, debating her emotions.

In the uneasy silence, the voice of railroad baron Henry Villard echoed from behind them: "We have striven to do our full duty, and to obtain the greatest effort of which human brain and muscle, stimulated by unlimited capital, are capable. . . ."

With that, the golden spike was hammered into place. And the Northern Pacific Railroad was completed through the Northwest to Washington Territory.

At the same moment, Tavish straightened to leave the platform. Ember stood, her heart racing, and began moving through the crowd toward him.

The throng surged between them, oblivious to the emotion that burned white-hot in their eyes.

Ember moved slowly down the pavilion steps and faced the foreboding black train with the Montana sky looming behind. The wind tugged at her, edging her forward.

Tavish stood with the wind tossing about his dark coat, the gun belt showing. His riveting gaze held hers.

"We're back where we started. Only thing missing is a covered wagon and Sitting Bull," he said.

She remained silent, leaving the distance between them questionable.

He respected her silence, but made clear his motive for coming. "I can't lose you," he said.

"You lied to me," she challenged.

She saw his flicker of pain, but it brought no satisfaction to her, only mirrored pain. How could it be otherwise?

"I never lied to you," he said.

"You didn't tell me about Kain."

"I'm not making excuses. I should have."

He took a step toward her but she stepped back, tears wetting her eyes. "No. Stay where you are."

"We've got to talk. Come inside the train."

She hesitated a moment, torn between conflicting emotions, then walked to the train and entered the Pullman car.

The private car was quiet and offered emotional reprieve after the noisy hours spent on the platform. She removed her stylish hat and gloves, aware that her fingers were cold and trembling.

"You're wrong about me," he said. "I didn't marry you to get back at Mack and Cleo."

"Then why didn't you tell me the truth? Why was I the last one to know? I should have been the first—I was your wife."

"I didn't want to lose you. I knew you'd suspect ulterior reasons. It was wrong not to tell you. I, above everyone else, could quickly give the biblical reasons why I behaved badly. But the fact we're standing here now, like this, is answer enough. In keeping the past a secret, I allowed the situation I hoped to avoid. I should have believed in you more. You're worthy of a man's finest trust, Ember. I'm asking you to forgive me."

She turned to look at him, but kept her distance. "Mack's here," she said, searching his eyes. "So is Wade—and Cleo."

His expression did not change. "I'm not searching for Mack, or the others. It's you I want."

Her heart beat faster. "He had nothing to do with what happened that night."

"I know that now. Cleo arranged with the railroad to take the land."

"Even she didn't plan for what took place. She didn't want your father harmed."

"I know. It was Riley. He always did have it in for me—a preacher's kid, he used to call me. I almost busted into him a few times. Looking back, maybe I should have. It might have saved a good deal of trouble later."

"You did what was right back then," she said quietly. "But what about now, Tavish? What are you going to do, about Riley, and my family?"

"Cleo has herself to face every morning. Not a happy prospect, I would think. Guilt can be a worse avenger than a hangman's noose. And Mack's absorbed in the railroad, and Wade in timber."

"And Riley?" she whispered.

The noise of the celebration continued. "I found him. He's a drunk. More to be pitied than an object of revenge. Injustice is best left in the hand of God. I'm through with Riley—with a whole lot of things, but I'm curious about what happened to Cooper."

"He arranged to cover matters because of his loyalty to Cleo. Cleo said he had no active part. She doesn't know where he is. I thought he might have been working with my father, but I haven't seen him since I arrived in St. Paul. If you do find Cooper, what will you do?"

His eyes held hers. "Nothing."

"You mean that?" she whispered.

"I've too much to live for, to be thankful for, to allow the past to enslave me. In saying this, I'm not excusing their actions. They'll answer for their deeds one day, but not to me. I've already yielded it to the Lord. It's been over for a long time. I came home to tell you, but you had already left with Lottie."

There was a tenderness in his gaze that convinced her he was telling the truth. She had not seen him look this way since the first night she saw him outside her wagon.

"Ember?" He took a step toward her and again she wanted to sway toward him, but fought back the feelings that sprang up. She found herself saying, "It's over for us too."

"It will never be over for us. What we feel has been there from the moment we met."

"Confident, aren't you," she stated.

"Maybe I have confidence in us both, in the Lord. Marriage

is a commitment," he said quietly. "You can't just write a note and say goodbye."

"But I did," she challenged.

"But even if you did—you're still a part of me. I think I'm still a part of you. We can't forget, pretend we didn't love once, that we don't love now. I do love you. You know it."

"I don't know—"

"Yes, you do. We belong together. I meant it when I saved you from that Cheyenne for myself. I might have ridden out then, but in my mind it wasn't permanent. I had nothing to offer you. Kain, Julot, and I worked our way to Washington. When you returned to Port Townsend, I planned to have a timber enterprise of my own. I knew I had that land on the Hood. Then Julot and I were shanghaied by Edmund Clark and Riley."

Her heart wrenched. "If only you had told me."

"I'm laying my heart open to you now. No more secrets, no more suspicions."

Ember stood there hurting, yet knowing she must place their past—with all of the pain, and the deceit, and the betrayal—into the gentle hand of God. *I love this man. And love hopes all things. Endures all things. . . .*

Under his gaze, her eyes misted. He pulled her into his arms and she came with sudden relief, returning his embrace.

He was kissing her, passionately, and she found herself clinging to him, returning his kiss, the tears running down her cheeks.

"I'm sorry," she whispered, but heard him saying it at the same moment, and they clung to each other.

"Nothing must ever come between us," he said.

"Nothing," she repeated.

Outside, the cannon boomed, and the band began playing again.

"I love you, Ember darling. There'll be more struggles, but we'll commit to working through those times. He held her ring finger to his lips for a tender moment. "Until death do us part," he whispered.

She added, "And for richer or for poorer."

He smiled and lifted a brow. "Sure about that last part?"

She kissed him lightly and closed her eyes, enjoying his warm embrace. "Mmm. . . . Why do you ask?"

When he said nothing, she slowly lifted her head and looked at him. His eyes took on mischievous humor.

"What would you do if the NP suddenly went bust again, this time under Villard—and your husband went with it?"

She searched his eyes for any hint of truth. His gaze was full of amusement, but something else too. Sobriety? Irony?

"You are teasing me," she murmured.

"Maybe not. . . . Did you ever think about singing solos in train camp revivals?"

She smiled. "Do you still have your guitar?"

"A string is busted, but I can fix it. Julot might lend me his harmonica."

"I always did like you in those dusty black jeans and buckskin coat."

"Did you?"

"Uh-huh."

"Better than a derby hat and a frock coat?"

"Well, I don't know. . . . I like you both ways. But—tell me you're teasing me, Tavish."

He smiled. "Villard arranged this grand excursion to convince the Europeans to invest more needed money into the railroad. I don't think they're impressed all that much. Maybe I'll sell out when we get back to Port Townsend. Whatever happens, I've learned that money doesn't buy contentment."

She rested the side of her face against his chest, her palm on his coat. "You're right."

He lifted her face and searched her eyes. Seeing what he wanted, he held her more tightly. "The Lord has given us the future. Now we must use it wisely. I keep thinking of a verse my father used to quote so much. 'Forgetting those things which are behind, and reaching forth unto those things which are before.' "

He looked down at her. "Ready to build the future, Mrs. Wilder?"

"I'm not afraid if God is with us. He brought you back into my life," she whispered. "It's enough."

"With Him, I know we can make it," he said.

She smiled up at him. She knew it too.